A Spell For a Duke

Spellmaidens of Coven Square
House Animus
Book 1

AMY QUINTON

ARE YOU SIGNED UP FOR DRAGONBLADE'S BLOG?

You'll get the latest news and information on exclusive giveaways, exclusive excerpts, coming releases, sales, free books, cover reveals and more.

Check out our complete list of authors, too!

No spam, no junk. That's a promise!

Sign Up Here

www.dragonbladepublishing.com

Dearest Reader;

Thank you for your support of a small press. At Dragonblade Publishing, we strive to bring you the highest quality Historical Romance from some of the best authors in the business. Without your support, there is no 'us', so we sincerely hope you adore these stories and find some new favorite authors along the way.

Happy Reading!

CEO, Dragonblade Publishing

hell, so beguiling.

But that kiss…

But how much more *could* they be *together?*

Once a Lycan kisses his mate, he's compelled to complete the Mating Ritual lest he go, quite literally, insane. (Talk about morning after regrets.) If that wicked minx is as clever as she seems, she is **far** from London right about now. Because all it would take is one whiff of her scent and even this magically sealed cage couldn't keep him from her.

Josie Bell isn't concerned. Witches aren't compelled by Lycan Mating Instincts and fending off *alleged* murderous scoundrels is just another day in the life of a Spellmaiden. An impulsive, kissable Lycan doesn't even merit a raised brow. She's far more concerned with saving the world, though admittedly, a searing kiss (or two or ten, but who's counting) does have its—perks.

But when Josie and Lachlan discover how certain random events aren't quite so accidental, insignificant oddities aren't quite so trivial, and the true villains aren't quite who they expected, they must learn how to work together before the next Potential Extinction Event becomes very, very real.

It's a busy time to be a witch in London.

Dedication

To the Scott and Erin Rappold...thanks for the use of your family name.

To Erin Rappold, thanks for helping me make this book better than ever...You are brilliant.

To all the witches out there...be marvelously witchy!

Prologue

Josephine Caroline Bell: Orphan, Petty Thief, Tenacious Brat
Diary of a Willful Witch

I KILLED MY first demon by the age of nine. Knew I wanted to be a Spellmaiden by thirteen. I was destined for it, really, though it had taken 10 years, 9 failures and 17,520 hours of training and practice to prove it.

But I digress. Where was I? Ah yes, the demon.

I had been on my own, surviving the streets of St. Giles for around three years when it happened. And by surviving, I mean I'd been existing more out of sheer stubbornness and pure dumb luck than any sort of actual skill. I wasn't even a witch…yet—hadn't so much as a flicker of magical power (or so I'd thought) and certainly no one around to train me.

The demon had it coming though. It was the fourth time that week it had tried to eat me, and I had grown tired of running.

Now, that is not to say that all demons are chronic rot. Like humans, or really any species for that matter, demons come in all sorts of varieties—good, bad, beautiful, ugly, short, tall, spindly, corpulent, horned, intelligent, idiotic, and every combination in between.

Fortunately for me, this demon was of the extremely bad,

straight-out-of-hell-no-chance-for-redemption variety. (Truth be told, all demons came from hell, so I couldn't really pin that part on him.)

Unfortunately for me, being only nine years of age, I didn't have any sort of license to kill, detain, assassinate, or even subdue…well, anything…and so my actions invited the type of scrutiny an orphan surviving on the streets of St. Giles could ill afford to summon.

The details of the demon's demise are rather irrelevant. What is important to this story is what happened after.

I stood trial.

I spent time in gaol. (In truth, that part had been simply a matter of time, and really, only a matter of procedure.)

I spent time in Hades. (A bureaucratic error, but one in which the deceased demon's friends made colorful promises about how they intended to wipe me and all my future heirs from existence. I'd like it noted I refrained from pointing out the sheer ridiculousness of such a statement—an impressive feat for a nine-year-old going on twenty.)

But I digress.

More important than all those things put together?

I attracted the attention of the White Witch.

And from there on out, my life had changed irrevocably.

Whether that was good or bad though?

That part remained to be seen.

Chapter One

Josephine Caroline Bell, Witch (Still Willful)
Speaking of Bureaucratic Blunders...

March 1897
London, Mayfair, Number Twenty-Seven Brook Street to be precise.

I STEPPED OUT the door of number twenty-seven Brook Street—a deceptively harmless looking domicile owned and ruled by a sadistic incubus bent on honing a witch's physical strength through regular applications of torture, or exercise as he liked to call it—and crumbled the missive in my hand as I watched the White Witch's messenger beat a hasty retreat.

Probation...

Investigation...

Enquiry...

Again.

The pertinent points inscribed on the notice currently crushed in my fist raced through my mind on repeat, but more importantly, I wondered...*why?*

Or more specifically, why *this* time?

I *always* followed the rules.

Or tried to.

Er, mostly.

Really, I couldn't afford not to follow them. Unlike every other Spellmaiden, I wasn't from the nobility. Too many wanted me to fail on that fact alone and would use any excuse to have me ousted from the coven.

I swallowed, then quickly shoved the crumpled missive into one of my pockets and glanced to the sky, squinting against the all-too-cheerful morning sun.

Bright. Unusually warm. The very air shimmered with hope and a sense of fresh beginnings. Safety beckoned and innocence presumed. Optimism whispered upon the casual wind.

Out of habit, I patted my skirts, double-checking that my blades were secure in my modified bustle, and relaxed a spare inch as I fingered their familiar shape. Only then could I take a deep breath.

Some considered the ability to wield magic to be more than enough protection but truthfully, having two eight-inch daggers at my fingertips felt infinitely better.

Magic could be unreliable.

Knowledge, determination, and skill? Far more dependable.

Along with the knives in my boots, a stiletto up my sleeve and another secured in my corset, plus the lethal additions to my unassuming hat, and I should have felt unstoppable.

Should have *been* unstoppable.

And I *was*, though every so often, I felt like a charlatan waiting to be found out.

Like right about now.

I shifted the stack of books presently balanced on my hip and tapped an impatient rhythm with the toe of my sensible leather boot—standard-issue, complete with retractable blades and two secret compartments—as I waited for my roommate, and fellow tortur*ee*, Daphne—or more appropriately *Lady* Daphne.

I tried to keep my mind from dwelling on the crumpled paper in my skirts until I had time to *do* something about it. My roommate wouldn't know about my probation. Yet. I had time, even if only a very little, to figure out what, exactly, I should do.

Below, on the pavement, a gentleman approached, whistling a jaunty tune, and he dipped his head with a smile as he passed. "Beautiful day, my lady."

"Indeed," I replied. What else could I say?

Briefly, I wondered if the gentleman would still feel the same had he been here last night, in this very spot, as I'd dispatched three five-foot, two-headed hellhounds—all of them descendants of a lesser-known line of creatures who considered Cerberus a close fourth cousin, thrice removed.

Occasionally, whenever the wind shifted just so, I swore I could smell the lingering scent of sulfur and, to a lesser extent, the malodorous stench of burnt dog hair. It brought to mind the satisfying sense of a job well done, even if it was a near thing, particularly when much of my success last night had relied upon pure obstinacy and unrelenting fortitude.

Or perhaps just plain old luck.

I could well imagine the look of horror on the gentleman's face had he been present to witness such an event. To glimpse just how easily the lie could all fall apart.

Fortunately for him, he remained peacefully unaware.

Alas, I was not so unenlightened and had long perfected the art of questioning optimism in any form, particularly when it came in the shape of deceptively brilliant blue skies and warm spring air.

Death didn't *only* dwell in shadows.

Danger could be found at any given time, around any given corner, and often summoned one into its lethal arms with a bright smile and a melodious voice.

Even in the heart of Mayfair.

I pulled myself out of such maudlin thoughts and checked the small clock pinned to my jacket—*ten o-clock*—and resisted the impulse to pound on the door behind me. Perhaps, I should bribe the large raccoon currently sprawled out upon a windowsill across the way, a half-smoked cheroot dangling from its lips while he crooned a naughty catchpenny.

Would a crown be enough to convince him to trespass onto the premises of number twenty-seven and speed my roommate along?

As a rule, raccoons required very little incentive to act upon some mischief or other. And a caroon—every raccoon in my acquaintance referred to a crown as a caroon—was a great deal more than a little. Better still, Daphne (I never actually used her honorific between us), rather liked raccoons, particularly because her nemesis, the Duke of Anglesey and the aforementioned sadist who *tortured innocent witches* at number twenty-seven, most definitely did *not*.

I heard the scrape and scramble of numerous tiny, clawed feet and smiled as I glanced over to see a dozen or so squirrels intrude upon my random musings as they climbed the trunk of a nearby cherry tree and stationed themselves upon the branches amidst all its full-bloomed glory. They twittered and bounced in place, jostling each other in their excitement, some barking, others gesturing my way.

Eager for an audience, they all started speaking at once.

"Miss Bell—"

"Heard about the Lycan?"

"Are the people safe, love?"

"Fancy a comfy coze and a nice spot of tea?"

"How many were murdered?"

"Have you heard the one about the vampire with a wooden leg named Smythe?"

"I filed my complaint with the Ministry of the Magical Realm more than six weeks ago, and I *still*—"

I felt my lips twitch as I suppressed an outright laugh.

Squirrels were *always* impatient for a bit of conversation or gossip, or to catalogue a list of complaints, worse even than badgers. And they forever followed me on the off chance I was up for a quick *tête-à-tête*—the curse of an Animus Witch, depending on who one asked—no matter the location or time of day; doubly so when there was *news* to be had.

They spoke of murder with as much enthusiasm as when they'd managed to swipe a blueberry scone from a picnic in Hyde Park. As if death was just another rote bit of juicy gossip.

And while the topic was very serious, I couldn't help but release a slow breath and thank the gods they no longer looked askance at *me* whenever the subject of murder arose.

Still, they very well knew I couldn't discuss coven business, but it didn't stop them from trying.

Now that they stood silent, their hands clasped in eager expectation, I forced a smile, dipped my head to the first squirrel, and acknowledged each query in turn. "Madame. I have not. Yes, of course. I cannot, at the moment, thank you for the invitation. I do not know. What was the name of his other leg? Current wait times are eight weeks, I do apologize for the delay." I gestured broadly to the lot of them and added, "Thank you, there will be no further questions today, please."

Seemingly satisfied, the squirrels scattered anyway, thoroughly unaffected by my abrupt dismissal, but I knew they'd simply return before long. Shaking my head, I checked my timepiece once more, then snapped the lid closed with a solid *click*.

It was a busy time to be a witch in London.

Or Spellmaiden if one preferred the technical term.

The door behind me slammed, rattling the townhome's very foundation with its force, and I had to resist the urge to pat my skirts to see if the crumpled missive was still in my pocket and hadn't randomly fallen out to the ground for my roommate to discover. It hadn't, so I plastered on a tight smile and neatly glanced over my shoulder just as Daphne joined me on the front stoop in a huff.

"I swear that man has a vicious streak longer than the River Thames." Daphne glanced over her shoulder and stuck out her tongue. "He takes entirely too much pleasure in torturing us. How long did we suffer this time?"

Desperate to be on our way, I was half-way down the steps when I answered, "Three hours and fourteen minutes."

"See?" continued Daphne, who kept apace while employing a small towel to dab away the sweat glistening along her hairline. "Who exercises for three hours unless one is being pursued by the likes of an eight-foot demon—at least eight-foot, shorter if they employ more than two legs and arms? Or while under the influence of some sort of evil curse?" Daphne tsked. "Or, for that matter, while heavily disguised after imbibing a substantial quantity of alcohol? Absinthe, anyone?"

Daphne slowed me with the briefest touch to my arm. "What if he's an *addict?*"

Bemused despite myself, I shook my head and carried on. "Opium? Anglesey? Don't be silly."

Daphne nodded and resumed walking. "Quite right. What was I thinking? The man is far too…," she gestured broadly with both hands, "large. Though I suppose with a sizeable enough fortune and access to a powerful enough witch, one could procure a spell to stave off at least some of the physical side effects of opium addiction easily enough."

I glanced at my friend as we advanced down the pavement toward Hyde Park. "Do recall the White Witch hired him."

Daphne rolled her eyes. "Naturally."

The White Witch worked for the Ministry (formally, the Ministry of the Magical Realm, or the M.M.R. if one were inclined to brevity) and dictated the lives of thirty-six Spellmaidens, among other beings. She demanded absolute proficiency in all the magical creatures she employed. One too-many mistakes and you were removed. No consideration for exceptional past performance. Just finished. Out. Gone.

Which didn't explain why I was on probation *again*. Not to mention the problems it caused when the witches in other houses gave me a pointed look while whispering behind their wands.

So why me?

Not that I was complaining. Much.

Our third housemate certainly hadn't been offered probation, leaving Daphne and I among the few residents of our home on

Coven Square.

Well, not counting the cats, frequent day visitors, recurrent overnight guests (some of whom seemed disinclined to leave), thirteen resident ghosts, and a full menagerie of year-round inhabitants of the four-or-more-legged or winged variety...animals who called our house on Coven Square—The Kameleon—home.

Or the house's sentient soul, who went by the name of Mac, if one wanted to be particularly precise.

This enquiry I faced could throw our home into turmoil all over again.

I blew a loose lock of hair from my eyes and dabbed at the sweat collecting on my brow as Daphne carried on, "Well, I'm sure there *is* such a thing as over-competence, and Aiden is the very definition of it. It's right there in *DeBrett's* next to Aiden Locke, Duke of Anglesey; I made note of it while visiting the circulating library only just this week past."

Since when had Anglesey become Aiden to Daphne?

Daphne continued, "Honestly, that man is one wave of a wand away from a wicked, centuries-long hex, I daresay; I don't care if he is an incubus. Or a duke for that matter. And I'd have happily done the honors myself this morning if he'd even thought for a moment to make me do one more chin up on *The Bar*."

The Bar was a five-inch diameter pipe covered in grease that smelled of rotting fish and several other things we refused to consider. It took a decent spell just to wash the smell from our hands, and still, it lingered in our noses for *hours* after.

Nevertheless, I said, "Better 'The Bar' than losing a battle with an eight-foot-tall demon brandishing ten swords in as many arms."

"Perhaps, I should set down a wager at the club?" Daphne queried.

"I would happily take that bet."

"Fancy having the nerve to hire a sadistic incubus as a trainer to thirty-six *women*—"

"Incubus or not, Anglesey is just a regular demon doing his job."

Daphne snorted. "Imagine having the cheek to *be* the sadistic incubus who agreed to do that job. And for the White Witch of all people." Daphne shook her head. "What was she thinking..."

Daphne's complaints fell away as a horse pulling a wagon laden with crated milk reared on its hind legs with an overwrought whinny of protest, sending the driver to his feet and scrambling to calm his noble steed. Around them, several private carriages took evasive maneuvers to avoid a collision, their own cattle tossing out colorful complaints as they passed and generally cursing and shaking their equine heads at the horse pulling said milk cart. Numerous pedestrians stopped, necks strained, to gawk at the misbehaving horses in the hopes of witnessing an accidental catastrophe. Little did they know, real calamities never made for good sources of entertainment. Something about the reality of imminent death tended to call a halt to one's morbid curiosity.

Most of the time, anyway.

In all fairness to the milk cart horse, it wasn't every day one experienced an enormous purple paper elephant cutting you off in the heart of Mayfair while you were just doing your job and minding your own business. This fact appeared to be the horse's general complaint, more or less, regarding the entire, unruly affair.

To add to the pandemonium, only animals and creatures of a magical nature could even see the elephant. To everyone else, *well, to humans in particular*, the scene playing out must seem like utter chaos.

The elephant, or in truth, a collection of purple papers folded into the *shape* of an elephant, stood as tall as the horse, and suddenly surrendered to the irrational urge to rear up on its hind legs—a definite obscenity levelled at the offended horse—its trunk gesturing wildly in the air along with a few more colorful invectives thrown in...something about the horse's parentage was involved.

Really, the M.M.R. had no sense of humor they were aware of, and thus, their missives tended to act accordingly. But they'd *never* before been so conspicuous in public.

Without warning, the purple elephant dropped to all four feet with a loud crash that shook the ground, sending several birds into a wild panic before they took to the air.

Well, apart from the one that mistook a window for the open sky, who now squawked like a drunken sailor and glanced dazedly about from a nearby windowsill.

Eventually, the elephant shifted left, then right, then adjusted course, somehow missing every pedestrian, horse, and cart in its way, and turned towards Daphne and I as we stood rooted in place on the pavement in case the situation escalated to a point requiring specialist (re: magical) intervention.

Daphne clapped her hands together. "Oh! An assignment and a rather large one as well…"

I crossed my arms. "Indeed. Er, Daphne?"

"Yes?"

"Have you ever seen one so—," I gestured broadly at the oversized elephant.

"Can't say I have. I've never gotten an assignment larger than a magpie before. And never in public. Must be serious. Do you think it's about *him*?" Daphne waggled her brows as if I had any clue what she was talking about.

"Who?"

Daphne's brows crept up to her hairline. "You know. *Him*. The Lycan. Naughty Wolf. Recently dubbed 'Murderin' MacKeane.' Sex God. Likes them in pairs, doesn't limit himself to Lycans. Or females for that matter…" Her voice trailed off with a dreamy sigh.

I shook my head, slowly.

"Really? Don't you keep up with the latest *on dits*?"

Daphne well knew the answer to that.

"Wealthy. Handsome. Sexy as sin. Champion of the Highland

Games for the last six years running. I hear the ladies still swoon at his feet despite his murderous propensities. Doubly so when he dons his kilt—"

I snorted, "Sounds like a regular celebrity. If he is that much of a scoundrel, I suppose the age-old question of what a Scotsman wears beneath his kilt has been laid to rest quite satisfactorily…"

"Personally, I still think it would be prudent to confirm—"

"Daphne. He's a *murderer*—"

"Alleged—"

"Lycans and Spellmaidens shouldn't mingle—"

"I prefer the term *professional adversaries*, myself—"

"*Daphne.*"

"Josie. They're not *all* bad."

I scoffed. "Of course not. Just impulsive—"

"I like to think spontaneous—"

"Violent—"

"Or formidable—"

"Lusty."

"Ooh, *agreed.*"

We shared a laugh, and I soberly added, "But worst of all, when it comes to *The Law*, they're subversive at best."

Daphne shrugged. "What you call subversive, I call carefree. And why the world is so perfectly colorful." Daphne gave me a brief, one-armed hug. "Fortunately for the Lycans, *you* are first and foremost, honest. And a great believer in upholding the Law—the perfect Spellmaiden."

If only she knew.

I cleared the unexpected catch in my throat. "Precisely." I felt like a fraud saying it, and for a very brief moment, an awkward silence followed, which was silly. I always followed the rules…when I could. And I *was* good. I had the results to prove it. Right?

I shook off my feelings of doubt and trained my eyes on the purple elephant, which had stopped to investigate a patch of clovers at the base of a nearby tree.

Though humans were incapable of detecting that sort of magic on vivid display, or any magic at all, really—and indeed, the milk cart horse had finally settled, and the driver, including every human present, simply carried on their way as if nothing untoward had ever occurred—such things always carried a tangible, potentially devastating risk.

As a Spellmaiden, it often felt as if the entire world were one magic spell gone awry away from total annihilation. P.E.E.'s, Potential Extinction Events, were an almost weekly occurrence. The White Witch had a sign in her office showing the number of days since the last P.E.E. had occurred. I had never seen the number reach higher than eight.

It currently stood at one.

Fortunately, most people, especially humans, bloody well never knew it.

And for that, they could thank their local Spellmaiden.

With such a constant threat against life as everyone knew it, unsurprisingly, exposing the magical world to the human one constituted treason. No matter the reason. Even if you were acting under orders of the M.M.R., which was a sobering thought.

If guilty, you were put to death. Immediately. No chance for parole, which everyone agreed was rather *disagreeable,* but it was the law, nonetheless.

Not even the Fae could save you if convicted, and the Angels, being Judges of *The Law,* wouldn't even dream of it.

Ahead of us, the paper elephant finally decided to quit procrastinating and approached. It reached out with its trunk and investigated both of us by touch and smell—which tickled, forcing Daphne and I to bite back uncontrollable fits of laughter. Then, it bowed before me, and I exhaled a nervous breath as I once more recalled the crumpled paper in my pocket. Though I daren't say so out loud, there must be some sort of mistake, and yet the elephant continued to stare at me expectantly.

Should I take the job?

"Josie?"

Ignoring my roommate, I imagined I could feel the burden of the crumpled notice in my pocket weighing me down, burning a hole right through my skirts and lighting me up like a beacon for the world to notice and point at while boldly exclaiming "Fraud!" in no uncertain terms.

Rather than succumb to startled panic, I swallowed my fears and calmly handed my stack of books to Daphne. Then, I sucked in a slow, steady breath and only just refrained from wiping my damp palms on my skirts. I probably shouldn't accept the assignment—who was I kidding, I *know* I shouldn't accept the assignment.

But what if I could use this to somehow prove my innocence? What if this was the key to *saving* my job instead?

That was assuming I ever learned what I was being investigated *for*. The missive hadn't said, which was peculiar and something to consider…later.

I opened my mouth to speak up. To deny myself the opportunity. To do the right thing.

Instead, I held out both arms, palms up signaling my acceptance of the mission.

The elephant stomped one foot, then flapped its rather large ears, screeched once with an ear-splitting shriek not remotely reminiscent of any sort of real elephant, and took flight, unfolding and refolding in on itself and generally twisting about in mid-air until it settled into my outstretched arms in the form of a folder at least an inch thick.

"You have the devil's own luck," murmured Daphne.

I smoothed one hand down the file, relishing the weight of it in my hands, as a surge of excitement hummed through my veins. "Luck is a sentiment for the unprepared."

Though at times I agreed it seemed as if I really did have the devil's own luck, though I suspected I survived more out of pure obduracy than any sort of random good fortune.

Always had, and I didn't anticipate that changing.

I was already starting from the back of the line. Whereas

most Spellmaidens came from the ranks of the aristocracy...I didn't.

Which was why the rules were important. And why I pushed myself to go further, be faster, work harder.

Just to be *as* good.

Just to keep from being tossed back to the streets as many *purists* would no doubt relish.

Daphne shook her head. "You cannot fool me, Josie Bell. I can see you fighting back a smile. I've never known anyone as work obsessed as you. The more dangerous the job, the better..."

"And you aren't?"

"Well, naturally, I love my job, but...'

I raised one brow.

"You're the best, Josie Bell, deservedly so. You never fail." It wasn't what she'd meant to say, and we both knew it.

I shook my head in denial. I failed all the time, sometimes quite spectacularly, and that knowledge had me feeling more like a charlatan of late than ever before, and yet, I kept my mouth closed and shoved aside any further feelings of inadequacy because such feelings *were* absurd.

Most magical folk found being a Spellmaiden a hard but respected life. And isolating. But Spellmaidens were the best of the best and the last line of defense protecting both the magical world and the human one from evil in all its forms, while keeping humans blissfully unaware of the potent magic amidst them.

It was a code—*a responsibility*—I respected, and I did my best to incorporate its tenets throughout every aspect of my life.

I was born to *be* a Spellmaiden. I worked hard to *become* a Spellmaiden.

And I would *die* a Spellmaiden as well.

Daphne settled a hand on my shoulder and squeezed. "I'll meet you back home?"

I cleared my throat, which felt unexpectedly tight all of a sudden, and nodded. "Yes. This afternoon, likely. Will you take my books?"

"Yes, alright, see you then."

Despite her earlier questions and suppositions, Daphne well knew the rules and didn't ask to see the file or push me for answers. Assignments were strictly need-to-know.

I held my breath and carefully gripped the folder, running my finger along the long edge while fighting the urge to lift the cover and start reading right here on the pavement in the middle of Mayfair.

What if I just took a quick peek? A glimpse, no more.

I'd risked much by accepting this assignment while on probation, and I wanted to know—*needed* to know—what it might cost me.

Ultimately the urge to look proved too difficult to resist, though it really oughtn't have been so difficult.

So, with a final, bracing exhale, I flipped open the file.

And stared, almost in disbelief, yet somehow, I'd already known what I would find, for there, in the middle of the first page in a glittering purple, almost glowing, ink was a name. A single name. *His* name. My latest assignment.

Lachlan Connor Daire MacKeane

I might have wondered, if only for a moment, whether I was ready to take on an assignment of such magnitude... the man was practically a celebrity and beloved, it seemed, by all womankind...and I well knew he wouldn't be an easy mark. And while I hoped this assignment might help me with the enquiry I faced, it could just as easily backfire.

But rather than concern myself with such possibilities, I felt a smile begin to tilt at the corner of my lips as anticipation and, dare I think it—excitement—surged, and I knew I couldn't wait to get started.

Tick Tock, Lachlan MacKeane. I'm coming for you.

Chapter Two

Lachlan Connor Daire MacKeane, *The MacKeane*, 7th
Duke of Skye
Bounties, Bounties Everywhere and Not but Swill to Drink

Yesterday
The Cock and Bull Tavern
Little Walrus, Hampshire

THE STENCH OF stale ale coupled with the sour smell of Bags o' Mystery stew permeated the already fetid air of the Cock and Bull Tavern, while the sound of laughing men combined with the words of a raunchy sea ditty drowned out the murmur of conversation apart from the occasional burst of laughter and raucous good cheer. The place was rather crowded for such an out of the way tavern and filled with an interesting combination of both human and supernatural beings.

From my position in the furthest corner of the room from the main door, I identified at least six different species of demons: three classes of shifters, not counting my two packmates, an incubus, an elf, four brownies, and some strange entity in the far, opposite corner I had never seen in my life, that definitely wasn't human. Possibly a vampire, though those usually kept themselves so far removed from society; they were practically myth.

In other words, nothing *truly* out of the ordinary.

I stretched my legs beneath the table and eyed my companions over a glass of what the bartender claimed was whisky. I wish we'd brought our own, as the swill the Sassenachs served this far south wasn't fit to be called whisky, much less be imbibed. Though I could probably strip the paint from my traveling carriage with the Cock and Bull's finest, if I were so inclined.

Alas, we'd left Scotland in quite the rush and hadn't even so much as a dram amongst us.

My best friend and packmate, Hugh MacKeane, frowned into his glass, his stiff shoulders nearly touching his ears with building tension. My brother, Jack MacKeane, sat backwards in his chair, his glass hanging loosely from broad fingers as he watched a trio of two men and a woman as they sang, oblivious to the strained atmosphere behind him. The song was a familiar one, and I realized right away why. It had been our uncle's favorite.

I shut the door on that line of thinking before my mood soured. I refused to consider how different things would be if he were still here. If it hadn't been for my own recklessness in my youth—

Damn. Years had passed. I had moved on; I no longer blamed my youthful impulsiveness. Mostly.

Besides, we weren't here on holiday. I didn't have the luxury of time to dwell on past mistakes, no matter how badly I wished I could undo them.

I tossed back a finger of whisky in my family's memory, then nudged Hugh with my booted foot, desperate to restore my normal good humor. "Relax, my friend. They're no' going ta arrest me at the Cock and Bull in Little Walrus."

Hugh snorted. "Relax? *Relax?*" He jammed the table with his finger as if to punctuate his concern. "Ye're wanted fer murder, Lach. *Murder.*"

I calmly swirled the whisky in my glass a moment before replying. "Och, aye. Precisely why we're headed ta London."

Hugh scoffed. "Yer daft, man," his voice was gruff with frustration yet tinged with obvious concern, which I appreciated.

I tried to soothe his ire. "Neither the London Metropolitan Police nor Scotland Yard's Division X concerns me."

"I still think ye should have listened to yer solicitor's advice and hired a private investigator."

"I'll no' leave my future—my freedom—in the hands o' someone else. Ye ken I like to make my own choices when it comes ta my life." It was true, I fucking hated the entire idea of fate or anything like it. And I certainly didn't want someone I didn't know handling something as important as determining who tried to frame me for *murder*.

Hugh rubbed at the back of his neck before adding, "Yer a Lycan and a duke. Ye ken they willnae send this to Division X or the L.M.P. They'll go directly to the best, and a Spellmaiden'll have ye locked in Marshalsea before ye can fully inhale one breath of the foul London air."

I raised my glass in a mock salute and winked. "I appreciate yer vote of confidence." We both knew the chances of me being caught were slim, but Hugh did have a very good point. "Let them send their very best; ye know hiding is no' how I operate."

Hugh tossed back his drink and slammed his glass on the table, which was honestly out of character for the big man and more a reflection of the strength of his concern than any resemblance to his general personality, which was normally more adventurous and laid-back.

Hugh's voice was low as he bit out, "According to the dragon at the far end o' the bar, word on the street is, they already have."

I glanced across the room to the being in question, my Lycan eyesight and heightened senses taking in far more detail about the stranger than most...including those standing right next to the man. Even from across a crowded, smoky barroom with so many competing, and mostly foul, smells. The dragon was in his human form, though if a bit dated in his attire. He wore clothes from earlier in the century: a cravat, waistcoat, knee breeches, tasseled boots. A regular lord of the manor type. The effect was ruined by the way he hovered over his drink as if hoarding it. *Typical dragon behavior.*

He didn't look like your garden-variety informant.

I couldn't deny I felt a surge of excitement at the very thought that the M.M.R. might have already assigned one of their precious Spellmaidens to bring me in—I always did enjoy a good challenge. Life as of late, had been unusually confrontation-free...well, until now; the potential for insanity all Lycan's faced notwithstanding. It's why I'd never take a mate. I didn't deserve one and I hated the entire idea of Lycan matehood. I wanted everything to be mine through my own choice.

Still, I forced a shrug. "Words on the street say all sorts of things...from the mundane ta the truly outrageous, most of it utter tripe."

Hugh glanced over his shoulder as if to check for listening ears, then leaned closer and whispered two words. "Josephine Bell."

As if saying her name too loudly could conjure her to this run-down public house in the middle of nowhere. It was a humorous sight to see coming from a man who was not only as broad as a house—only a slight exaggeration—but a full-fledged Lycan in his prime to boot.

There was a reason we were at the top of the food chain; though one would be wise not to express such a sentiment to the Drakaina, dragon shifters, who were technically the head of all the various shifter species.

For now.

It was complicated.

"Ye've confirmed this?" I asked.

"Nae. So far, it's only strong speculation."

I rubbed at my night beard, the better to hide my grin, as I considered Hugh's revelation. Josephine Bell. "I cannae say I've had the pleasure," but I'd heard of her, and damn if I didn't feel an unexpected surge of anticipation at the possibility.

"But ye have heard of her..."

"Who hasnae?" I drank more of my whisky, savoring the burn...at least it had that going for it. "Earned her spot as a Spellmaiden through pure grit. Highest number of arrests, captures, kills. Orphan." *Beautiful.* "Does that about sum it up?"

Hugh snorted as he relaxed back in his chair, but his shoulders stiffened once again as a barmaid walked up and rather nonchalantly slid onto my lap.

She wrapped both arms around my neck and with a suggestive purr exclaimed, "Lachlan! It's been an age." Then, she leaned close to whisper, "I get off in an hour, lover...," her voice trailed off suggestively as she playfully walked her fingers up my chest, and I smiled in fond remembrance.

The hours I'd spent between her ample tits and fleshy thighs were a marvel, but this time, my friend had the greater need. The man was far too tense, and at this point, only fighting or fucking would help alleviate some of his obvious tension.

I knew which *I'd* prefer.

I playfully swatted the barmaid's arse. "Och, lass, I'd be honored to reacquaint myself with yer charms, but my friend Hugh here could really use yer special talents more than I this eve."

At my suggestion, she twisted in my lap to face Hugh, a wide, naughty smile curling her lips. Hugh's scowl hardened in response, and yet she leaned back into me to say, "Mmmm... He does look like he'd be a beast of a man in bed. But a delicious beast, for sure."

"Och, aye. A gentleman beastie...," I clarified, and I had to stifle a chuckle at Hugh's snort.

Her eyes locked on my friend for only a moment longer, before she nodded and quickly stood, practically dancing over to Hugh before straddling his lap. The big man's hands lifted automatically, coming to rest on her generous hips.

Unfortunately, knowing my packmate well, I could see Hugh was about to gently decline her advances...

But then a large, ugly brute of a man in torn, filthy trousers along with three of his equally unkempt friends crowded over our table. The apparent leader of said group of miscreants wrapped one meaty hand around the barmaid's upper arm and squeezed. "Janine. Ye're meant to be seeing to *our* needs this eve."

Judging by the subtle waft of steam coming out of the man's ears and the small, boney nubs running down the length of his big blue bald head, he and his friends were some type of demon. Not the classified types, which were more animal than anything that could pass as human, but definitely demonic in origin, though judging from appearance, barely civilized.

Hugh growled low, his rumble deep and not at all subtle. When he spoke, his voice was harder than stone. "Remove yer hand from the lass afore I rip yer fooking arms from yer shoulders."

While the leader focused on Hugh, one of the demon's friends nudged him in the arm and pointed rudely in my direction. "Blimey, Nigel. Isn't that…"

Damn and blast, I sighed to the heavens, knowing what was to come. Couldn't a man just enjoy a drink—even if it was only a small step up from rat's piss—in relative peace anymore?

Nigel turned to face me and narrowed his eyes. "You Lachlan MacKeane?"

I finished off my whisky, then shrugged. "Depends on who's asking."

The man smiled revealing sharp blackened teeth, and he let go of the barmaid, his interest in the lass forgotten. "Boys." He clearly spoke to the two miscreants at his shoulders. "It appears to be our lucky day."

The two men behind him laughed like a pair of imbeciles, and the leader cracked his knuckles, then rubbed one hand down the nubs on his head as he asked, "What's the latest bounty on this man's head, Shorty?"

The demon to his right replied, "Fifty pounds, boss."

I glanced at Hugh who shook his head in exasperation. I could practically hear his silent groan. "Do ye hear that, Hugh? Only fifty."

Hugh snorted.

"Well, it's an outrage," I scoffed.

This confused the trio as their gazes bounced back and forth between my friend and I.

In fact, they were so stunned, they didn't react when I stood and put a friendly arm around Nigel's shoulders and offered my unsolicited opinion on the matter. "Ye really should hold out for far more than fifty, lads."

The man nodded his head and rubbed at his chin as if taking my sage advice under serious consideration. From the corner of my eye, I saw Hugh beseech the ceiling, and I had to choke back a laugh.

"In fact," I continued, "ye see that gent over there by the stairs?"

The three men swung their gazes towards the stairs in unison; it was almost comical to witness.

"Aye?" the leader confirmed.

"He claims he knows someone offering two *hundred* and fifty pounds." I slapped the man's chest as if to punctuate the truth of my statement, my actions all companion like. As if we stood on the same team.

The man looked at me, then back at the gent by the stairs, then looked at me again.

I gave him a toothy grin.

The other man's smile fell.

So, perhaps, the demon wasn't quite such an imbecile after all.

I ducked just as the demon took a clumsy swing, then glanced over my shoulder to note a wavering knife embedded in the wall right where my head had been.

Ah. It seemed other bounty hunters had arrived. I supposed word on the street had gotten around after all and knowing the magical community like I did, we could add all sorts of bounty hunters to the long list of people I needed to avoid for a while.

I slapped my hands together in anticipation as Shorty took his own ineffective swing, while Nigel tried to remove a screeching Janine from his back.

Then, Hugh stood and grabbed his chair, swinging it at the third demon's head, and I grinned.

Fighting it is, then. Hell, I needed the exercise anyway.

That's when all hell really broke loose.

Chapter Three

Vincent von Rappoldstein, the Greatest Villain Ever Known. Ever.
An Unexpected **Cat**astrophe

Meanwhile…
von Rappoldstein's Lair,
London, England…

IT WAS MID-AFTERNOON, and thus far, I had successfully managed to avoid glancing at my soul scales all day, even going so far as to sit in this interminably long meeting in my office with my back solidly facing the hated device. In truth, after the prior day's events, I hesitated to look.

Some days, I didn't want to *know* just how bad it was.

Yet as I contemplated murdering my first lieutenant for the third time in less than an hour, I regretted not looking in on the state of my soul at least once. I needed to know how much play I had before—catastrophe struck and the world came to an end.

To say I was near the very end of my patience was an understatement.

But who could blame me? Hadn't I specifically requested someone *not* boring for the position of first in command? Someone with more than one or two cells in their oversized brainbox? Would anyone truly fault me for embedding my brass letter opener into my first commander's dull and withered heart?

I certainly thought not.

I idly stroked my pocket watch, no ordinary watch by any stretch of the imagination, my fingers itching to flip open the lid and *check*, which, whenever they noticed this behavior, always managed to make my commanders nervous.

My previous commander would piss himself at the mere sight of my watch, whether I opened it or not.

Needless to say, *that* man hadn't remained in my employ for long.

Was it really so difficult to find good help these days? What was the world coming to when a formidable villain couldn't find competent people who didn't balk at a little murder and mayhem? Why even apply for the position in the first place when everyone who was anyone knew I excelled at wreaking havoc of the very worst kind?

As such, prospective employees should expect to get their hands dirty from time to time whilst in my employ. I'd always made that pertinent point perfectly clear right up front—in the initial interview even. Yesterday's events were practically an everyday occurrence in my world.

Usually because I orchestrated them.

I smiled a little in fond remembrance of yesterday's pandemonium. Pissing off Cerberus had been, quite frankly, inspired. And using Josephine Bell to do it—brilliant, the veritable cherry on top of a well-laid plan. I nearly purred with glorious satisfaction.

I wasn't sure what sort of look had crossed my face just then, but I noticed when my first commander stumbled over his words. Yet when I glanced his way, the man simply continued to drone on and on and on.

And *on*.

If a bit slower, even.

And in that same monotonous tone, which seemed employed

specifically to drive me to the edge of sanity.

I would rather watch paint dry.

Unable to bear it any longer and before I did something rather rash, I flipped open the lid of my watch—which served as a sort of portable soul scales, among other things—and glanced down. My smile fell as I regarded the specific dial showing the current state of my soul.

It was solidly in the yellow—on the side of evil, naturally—a mere tick away from red, in fact, which was bad news for the world.

Dammit.

Truthfully, being in the red on the side of good was equally as bad for the world…it was all a matter of balance.

Personally, I preferred to be near the red side of bad than the red side of good, but regardless of my preferences, I had to do something to swing the pendulum of my cursed soul back in the opposite direction. And soon.

Ugh. I would have to do something *nice*—perish the thought—to bring my soul back into balance, or else—*boom*—goodbye cruel world. And everyone in it.

Even *dirt* would cease to exist.

It was a damn effective spell, and I could appreciate being cursed so very thoroughly, the White Witch be damned.

It took a moment or two of quiet contemplation, while I considered and discounted several approaches to address the state of my soul, before it dawned on me that the room had gone peculiarly silent, and I glanced up to see my second in command mopping his brow with a small, damp cloth; his eyes wide with fear.

I glanced to the man's right, then leaned forward a bit to peer over the edge of my desk to discover my first in command had fainted.

Seriously?

I shook my head, a small tension headache beginning to make its presence known, before I shifted my attention and directed a small, if forced, smile towards my former second commander. Folding my hands together atop the desk, I said, "Congratulations. You've been promoted."

My new commander—what was his name? Bob? Jerry? Nigel? James?—I really wasn't sure—but whoever he was, his head bobbed as he swallowed hard. He opened his mouth to speak, but then seemed to think better of it and instead, slammed his lips together as if in a vow of silence.

Perhaps, this one wasn't a complete imbecile after all.

I squeezed the letter opener in my grip—when had I reached for the blasted thing?—then glanced up sharply when out of the corner of his eye, I saw the larger set of official soul scales shift a hair further towards red.

Towards evil.

Blast and Damn.

I glanced to the heavens with a growl. "Oh, so now I am penalized for merely *thinking* about murder?" Never mind the fact I had a white-knuckled grip around a veritable weapon.

My query was punctuated by a loud thump, and I rubbed at the building tension in my head, well-knowing the thump had been the sound of my newly promoted first in command falling to the floor in his own dead faint.

As I stared at his prone form, I made a mental note to put an advertisement in the paper for a pair of new commanders while I was out working to bring my soul back into balance by way of—*shudder*—a few good deeds.

I closed my watch and dropped it into my waistcoat pocket as I stood. All would be fine. Helping a little old lady or two across the pavement should do the trick to bring me back into balance and appease the powers that be.

Good deeds always seemed to carry more weight than the bad. For whatever reason.

But that was an observation to ponder another day.

IN HINDSIGHT, I should have stuck with my initial plan: to help a couple of old ladies cross the street. But who could really fault me for choosing, instead, to rescue an innocent little cat stuck in a tree who just happened to be there, howling pitifully, as I passed?

Who could have possibly *foreseen* the consequences of my impulsive actions? It was a mere cat for crying out loud. Never mind how she found herself so very conveniently placed in my path. Cats got stuck in trees every day, right?

At the time, I certainly hadn't anticipated what would happen, else I'd have happily left the cat to die—perhaps, even hastened things along—then, merrily held the skeins of yarn for a dozen little old ladies while I listened to them talk of boils and ulcers and gastronomical issues...all while they crocheted a thousand doilies and hats for the needy and destitute.

But no. I had to help the damn cat out of a tree. A monumental mistake in retrospect.

I should have known. I preferred dogs, myself—Hellhounds to be precise—cats being a blight on the Earth. But I was too concerned with balancing my soul to take pause and wonder at the convenience of this good deed practically falling into my lap, and I rarely, if ever, second guessed myself.

The thankless feline clawed my face for all my efforts, the wretch, then 'followed' me home by clinging to my back with twenty fully engaged claws.

I really had no one to blame but myself for what happened next, but I'd simply had enough. So, I made another, I admit hasty, decision to rectify my blunder of rescuing Satan's hell maiden in the first place.

Surely, I reasoned, my soul could afford to feed Lucifer's feline to my Hellhound, Bob. Bob was such a good boy and had earned this prize. Honestly. Besides, the cat was a right *bitch*—a cute and cuddly monster with retractable blades hidden between every delightful little kitty toe. A floofy killing machine. Empirical evidence all cats were evil, and under better circumstances, I might have appreciated the effectiveness of such a clever killing machine.

Note to Self: Never follow through on a plan if one began one's justification for said plan with the word 'Surely.'

Without an ounce of remorse, I tossed Satan's mistress and Bob into the back garden and slammed the door, relying on Bob to sort things out in his own way.

Imagine my surprise when, less than ten minutes later, that damned feline waltzed back into my house with nary a hair out of place. I could barely believe my own eyes.

Bob had *lost?* To this oversized rat?

Leaving me in the market for a new hellhound?

*Blast and Damn...*a real pain in the arse that. One couldn't exactly walk down to Long and Sons in Piccadilly Circus and just buy a replacement hellhound, they were deuced hard to come by even in the magical world. Not to mention ludicrously expensive.

Then there was all the *training* involved.

And the safety gear to stay alive whilst engaged in said training.

It had taken *years* and many months of recovery to train Bob; may he rest in hell.

I rubbed at my chest. Poor Bob was never going to live this down. The other Hellhounds were going to *laugh.*

I swallowed a small—very small—lump of remorse and turned my back on the all-too-pleased cat, but not before flinging the murderess my most ferocious scowl then tossing back two fingers of whisky. I had just poured myself another when the killer in fluffy disguise with stupidly cute pink toe pads spoke.

"Why thank you for that, young man. I quite needed the exercise."

I snorted, for if my suspicions were correct, this feline hadn't had to put forth much effort to win, but I kept such suppositions to myself. Instead, I glanced over my shoulder, asking, "My pleasure. I presume our meeting today was no accident?"

A small smile was the cat's only response.

I tossed back my second whisky and slammed the glass to the counter before crossing my arms and turning to fully face my adversary. "You could have just knocked, you know?"

The cat shrugged. "I hadn't intended to, er, reveal myself just yet."

"But did you need to employ every single one of those daggers you call claws, though?" What I really wanted to ask was, "Did you need to kill Bob?"

I rubbed at the sudden pang in my chest.

The cat investigated said claws, cleaning one with a pull of her teeth before saying, "I needed to act the part. You would have been suspicious otherwise."

I refused to acknowledge she had a point. I took a moment to study my newly discovered rival.

"Well, then. Why don't we start with introductions. Vincent von Rappoldstein, at your service, apparently." I gave a slight bow, then relaxed back against my desk. "And you are?"

The cat dipped her head. "Lady Sophia Tewkesbury-Smith. I've come to claim you as my familiar."

I laughed without an ounce of humor to color my tone. "You've come to claim *me* as *your* familiar?" I scoffed. "Now, why in the world would I allow that?"

Most unnervingly, Lady Sophia merely tsked in response. "Oh, son, you seem to think you have some say in the matter."

She blinked once. Twice.

I stared, refusing to blink.

And then all of a sudden it was done.

The entire "claiming" was peculiarly uneventful and over in a second. I knew she'd done it. I could feel the bond snapping into place, could almost sense Sophia's presence before me in a different way than before.

She smiled, then, showing her gleaming white fangs and asked, "Now, shall we discuss the bounty you posted for Lachlan MacKeane's head?"

Chapter Four

Josie
Mmhmm... What a Delicious ~~Target~~, er, Cup of Coffee

The Twisted Vine
Messers Nutterfield and Shaw
Purveyors of Fine Coffees and Exotic Teas

WITHOUT QUESTION, THE Twisted Vine brewed the best and hottest coffee in the world, or at least, the best on Piccadilly Circus, formerly known as Regent Circus South. I stepped inside the dim coffee shop, setting off the little brass bell over the door, the sound of which was barely discernable over the din of patrons crowded near the bar awaiting their orders. I closed my eyes and drew in a deep, calming breath. The air was saturated with the remarkable scent of fresh coffee, earthy spices, and the subtle suggestion of magic.

In other words, heavenly...

I removed my cloak and hung it on a hook by the door, though I kept hold of my fingerless gloves; then I pushed my way through the crowd of milling people until I reached the bar where a tall and equally broad mustachioed man of middling years wiped out a stoneware mug with a clean, if damp, rag. His mouth split into a wide grin. "Gorblimy, Joe! Look at what the demon brought in."

A few customers—decidedly human—darted an uncomfortable glance his way, but ultimately seemed to shrug off the man's words as owning to a peculiar sense of humor rather than a statement of literal fact.

If only they knew that the co-owners of this establishment were both demons who employed a couple of well-placed spells that only made them appear human when they were anything but.

A short, lean man—the opposite of the barkeep in every way—stepped into the open doorway leading to the kitchens, wiping his hands on a dingy, grey apron with oversized pockets. "Well, bless me soul, indeed. Morning, Ms. Bell."

"Good morning, Mr. Shaw, Mr. Nutterfield."

Mr. Nutterfield nodded. "Let's see. The usual? A medium roast with cinnamon, nutmeg, and allspice?"

I dipped my head. "Yes, please and thank you."

Mr. Nutterfield nodded his approval, then moved along to help another customer with a boldly barked, "First time? What'll it be, good sir? Coffee or condoms? We offer both, including a special commemorative edition mug in honor of the Queen's Diamond Jubilee."

"How about a commemorative condom?" someone shouted out, which was followed by a dozen snickers all around.

I shook my head and turned my back on the bar, and out of habit more than anything, I scanned the room with my eyes and my magic, but apart from two Lycans in a shadowed corner on the far side of the cafe, the patrons were harmless humans. Well, mostly.

Confident no threats were lurking in the shop, I threaded my way through a motley assortment of tables in various sizes, colors, and shapes while behind me, Mr. Nutterfield called out to patrons by name as their orders were readied. At the back of the little cafe, my favorite table beckoned, and it was with a deep sigh of contentment that I dropped the file outlining my new assignment on the surface and settled into the sturdy wooden chair, my back to the wall, my gaze once more scanning my surroundings for trouble.

Not five minutes later, Mr. Nutterfield placed a steaming mug of coffee on the table and settled in the seat across from me, nodding at the file to my left. A file I longed to open but hadn't yet dared after my initial peek. I was...readying myself.

"New assignment?" he asked while he absentmindedly cleaned the table in front of him with his ever-present rag.

Once again, I darted a glance at the innocuous purple folder and had to suppress the urge to reach over and run my hand down the cover. Instead, I gripped my coffee with both hands, holding on to what was surely the elixir of life.

Ignoring Mr. Nutterfield's question for now, I inhaled, taking in a full breath of the delicious aroma of my favorite drink, the exotic scents a balm to my soul, before I took a bracing sip. "Mmmm..." Then with exaggerated care, I set the mug before me, though I continued to embrace it with both hands. "You know I cannot discuss Spellmaiden business," I chided.

He laughed, a deep familiar chuckle, and replied. "Eh, I know."

Without conscious thought, I glanced at the file again, unable to help myself. Tearing my gaze away, I looked Mr. Nutterfield in the eye and asked, "Have you seen Belmont lately?" Belmont was a font of information—if the price was right—and I often employed his services whenever I landed a new assignment.

Mr. Nutterfield scratched at his chin. "I'd say it's been a couple o' weeks, a least."

Interesting. "Well, then, I suppose he's due for a visit."

Mr. Nutterfield nodded his agreement. "Should I let 'im know ye're looking for 'im?"

I considered this, but in the end, I felt it far more prudent to lay low—the White Witch had a long reach, and I couldn't forget I was supposed to be under enquiry. I was taking a huge risk by even talking to Nutterfield, much less Belmont. "That won't be necessary but thanks anyway."

The barkeep rapped the table with his knuckles, once, as he stood and said, "Well, you let me know if ye change yer mind. In the meantime, be safe, little wren." It's what he always said at the end of our little chats.

I dipped my head, adding, "Whenever possible."

Well, I *was* honest, if anything.

He nodded toward the mug in my grip. "I'll start a second cup for ye."

I smiled my thanks, took one last bracing sip, draining my mug, then, slipped on my spectacles. A sense of anticipation filled me as I slid the purple folder over and flipped open the cover, automatically turning to the second page, unable to wait another moment to dive into the details.

ASSIGNED SPELLMAIDEN: Josephine Caroline Bell, Kameleon House, One Coven Square, London

I grinned. Regardless of everything I'd achieved that part never got old.

TARGET: Lachlan Connor Daire MacKeane, 7th Duke of Skye

Lachlan MacKeane…Lachlan MacKeane…Lachlan Mac—Come to think on it, I *had* heard of him. If memory served, rumor had it he'd been caught *in flagrante delicto* whilst entertaining five women in his rooms during the Duke of Abernathy's annual Christmas house party.

Five women at once.

Purportedly, the man had simply shrugged when he'd been found out and asked his hostess to rustle up some more cham-pagne and join them.

And by all accounts, the hostess and her husband *did*.

I cleared an interesting and unexpected catch in my throat and carried on reading.

SPECIES: Lycan

I had to admit the Lycan clans and I clung to a tenuous truce at the best of times, seeing as I was forever having to hunt them due to their impulsive behavior coupled with their extraordinary strength. Far more so than all the other shifter species.

Not to mention the fact that every single one of them went insane, eventually, unless they died prematurely in battle or at the hands of a cunning adversary. Or never took a mate.

In fact, it was a surprise, really, that in all my dealings with Lycans, I'd never met the head of the MacKeane clan.

I glanced at the Lycans seated in the opposite corner. At present, one of the men faced away from me; and with his massive back, old-fashioned attire, and thick, red hair, which hung loose over extraordinarily broad shoulders, he was utterly unremarkable…broad shoulders and unruly, red hair being typical of many Lycan males.

It was the other man, the one enveloped in shadows, who piqued my interest. Or perhaps, caution, was a more accurate descriptor.

I could see very little of the second man, apart from a couple of somewhat intriguing details. Broad, blunt fingers, unexpectedly buffed and trimmed, toyed with the steaming mug of coffee before him, his touch upon the stoneware reminiscent of a bold caress, which was a patently absurd observation and wholly irrelevant.

Down below, long legs stretched the width of the table, casual like and crossed at the ankles. He wore black leather boots and thick woolen socks, but from the angle my view afforded me, I could discern nothing else.

Which was suitably inspiring, truth be told. I did have an active imagination…when I chose to employ it…and it threatened to entertain me now.

Not that I would ever admit that to a soul.

He had perfectly shaped knees—another peculiar observation—and lean, muscular thighs liberally dusted with hair and carved to exquisite perfection. The table itself hindered my view, preventing further visual exploration, though I understood were I to investigate more thoroughly, I'd discover a kilt somewhere amidst all that darkness, likely a match to the one his friend wore (thick wool woven in colors of black, blue, and green—and most importantly—*not* the tartan belonging to the MacKeanes of Skye). *Pity.*

Despite the mystery and shadows surrounding the two men, nothing about the pair felt particularly threatening in the least, and I dragged my attention away from them, if reluctantly.

Besides, what idiot would present himself in public—in London, no less—while being hunted by the government to such an extent they'd hire a Spellmaiden to apprehend him? Lycans were accountably clever, after all, even if I hadn't necessarily seen a sign of their infamous wit myself.

And while I may not care for the breed, I didn't think a man like MacKeane would be so daft. In fact, I'd be quite put out if he were.

Shaking my head, I pushed my glasses up my nose and returned my attention to his file.

NATIONALITY: Scotland

FAMILY: Parents – Both Deceased.

    Siblings – Two. Jack MacKeane, younger brother. Owain MacKeane, younger brother.

    Other Family – Uncle and His Family, All Deceased.

ASSIGNMENT: Capture and Present Fugitive-at-Large to Gabriel, head angel, Marshalsea Gaol

Marshalsea? Well, someone really, really *wants this guy.*

WANTED FOR MURDER

That made it official. And partially explained Marshalsea. While there were several magical gaols in use, Marshalsea was particularly brutal and rumored to be impossible to breach.

I read on:

Outmaneuvered five runners; wounded three. Outran a Class III Demon. Overpowered a Titan. Captured a gorgon. Sniper. Boxer. Fencer. Rumored to have escaped purgatory. The only person in the world to neutralize a Class I Demon.

Impressive.

Strong. Clever. Lethal.

Seriously…

Extremely Dangerous.

And that little wolfie, explains me.
I didn't even try to mask my pleasure now. I smiled, allowing myself a moment to relish the thrill of the chase. The challenge. He sounded like a worthy opponent, a dastardly villain.
He sounded *perfect.*
While I did occasionally suffer from self-doubt, deep-down I knew I could do this. What I lacked in luck and skill, I more than made up for with sheer determination, which was equally as valid as relying purely on skill and magical talent.

MOTIVE: Unknown.

This wasn't a surprise. Lycans truly were the most impulsive lot of beasts in existence for all that they were notoriously cunning.

WHEREABOUTS: Unknown.

ADDITIONAL REMARKS: UNMATED. DO NOT KILL.

Thank the gods. The only thing worse than an unmated Lycan was a mated one.

I scanned the rest of the page, which listed known aliases, biographical details, known residences, net worth... I whistled. *Four hundred thousand pounds.*

Also, *Tattoos* **and** *piercings? Six foot seven?* Even for a Lycan, six-seven was brow-raising.

I glanced over to the Lycans in the opposite corner once again. While broad, the man with his back to me didn't appear to be anywhere near six-seven. Six-two, maybe. The other one, alas, remained a mystery.

To be safe, I closed my eyes and plucked out a thread of magic, running figurative fingers over its length as it flowed toward the Lycans. Though a low hum skated across my skin on contact—which wasn't completely unusual, *per se*, since I knew the coffee house employed several levels of magic for security purposes and to protect their identities—no sense of a threat nor hint of animosity disturbed the thread of power flowing beneath my hands.

Then again, the most direct line of magic flowing toward them, purple in color, seemed to hold a hint of grey...a neutralizing color, the result was an almost indiscernibly less vivid hue than it should have been. A sign some sort of masking spell was involved, different from the ones I knew The Twisted Vine employed.

Curious, I began to pick at the dulled thread—

Or I did right up until someone slid into the seat before me with a small grunt. I opened my eyes. *Belmont.*

I slammed the file closed and locked eyes with the creature—man was a misnomer for certain. For long moments, we stared at each other in silence, our gazes narrowed, until Mr. Nutterfield appeared and dropped two steaming mugs of coffee between us.

Before leaving, the barkeep rapped the table in warning. "I don't want any bloodshed."

Mr. Nutterfield gave me a pointed look, and I felt my lips twitch. What can I say? I have a bit of a reputation.

I otherwise ignored the barkeep and instead, tossed my unwanted colleague a false smile.

Belmont smirked in response. "Josssie Bell—it'sss been awhile."

I reached for my mug, drew the cup before my mouth, and blew at the rising steam. "Miss me?"

His eyes flicked to the closed file before meeting my gaze once again. "Like an unwanted rasssh."

"Oh? Are there other kinds of rashes that are wanted then?"

A long, forked tongue darted from between his reptilian-like lips, as if to taste me on the air, before recoiling once more between cold, thin lips. "Funny."

I shrugged. "I thought so."

He slid further into his chair and crossed his arms, leaving his mug untouched on the table.

Knowing the walls had ears—though in truth, I was really just anxious to return to the file before me and the juicy details therein rather than spend a moment more of my time than necessary facing a creature like Belmont—I decided to get directly to the point. I pinned him with narrowed eyes. "I didn't summon you, so you must have information you think I'd be willing to purchase." We both knew real information didn't come for free.

He smiled. "What'sss it worth to you, Josssie Bell?"

"You know as well as I that depends on the quality of the information you have to offer."

He shrugged. "Word hasss it you acccepted a rather im-presssive asssignment today."

Damn the M.M.R. and their, at times, apparent lack of intelligence. Of course, a large paper elephant didn't charge down the main thoroughfare of Mayfair without attracting notice. I feigned an expression of ignorance. "Oh?"

Belmont clearly wasn't amused. "There'sss already been quite a bit of sssspeculation asss to the nature of thisss asssignment."

I shrugged. "Speculation isn't worth a farthing. You're going to have to do better than that."

He continued as if I hadn't spoken. "Interesssstingly, a sssurge of wagersss and more than a few bountiesss—with ssstaggering returnsss and incccentivesss—were posssted immediately after."

I hesitated. "Define immediate."

"I meant that quite literally."

"Alright, I'll buy. A halfpence apiece."

"A caroon."

I laughed at that. A crown? No. "If these bounties and speculations are as outrageous as you claim, I can find out for myself easily enough. And for free."

Posted bounties were never secret—they were meant to be broadcasted by their very nature—I was paying for expediency more than anything else.

"Four ssshillingsss."

"How about we start with one"

He seemed to think it over, but I well knew he would take whatever I offered.

"One shilling? Deal."

"Alright." I pulled my wand out of thin air and with a flick of my wrist, twelve pennies landed on the table in front of Belmont with a melodic clink. Oh, I hadn't conjured the coins up from nowhere, I had the coin, I just wasn't idiotic enough to openly carry money on my person…not with the sort of places I often frequented in the course of my duties. "Now, talk."

Belmont's tongue whipped out and the coins disappeared as fast as a frog capturing a fly.

"Lachlan MacKeane…." hearing the duke's name on the lizardman's lips was both promising and worrying for an entire host of reasons.

I waved off whatever Belmont intended to say. "He had bounties on his head the moment he was charged with murder." I didn't actually know, but I could make an educated guess.

Belmont dipped his head. "And yet, every sssingle one of thossse bountiesss tripled in sssize asss of about an hour ago."

About the time I accepted the assignment then. "How many bounties are on his head? And how much are we talking about?"

"There are currently thirty-ssseven different bountiesss float-ing about…" Belmont cocked his head as if listening to something only he could hear. "…make that thirty-eight. The sssmallessst of thossse is offering one—"

"Shilling?" I could clearly start a side-hustle as a comedienne.

"—thousssand poundsss."

I kept my face neutral, pretending that amount wasn't stag-geringly obscene. "Dead or Alive?"

Belmont shrugged, "In thisss inssstanccce, alive, but thessse bountiesss run the gambit…from roughed up a bit to packed up into individual, bite-sssized piecccesss."

Belmont's slithering sss's were starting to grate on my nerves, and I forced a polite smile. "And the highest bounty?"

"Fifty thousand."

Well. That was unfortunate. "Anonymous?"

Belmont shook his head. "Von Rappoldssstein."

Of course. I really should have known. *Blast.* These bounties were going to make my job infinitely more difficult because every Tom, Dick, and Harry was going to be hunting my mark.

"Anything else?"

"One more thing, though thisss one'sss on the houssse."

Belmont leaned across the table, his voice low. "Rumor has it, there's been a spot of trouble in paradise for you."

I narrowed my eyes. Did he know about my probation? I couldn't see how, and I wasn't about to reveal my concern. "Is that all?"

Belmont stood. "I'd watch your back if I were you, Josssie Bell."

I always watched my back.

After he left, I debated packing up and going someplace more secure, but honestly, I'd already covered the coffee house and who knows what might be lurking on the streets in wait. Better to finish going through the file to understand the full extent of what I faced first.

And on that thought, I reopened the file and continued reading.

NOTES: Suspected owner of Wolffe and Sons L'Arène de Bataille.

Now *that* was an interesting possibility. Wolffe and Sons L'Arène de Bataille was an illegal club—to say they engaged in unlawful fisticuffs was a gross understatement.

The club was all but impossible to find. Powerful magic protected it, and the list of people who would sell their souls to the Fae to control such power was long and distinguished. One could be arrested simply from *trying* to enter the club.

Yes, Wolffe and Sons was the magical world's worst best-kept secret.

And in that moment, I rather hoped I'd be required to drop in unannounced.

As if reading my thoughts, four words inked in oxblood red appeared in the empty space near the bottom of the page:

GO TO THE CLUB.

I *should* be properly concerned. Never mind my recent probation and despite the clear directive, I'd be arrested if caught, which naturally begged the questions: Who, exactly, was Lachlan MacKeane? And why did so many people want him so badly, besides the obvious? I was beginning to think that the possibility he murdered some people was the more insignificant part of what was happening here.

I flipped to the next page, to find the first of many drawings and photographs of my mark and had to actually fight the urge to fan myself.

Oh…

Well…

He is…

I swallowed. Kilt inspector, *indeed…*

A handful of seconds passed, perhaps more, and in those

handful of lost moments, I catalogued an incredible number of details about the man whose likeness I perused. Like the black hair, and the eyes of molten lava. The dimple in his left cheek, or the Celtic wolf tattooed on his left shoulder. The small round space peculiarly devoid of any tattoo directly over his heart.

The tiny gold hoops piercing his nipples.

Several thoughts, absurd thoughts really—*miles* outside the basic facts—teased, seeking to distract me. I dismissed them all, though admitted it hardly seemed fair a creature so viscerally *male* should be so very wicked.

So appealing, yet so bad.

Might he be part incubus?

Thinking back to my conversation with Daphne—and from a purely occupational standpoint, mind you—I admitted I could see the appeal, more's the pity. Perhaps, it was the unexpected twinkle in his eye?

For a *murderer*, that is. Why did I seem to keep forgetting that pertinent fact?

Still, I smiled, and the hum in the air intensified the tiniest bit, barely perceptible and thus one might forgive oneself for ignoring what one oughtn't...and I might not have ignored it were I not, at that moment, effectively bouncing in my standard issue shoes whilst savoring the thrill of the upcoming hunt.

Unfortunately for MacKeane, no matter my thoughts—and MacKeane could be all the things people said and more. Good and bad. He could even be *innocent*—

I was still going to arrest his *arse*, fascinating piercings and all.

And maybe, just maybe, have a little fun in the process.

Chapter Five

Lachlan
One Coffee with a Side of Bollocks, Please

AFTER ALL HIS cantankerous grumbling and bellyaching about traveling to London whilst there were so many bounties on my head, I don't know why Hugh insisted on meeting me at a public coffee house once we got here, but here we were, taking up quite a lot of space at an oversized table situated along the back wall of The Twisted Vine.

And when Josephine Caroline Bell just so happened to waltz through the front door with a broad smile on her face and hung her cloak on a hook by the window, I no longer cared about the whys of it.

I drew a sip of exquisitely brewed coffee, then mumbled to Hugh, "Do no' turn around now, but the verra last Sassenach ye'd prefer me not ta see just walked right through the front door."

The expression on Hugh's face swung from skeptical to comically panicked and back again, and I had to bite back a laugh as the coin he'd been rolling over his knuckles clattered to the table with a loud clank.

"And here I didnae think ye cared…"

Hugh cursed, the word "Fook" all but exploding from his

mouth on a low huff of frustrated air, and I knew he'd spotted my Spellmaiden. But then he simply picked up his silver shilling and began spinning it on the table between his hands, and I watched in silence until his gaze met mine.

"Problem?" I asked.

Hugh swiped up the coin and reached for his coffee. "Nae."

I nodded, once, then sought out Ms. Bell, while testing the air, only to be left feeling strangely disappointed when I couldn't detect any sign of her scent. Though considering she was a Spellmaiden, it wasn't a stretch to think she might suppress her natural scent through some sort of amulet or spell. That would make sense considering the nature of her job, though I didn't have to like it.

I tracked her with every sense at my disposal, drinking her in as she approached the bar and placed her order. When she turned to face the crowded room, my breath caught at the sight of her worrying her plump bottom lip. I was spellbound and found myself strangely holding my breath as she scanned the room, passing right over our table twice, before making her way to an empty seat in the back. As if I longed for her to spot me hidden in the shadows.

Worse, I had to stifle the urge to follow her, like a lost dog begging for some scrap of attention, which would be a monumental mistake for obvious reasons.

I forced myself to focus. To size up the biggest threat to my continued freedom: the notorious Josephine Caroline Bell. Here. In the flesh.

Witch. Spellmaiden. Huntress. Orphan.

Expert tracker. Brilliant tactician.

Powerful. Athletic. Beautiful.

Authorized to kill.

She looked exactly as my file on her suggested.

I shifted in my seat; a slow smile curling the corners of my mouth as I scrutinized the woman the M.M.R. thought to employ to hunt me down…Hugh had somehow managed to confirm the assignment. I could scarcely credit my good fortune at being here at this precise moment, assuming it was an actual coincidence.

Cat-like spectacles perched on the tip of her nose, hair bound and tightened in a simple, yet severe top knot, high-necked collar secured with a lacy jabot and pinned with a large, black cameo… she walked and moved with purpose. On the surface, she appeared more rigid librarian or austere governess than the most successful—and deadliest—Spellmaiden in history.

Only the unexpected shock of bright, red hair and wide, cerulean eyes stopped her from appearing too severe.

I stroked my stubbled jaw as I followed the intriguing lines of her shirtwaist and down her expertly tailored skirts. How many weapons did she have on her person at this very moment? I guessed a dozen at least, and I grinned with unexpected delight at the very idea.

Upon further reflection, I'd never met a librarian or a governess with curves like *that*, and I found the combination of effortless sensuality, lethal skill, and allusive innocence *damned* erotic.

Pity she was a witch.

I shifted in my seat once again, feeling uncomfortably tight all of a sudden, and covered my unease by raising my mug of coffee to my lips. It wouldn't do to lust too hard after the woman sent to toss me in gaol.

Then again, it could only enhance my carefully cultivated reputation if rather than arrest me, we became lovers instead. The idea certainly had merit, and judging by the hum simmering beneath my skin, making love to her would definitely not be a hardship either.

I narrowed my eyes when a short, lizard-like individual dressed to the nines slid into the empty seat across from her. He had a short mop of hair on his crown and small, thin lips with widespread eyes that nearly wrapped to the side of his face and his skin was roughly textured; I had to imagine he had some sort of magic which enabled him to appear amongst humans without causing a stir.

"Who is this shifty-eyed creature?"

Hugh didn't turn around, just continued to roll his coin across his knuckles, but he knew precisely who I meant. "Name's Belmont. Trades in information."

Their voices were low, but I didn't have to tax my preternatural senses to hear their conversation, even over the din of the overcrowded coffee house, and I was wholly unsurprised nor bothered when I quickly became the topic of their conversation. I was too busy being impressed by how Josie Bell so easily managed a creature like Belmont, which only made my anticipation of our eventual meeting—and we would be meeting—soar.

With the way she kept shooting glances down at the file before her, which I had no doubt documented my entire life's history, I suspected the feeling was mutual.

Eventually, Belmont stood, and I followed him with my eyes as he threaded his way back through the tables. "Hugh. Why dinnae ye intercept our new friend. Make him feel at home, until I can catch up with ye." I had a few questions of my own to ask the man, and I couldn't do that here, not with Josie Bell in the room.

And I definitely wasn't ready to quit her presence.

Hugh left without a word, surprisingly leaving behind his coin, and I resumed watching my quarry.

Before long, a middle-aged human male, ruddy and covered in filth, slid from his seat at the bar and shuffled unerringly toward Ms. Bell's table, the leer contorting the man's lips unmistakably suggestive and lewd.

The shop's patrons quieted, and with my heightened Lycan senses, I scented the air. I could smell the man without much effort—he reeked of horseshit and opium and gin, among a fair number of other questionable things.

Still, I couldn't help but smile. If even half the rumors about her were true, the patrons of The Twisted Vine were in for a treat.

Not counting the day he'd been born, the drunk human made his first mistake when he leaned over Ms. Bell, crowding her, one hand seized upon the back of her chair, the other splayed across her stack of papers, halting her study of my biography.

Ms. Bell, a simple, serene smile situated upon startlingly full lips, calmly brushed away whatever filth had fallen from the man's ragged sleeve—or equally likely, from his greasy, unkempt hair—and onto the surface of her papers. I appreciated how supremely unruffled she appeared as she locked eyes with the blighter, while primly dusting her hands free of dirt, directly over the man's feet.

Who was I kidding...she made me *rock hard*, and I rubbed a hand down my face as I fought valiantly for self-control, which I could feel fraying around the edges.

The ruffian made his second mistake when he propositioned her with vulgar, degrading remarks.

The crowd watching froze in silent horror, but I simply smiled, anticipation humming through my veins along with my desire. She wasn't accounted the best for nothing, and I knew she would handle this miscreant without even trying very hard.

The entire affair was over in a matter of seconds, and Josie Bell did not disappoint.

Her bored but confident mien never faltered, not even while she whipped out her arm and twisted the blighter's balls with one fisted hand. All the men in the cafe winced at the sight, and a few even crossed their legs in sympathy, but no one looked away.

The man's face, now an alarming, and well-deserved, shade of dark purple, greeted the top of her table on his way to the floor. As he succumbed to gravity, the man held one hand to his nose, the other buried between his legs, while he shrieked a lengthy string of high-pitched curses and squeals. Rather like a stuck pig.

This clearly did not ruffle Josie Bell's feathers as she expertly demonstrated when she casually retrieved a kerchief from her sleeve and mopped up the splattered blood from her table, then reached out and dropped the soiled cloth to the floor. It landed in a crumpled wad on the man's shit-stained waistcoat, then slid off his belly as he rolled onto his side, groaning and whimpering with dogged commitment.

"Oh, do shut up." Ms. Bell ordered as she flipped another page of my file. She reached for her coffee as she read, her gaze never straying to the incapacitated man as he lay on the floor, forgotten, at her feet.

This was the renowned warrior I'd expected, and I couldn't help but be suitably impressed. The woman was *good.*

Effortlessly good.

I studied her at my leisure while the rest of the room, including the owner, diligently avoided glancing in her direction. The unwelcome erection I found myself enduring, while not wholly unexpected, threatened to thrust me into a black mood, and I eventually dragged my gaze away with a low growl.

"I doon care fer the scowl upon yer face. I've seen that look before."

My eyes flicked to Hugh as he approached the table. "Where's Belmont?"

"Gagged and trussed up in our carriage."

I nodded my head in approval.

Hugh darted a glance over his shoulder, then looked back at me. He dragged a hand down his face and shook his head, then swiped up the coin he'd left behind. "I cannae believe I'm aboot ta say this after tryin' and failin' to soften yer stance for *years,* but eventually, ye're going to recall how much ye despise witches, particularly Spellmaidens, and then I'll have ta listen to yer belly-aching fer a week—maybe two—for forgetting that fact, even for a moment."

Hugh was not mistaken.

"I've no' forgotten. This is merely reconnaissance."

Hugh scoffed. "Och, aye. But the look on yer face says otherwise, mate."

I resisted the urge to launch my fist into Hugh's great big

flapping jaw, unaccountably irritated all of a sudden.

Unconcerned, my friend leaned forward in his seat. "Call me a liar. I dare ye."

"Fook off."

There was no real heat behind my curse, and I found myself glancing around Hugh, who easily blocked part of my view of Ms. Bell with his ridiculously expansive self. "Demme, but ye've got broad shoulders brother."

Hugh snorted. "Aye. Ye just remember that when ye try to take off my head later. When yer overrun with remorse for whatever it is ye've been thinking about but should no'."

"I'll bear that in mind." I nodded towards the woman across the room and grinned, "While you bear in mind that the government found it necessary to send their verra best."

Hugh chuckled. "She *is* the best. And if I shift over the tiniest bit, I wager she'd have even *ye* trussed up on the floor and at her feet in a matter of seconds. Ye're a demmed fool for still being here, MacKeane."

For a split second, I imagined Ms. Bell doing exactly that—straddling me, one knee buried in my back as she bound me with ropes. The very idea was rather delicious to imagine, inspiring even.

Bloody Hell.

"Drat it, Lach," Hugh's voice was an urgent whisper now, "If ye refused to heed the fact she's no' just some chit assigned to arrest you, can ye at least recall she's a Spellmaiden, an *Animus* Witch. Tell me ye havenae forgotten?"

I shook my head. "No' a fooking chance."

How could I forget? I'd earned a first in Witch Studies at Oxford. What better way to understand my enemy than through dedicated study? Sure, they were working for the *law*. But by all accounts Spellmaidens were my enemy as they seemed to make arresting members of my clan a regular occurrence.

Though it was a very long time ago, more than fifty years to be precise and a drop in the bucket of time for a near-immortal like myself who had the looks and strength of a Lycan male in his prime, every fact and supposition and rumor regarding witches—from biology to history to mythology—was as fresh in my mind now, as the day I'd graduated.

Hugh growled. "She can talk to animals, and ye've the wolf inside ye—"

I waved off my friend's warning and cut him off before he could continue with such ridiculous notions. "That's a myth."

Hugh referred to the idea that an Animus witch could read the thoughts of a Lycan's wolf even while the Lycan was in human form. It would be worrying if not for the fact that in all our historical dealings with witches, a few of them being Animus, it had never come up as something they could use against us (and given the popularity of this particular rumor, they would've certainly tried to employ such tactics if there was any truth to it.)

But, Hugh was worried and that usually meant he could get overly panicked.

Hugh snorted. "Such myths always begin with a kernel o' truth. Besides, it makes perfect sense—"

I shook his head. "It willnae be a problem."

Hugh raised a brow.

"It *willnae.*"

The grate of a chair as it slid across the floor sliced through the heavy atmosphere, and I chanced another glance to the far side of the room. Josie had stood, the purple folder held tight in one arm as she dropped a few coins on the table. I followed her movements, bit back a chuckle when she stepped squarely on her earlier victim's groin as though it were a perfectly normal thing to do, before crossing the room, her mouth drawn in a firm line, her eyes focused. Determined.

Fooking lethal, that one.

Tall, graceful, fierce, confident. She would be a worthy opponent, for a witch.

And yet I found myself strangely disappointed when she left without a confrontation when I was sitting here beneath her very nose.

Something wasn't right about that; she was far too skilled to miss me sitting here in the shadows. And my sense of her was strange. Complicated.

Once the door closed behind her, I looked up at Hugh, whose eyes quickly shifted away from mine. *What the fook.* "Hugh?"

The coin he'd been toying with once again clattered to the table, landing upright in a rapid spin.

I trained my eyes on Hugh, who rubbed the back of his neck before he finally glanced up and met my gaze. I stared at my most trusted friend, the sound of the spinning coin marking the seconds as they passed.

"What did ye do?" I growled out.

He rolled his shoulders before saying, "It's just a small spell."

Aw, fook.

I rubbed a hand down my face. He knew how much I hated using magic. Especially the witch kind for it was a witch's spell which had led to the deaths of my parents. As if divining the direction of my thoughts, the coin flared in my peripheral vision, and Hugh and I glanced down at the spinning shilling.

I raised my hand, intending to slam it down on the damn coin, but Hugh managed to swipe it up before I could, and the flat of my palm met the table. A small crack appeared in the surface, traveling lengthwise, straight down the middle. The table creaked and groaned but held together.

As one, we stood, our chairs sliding back with a loud scrape. Facing each other, we leaned across the table, and my hand slid behind his neck dragging him closer until our foreheads touched. It wasn't sexual; he was my pack. But we were Lycan, and Lycan thrived and communicated through affectionate touch.

My eyes bored into his. "Talk to me."

"Ye break that coin and every single person in this room will know precisely who ye are."

My voice was a low, thick growl. "I'm no' worried about anybody left in this building." I rubbed my thumb on his neck, a small sign I understood he only sought to protect me, but I was also pack alpha and chief of Clan MacKeane, and I would not be kept in the dark, especially in matters involving magic. "Where'd ye get it?"

"A witch."

Hugh knew I'd hate that. Hate hiding. Hate using witches to help. I'd rather seek out the Fae.

"What type of witch?" I asked.

"Sermo."

Of course. Witty and clever, witches from House Sermo drew their power from words themselves. Not to mention they were notorious for possessing several potent magical books. As such, their spells and curios were highly sought after. "Where?"

"I didnae go to their House if that's what ye're asking."

I relaxed a bit upon hearing that. By all accounts The Dikter—the home on Coven Square which housed the Spellmaidens from Sermo—was the most innocuous looking yet deadliest house in all of England, Scotland, and Wales.

"I ken how ye feel aboot witches, but it's my job to protect ye even though you no' need it."

"I ken, my friend. I just…I need ye to trust me."

"Trust goes both ways."

I slapped him on the back as we stood back. "I ken, I ken."

I glanced around then, having noticed the room had gone silent. The patrons of The Twisted Vine held their collective breath as they eyed us uncertainly. I couldn't look at Hugh lest I burst out laughing at the sight, yet I heard him clearly as he whispered, "Why dinnae we go check on our trussed-up friend."

I nodded. "Good thinking."

As I passed the bar, I dropped a pile of coins on the counter and said, "Sorry about the mess."

As if on cue, our table crashed to the floor behind us.

ONCE OUTSIDE, WE walked the few blocks to our awaiting carriage, both of us deep in our thoughts. The carriage we'd arrived in, while one of mine, was unmarked and plain so as to remain inconspicuous, and was waiting right where we'd left it, not two blocks from the coffee house, my driver still perched on top and reading a novel.

As we approached, Hugh said, "It'll be verra crowded with the three of us in there… Want me ta ride up top while ye have a talk with our guest?"

"Nae, we'll manage. Besides, we wouldnae want him to get too comfortable."

I opened the carriage door and leaned against the frame; a quick glance showed Belmont trussed up on the floor, just as Hugh had said.

I slapped on a congenial grin and asked, "Well, hello, there. Mind if we join you?"

Belmont's reply was muffled seeing as how he had a wadded-up handkerchief stuffed in his gigglebox.

"Here." I reached out and lifted a cursing and squirming Belmont. "Lemme give you a hand." Seeing as Belmont had both his arms and legs tied, he was bound, I chuckled to myself as I realized the double entendre, to struggle to situate himself upright and out of the way so Hugh and I could enter the carriage.

Once I'd settled Belmont on the rear facing seat, Hugh climbed inside and with a rapid knock on the roof, we took off.

I removed Belmont's gag and waited patiently while he stretched his mouth, before saying, "I couldnae help but note yer little conversation with a certain Spellmaiden back at the Twisted Vine."

Belmont turned his nose up somewhat—a bold move all things considered—before muttering, "Our conversssation ssstrictly fallsss under client/informant confidentiality."

I laughed. "I dinnae need to ask ye *what* was said." I gestured at my ears. "Lycan, aye? Besides, she's no' yer client."

Belmont shrugged, and though he acted utterly unconcerned, a nervous sweat broke out on his forehead, and for a moment I was distracted by the idea that a half-human/half-lizard creature *could* sweat.

"I know she dinnae summon you, so why the peculiar interest?"

Belmont scoffed as if offended. "I *trade* in information, sssirrah. Naturally, I'd be interesssted in information regarding a high-profile duke who isss wanted for murder."

I glanced to Hugh. "Ye hear that, Hugh? Our friend appears to be putting on airs far above his station." Not that I cared about station, to be honest, the dukedom was mine through no skill of my own, but I still found it funny that a man who made his living off gossip and innuendo—hell, off the ruination of others—could sound so *put out*, "and that's *Yer Grace*," I added.

The man looked confused and glanced to Hugh as if to gain confirmation, while Hugh glanced to me with a look that said, *strange*.

I nodded to Hugh, who understood what I wanted him to do without my having to say it.

Hugh answered Belmont's implied question and took over the interrogation. "Och, ignore the puir bastard," Hugh made a motion that suggested my disposition might improve with a visit to Bedlam (a suggestion Hugh was going to pay for later.) Stifling a laugh, he continued, "Tell me. What do ye know aboot Murderin' MacKeane?"

Belmont eyed Hugh a moment, then dipped a glance at his own tied hands. With a sigh, Hugh freed the man, then commanded, "Now, talk."

Belmont rubbed at his wrists, saying, "What I know about the duke? That'sss a big asssk. I know quite a bit about him, actually."

Hugh and I exchanged a glance. "Oh?"

Belmont shook his head with a smirk, his lizard-like tongue darting out once, then back in, and then he made a gesture with his hands that made it clear he wouldn't speak without payment.

Hugh grinned, a grin that if you knew him, would put you on instant alert. "How about ye just tell me, and I willnae plant my fist in yer face?" a pause, "Would ye recognize the duke if ye saw him on the street?"

Belmont sat up straighter. "Of courssse." He almost seemed put out we'd asked.

"Who's posted the biggest bounty?"

We already knew the answer, for we'd heard him tell Ms. Bell, but this way, we'd know if he lied.

Belmont lifted his chin with pride. "Normally, even *I* wouldn't know the anssswer to that; they're generally anonymousss, but von Rappoldstein hasssn't been quiet about hisss offer."

"How did ye first hear aboot it?"

Belmont scoffed. "I couldn't posssssibly reveal my sssourcesss. I'd be out of a job. Or worssse."

Hugh smirked. "I have ten fingers that tell me ye can, actually."

Hugh took that moment to crack the knuckles on both his hands, and once again, I had to stifle the urge to laugh… I could see we were both enjoying this far more than we should despite the seriousness of the accusations I was up against, but then I knew I was innocent and eventually we'd prove it. For all of Hugh's worrying, we were safe enough for now.

I turned to open the carriage window as the air seemed a bit musky all of a sudden. "Just answer the question," I added.

"Asssk your friend," Belmont gestured at Hugh, "he wasss there earlier today…"

At that, the smile on Hugh's face fell, and I knew I wasn't going to like what we'd inadvertently uncovered.

I had barely finished that thought when Belmont abruptly stood on the seat, then leapt straight out the window, which without whatever magic he had, would have been utterly impossible based on size alone.

I rapped on the ceiling and within moments, the carriage

pulled to the side and stopped.

I leaned out the door, one arm braced on the frame as we watched Belmont all but sprint down the pavement.

Egerton, my coachman, leaned over and asked, "Should we give chase, Your Grace?"

"Nae."

I rubbed my scruffy chin and asked Hugh, "Notice anything off aboot that entire confrontation?"

Hugh laughed. "Only *one* thing?"

We shared a quick smile. "Seems to me that it's one thing for the patrons of the Twisted Vine to no' recognize me sitting deep in the shadows, quite another when I'm sitting directly across from someone like Belmont."

Hugh agreed. "He should have recognized ye on sight. Do ye think he was telling the truth?"

I pulled back into the carriage and shut the door. "That he didnae know me? Yes." I settled back in my seat and rapped on the ceiling, communicating to the driver we were ready to go.

Meanwhile, Hugh pulled the coin out of his pocket and held it up.

For a moment, we both stared at the thing, a shiny new silver shilling, minted in 1897. So normal looking, so benign. At least, on the surface.

"Hugh?" I asked, "What the fook have ye done?"

He shook his head. "Hell if I ken, but I suppose we'd better find oot."

Chapter Six

von Rappoldstein
Once Bitten, Twice...Cursed

Back at von Rappoldstein's Lair...

I MADE A mental note that if I ever successfully ruled the world, I would extinguish every single cat from my realm, then I turned to my unwanted guest. "What the hell did you do to me?"

"Claimed you as my familiar, as I said."

"How do we undo it?"

"We don't."

Rather than repeat myself, I summoned a ball of fire in one hand, its flames of graduating purple—from the deepest eggplant to the palest lilac—a perfect match for the color of my magic.

Had I mentioned I'm a witch?

Sophia tossed a dismissive glance at the swirling, flaming orb in my hand and said, "Well, for starters, I could kill you."

At my growl, her eyes flashed as if in warning, and a red glimmer seemed to light up their depths, but it was there and gone so rapidly, I questioned whether what I saw was real.

I filed that thought away for later and smirked. "Or I could kill you."

She shrugged, "You could try…"

Without warning, I unsheathed the knife I always carried and threw it straight at her heart with exceptional skill. I grinned; I *never* missed.

My smile was short-lived. Inexplicably, the dagger landed at her feet with a heavy clang, which should have been impossible.

For her part, Sophia hadn't moved, not even so much as a flinch of concern.

Hell, she hadn't even looked at the knife until it landed at her feet, and even then, she merely responded with a soft *Tsk*.

"Tell me," I compelled.

Sophia chuckled softly. "You should know your magic doesn't affect me now that I've claimed you, so you can save your mind powers for someone else."

I thought harder, directing my multiple commands at her with my power: *Dance. Jump. Strangle yourself. Bite your arm. Lick your nose.*

She didn't move, only to raise a brow as if to say, *Are you finished?*

Well. It seemed she was telling the truth, not that I wouldn't keep trying for when she wasn't already on her guard. I knew she hadn't told me everything. There was always a way.

For now, I decided to change tactics. "So, what does my being your familiar involve?" I narrowed my eyes and thought, *Bark like a dog.*

For a moment, she looked as if she intended to answer, or bark like a dog, but alas, she merely glanced to the door a few seconds before someone knocked.

"Enter," I called out, my eyes never straying from hers.

Baldor, my butler/valet/coachman/do-whatever-the-hell-I-ask servant, entered. "Your Worshipfulness," I sighed at the ridiculous honorific. I'd repeatedly asked him to merely call me Your Highness to no avail. "You have a visitor."

I glanced at Baldor. At least this time, he was wearing my livery: black lederhosen with purple embroidery. "Who?"

Baldor glanced over his shoulder, then lowered his voice.

"He's a *hedgehog*."

A distant voice called out, "Not a hedgehog!"

Baldor's eyes widened, and he slowly shook his head left and right. "Lies," he mouthed.

This should be interesting. "Why not? Send him in."

When I turned back to the room, Sophia was curled up on the rug in front of the fire, asleep, as if she were a normal cat. She'd even magicked away all her clothes.

I narrowed my eyes but arranged my face in a non-threatening manner just in time for Baldor to enter the room with my guest.

A guest who was definitely a hedgehog, a rather large one, the size of a raccoon in fact. One wearing a three-piece suit, which was quite the accomplishment considering the spines along his back and carrying a flat cap between his paws with an unlit cigarette tucked behind his ear.

Baldor cleared his throat, "Your Illustriousness," I glanced pointedly at my soul scales, which were back in the green of good, meaning I had room for a little vengeance against one disobedient servant.

Baldor ignored my look and continued, "A Mister Harold Quill to see you."

The hedgehog held out a paw and grasped my finger for a shake. "Your Highness," I flashed a smug smile at Baldor and gestured toward the bowing hedgehog. Baldor simply left.

"You can call me Harry," continued my guest as I finished burning a figurative hole in the back of Baldor's head.

In a much more congenial tone, I said, "Have a seat, Harry," and directed him to one of the chairs facing my desk. "What brings you to see me this fine evening." A blast of thunder punctuated my statement as I skirted my desk while Harry climbed into the seat I'd indicated.

"I understand you're looking for a first commander. I'm here to apply for the position."

I steepled my hands before me. "I see." Mr. Quill's head barely cleared the top of the desk. "Most people send around a letter outlining their qualifications and await an invitation."

"Can't write."

"I see."

"Can't read either for that mat'ter. Can't afford the paper e'fin if I could."

"How did you hear about the position then?"

"I haf' my ways."

I glanced over toward the fireplace. Lady Sophia still appeared to be sleeping, but one ear was most decidedly trained our way.

"Do you have an idea of what the position entails?"

Harry dipped his head. "Bit of everyfing, yea? I get the general idea."

"Are you prepared to do anything I ask? Even if it's...despicable?"

Harry lifted his chin. "I am."

"Spying?"

A head nod.

"Lying?"

Nod.

"Murder?"

Nod.

"Even children?"

Pause.

"Don't answer that. Good deeds?"

Slow nod.

"What do you do now?"

"Primarily, I'm a moonlighter."

"Petty crimes?"

"Mostly. A Bit Faker for a while. Some bareknuckle boxing."

I glanced at his tiny paws, then mentally shrugged. "Why should I hire you?"

"I can get the job done. I'm willing, and people always underestimate me."

I narrowed my eyes, ready to deliver the real kicker. "Has anyone ever called you…boring?"

Harry lifted his chin. "I'm also a comic poet. Been in a few performances at The Rusty Spirit. You might have seen me mug before…" Harry lifted his brows and mimicked a hardy laugh.

I shook my head.

"No?" Harry made another face. "'ow about now?"

Another head shake.

Harry covered his eyes with his paws. "Now?"

I waved off his attempts. "Never mind." Still, I might not have seen him perform, but I couldn't deny I was somewhat entertained. I stood and pulled the bell pull to summon Baldor. "You're hired. Come back in the morning, and we'll discuss the finer details."

Harry stood on the chair and raised his paws in the air. "Really!? Fank you, Your Highness. You won't be disappointed."

If I ignored the hint of madness behind his eyes, which I did, I felt confident in my decision.

I rang for Baldor, who arrived with great punctuality and one spoken, "Yer Munificence?"

"Ah. Yes, See that my new commander is gifted a cant of togs and added to the payroll, will you?"

My butler bowed. "As you wish. Is that all, Yer Largesse?"

"Yes, Baldor, that will be all."

After they left, I turned from the door and was startled to find Lady Sophia dressed and seated in Harry's vacated chair as if she'd been there all along.

I wasn't surprised by this. Definitely not.

I dropped the hand that had involuntarily reached to cover my heart, which felt like it had nearly leapt out of my chest and into my throat. *By the gods.*

Lady Sophia shook her head as if in exasperation. "You need help, young man."

I returned to my seat and asked, "Why do you keep calling me young man?"

"Why did you put a bounty on MacKeane?"

"It amused me to do so. Why did you call me young man?"

Lady Sophia crossed her arms. "How old are you?"

I shrugged. "That's a tricky question, actually. I was a couple of centuries old when I was cursed the first time." I sighed in fond remembrance. "That was some curse…"

"You sound impressed."

"It was an impressive curse. I had to relive the last decade or so of my life…but going backwards in time."

"Sounds like an interesting curse."

"Each year, I died."

Lady Sophia winced. "You must have really pissed off someone powerful."

I nodded. "And each year, I reanimated with gaping holes in my memories… with no memory of the previous year in particular."

Sophia whistled, and I briefly wondered how that was even possible without lips. "Each year, I was armed only with the knowledge that I was reliving some year from my past and that I had to correct some egregious mistake I'd made the last time, or I would have to keep reliving that year until I got it right."

"Ouch. Did you have to repeat any years?"

I shrugged and tapped the side of my head. "Tampered memories, remember?"

"Ah. Yes, that explains a lot…"

"What are you trying to say?"

Lady Sophia gave me an innocent looking smile. "Oh, nothing. Do carry on."

"Occasionally, I would remember certain people, events. Believe me…discerning what was real and what wasn't was…interesting. I smoked a lot of opium back in those days. I think."

Sophia glanced away as she said, "I bet that helped," her tone definitely dripped with sarcasm.

I shrugged. "Every year, I forgot many of the people and

events in my life…and I actually knew I was forgetting those things, just not who or what I'd forgotten. I think I went a little insane."

I'm quite sure Lady Sophia mumbled, *You don't say.* But then she smirked and said, "It's definitely all starting to make sense."

"What makes sense?"

"You pissed off a woman."

Startled, I stared at her a moment. *This feline is clever.* "Each year, I got younger. Like I was going backwards in time physically. Unaging."

"So, perhaps a couple of centuries, but physically, more like thirty-eight?"

I nodded; that sounded about right.

"So, I was correct…*young man.*"

And in that moment, I saw an ancient, almost unsettling, wisdom deep in her gaze. *Interesting.* Still, "In our world, age is really just a state of mind…"

"…and a compendium of experience—wait," Sophie held up a hand, er, paw, "are you still trying to break this curse?"

"Oh, no. In the end, I beat the curse."

Sophia glanced pointedly at my soul scales. Naturally, the feline wouldn't miss a thing. "What can I say—I beat one curse only to be cursed anew. Hence, the scales."

Lady Sophia actually laughed. "Gods, I almost feel sorry for you. So, who did you provoke this time?"

I shrugged. "The same woman I pissed off the last time, actually."

"Yes?"

I nodded. "The White Witch."

Chapter Seven

Josie
How Many Larks Does It Take to Create a Disaster?

Two Hours Later,
The Kameleon, Number One Coven Square, London

I DISEMBARKED FROM my hired hack directly before the arched gates of The Kameleon—the home for Animus Spellmaidens. The gates, a masterpiece of ornate ironwork and magic, soared ten feet in the air, sometimes higher if the occasion warranted it. Two three-foot wide, brick columns supported the massive structure, and atop each pillar of bricks, cast iron gargoyles stood sentinel, their faces and stature permanently etched with menace; their narrowed eyes locked on anyone who drew too close.

No one escaped their notice. Nor their dedicated scrutiny.

Not even the Spellmaidens who called The Kameleon home.

The gargoyle on the left, Justice, was irreverent and unpredictable at best, sour and malicious at worst, and I simply saved myself the trouble and avoided him whenever possible. The one on the right, Mischief, was—*oh*, missing.

I searched the nearby trees and found him eventually, high up on the branches of an English Oak, his nose buried beneath one wing as he groomed himself. A ragged cut marred the precision of his wing, and I suspected he and Justice had been at it. Again.

I cleared my throat.

Slowly, irreverently, Mischief glared down, his eyes flaring red.

Other than that, he ignored me, as usual…as he did everyone, though he knew full-well I intended to pass. I reached for my clock…slowly…as if I had all the time in the world to wait. When I glanced up again, Mischief just stood there, wings on his hips. I'd heard him move, naturally. Cast iron birds don't move an inch without making a lot of screeching and grinding. Eventually, he rolled his eyes and huffed, "Oh, all right," and flew down, grumbling beneath his breath all the way.

His impertinence didn't bother me; not with the thrill of my assignment still fresh in my mind, and I waited with more patience than usual while he settled himself on his perch.

Once steady, Mischief flashed me a look. "Rumor has it Cerberus has hired an assassin."

When I failed to respond, he added, "You don't seem suitably impressed. Or concerned for your own welfare for that matter."

"Should I be? It isn't the first time. And it certainly won't be the last." Someone *always* had a bounty on me; it sort of came hand in hand with the job.

"Eh, fair enough." The gate on his side began to open, the hinges screeching their protest the entire way. "Just thought I'd warn you. Cerberus is furious about the death of his cousins. Listen," Mischief glanced left and right as if to check if anyone was listening, then met my gaze again. I raised my brows. "I'd appreciate that pendant of yours should you die."

I resisted the impulse to grab hold of said pendant, only briefly wondering how he even knew of its existence or more precisely, *what* he knew about it. He may only be guessing. It didn't matter; I dipped my head toward the slow-moving gate as it screeched in protest but continued to open at a snail's pace. "Might want to get that fixed."

I would never acknowledge the existence of my pendant.

Instinct told me this was important. It's why as an adult, I never took it off, and I hid it from everyone with my magic.

Justice snorted from somewhere to my left, and Mischief sniggered. "Sure. Right on it."

We had the same conversation nearly every time I passed, yet the hinges still creaked as rust-coated metal threatened to seize at any given moment.

Perhaps I should bite the bullet and take the issue up with Mac, the Kameleon's sentient soul.

Or maybe not.

I stepped onto the long and winding path leading home, and discovered once again, a line of squirrels had stationed themselves upon a nearby log, twitching their tails and leaping in place and generally kicking up a bit of a ruckus in their efforts to gain my attention. A particularly tenacious squirrel named Sherman darted in front of me, nearly finding himself launched to the distant porch for all his daring.

I contemplated scolding them away. But squirrels were a persistent, optimistic lot, and they weren't to blame for their nature, nor would they give up so readily. Instead, I tossed them a small smile as they scurried by my side, but I carried on, chin raised, eyes forward…focused.

By the time I spotted my home through the distant trees, sweat trailed down my neck and back, owing to the blazing sun, which found me unerringly despite the overhead canopy of green. Worse, my bustle itched, my red hair was more than half-way toward successfully overpowering its pins, and the muscles in my arms and legs trembled from pure physical exhaustion—both from this morning's marathon training session and last night's grueling work.

The aches and bruises would come later.

I wanted nothing more than a long soak in a deep tub right about now, a secret indulgence of mine. Notoriously practical, I would deny any knowledge of such an extravagance, even upon pain of death, were someone to question me on it.

The Kameleon stood situated upon a slight hill, shielded from view of the street by a thick wood through which the path to the house meandered for the length of a good two city blocks. The house was Gothically Victorian—somewhat—with turrets and windows and roof lines and even porches slapped on haphazardly as after thoughts since they existed purely for the sake of the ever-changing rooms inside.

Function over form—or better yet, function, never heard of form—was the rule of thumb at the Kameleon, inside and out.

To my mind, the house had character, and I *loved* it.

It constantly changed, depending on the mood of the various residents and guests, or whether unexpected events required special accommodation. Or it was a Wednesday.

I stopped before an elaborate ironwork sign affixed to a column to the left of the front steps. The Griffin perched atop the intricate metalwork bore one head, as expected, and I absent-mindedly tossed him the key, a lock of my hair, which he caught easily, then returned to his vigil.

The man or woman who looked upon the Griffin and saw two, or worse, three heads rather than one, would face far greater difficulty gaining entrance to the house, if they survived at all.

If they even made it this far. Which begged the question—

I drew to a halt and scanned the skies, one arm shading my face from the blaring sun. Why hadn't I been set upon by the house's defenses along the way? I could usually count on at least one dragon trying to incinerate me as I made my way to the door. *Curious...*

I turned to face the steps. Before me, a shimmering wall of air parted like drawn curtains as the magic barring entry opened to allow me safe passage, and I marched smartly up the granite steps, the staccato click of my boot heels keeping time with the steady thump of my heart.

Once beneath the overhang, I welcomed the cool relief of the shade with a low sigh, a feeling short-lived and at odds with the cannonade of chaos I heard coming from inside the house.

I entered, and after magicking the purple file folder away, immediately tuning out the usual noise and chaos of hundreds of guests, visitors, and staff of every species coupled with random floating objects and odd bursts of magic.

Instead, I tracked the echoes of *unusual* pandemonium—up two flights of red stairs whose walls were papered with red animal paw prints which changed randomly to a different type of animal every ten minutes, down the crooked hall with walls of green tiger stripes, down one flight of black stairs with vines hanging from the ceiling, up the curved blue hall with the jungle themed walls, up two flights of striped, yellow stairs, and back down another flight of red stairs.

Eventually, I drew to a halt before my own bed chamber. *Naturally*, the chaos would lead here.

I surveyed the scene while resisting the urge to press my fingers to the bridge of my nose.

Before me lay absolute destruction and utter chaos juxtaposed upon a backdrop of peaceful silence, as if the bluster of recent anarchy had decamped through the nearby open window mere seconds before I'd arrived.

It probably had.

Feathers floated about the room as if a full pride of fairies had blessed a thousand wishes in the space of a few seconds, and I supposed somewhere a pillow or two could be found beneath the destruction, minus its stuffing.

Clothes, including my favorite black cloak, littered the bed, floor, and furniture, and my curtains fluttered in the cross breeze of open windows.

Empty glasses, full glasses, and everything in between loitered about upon every available surface. One brave goblet tottered precariously on the edge of a windowsill, ready to tumble to the floor with nothing more than the strength of a delicate sneeze.

Something, somewhere dripped.

And scattered leaves covered the floor beneath my radiator,

next to a bowl of ashes, a handful of burnt filters, and the remains of spent Lucifer matches. I tested the air with a sniff.

Catnip. Of course. Dammit, George.

I glanced to the bed and spied the indisputable source of chaos atop a mountain of discarded chemises, drawers, petticoats, and corsets—none of them mine.

George Augustus Fletcher Bram, III, my catnip-addled feline, basked in the warmth of the sun, his body in full recline with legs spread wide, probably high on catnip whisky. At some point, he'd lost hold of his ever-present top hat, for the fur atop his head remained matted and twisted as if he'd only just removed it, though the hat was nowhere in sight. The dark stripes threaded throughout his buff-colored fur formed an intricate and bizarre pattern—as if he'd been marked by a curse—and in that moment, I realized I'd never before seen George bareheaded.

I filed that thought away for future reflection and planted my fists on my hips.

One buff ear turned in my direction, and the toes on all four paws curled slightly, but his green eyes remained closed, though he fooled no one. For whatever reason, even at the youthful age of 86, a young man, er—cat, in the magical feline world, George still liked to pretend he hadn't noticed my presence when we both knew better.

The clock on my mantle sounded the quarter past chime. And still, I waited.

Eventually, George drew in a great, big yawn and sighed. One lazy, green eye peeked open, found me, and noted my frown. His sigh, drawn-out and exaggerated, ended with another yawn. "It was just a lark, Josie. You *know* how irresistible they are...," he drawled, as he twisted his body, four paws in the air now, two straight out above his head, tongue lolling about as if he'd simply forgotten to tuck it back in.

It was *always* a lark. A mistake. A misunderstanding.

I didn't care to enumerate the number of pranks gone awry at the hands of my catnip-addled feline. I whipped my best cloak from the bed a second before George rolled atop it—velvet being another thing he found irresistible.

Having noticed the movement, his feline eyes flared, his pupils blown wide, and he swiped for a corner but missed.

"George. What did you *do*?" I turned to hang the garment on the peg by the door. "Might I remind you we only got off probation Tuesday last?" *Did he know I was back on probation already? Was he the reason yet again?*

I turned back only to note George had removed his jacket and was now in the process of grooming his hindquarters; one rear leg pointed heavenward as if directing my attention to the ceiling. Ignoring me, he carried on grooming, listing further and further to the side in the process.

I crossed my arms and waited until he'd listed one step too far and tumbled off the far side of the bed with a graceful if drunken thud.

When he didn't immediately launch himself back on the bed, I skirted the end of the four-poster only to find George flat on his back, arms folded behind his head, as he contemplated the ceiling. As if every move leading up to this point had been perfectly executed by design. *Typical.*

To the ceiling, he cocked his head and murmured, "I say, how was I supposed to know it had a taste for leprechaun?" *Hiccough.*

I pinched the bridge of my nose to stay the onset of a headache as I recalled there were two leprechauns staying in the attic guest rooms for the week.

I shifted my hands to my hips. *"George—"*

The cat twisted to see me, his front paws gripping the toes of the rear. "Oh – did I say that out loud?"

I drew upon the shredded remains of my patience. "By chance, is there something more you're not telling me?"

George shrugged and rolled to his feet.

I raised a brow.

"I just wanted to play with it, you see." He swiped up a glass from my bedside table, tossed back two fingers of, most likely, *more* catnip-laced whisky, and wiped his mouth on his lacy sleeve. "We were having such fun and then...," shrug, "...oops."

"Oops," I repeated and wondered, not for the first time in two antagonizing years where he'd nearly destroyed my career as a Spellmaiden a dozen times over, why George had chosen *me* as his familiar.

George leapt onto the bed and crawled to the center where he began kneading the colorful quilt, mumbling, "I *suppose* a few of the house guests *might* have gone missing in the night—"

"*Drat*," I spun on my heel, calling out, "Why didn't you lead with that bit of information, George?"

I snatched my bow from the wall on my way out. As if in apology, the house shuddered, then flung my bedchamber door wide.

Eyes lifted to the ceiling, I called out, "A little late for that don't you think?" as I marched down the hall.

The black walls surrounding me seemed to lift, then settle as if the house shrugged, and a Scottish brogue floated in on the air. "Och, lass. All the chimneys on the seventh floor are clogged, so my hearin' was no' so good last night, and I could no' smell a thing but burnt wood, old ashes, and soot."

The Kameleon's soul had once belonged to a Lycan named Mac who had roamed for decades untethered until settling here, replacing the last soul, who'd grown tired of it all and left. Or that was the story, depending on who you asked.

"Isn't it *your* job to fix that?"

Mac belched, and I stopped to glare down at George, who seized upon the opportunity to rub against my legs. He paused to stare at me in absolute devotion with large, liquid eyes. "I only shared a wee dram, love..."

But George couldn't hold such a sincere face for long, and within seconds, his face cracked, and Mac and George both snorted.

Then, the snickering began in earnest.

It seemed George had poured quite a lot more down the pipes than a drop or two.

I didn't have time for this. I neatly sidestepped the cat and proceeded down the stairs. "What am I searching for?"

My question met with silence, and I drew to a halt but didn't turn, waiting.

Somewhere, a clock tapped out the time in measured beats. One, Two, Three, Four.

Eventually, from somewhere behind me, George spoke, his voice barely above a whisper, "A gorgon."

A puff of air burst from my lips.

"I meant it as a gift."

I unclenched my jaw, lifted the pendant hanging from the chain round my neck, and pressed it to my lips. From George's perspective, he'd just think I was pressing the tips of my fingers to my lips.

"A sign of my devotion, Josie Bell."

I drew in a deep breath. "George, if you continue to be *this* devoted to me, I'll have no choice but to turn you into a three-legged dog. With mange."

George gasped. "A *dog*, Josie—"

I dropped the small disc. "You can clean up the mess while I'm gone."

I froze mid-step when I heard the telltale snap of his fingers, and I knew my room was already set to rights in the space of a second. I squashed a petty, disgruntled snort, squared my shoulders, and carried on without a word.

"You're no fun, Josie," George called, "Stiff as a board with far less feeling, I daresay…"

He was all but shouting to my receding back, though a note of doubt softened the edges of his words a moment before the terrace door swung close behind me with a conversation-ending thud.

I REMINDED MYSELF George wasn't really angry—never that. I didn't think he *could* get angry. Could a person who never took anything seriously even *get* angry?

Besides, I'd been called worse; all of it true, so it wasn't as if he were saying anything I hadn't already heard a dozen times before.

Such truths were the reason I still hadn't discerned why George had chosen me as his familiar.

He worshipped the sun, albeit whilst lounging on his back, legs spread, high on catnip.

I found sober strength only on the darkest of nights.

He flouted the rules; I furiously embraced them.

According to George, the entire affair of his claiming me had been an accident, another precarious *lark*.

At the time, he'd merely *hiccoughed* and said, "Oops." And rather than try to undo everything—*as he should've*—he'd shrugged, rubbed his paws together, and proclaimed, "Ah, well. This should be fun." Then, he swiped up a glass and tossed back his favorite whisky, indifferent to the absolute havoc he'd wrought.

Destruction only he could undo.

Destruction he refused to address.

And no one, *no one*, believed for a minute it all hadn't been his plan from the start.

But why?

A question that remained unanswered two years later.

Two long antagonizing years where he'd nearly destroyed my career as a Spellmaiden a dozen times over.

Oh, I'd asked him. More times than I cared to consider. My *favorite* answer was the day he'd up and declared I needed to unwind, and he was "just the mouser for the job."

Being a Spellmaiden for the M.M.R. required absolute dedication. They upheld a strict code of conduct. Spiritual, mental, and physical health: prioritized. Personal attachments outside the Coven: discouraged.

George threatened my position on a weekly, almost daily, basis, and I admit, I resented it. It was a miracle I still had a job. A job I loved. A job I *needed*.

A job only I was allowed to ruin.

I clenched my bow. It simply made no sense for me to be George's familiar. Of all the cats about looking to make a Spellmaiden their familiar, he was the *least* suitable of the lot. Besides, what had he gained out of the entire affair? Nothing, so far as I could see.

I stormed across the paved stones making up the rather large, rear terrace, intent upon settling my mind before I reached the steps leading to the gardens; steps one couldn't even see from any of the rear doors leading outside, the terrace was so large.

The entire space was utter chaos, like the house, and I dodged at least a dozen guests (and ducked numerous flying objects and stray shots of magic) with a forced smile as I made my way to the rear gardens.

Oh, the guests weren't reacting with any sort of obvious terror...no one was running away screaming and there was no sign of blood or panic. There were simply a great, many of them and not all of them were species who were, shall we say, *compatible* in the same social settings. There were squawks and growls and barks and laughs and shouts of anger alongside a healthy dose of general polite conversation.

Visitors often remarked upon the sheer size of the patio—but how else were we to accommodate the colorful menagerie who resided upon the grounds of The Kameleon at any given time? Not to mention the many guests who traveled from the far reaches of the globe to experience our well-known hospitality. Many residents and guests enjoyed their morning coffee or their evening aperitifs on the terrace.

Our resident elephant liked his coffee, black, promptly at six in the morning and arrived precisely at six every evening to sip his afternoon sherry. Sometimes his entire family traveled here for a visit and liked to join him for his repasts on the terrace. His overprotective mother always hovered, exclaiming over this and that as if he were still a young calf and not a full-grown bachelor with his own accommodation. The point is…they alone took up a lot of space.

Eventually, I reached the steps leading down into the rear gardens and descended them at a fast clip. Almost immediately, I heard an interesting chirp, and I leaned into the shrubbery to investigate the disturbance while relentless heat from the afternoon sun bore down upon my shoulders and back, making me regret not taking time to change into garments more suitable to the task at hand.

The disturbance proved to be nothing more than a family of grasshoppers settling into a new home, none of whom had witnessed anything amiss overnight.

I thanked them as I stood and wiped my brow on my sleeve, then pulled at my ruffled jabot until it loosened. I folded the frilly piece, laying it atop a nearby log, then shrugged out of my cropped jacket, placing it gingerly beside the jabot, before reaching for the train of my skirts and launching myself one-handed over the newly fallen log, its horizontal state the reason the grasshoppers had needed to find new accommodation.

I dusted my hands and made a mental note to work out an arrangement with the Beavers' son, Joseph, who resided at the far edge of their pond. He'd take care of the fallen log in a thrice, though of late, his fees had become rather exorbitant and his attitude, cocky.

Partly due to our frequent need of his services.

And partly because he was just plain greedy.

I would investigate later, but the large trunk of wood was most likely a causality of our resident rhinoceros, who picked a fight with his neighbor, an African elephant, nearly every day. Usually over which of them had the better view—or had captured the eye of one of the flirty trio of flamingos across the way... the flamingos being what qualified as 'the better view.'

Fallout from their repeated disagreements wreaked havoc upon the flora and fauna of The Kameleon—while providing plenty of money-making opportunities for enterprising young beavers and the witches of House Planta, who had not just a green thumb, but ten green fingers and toes, figuratively speaking, of course.

Still, their disagreements were relatively harmless.

Unlike the creature George had unleashed upon Coven Square.

I trusted the creature hadn't crossed over the wards surrounding The Square and waltzed right into Mayfair, confident an alarm would have sounded if it'd tried.

And I *would* prevent it from doing so now.

I shook my head. I'd only just gotten off probation on Tuesday. A punishment courtesy of George's *last* lark, which marked the third time this year alone... and it was only early March. And now I was on probation again, probably due to another of George's classic tricks. I released a long, exasperated breath.

Unfortunately, other than the discussion with the grasshoppers, my hunt through the gardens and further through the maze of 20-foot hedges, which separated the formal gardens from the mews beyond, passed without incident and placed me an uneasy minus-one-hundred yards from the wooded and warded boundary separating Coven Square from the humans of Mayfair, the majority of whom were wholly ignorant of what lay at the very heart of their precious and highly coveted slice of London.

But as I neared the end of the hedge, a trickle of awareness skated over my skin, raising the fine hairs on my neck and arms.

I pressed back against the towering hedge and closed my eyes, reaching out with my senses, seeking something—anything—off. That which didn't belong.

I knew the answer in an instant.

Everything was wrong.

NO SQUIRRELS SCURRIED about in the trees. No birds chirped out warnings. The usual racket of our resident menagerie could not be heard—not even the peacocks, whose echoing cries could usually be noted anywhere on one of the properties making up Coven Square.

The very air itself seemed oppressed and *unwilling* to bestir itself.

Worse, the flow of magic trickled by like concentrated sludge. And the auras of nearby things reflected a greyish hue overtop their usual, brilliant plethora of colors, dulling them noticeably.

I lifted my chin and scented the air, then promptly pinched my nose.

The smell of sulfuric leaves poisoned the air… definitely not the *earthly* variety.

No. This was a malodorous stench straight out of hell.

I mouthed a quick spell—protection from the noxious fumes—then took a cautious breath, chanced a peek around the end of the hedge…

And discovered my quarry.

I drew an arrow from my quiver and lifted my bow into position at a veritable snail's pace. With great care, I nocked the arrow, then held steady, the string taut, watching the distant beast as it *hunted,* weaving its way in and out of the edge of the wood marking the east side boundary of Coven Square like a giant asp with legs. And teeth as long as a *sgian dubh.*

Its silvery scales winked in and out of view among low hanging branches, helping me track its movement.

Thankfully, it hadn't crossed into Mayfair, or by now, there'd be nothing left.

But all too soon, the gorgon froze, and its silver scales rippled and flashed in the afternoon light before they, too, stilled, then began to transform.

Drat!

The beast had sighted prey, and in a blink, the gorgon vanished.

Too fast.

Normal Gorgons took thirty seconds or *more. This* one disappeared in an instant.

I had no time to ponder the reason. I tossed aside my quiver
and bow, both now useless, ripped the knife from my boot, and
ran after the creature.

"Over here, you big bloody beast!" I shouted as I ran, dodging
uneven terrain wearing impractical heeled boots, determined to
capture the gorgon's attention. I wouldn't know if I'd succeeded
until—

I launched myself into the air at the same time a sudden blast
of hellfire nearly melted the hair from my head, or worse, all the
while twisting to the side midflight. I used my left hand to
perform the complicated gestures of a freezing spell while I swept
out with my right, the one with the knife, which sliced across
what my eyes told me was nothing but air, and no corresponding
resistance slowed the arc of my swing, providing not even the
suggestion of a glance against the gorgon, much less a direct hit.

But that meant nothing while a gorgon was invisible.

I landed hard on my shoulder, tucked into a twisted roll—
skirts up, drawers exposed to the elements—and allowed
momentum to land me upright once again, though squatting and
facing the direction I'd come from.

It was over in mere seconds. *Too many* seconds.

I summoned my magic, drew my hands up, and darted my
gaze left, right, then straight-ahead—knowing if I'd missed, the
attack could come from anywhere at any time.

And I would likely lose.

But I'd die giving my best.

Ten seconds passed. Fifteen. I held my breath; every one of
my senses on alert.

A shimmer of light flickered about twenty yards away, and I

stiffened, ready. But the gorgon's body didn't move and appeared streaked with blood, its body twisted unnaturally—

And missing its head.

That bit turned up a few seconds later and about five feet to the right.

It was only then I allowed myself to slide to the ground, until I was laid out flat on my back, and from there, I relinquished one great big exhale of relief.

That was close. *Too close.*

THE WORLD AROUND me exploded into sound, the normal sounds of the wood and our home returned indicating the threat was gone.

But the prattle immediately surrounding me surged, reached a crescendo, then ceased altogether a moment before every squirrel and small animal broke form and scattered. The breeze picked up, rustling the leaves, and the air, now fresh—or as fresh as could be considering the veritable zoo on the grounds surrounding The Kameleon—smelled familiar, a welcome relief. Even the magic ebbed and swirled like normal, but apart from a few intrepid fellows who barked and twitched their tails at this new threat, all stood relatively silent.

I closed my eyes and reached out once more with my senses, probing my surroundings. I could smell the humans of Mayfair, hear the clop of horses' hooves and the rattle of carriages.

Blast, but I'd rolled to a stop uncomfortably close to the border.

Only witches and certain magical creatures could find Coven Square at all…for the safety of humankind, and in that moment, I understood just how close this entire disaster had come to exposing them all.

I probed the wood but found nothing truly threatening. I

reached out in the opposite direction, perceiving the roars and twitters and *smells* of meandering houseguests in the far distance.

I set aside the reminder and focused to my left, but shied away when I came upon the saccharine scent of gardenias. Further along, I discerned the distant lap of water and the sound of the resident beavers hard at work in their pond. And then a trace of—

Ah, yes, Sophia.

I opened my eyes in time to see a mockingbird plunge toward the earth, disappearing from view on the opposite side of the distant hedge, cursing like a well-worn sailor all the while, and I allowed a slight smile at the disembodied but very proper reply to all the swearing, "Pardon me. Some of us have work to accomplish."

I'd only ever heard such colorful language from gulls down by the docks before making the acquaintance of our resident mockingbird, and the elegant upper crust accent meant Lady Sophia was close to rounding the hedge and coming into view.

I rose and attempted to brush the dirt from my vest and skirts, a futile act, and one I attempted for far too long before accepting defeat. I pulled upon the energy—the magic—flowing around me and murmured an easy spell which set my clothing and hair to rights, removing all traces of my battle. My jacket and jabot returned a few moments later, riding high on a gust of wind.

The garments circled me, gesturing wildly and nudging me persistently until I spread my arms and allowed them to settle into place.

My bow and quiver alighted gracefully at my feet.

I glanced over my shoulder as a grey tabby sauntered around the hedge maze and into the mews, her tail high. I could just make out the sound of her pocket watches and pearls, clinking together in time with the rhythm of her graceful steps.

Lady Sophia—or, more formally, Lady Sophrosyne Johanna Tewkesbury-Smith, though no one dared utter her real name within hearing distance—was a meticulously groomed and discerning feline of refined tastes. Today, pearls, white as newly fallen snow, wound gracefully round her neck, providing a pleasing contrast to the sharp grey of her fur and matched precisely the pristine tips of each paw. Her hat sat perched upon her head just so, the perfect angle so as to suggest an impudent air, a quality of manner at which Sophia was especially skilled in evoking. As usual, her elaborate top hat complimented her corset to an exacting degree, and despite every known rule to the contrary, its paisley pattern flattered the stripes marking her body and brought out the green undertones in her feline eyes. No one else could pull off such a look.

No one else dared.

Sophia took her time, every step deliberate and precise. And utterly silent. She ignored the dead gorgon as she wove a neat path between its body and head.

Eventually, Lady Sophia reached the edge of the wood. There, she rose onto her hind legs and took up residence against the squirrels' oak, before turning her attention to her claws.

"Don't mind me," Lady Sophia purred, never once glancing my way.

I had no idea how old she was, but despite her youthful, almost sultry voice, she phrased everything as if she were on the upward side of ninety, in human years, which was entirely possible.

I straightened the lace cuffs of my sleeves. "You have my undivided attention, Lady Sophia."

The cat merely inspected another claw, her attention fixed upon her grooming, a deception one would be foolish to believe.

I waited with practiced patience, knowing Lady Sophia would speak when ready.

After a few moments, she angled her head as she examined her next claw. "Heard about your new assignment, dear."

I raised a brow; a move guaranteed to provoke Lady Sophia, who found the affectation crass, but I wasn't so foolish as to inquire how she came to learn the Oracle had assigned me the task of apprehending a dangerous, murderous Lycan.

And a duke, no less.

Did she also know about the enquiry?

Lady Sophia maintained focus on grooming her already pristine paws. "Lycan's are notoriously difficult to find, much less apprehend. It's the nose, you know. He'll smell you before you're even aware he's there."

I snorted and had to bite back a curse.

Lady Sophia's head snapped up, her pupils dilated as any cat who'd just discovered a mouse dangling in front of them might do, reminding me that she was very much a predator in her own right.

Lady Sophia narrowed her eyes; her feline gaze intent as she scrutinized me. "That was uncharacteristic of you," she admonished.

It *was*.

Yet I refused to address the infraction and mutely returned her stare. Not a defiant expression, but I refused to prostrate myself either.

Unfortunately, Lady Sophia's patience was unsurpassed. Eventually, I relented. "I have a plan."

I said with as much confidence and bravado as I could muster. It was also *A Lie*.

I didn't actually have a plan, *per se*. Yet. And I *always* had a plan. I was meticulously detailed. Focused. Firm.

This time would be no different. Eventually.

"I've booked passage on the 6 o'clock train to Glasgow." I hadn't yet, but I would.

A trace of exasperation tinged the edges of Lady Sophia's voice—and as always, disappointment—when she said, "'Travel to Scotland' isn't a plan."

"A murderer on the run and wanted by the M.M.R. would be an idiot to openly prance about the streets of London while there is a price on his head. And a man like Lachlan MacKeane would never be so thoughtless. Most likely he's lounging about his estate on the Isle of Skye, eating raw, red meat, fornicating with all the lads and lasses in the vicinity while rubbing necks and petting and pawing the members of his clan—when he's not murdering them in their sleep, that is—and generally being a reckless, unkempt, *arse*." I crossed my arms. "Traveling to Scotland is a fine *start* of a plan."

Scotland was where all Lycan clans called home, with only a few maintaining houses in London purely for the social season. Plans based on pure logic were bound to succeed.

Lady Sophia pursed her lips, unimpressed.

I bent to retrieve my bow while adding, "I'll work out the details on the way; there's plenty of—"

"He's here."

My head snapped up. "In London?"

Lady Sophia could have frozen the Thames with a look, like the one that claimed her face in that moment.

Unlike most cats, Lady Sophia was a no-nonsense feline. And utterly without fault, her knowledge vast and undeniable. To question her… it simply wasn't done. It wasn't *healthy*.

Normally, at this point, Lady Sophia would walk away, insulted and with good reason. I could tell she wanted to do that very thing. Instead, she remained in place against the log. "Yes. *In London*," she bit out, "His close friend, the Duke of Abernathy, is throwing a grand ball on Wednesday. I suspect he'll be there."

"What. An. Idiot."

Lady Sophia harrumphed, an unusual response for the feline, and I wondered at the tiny break in her composure.

"Well… good. That'll make my job much easier."

Despite my words, a twinge of disappointment nipped at me. I imagined the brawny Scotsman depicted in the file on my desk. I felt a surge of *something* and frowned.

Lady Sophia interrupted my thoughts. "Lachlan MacKeane doesn't make a move without a reason."

It was my turn to scoff. "In my experience, Lycans are disgracefully impulsive."

"True. But they're also clever… He's taunting us."

"You sound impressed."

"Merely curious."

Why did that sound like a lie? "Whatever for? And why would he be taunting *us*?"

Lady Sophia smoothed the front of her corset, then tossed me a speculative look. "My dear, I've been pondering that question all morning. By now, he knows you've been assigned to detain him. And your reputation, a credit to your kind, I admit, will certainly precede you. He's likely got a file on you two inches thick."

The unexpected compliment surprised me, suffusing me with warmth, and in that moment, I wondered what *he* thought when he glanced over my file.

I collected myself and peeked at Lady Sophia who watched me with an unsettling stare. She had a talent for discerning a person's true motive, but somehow, I didn't think *that* was the source of her disquiet.

And at the moment, I hadn't the time or inclination to work it out; Lady Sophie would speak her mind when ready. For now, I needed to focus on the assignment. "Well, whatever his reasons, I cannot complain; he's made my job easier, it's almost criminal to collect my fee." I secured my bow in place on my shoulder. "Almost. As it stands, I'll be back well before Evening Circle on Wednesday, while Lachlan MacKeane becomes intimately acquainted with his cell in Marshalsea Gaol."

Lady Sophia didn't bother to hide the doubt written plain upon her face. "Josephine. Caroline. Bell. That ball will have no less than a thousand wards. It's being hosted by the Duke of Abernathy, a man as rich as Croesus and backed by MacKeane himself. Together, they have access to all the best wards money can buy. Not to mention *he'll* be looking for *you*. They will capture you before you step one foot inside those doors."

I crossed my arms, and Lady Sophia pressed on. "My dear, do

not underestimate the man. I'm quite sure he knows precisely what he's about. By all accounts he's quite keen. And a Lycan's sense of smell is unsurpassed."

Lady Sophia's tail began to twitch restlessly, which was interesting. Surely, she wasn't hiding something?

I decided to test that theory. "What about *Wolffe & Sons L'Arène de Bataille*...there's an event scheduled this very eve, yes?"

Lady Sophia's head snapped up, and it appeared that this unflappable feline only just hung on to her composure though her voice was even when she finally spoke. "I'm surprised you know of it. But really, you cannot be serious." She narrowed her eyes. "I presume you know of his suspected connection?"

I nodded but remained intrigued. Lady Sophia well-knew the answer to that question. "Some say he's one of the major sponsors. Some say he merely makes it his habit to attend."

"But what do you say, Josie Bell?"

"*I* think he owns the whole rotten enterprise."

Lady Sophia's eyes flashed but it was a fleeting thing, and once more I had the peculiar feeling she held something back.

The cat smoothed her perfectly aligned waistcoat. "I'm surprised at you, Josephine. It's *illegal*."

"I don't intend to be a contestant."

"Of course not. Besides the legalities, contestants cannot use their magic."

I didn't fool myself into believing Lady Sophia's remark had been careless. No, it was deliberate, and to be honest, it bothered me. Did she think so little of my skills? Or was there another reason for the seemingly careless remark they *both* knew to be anything but? Did she *want* me to enter the contest?

Lady Sophia tsked before dropping to all fours. It seemed the conversation was over.

I watched as she sauntered off in the direction of the house and found myself more bothered by the fact that she seemed unaware of the most interesting piece of my assignment rather than the fact that she even knew of my assignment at all. Had she known of the Oracle's command—a direct order for me to attend the illegal fights—this conversation would not yet be over.

Lady Sophia paused by the dead gorgon, studied it, then pinned me with a curious stare. "Do you happen to know where George picked up his little plaything?" Lady Sophia nodded toward the creature's remains.

I shook my head. "I only just learned of his perfidy half an hour ago."

She glanced back down. "Interesting…"

Her voice sounded smooth and calm, but her tail stood straight, the fur subtly lifted and no longer sleek. And her back arched, almost imperceptibly.

I filed her quiet observations away and watched as she resumed picking her way past the remains, careful to steer well clear, for the beast's carcass would only grow *more* dangerous until I cast the spell that would send the bastard back to hell.

I didn't have time to consider her strange reactions further.

I had an illegal fight to attend.

$$\text{\large\symbol{}}\;\longrightarrow\;\text{\Large\symbol{}}$$

Chapter Eight

Lachlan
Accursed Curios and Oddities and Trinkets, Oh My

Willoughby's Curiosities
Deep in the Heart of the Rookeries
North Phoenix Street, St. Giles, London

T HE PLACE REEKED of magic and sulfur and rot, a downright fetid combination that was highly offensive to our sensitive noses. And that was just from the *outside*.

Then again, we were deep in the rookeries of St. Giles, what else should I expect?

The Rookery was a dismal stew of misery and desperation, with a diverse assemblage of bit fakers, harlots, lurkers, lushes, shirkers, and sharps, just to name a few…not all of them human, most of them simply waiting for the opportune moment to exercise their villainy, or so Richard King would have one believe. I could feel their eyes upon me when I passed, yet for the most part, I simply sensed the substantial weight of their despair.

The gin shops and bawdy houses and workplaces of all sorts practically stood atop of each other, vying for room in this dark pool of humanity, crowding out the sun…or would have, if one were able to see the sun through the ever-present London

Particular, and it all contrived to make my skin crawl with visceral discomfort. Being a Lycan, I preferred wide-open spaces—places I could let loose my wolf and *run*—and fresh air.

The Rookeries of St. Giles were the opposite of that in every way.

I could feel the same tension building in Hugh, yet we marched on towards our destination. Despite the fact nearly every shop we passed had a notice in their front window announcing: "Beware Murderous MacKeane!" above a scowling, yet remarkable likeness of me, and beneath my narrowed gaze, the words: "Don't be another victim!"

For those a part of the magical community, my visage alternated between a scowl and a come-hither wink, which my image aimed at every passerby unless it happened to notice *me*, in which case it would start gesturing and pointing wildly as if to point me out to anyone who might be inclined to notice or care.

No one did.

On occasion, I caught my likeness winking at the other notices sharing the same window, which were almost always an announcement regarding Queen Victoria's upcoming Diamond Jubilee…and in those cases, she always directed a look of abject horror at my image's cheek.

It seemed, upon occasion, that magic itself demonstrated a very British sense of humor.

Nevertheless, it was going to take a hell of a lot more than misery and villainy and amusing advert antics to drive us away.

We took a right on Plumptre Street, then a left on Phoenix, followed by a slight right—only visible to the magical world—which split off from the main road and was marked by a purple sign built into the brick of the corner shop which read: North Phoenix Street.

The door we sought was four down but one from the corner, a real hellhole in the wall, and as we stopped before it, Hugh barked out a choice word.

The door was covered in curses and runes and other indecipherable things, what paint had been present was long gone. The sign above the door was dingy and barely legible, though likely on purpose as only those who really wanted to enter would ever care to do so and would already know the name.

Still, with my Lycan sight, I could read the sign, which boasted:

Willoughby's Curiosities
Oddities and Trinkets for the Macabre at Heart

Hugh turned away and raked his hands through his hair, then faced me with his fists on his hips. I was shocked, to be honest, that he would go here for such a purpose…the place definitely didn't exude warmth or invite one to trust. "Ye went *here* ta get ye're coin?"

"It didnae look like this yesterday."

I wanted to tease him about it, suggest the door had been painted brightly with sunshine and rainbows with pots of daisies in the window, but even for two Lycans, it wasn't a healthy idea to remain standing on the pavement for too long, particularly outside a place like this. Besides, I could see my friend was more distressed than he let on, though I knew Hugh wasn't easily fooled.

I put one hand on his shoulder and leaned in until our foreheads touched. "It's alright. I trust ye. Those witches are bound to be long gone by now, but someone in here will have answers."

Hugh released a long, slow sigh then stood back. He dipped his head once and followed me inside.

The interior was dusky and antiquated, a thick cloud of smoke lingered in the air as if the London fog worked diligently to reclaim the space inside. The smell was similarly old, though less foul, completely at odds with the decayed look of the outside.

A display case ran along the wall to my left, behind which an employee stood with a passive smile on his face. Along the front and right side of the store, were more cases and on every wall, shelves were crammed with objects of all sorts, some of which defied the imagination. Tables were set up in the back, a few occupied with creatures of various ilk, and the magic on the air was so potent, it could be felt like a hum beneath the skin.

The place itself was quite narrow, barely wide enough for Hugh and I to walk down the middle, and though there were at least two dozen people at the counters or seated at the tables, it was as silent as a church on a Saturday afternoon.

I turned to the employee waiting expectantly to my left, while Hugh kept an eye on the room at large.

The man was of medium height and unnaturally thin, dressed neatly in full on black. His hair, eyes, lips, and even his nails were black. He was meticulously clean shaven, every hair cut short and smoothed into place with some sort of pomade or spell. His hands rested upon each other atop of the display case, and for a moment my attention lingered on his long fingers, which were unnaturally white and smooth, made more obviously so by his ebony-painted nails.

I lifted my head and returned his smile with one of my own false grins. "I'm looking for a trio of witches."

The man's falsely pleasant demeanor never faltered as he replied, "I'm afraid we don't sell witches here."

I let out a low growl at the deliberate misunderstanding and tightened my hand into a fist where I'd rested it on the cabinet's surface. "They belong to House Sermo."

There… I saw a slight tic, a minute loss of composure, but the man regained his sangfroid demeanor remarkably fast.

He opened his mouth, likely to deny me once again, but was forestalled by a short woman wearing flamboyant layers of colorful fabric, which swirled about her in every direction despite the nonexistent breeze. As she approached, her arms waved about randomly in the air as she walked. *Was she wearing bells?*

The man continued to stare at me as I watched this curious woman's arrival, though she never once glanced my way. She stopped right next to him and pulled on the sleeve of his jacket—she *was* significantly shorter than he—and he bent to listen, though his eyes never left mine as she whispered, "Lady Ivy will see him."

At the news, the man scowled, but for my part, my grin turned genuinely smug.

The man's mouth barely moved when he bit out, "Black table in the back."

I glanced to the back of the store, then back to the man behind the counter. "They're all black."

I wanted desperately to reach across the counter and pull him up by the lapels of his jacket, but decided I needed answers more than the release the bashing of his head would provide, and so I refrained. "Never mind, I'll find Lady *Ivy* myself."

The man smirked as I turned to head toward the back, but I didn't care.

Hugh and I stopped before a table where a lone woman in a leafy green ensemble sat shuffling tarot cards, her gaze intent upon us…well, really, her gaze intent upon Hugh.

When Hugh just stood there like a mindless imbecile, I nudged him hard in the arm. He jumped as if jolted out of a stupor, and then reached in his pocket for the coin.

He slammed it on the table, and I asked as I seated myself in the chair across from her, "What can ye tell us aboot this?"

A few heartbeats passed before she dropped her gaze to the table, then another beat before startled eyes met mine. "Where did you get this?"

Arms crossed, Hugh answered for me, "Last night, right here."

Lady Ivy turned to Hugh. "That's not possible."

My pack mate leaned over, his fists planted on the table, an aggressive stance to be sure. "I can assure you, madam, I ken where the fook I got it."

The witch didn't take kindly to Hugh's antagonistic attitude, which to be honest, was decidedly out of character.

She eyed him a moment, lingering a bit too long on Hugh's broad shoulders and had we been here under different circumstances, I'd have given Hugh good-natured hell about attracting the notice of this petite little witch, but we weren't and clearly neither of them was in the mood for some good-natured ribbing.

Lady Ivy narrowed her eyes. "Did anything seem off to you when you arrived?"

Hugh narrowed his own eyes, then said, "Everything was different. Particularly the front door. It was bright and clean, no smell."

The witch relaxed and shook her head. "Ah. That explains it."

"Och, aye, of course," I said, "Clear as mud."

Lady Ivy glared at me. "Your friend here walked right through a portal."

"How the fook could I walk through a portal and no' know it?"

The witch glanced at Hugh, her face plainly saying she found his idiocy astounding, but she said nothing before returning her attention to me. She pulled a long, thin sliver of—*was that bone?*—bone, I supposed, out of thin air and pointed at the coin on the table between us. "This isn't an ordinary coin—"

"Ye dinnae say…," volunteered Hugh, the sarcasm practically dripping off his tongue.

I laughed, "Careful, Hugh, she looks prepared to remove a piece of yer hide."

Ignoring us both, Lady Ivy continued, "Look at the shield with the three lions…notice the middle lion's tail is pointing in the opposite direction? That's not normal, and look at this," she reached in a pouch at her waist and pulled out a pinch of powder, which she sprinkled liberally over the shilling. Before our eyes, the coin shimmered, then the lion with the redirected tale turned red right along with the Latin words surrounding the engraved shields and the rose between the two top shields. "Even the words are incorrect. *Pallium* should be *Pence*. And the flower in the middle, which should be a rose, isn't even a rose at all…"

"Fook," Hugh cursed.

Lady Ivy nodded in agreement. "Or in intelligent circles,

Atropa belladonna…deadly nightshade."

"Ye havenae touched the coin…," I noted.

Her eyes briefly flashed to Hugh rather than me. "Because *I'm* not an imbecile."

I stifled a chuckle. "Can ye divine what the coin does?"

"Not with the tools I have on hand," Lady Ivy glanced to Hugh, "What did they *tell* you it would do?"

"Cloak him…," Hugh jerked his thumb at me, "from those hunting him."

"So pallium, which means cloak, makes sense." Lady Ivy looked at me. "Have you touched this?"

"Nae."

"Did it work in any way?"

"It appears so."

"Interesting…," Lady Ivy looked away, deep in thought.

"Why do ye say that?" I prompted.

"Well, if it works and you haven't touched it; it either works by proximity, which is wildly unreliable, unpredictable, and weak, or… they created it using your blood."

Hugh held up his hands. "I'm no' that stupid. I was told it would work by proximity powered by my intent: ta see him safe."

Lady Ivy shook her head. "Highly doubtful… for that to work, I mean."

I glanced at her, "Suppose they do have my blood…what does that mean?"

"Depends…it could do exactly as they said, or it could be very, very bad…magic can be unreliable and chaotic if misused."

Hugh snorted, "To the tune of two crowns."

"Yes, well," said Lady Ivy, "you should have been more careful with the details and who you procured it from."

"How do we destroy it?"

"Without further testing, I don't know."

"So, it's more like a curse," at her nod, I added, "How much?"

Lady Ivy seemed to understand that I meant how much to get her to find an answer and destroy it, and yet as she considered her price, she had eyes only for Hugh.

"I'll do it," she said, "for the price of a favor, to be collected at a time of my choosing."

"Fine—"

"Not you, Your Grace," so she was aware of who I was, "I'll do it for a favor from *him*." She turned to look at Hugh.

I opened my mouth to speak; Hugh beat me to it, "Done."

I glanced at him. "Are ye sure?"

Hugh nodded. "I got us inta this mess; it's only right."

And with that, Lady Ivy stood, collected her cards, and with a wave of her baton, disappeared the accursed coin. "It's been a pleasure doing business with you gents; Mr. Hugh, I'll be in touch."

And with that she marched out of the shop. We both remained silent as we watched her depart.

"Hugh—"

"Dinnae ye have a battle tonight?" Hugh bit out.

So, he didn't want to discuss it…interesting. Deciding to leave the topic off for now, I nodded. "And since it appears we'll have no more answers today, I might as well find my arena."

Because there was no way in hell the damned thing was still parked where I'd left it; the place had a mind of its own.

Literally.

Chapter Nine

von Rappoldstein
An Unexpected Visitor

von Rappoldstein's Lair
London

L ADY SOPHIA LEFT with remarkable haste after I revealed the author of my curse. A move which was likely important, but I was too relieved to be alone with my thoughts, despite how rattled with holes and a touch of insanity they might be at times, to fully question the timing.

Prepared to make the most of some unexpected alone time, I settled before the fire with a full glass of hellfire whisky. I had yet to take the first sip, and the smoke still oozed over the rim of my glass, when Baldor knocked on my study door.

"Go away!" I called out, eager for my first mouthful of Satan's brew.

Baldor entered without pause, and I nearly launched the potent draught at his head. "Your Effervescence, you've a visitor."

I glanced at the clock over the mantle; it was half-past ten in the evening. "Tell them to return during visitor's hours; I'm busy plotting nefarious misdeeds."

"You don't have visitor's hours. Besides, you're going to want to meet with this one."

"Who is it?"

"He refused to give his name."

I glanced over Baldor's smooth head; tall, lanky form; and droopy eyes and wondered if it wasn't time to finally replace him with someone more *obedient*. "How long have you been in my employ?"

"A day too long, yet not nearly long enough, Your Vibrancy."

I mimed the words alongside him; it was the same answer he always gave and I waved him away to go retrieve yet another unexpected visitor.

I tossed back a bracing swallow of hellfire whisky, relishing the exquisite burn in my mouth as it went down my throat, followed by the scorch of smoke as it emerged out of my orifices. In the mirror across the way, I could see the telltale flare of red deep in my eyes as I savored the scalding fire of the infamous whisky.

Baldor entered then, a Scotsman—clearly a MacKeane, though not *The* MacKeane—on his heels, and my interest was definitely piqued.

I gestured to the chair beside mine. "Won't you sit?"

The man was immense and practically shook the foundations of my home as he stalked across the room in well-worn boots, the MacKeane kilt swaying at his bared knees, his hands clenched into fists at his sides. His eyes met mine and held me captivated, which really wouldn't do.

For all that I was notoriously immaculate in my attire, this man was my opposite in every way, and I had to admit, if only to myself, I was intrigued. The man was familiar in a way, but I couldn't place my finger on why, but then that was par for the course for me. His dark hair was overly long and wildly disheveled and his kilt had seen far better days. He wore no weapons that I could see, but then he was *Lycan* and hardly needed them in the first place.

The man sat with a grunt, nearly overwhelming the chair almost as if it were made for a child. And yet the chair that was in truth oversized for my own comfort, as I wasn't a small man myself.

"Drink?" I asked, and with a wave of my hand, a second glass of hellfire whisky appeared on the table between us.

"Nae," was his curt response.

I always did fancy a Scottish brogue. "I don't believe I've had the pleasure…"

The Scotsman snorted. "Nae. But I ken *ye*."

I smirked at that. Who didn't know me?

His scowl deepened. "I need a spell—"

Well, that was depressing. I waved him off. "They've witches who trade in that sort of thing."

"No' the kind of spell I need."

I raised a brow.

"Rumor has it ye're unafraid to use dark magic."

He was right. I had used dark magic before, but even I didn't do so lightly. "Dark magic, you say? And you're willing to pay the price for such a trick."

"Aye."

I looked him up and down, noting every detail…and making a point…dark magic didn't come cheap. "And what are you willing to offer in exchange?"

"I have—"

"I don't *need* money."

The man smiled then and folded his arms across his broad chest. "I have something better; something I ken ye want."

I doubted that but gestured for him to continue.

"Ye ken my family's arena—"

I nodded. Wolffe and Sons L'Arène de Bataille was the world's worst best kept secret, and the magic surrounding the ever evolving, forever relocating arena was the stuff of legends. There wasn't a soul in the magical community—or at least on the underworld side—who wouldn't give just about anything for a piece of its magic. Many have tried—none succeeded. I didn't want to risk showing just how interested this made me, though I suspected this MacKeane well knew…though maybe not quite to what extent.

"I can get you a piece of the magic."

I nearly salivated at the thought. *Oh, the possibilities…* I'd dabbled in alchemy for decades and with the strides a certain studious duke—a human, no less—was making in the scientific community—attempting to turn metal into gold—coupled with the MacKeane magic…the idea was heady. I might finally break my curse. I could be free to be fully evil. Or good. Or whatever. I wasn't even sure anymore. But that wasn't the point. I could choose.

I'd already had my eye on the alchemist, the Duke of West Sussex, but this…this changed *everything.*

I gathered the reins of my composure; it would not do to let this Scotsman see just how much I was enticed. "I'm interested about as much as a pinch of shite."

The Scot narrowed his eyes. "Are ye sure?"

So, the man wasn't fooled. "How do I know you can fulfill your end of the bargain?"

"Tonight, there's another battle." I nodded; I knew. "I'll be sure to arrange a demonstration you cannot ignore."

Chapter Ten

Josie

The Worst Best Kept Secret in All of England, Scotland and Wales

Between the Cracks
Somewhere in Southwark, London

TECHNICALLY, I WAS about to break the law, a serious infraction, particularly for a Spellmaiden.

But the Oracle's directive took precedence over everything. Therefore, an illegal action became legal. To a point.

If caught, I would still be arrested, directive or not. Worse, I'd be stripped of my status as a Spellmaiden forever. Shamed. Cut. *Banished.*

Seeing as how I was already on probation? I'd better not get caught.

I drew to a halt before a twenty-foot boulder that really shouldn't exist in this part of London, even if I was, technically, in the middle of the seedier side of Southwark.

It stood right in the middle of the pavement, and with a location like that one might be forgiven for thinking it wouldn't go unnoticed no matter how strong the magic being employed.

Nor how much gin had been imbibed.

Moss covered the sides of the rock where it was shrouded by the nearby buildings, and overall, the boulder was worn and pitted, dark-grey and black—clearly weathered over time as if it had resided in this location for thousands of years.

The pavement beneath it was a crumbled, disturbed mess as if the boulder was set in this exact setting with a rough and careless hand.

A jagged crack barely wide enough for the average adult witch to pass through followed the weathered lines of the rock face, and above it, carved gilt letters proclaimed in no uncertain terms: "Wolffe and Sons L'Arène de Bataille."

I snorted at the sight. A Scottish, Lycan-owned illegal fight club with a French Name.

The roar of a thousand magical folk crammed inside a giant cave echoed distantly from somewhere within the boulder and brought a smile to my lips. I'd definitely discovered the oft sought after but rarely found, ever moving Wolffe and Sons L'Arène de Bataille during an event. A *very* illegal event that wielded some of the most powerful magic in the world.

In the first place, a person could not find the arena, much less cross its threshold if that person had any intention, ever, of shutting down the event. Or of revealing anything about the event to the proper authorities. Tracing spells were utterly ineffective.

It was the magical world's worst kept secret, yet it remained impossible for anyone in authority to find.

And that wasn't even the most powerful of its purported magic.

Given that I was, in a way, a person of some authority, I possibly should have questioned the ease with which I found the arena…having all but stumbled onto it.

But considering just how desperately I needed to complete this job, I wasn't about to look a gift horse in the mouth.

I glanced around once more, but now, the familiar buildings of Southwark had disappeared, and in their place, a deep forest of towering oaks and various other hardwoods making up what looked remarkably like the Scottish countryside, surrounded me. The dirty pavements of Southwark no longer lay beneath my feet. Rather, dappled sunlight illuminated a lush, green forest floor. Gone were the odiferous smells of humanity, and in its place, clean, fresh air and pine sap tickled my nose.

The forest beckoned, tempting one to explore, and it was oh so persuasive. I could just imagine the hidden glens to be discovered, or if I were truly in Scotland, perhaps a fairy pool or two.

Alas, I had a job to do, so I ignored temptation, took a deep breath, and crossed the threshold.

Once inside, I found myself standing at the start of a small tunnel with only one way forward. Behind me, the entrance had already disappeared, and the tunnel was shrouded in near total darkness kept only from total obscurity by tiny dots of glowing blue embedded in the walls and ceiling and scattered across the tunnel floor. Those tiny speckles of light appeared to lead the way forward.

I tested the tunnel's magic by attempting to summon light to my hands with a spell, to no avail, despite the fact I could sense an extremely powerful magical current permeating the air.

I turned and reached out, only to discover a very solid cave wall where the entrance once stood. So, instead I followed the wall with my hands, then ran my fingers over the low ceiling finding the texture rough and damp. My hand came away wet, and I rubbed two fingers together, testing the viscosity, then put my fingers to my nose. Water. A drop landed on my forehead just then, and I laughed.

Bemused, I brushed my hands together and said, "Right. Nothing for it. Onward and, er, downward it is."

The tunnel twisted and turned steadily on a continuous downward slope. The sounds of a lively crowd still echoed in surges in the distance as the dots of blue light guided the way, but other than that, it appeared I was alone and there were no other doors or turn offs to consider.

I walked for twenty minutes before the narrow walls and low ceiling abruptly melted away, and I found myself standing before a motley collection of desks in various, shapes, sizes and colors. They stood at the bottom of a wide but narrow trench with soaring walls. Above me, fifty feet in the air at least, a brilliant blue sky shone down illuminating the room. I could hear the distant sounds of gulls calling out and the roar of rushing water making it sound as if we were close to the sea. There was definitely a hint of brine upon the air. I wondered if it ever rained down on the people in the trench, considering how often it rained in Scotland.

Before me, a tartan pennant declaring "Contestants Only" in ornate, gilt letters flapped in the nonexistent breeze high above a desk painted all over with peacocks at which sat a friendly-looking older woman with her hands folded together on the desktop. She wore an overactive floral blouse and a generous and eager smile as if my arrival had been the highpoint of her life. Packed in on either side of us, more desks and queues stood in a curved row which followed the line of the back wall of the trench, and creatures of every species stepped out of a dozen other tunnels, which, like mine, promptly vanished behind them the moment they crossed the threshold.

I approached the woman before me, and inconceivably, her grin widened, and her faded, grey eyes sparkled with delight.

The woman's hat—in a style familiar with many occultists— appeared to hail from the last century, as well as the frock she donned, which upon closer inspection appeared oddly formal, considering, as it was heavily trimmed with lace and pearls and embroidered silk, and overall made with an extraordinary amount of decadent, delicate fabric. Perhaps, it was a modern gown made by Worth after all, for such gowns were noted for their abundant use of fabrics, though I doubted a Worth gown had ever been so... tasteless.

Worth or not, it was *excessive* to put it mildly.

Still, the woman's mouth seemed carved into a permanent smile with generous laugh lines creasing the edges of her eyes. Eyes that suggested a fair amount of wisdom lurked in their depths. Sadly, the knuckles on her hands stood out in stark relief, like cabinet knobs, and her fingers were twisted with signs of arthritis, though these things did not seem to affect her greatly. Still, her nails were clean, her white hair neatly coiffed at the base of her neck, and her teeth, were almost unnaturally straight and bright.

On the whole, she was meticulously groomed, and according to the brass-colored tag pinned to her frock, her name was Mrs. Skettlebulb.

I nodded my hello, but before I could speak, the old woman, in perfectly pleasant, upper-class tones, asked, "Name, dearest?"

I tried my best to return an equally friendly smile as I replied. "Josephine Bell, but I'm not here as a contestant."

Mrs. Skettlebulb shook her head, though her beaming grin remained. "Not the most creative name, I daresay." The old woman sighed dramatically. "No, it simply will not do."

Next to me, someone snorted, and I glanced over to find a large half demon, half gnome dragging his lascivious gaze over my body. When our eyes met, he smirked, saliva dripping from his gaping, fanged mouth. "Vlad the Destroyer. Scared, Miss Bell?"

He followed his ill-advised comments with a snicker and a few rude gestures.

I reached out and slammed his face to the desk before him, breaking his nose on impact. As if on cue, the roar of the distant crowds surged, drowning out the beast's whimpers and cries as he wailed like a baby on the floor, hands clutched to his bleeding beak of an appendage. Green blood oozed from between his fingers.

Satisfied, I faced Mrs. Skettlebulb as if nothing had happened, and the woman dipped her head in approval.

I acknowledged the compliment with a quick smile and repeated, "Josie Bell. But I'm not here as a contestant."

"Of course, you aren't, dear."

Mrs. Skettlebulb unfolded her clasped fingers and lifted her right hand. An elaborate peacock feathered quill appeared in her grip, while a fancy piece of parchment and an inkwell full of golden ink materialized on the desk before her. With a flourish, Mrs. Skettlebulb dipped her quill and wrote, "Josephine, First of Her Name, Drawer of First Blood, Maiden of Death."

Mrs. Skettlebulb finished writing out the word death with an overly swirly and curlicued flourish, lifted her quill, and smiled down at her handiwork. With a voice all but oozing innocent charm, she said, "There. Much better, don't you think, my dear?"

Her question was clearly rhetorical, and she settled her quill on the brass stand accompanying the inkwell, which promptly disappeared, though the parchment remained. Then, she folded her hands and lifted her eyes, her ever-present smile firmly in place. "Now. To register as a contestant, you must agree to abide by the terms forthwith. Please answer aye or nay after each question. Question One. Do you, Josephine, First of Her Name, Drawer of First Blood, Maiden of Death, understand that entering the battle arena itself as a contestant is a binding, magical contract? An unbreakable contract?"

"Aye, but—"

My attention darted to the desk where the parchment fluttered as if ruffled by a gust of wind, and a checkmark appeared next to question one. My initials, which looked to be signed in my own hand, appeared next to the mark.

Mrs. Skettlebulb certainly hadn't moved, and neither had I.

When I looked up, the old witch continued as if nothing at all were amiss. "And do you, Josephine, First of Her Name, Drawer of First Blood, Maiden of Death, understand that once you enter the battle arena, you cannot leave until the battle is complete and a winner declared? For any reason whatsoever?"

"Mrs. Skettlebulb—"

"Please answer the question, dear." Her broad smile never dimmed.

I debated simply walking away. But a glance over my shoulder revealed a solid wall where my tunnel had been, and looking left or right, I saw there was nowhere else *to* go but forward. In fact, beyond the desk at which I stood, there was nothing but a large rock wall. I would work out my escape later, I supposed.

I turned back to Mrs. Skettlebulb, and her ubiquitous smile. "Aye."

"Excellent choice, my dear. Further, do you understand that while in the cage, you will be unable to use any magic? You will be fully human and only allowed to battle as a human with the tools and weapons available in the arena?"

"Aye." I'd heard about this part, and to be honest, that was my favorite part about this entire affair.

"Do you understand your opponent is whoever enters the arena opposite you, regardless of any size or power differences, no matter how significant or small?"

I briefly wondered what would happen if I said Nay but understood it really wouldn't matter. Somehow, I was entering this place as a contestant whether I wished to or not and couldn't help but marvel at—and respect—the astounding power of the arena.

Therefore, I held back a sigh and answered with the expected "Aye."

"Do you understand that each winner is determined by the Magical Orb of Medusa?"

Medusa? I hadn't but I filed that information away for later. "Aye."

"Do you agree not to hold Wolffe and Sons L'Arène de Bataille responsible should you die?"

I held back a snort, just. Mrs. Skettlebulb hadn't batted an eye at the absurdly morbid question. And really, how many people had access to a necromancer? They weren't exactly crowding the streets of London? Who could summon the intervention of an angel, which was even rarer, the only other way one might accomplish anything after death? One could approach one of the Fae from the Seelie or Unseelie courts, of course, but the cost was far too high a price to pay for anyone with a modicum of sense.

Still, I did nothing more than smile at the irony and replied, "Aye."

As soon as I spoke the word, I felt a swoosh push through my chest, then a twirling, purple ball of light shaped like a rotating question mark manifested itself above my head.

Mrs. Skettlebulb nodded to her right, indicating I should walk into the wall. "Have fun, sweeting. Your guide will be with you shortly."

"Yes, ma'am. Thank you."

Guide? A strange notion seeing as how, so far, there had been no options available to me but forward. How exactly could anyone ever get lost?

I stepped toward the wall, and another tunnel appeared and opened before me. This one was approximately double the size of the last, but instead of glowing dots of light, flaming torches spaced evenly along the walls led the way. I noted a bend to the left in the tunnel up ahead and that the ground seemed to be leveling off.

I proceeded forward and realized—with no small amount of exasperation, mind you—that the question mark remained with me, which I suspected would grow quite tedious before too long. I tried batting the thing away, as one might a pesky fly, but it simply leapt out of reach, all the while spinning on its axis, before returning to its usual position.

I imagined my quarry, MacKeane, thought it a hilarious joke and imagined giving him a swift kick for conceiving of such a torturous device. Assuming he did indeed own all of this.

Five minutes later, I rounded another sharp bend in the tunnel only to run nose first into the disembodied head of a cat, which hovered in the air precisely at eye level.

I brushed at the loose fur which lingered tenaciously about my face, particularly around my nose and mouth, while the feline's head, which seemed vaguely familiar, spun around with a start.

For a moment, I simply stood there and gaped like a fish out of water. Then, I blurted out, *"George?"*

Chapter Eleven

Lachlan
A Truth to Spar For

Meanwhile,
A Private Sparring Room,
Wolffe and Sons L'Arène de Bataille

SWEAT DRIPPED INTO my eyes as I brought my bare fists up to guard my face, but I ignored the effect, my focus trained on Hugh as he stalked me from the edge of our training circle. He feinted left a second before he launched himself at me, our shirtless bodies coming together in an explosion of sweat, slick skin, expanded muscle and pent-up violence.

"Stop projecting yer moves," I snarled, my voice taut with the strain of holding my pack mate back. I punctuated my command with a jab and a violent shove, which sent Hugh stumbling back a few steps. "And bloody hell, stop holding back."

Hugh swung his head to shake off the excess sweat dripping from his own thick mane of hair. "I'm no'. Ye're just too bloody fast."

He charged me again, managing to clip my jaw just before I swept him off his feet and onto his arse.

He followed through on the momentum, rolling to his feet

once more, though remaining crouched low in anticipation of me taking the offense.

I bided my time and the moment he relaxed a hair, I charged, tackling him to the ground, rolling with him this time in order to keep him planted there.

A knock on the door to the practice room had me cursing out loud in frustration. "This had better be good," I belted out.

The door opened and in walked my brother Owain. I hadn't seen him in months, and he was a welcome sight.

Hugh muttered a curse.

"Relax. He's family and no' going to arrest me either. I asked him to come."

Owain worked for the supernatural division of Scotland Yard, Division X.

I climbed off Hugh with a groan and together we walked over to a wooden cabinet in the corner. I grabbed a towel from one of the shelves and tossed a second at Hugh, who snatched it midair with a grunt of thanks.

Grabbing a fresh shirt from a nearby hook on the wall, I crossed the room while hooking the buttons, then enveloped Owain in a giant hug. "It's good to see ye, brother."

He pushed me away with a grin. "Lach. Ye smell."

I shrugged but backed away. "Talk to me."

"There's no' much to say. Though what I do know is definitely suspicious."

"Go on."

"First of all, no one from Division X was ever even assigned to yer case...which isn't wholly unusual...except that an assignment went out to the Spellmaidens before Division X even *knew about it*. Normally, someone from Division X makes the determination to bring in the Spellmaidens."

"Could it have been just a simple clerical error?"

"Nae. What compounds the issue is that no one seems ta know *who* submitted yer case."

"Or no one is claiming responsibility."

"Either way, something is no' right. Word is the White Witch is furious."

"I'm sure she is. She's known for her tight-fisted control over her Spellmaidens."

"Normally, when a Spellmaiden is assigned to a case, there is at least a record of who the oracle assigned to the case. This time, the assignment is blank."

"But I understand Miss Bell was assigned."

"I heard that, too. But technically, it's only hearsay."

"What about the crime itself?"

"The victim, a human man named Mr. Barnum Bailey, was mauled to death by an animal. But when authorities arrived, he was alive…just barely…and called out yer name just before he died."

"Who called in the authorities?"

"Another human, his neighbor, stopped a policeman and claimed to have seen a massive black wolf leaving the victim's residence. That's all they've got."

"What about the victim's remains?"

"Ah… the Seraph have claimed the remains, and they won't let anyone in to view them. I've tried."

I nodded my head. It wasn't a surprise, really…not with the suspicious circumstances surrounding the murder.

The door opened again and another member of my team entered. "Yes?"

The man bowed, a submissive greeting. "Your Grace, we've had an unexpected visitor."

I gestured for him to continue.

"Miss Josephine Bell is here."

Without my consent, a grin teased the corners of my mouth. *Well, well, well…* "Thank ye for bringing this to my attention; I'll see to her personally."

But rather than leave at my obvious dismissal, the guard looked a bit green and cleared his throat.

"Ye've more to say?"

The man all but reached to loosen the tie at his throat, before saying, "She's entered the contest—"

"No..." I glanced between Owain and Hugh, shaking my head, then began a march for the door. "No. no. no. no. no."

Bloody hell, this was not how our story was supposed to begin.

By the time I'd crossed the threshold, I ran as if the hounds of hell were after me.

But would I be fast enough?

Chapter Twelve

Josie
May the Odds be in Your Favor

I KNEW THE floating head before me wasn't *actually* George, but still, the resemblance was remarkable, even down to the way George would occasionally get that off-kilter look when he'd had too much catnip.

The head dipped before me as if bowing. "George Fletcher Augustus Bram, at your service. I am your interactive guide, your map, with a wealth of knowledge to satisfy all your most pressing questions."

Gracious. He even *sounded* like George. My eyes narrowed. "Are you going to behave like George as well?"

One of his feline ears flickered. "Naturally."

Great. George was difficult at the best of times. I supposed the map was tailored to each individual, but seeing as how George wasn't exactly my favorite person at the moment, I wondered, "Is there any way for me to adjust your settings?"

"In what way?"

"Do I have a choice of, er, heads?"

My guide shook his head. "No."

I tried a quick spell anyway, and not-George laughed. "Ooh, that tickles."

I decided to try some simple questions, though I knew better. I knew *George*. "Where does this tunnel lead?"

"Where do you want it to go?"

"That's not an answer."

My 'guide' moved as if it shrugged. "Depends on your point of view."

So like George to want to talk in riddles.

A paw appeared and not-George wetted it with his tongue, then began bathing his left ear with it as cats were wont to do.

"Bored already?" I asked.

George paused for a moment, his pupils widened, then narrowed before simply carrying on with his grooming.

I was growing impatient now, and I felt a compelling tug urging me to carry on down the hall. I resisted, only just. "So how does this work?" I gestured between him and I, then crossed my arms.

Not-George paused his grooming. "How do you want it to work?"

I narrowed my eyes. "Do you actually have any useful answers?" At this point, I was ready to bang my head against the wall, and I briefly wondered how they'd managed to capture George's essence so perfectly.

"Oh, loads."

I waited for him to expand on that; I even gestured in his direction.

"You have to ask the right question, don't you?"

A familiar leg appeared and I knew my *guide* was distracted washing his hindquarters.

"You know what? I think I'll figure things out on my own."

Not-George shrugged again. How I knew that? I did not know, but I was unsurprised when he said, "My, aren't you bricky? Well, then, carry on proper."

And with that, the floating head disappeared.

Without actually telling me how to summon him, naturally.

I shook my head—I didn't want to know; I couldn't imagine

needing his brand of assistance.

I carried on down the corridor. There were no turns or doorways, which once more begged the question why anyone would need a map if you could only ever go one way?

Finally, the cavernous hall ended at a flat, green wooden door with no knob, and marked with Nordic runes around the edges. The runes glowed with magic, and I could feel their potent almost seductive pull like a tug deep in my gut. I raised my hand—sensing the engravings, feeling them—and the runes glowed brighter wherever my hand hovered.

I couldn't read the runes, unfortunately, but I allowed instinct to guide me as I placed my palm against the door's surface where the handle should have been. I felt heat, searing heat, then the door turned purple, before opening.

I entered a long, curved room filled with a handful of creatures—all magic folk, like me—who all paused their conversations to glare in my direction for a heartbeat before dismissing me as, well, trivial, I supposed. Non-threatening.

The room was lit by more than a dozen ornate gas lamps along the back wall, which illuminated the room nearly as brightly as daylight could. To my left, a wall of floor to ceiling windows revealed a complete circle of similar rooms, four in total counting mine, with a round, caged arena in the center. At the moment, an angel without his wings and an eight-armed crocodile battled, circling each other, hunting each other. The angel bled from a dozen cuts along his arms, chest and legs, while the alligator limped...on account of only three of his eight arms being in working order.

The room directly across from mine looked to be filled with only a handful of half interested creatures, similar to the one I stood in. While the other two rooms were filled with stands of people drinking and eating and cheering and generally carrying on...clearly spectators. In that moment, it dawned on me that my room held the contestants.

And the one across from us were our potential opponents.

A few people, clearly Wolffe and Sons staff, circled the caged area where the battle raged on, and a very short queue of what appeared to be additional contestants lounged near the entrances to the arena, a few hanging on the bars of the cage, watching, all of them clearly waiting their turn and trying to look generally unconcerned about the danger, while simultaneously sizing up the competition.

Unfortunately, none of these rooms looked like a promising place to find my quarry. But there must be some sort of area set aside for MacKeane and any special guests.

I turned my attention back to my own room, not to size up the competition, but more to look for possible exits. There was a door on the far end, clearly marked, which seemed to lead to the arena itself. Along the back wall was a bar and two attendants offering drinks and other edible delicacies. A glance at the displays overhead revealed all manner of alcohol, tea and coffee were on offer, along with finger foods, some of which I'd never before heard of...cat's claws? Did they mean that literally?

I shook the question away. Next to the menu, was a listing of the current contestants, their probabilities—for the purpose of placing bets, I supposed—and a description of what constituted a win, which I was quick to understand varied per battle and was determined at the time of the match by some sort of magical orb, or so rumor had it.

I should have been prepared for it, but in truth, I was startled to see my name at the bottom of the list...just as the woman who had registered me entered it. Perhaps, I was startled because my odds of winning were staggeringly low, and I didn't quite know whether that made me *more* or *less* interested in actually entering the battle itself. Perhaps, a bit of both?

Alas, I had a job to do. I still hoped to leave this club with my target in custody, without ever actually entering the arena.

On that thought, I slowly turned in a circle, carefully taking it all in, and was surprised to find *two* doors behind me, neither even closely resembled the one I'd entered. The left one was as wide as it was tall and bright pink, and the right one was tall, narrow and royal blue.

A cheer from the spectators drowned out my exasperated, "George," and yet not-George appeared before me as if summoned.

Now, I could have asked where the doors lead to, but experience told me I wouldn't get a straight answer, so I decided to change tactics. "Where's Lachlan MacKeane?"

Not-George seemed to smile in approval, though all he said was, "He's here, naturally."

"You must know why I'm here, so why didn't you say so before?"

"You didn't ask."

I crossed my arms. "You know you're not exactly like George."

"I beg to differ."

"No. George isn't nearly so obnoxious."

"Hmmm… That's interesting…"

"Why?"

"Because I don't know George."

For a moment, I could only stare blankly, but my thoughts were anything but empty.

Still, before I could clarify, not-George huffed out a, "My personality is based on *your* view of George."

Well. The implications of *that* were a rather difficult charge to accept.

In fact, I rejected it thoroughly, shaking my head. "No. I suspect when you're not working, you're still obnoxious."

George scoffed. "And they say you're brilliant."

"Well, that's *quite* a thing to say…"

"Says the lady who thinks I exist."

I refused to dignify that with a response; I had a feeling I could race in circles, arguing with not-George for hours if I allowed it, but I really needed to know how much time I had to work with. "How will I know when it's my turn to fight?"

"You're called in the order you registered."

"Do I have to wait here?"

"No—you can go anywhere you'd like."

"Perfect, thanks." Of the two doors behind me, I chose to investigate the tall, blue one on the right.

But before I opened the door, George interrupted. "He's not in there."

Shaking my head, I turned toward the pink one on the left.

"He's not in there either."

I nearly threw up my hands, but instead I calmly replied, "I thought you said he was here?"

"I did. He is."

"But…"

"He's in the Family Wing."

"Well, where is that?"

"What?"

"The Family Wing."

"Oh, I can't take you there."

"Why not?"

"You're not Family."

I clenched my jaw, biting back a scathing retort, yet still I launched a small spell in his direction…one that should have at least compelled him to answer my questions seriously (a standard issue spell for a Spellmaiden, complete with license to wield it when necessary.)

For a moment, my spell seemed to work, and George appeared to grow serious—at least, for about a second—before he shouted out, laughing, "That tickles! Stop! You're killing me."

I wasn't laughing.

Eventually, not-George noted my expression, and he wiped the tears from his eyes saying, "Oh, were you being serious. Apologies."

He tried hard, and failed spectacularly, to adopt a more serious mien.

"How do I gain access to the Family Wing?"

"Oh, that's easy. You talk to MacKeane."

At this moment in time, it should be noted, I really, really wanted to shake not-George. "Marvelous. I would *love* to speak with him. So, take me to MacKeane."

"Sure. Let's go."

Not-George turned and hovered before the blue door, before stepping aside as if to say, *After you.*

I nodded my thanks as I opened the door and walked through, only to find myself back in the room we'd just left. George didn't say a word, as if nothing were amiss. I narrowed my eyes, and this time, tried the pink door.

Yet once again, I found myself back in the room we'd just left.

"George. We're still in the contestant's lounge."

"Naturally."

"I thought you were taking me to MacKeane?"

"Can't. He's in the Family Wing."

I turned my back on George and counted to ten. Slowly. Forcing my breathing to remain calm and steady, concentrating on the flow as it moved in and out of my body. Willing my frustrations to subside. It was a ploy I had to use quite often around the real George.

Once I'd rediscovered my equilibrium, I turned to George once again. "Every door I open takes me right back to this room."

"Naturally."

I refrained from pinching the bridge of my nose and forced a sweet smile.

George tossed me a pitying look. "Don't look so aggrieved. Really. Not everyone can be a genius like me."

"But you don't exist."

He huffed. "Well, there's no need to be rude!"

"Why do I keep ending up back in the same room?"

George held up a paw, which seemed to conveniently appear and disappear when the situation called for it. For a moment, George stared off into space as if listening for something, then finally he turned a smile in my direction. "Oh, well, the cave considers you a potential absconder. To be honest, I'm rather surprised you made it this far. I keep expecting the cave to kick you out of the arena altogether."

"I'm actually going to have to enter the fight, aren't I?"

"Naturally. Didn't they tell you that before you signed on?"

I didn't dignify that with a response; I'd clearly had no choice. "Blast!" I couldn't help a small curse over my predicament.

"Shhhh...," George glanced about, then admonished, "there are children about."

I tossed both hands in the air. "It's the contestant's lounge!"

George looked pointedly over my shoulder, and I followed his gaze. So, perhaps, some contestants did appear a trifle bit young, but I didn't for a moment underestimate their lethality.

"Why *did* you register if you didn't want to fight?"

It was my turn to shrug. "It was the only way to get in."

"That was brave of you..."

"Thank you."

"Or, mayhap, foolish."

I opened my mouth to send him away, though I didn't really know how I'd accomplished that feat the first time, when George said, "One moment—I shall return shortly."

"Not like I'm going anywhere," I murmured, as with a *Pop*, George's head vanished.

I walked to the wall of windows and looked across the arena to the opposite room, but it was of no use; I couldn't be sure of the types of creatures I might face. Within the arena, a battle between an orange demon and who knew what, was well under way. I hadn't even realized the last battle had finished.

I was just wondering whether the angel or the alligator had won their match, when not-George appeared next to me. He'd only been gone maybe five minutes.

"Where did you go?" I asked.

"To the betting room."

"Whatever for?"

George rolled his eyes. "To bet on you, naturally?"

"To win or to lose?" I asked, genuinely curious.

"Neither. On whether or not you are foolish."

"But… I thought the only bets were on the outcome of the fights?" I glanced to the board in our room.

George laughed. "Glad I put it all on foolish. You know the British—human or monsters alike—we'll bet on anything. The betting lounge is where the *real* bets are laid."

Truer words had never been spoken.

I glanced to my betting board and noted the final column which currently read, "First Blood."

"George, the last column." I gestured toward the board. "Each battle has a different goal?"

George nodded. "Let's see, I've seen: First blood, First severed limb, First tooth, First black eye, First to draw tears—"

"Fine. But how is the goal determined?"

"The arena chooses."

"When?"

"Once both contestants enter. Until then, there are odds as to which is likely to be chosen for each battle, so spectators can bet on what will be chosen, naturally."

"Has there ever been a fight till the death?"

George's face turned unusually serious. "Twice."

I fought the urge to ask about those two instances, but I had a more pressing matter weighing on my mind: All the other contestants had challengers listed. Apart from one. Me.

"George, why doesn't my name have an opponent?"

Not-George laughed nervously. "No idea, actually. It is unusual to be sure, but don't worry. There's nothing *much* to worry about—it won't be to the death."

Had he been capable, I would swear not-George would have tried to comfort me with an awkward pat on the shoulder.

"My, aren't you confident."

George shrugged. "Both times it's been called—the same man had entered the arena."

I didn't want to ask the question—I was afraid I well-knew

the answer—and yet I found my lips forming the question anyway. "Who?"

"MacKeane. It's why he doesn't enter. Ever."

Intrigued, I asked, "Why him?"

"Oh, no one knows. It's all just speculation really. Mostly rumors."

"Humor me."

My question was met with silence. Eventually, I prodded, "You've been quite talkative so far—why stop now?"

"Would *you* enter the arena if every time you did, you had to kill to leave?"

I snorted, murmuring, "I would have thought he'd like that."

George's horrified expression was comical, and I had to choke back a laugh. "What?"

"Well, now I'm glad I didn't take you to the Family Wing as my guest."

I narrowed my eyes. "Do you mean…all this time, you could have—"

"Oh! Looks like you're up. Well…may the odds be in your favor, Josie Bell."

"Thanks," I said, as not-George faded away.

I glanced at the betting sign, but it was as if it were possessed, the sign going haywire flipping between challenger names so fast, I couldn't read them, and the odds for me losing were climbing exponentially.

I glanced behind me, but the two doors were gone…the only way out was the far exit leading into the arena. It was only then that I noticed that the entire room had emptied of all remaining contestants, but I could hear, and just barely see, that the spectator rooms were filled to their limits, and I realized that considering the nature of my job, there were likely one or two creatures watching who would love to see me fail spectacularly.

With a short sigh and no other choice before me, I lifted my head and crossed the threshold into the arena itself.

I stopped before the gated entrance to the cage and noted a

nine-foot-tall demon with four arms was queued at the only other gate. He was grinning at me with an evil smirk I could practically feel across the hall, but rather than express any sort of trepidation, I chose to simply ignore him.

By now, the spectators were screaming wildly and beating their fists against the windows surrounding us. I ignored them as best I could and focused on surviving the next few moments. My apparent opponent certainly had me in the size department, but size didn't necessarily equate to skill, and with neither of us having access to magic? I guessed we were relatively evenly matched.

All at once, the light above my gate turned green and I stepped confidentially across the threshold, prepared to face my demon.

But when I looked across the open space, it wasn't a nine-foot demon standing opposite me.

No. It was *The* MacKeane himself. Lachlan MacKeane.

The very man I'd come here to find.

Chapter Thirteen

Lachlan
It's Just a Little Fight...

HURTLING MYSELF INTO the domed sparring field whilst cutting off the fae demon hybrid who'd been patiently waiting his turn had been an impulsive move on my part, I admit. Perhaps, a foolish one considering my own arena so often wanted to kill me. I might one day come to regret my rashness. Perhaps, even, today.

But as I looked across the pitch at the absolute warrior goddess walking towards me, in that moment, I couldn't unearth a single regret.

I examined Josie Bell's brazen entrance like a starving wolf eyeing nearby prey, attraction arrowing through me, burning along my veins, increasing exponentially with every bold, confident step she took. She looked as delectable and as fierce as ever, an intriguing combination I didn't even want to resist, the same as I'd noted back at The Twisted Vine, and in that instant, I felt as if I might combust like an exploding star.

She glanced around, taking in every detail of our surroundings, and my heart gave a swift kick each and every time her eyes flashed my way. *Thump.*

Her red hair was pulled back in a simple, society-approving

bun, though her attire was anything but.

She wore trousers for one, and I couldn't resist marking every ripple of fabric as it lovingly caressed her legs while she crossed the blood red floor in daring, self-possessed steps.

She wore a corseted top with fitted sleeves and straps, which crisscrossed her chest all but creating a perfect frame to encase and augment her flawless tits. I had to actively tear my gaze from the sight.

Gods. If I lost to her, it just might be worth it.

My attraction to her was disconcertingly fierce, my cock twitched beneath my kilt, and if I didn't know any better, I'd think she was my mate, a fact I couldn't verify with my currently bound Lycan senses (a requirement for the match), but also a slim likelihood I was determined not to entertain regardless.

I might be attracted to her on a base, animal level, but she was still a witch.

A witch, I might add, who intended to toss me in gaol, but not before taking a pound of flesh out of my hide first; I could read the intent in her eyes. Fate wouldn't—couldn't—be so cruel.

Besides, if she were my mate, I would have detected the scent by now, surely?

I tossed her a wink out of habit and ripped my gaze from hers, then turned in a circle, facing the crowds surrounding us, who were cheering wildly, all but losing their collective minds over my unexpected arrival, and with good reason. The last two times I'd entered had been battles to the death; the only two in the history of the arena.

I really hoped today wouldn't mark the third.

I raised my hands, encouraging their adoration, a showman giving his audience—my audience—precisely what they wanted. This was my family business, or part of it, and I knew my spectators well. I knew my business well.

Bets were being called out all over the place as the display overhead rapidly spun through various options that would define what constituted a victory in the battle between us, the words scrolling by too swiftly to make out. Yet.

We were the last fight of the day, and after so many combatants, the floor was a bloody, gruesome mess of gore and…limbs, many unidentifiable. Some of the weapons lining the walls of the cage were broken and bloody, with only a few remaining untouched.

Rule one of the arena: all magic was forbidden, which meant my preternatural Lycan senses—sight, smell, speed, strength, even my ability to transform—were bound and more in line with a human of similar age and build. I couldn't even heal like a normal Lycan while I was in the arena…

Another rule: All combatants could use weapons, but only the non-magical weaponry provided, which were available to either contestant…if you could reach one in time.

After mentally marking which weapon I intended to acquire first, I crossed the arena and met my combatant in the middle.

Josie Bell.

Face to face, in the flesh. *Finally.*

I clenched my jaw and forced myself not to close my eyes and test for her scent. As it was, a few tendrils reached me, and I tightened my hands into fists, desperate to resist following the path such a delicious scent invited me to travel.

Josie Bell adjusted her sleeves and asked, "Why did you do that?"

Candid, I liked it. My response was equally frank. "Damned if I know."

"Lachlan MacKeane." I held out my hand.

Without hesitation, she laid her palm in mine. "Josephine Bell."

I leaned in. "I know precisely who you are, Miss Bell."

I hesitated to release her, her hand feeling quite right in my broad grasp, and a half-smile curved one side of her mouth. "Then, you know why I'm here."

"Aye, lass, I ken."

I held her hand a moment too long, each second timed by the

beat of her heart, which I could see fluttering at the base of her neck. I wasn't the only one who noticed; I could practically feel the arena's magic figuratively sit up and narrow its eyes at our conjoined hands.

I dropped hers at once and braced both mine on my hips. "Why did you enter the competition?"

She shrugged. "I didn't seem to have a choice."

"Explain."

She raised one brow as if to demand I stop ordering her around; still, after a brief pause, she answered me anyway. "There's nothing to explain. I entered the cave, and it offered me no other path but forward."

"Not even at the desks?"

"When I argued that I wasn't here to enter, the woman helping me simply ignored me."

"Who?"

She laughed, a husky sound which I felt in my gut. "You think I'm going to tell *you?*"

"Why not?"

"For starters, I don't want her sacked because of me. I suspect it wasn't her fault."

I held up both hands. "Trust me; I won't bag her."

Josie laughed. "You expect me to trust *you*, a wanted murderer." She shook her head. "No, thank you."

Josie Bell lifted her stubborn, mutinous chin, and I couldn't help but admire her stance on the matter. I leaned in closer, whispering beneath my breath. "You do know the arena will not let us free until one of us is declared a winner."

She turned toward me, "I'm aware," her voice equally low and so close, I could feel her breath on my cheek.

I closed my eyes as if to savor her nearness. "If we do not fight as if we mean it, the arena will kill us both."

Josie Bell smiled then, a confident lift of her lips. "Not to worry, Lachlan MacKeane," and here Josie Bell did something quite unexpected, she patted my cheek with one elegant hand, punctuating each word with a touch. "I will absolutely mean it."

And just like that I felt my cock become rock hard.

Josie Bell noticed. Her eyes dropped, then returned to mine and she smirked, "Nice."

My rod wasn't the only one interested, and in other circumstances, I might savor our sexual attraction. Instead, I tore my gaze from hers and glanced up at the spinning words above me, wondering what the hell was taking the magic so damned long to decide.

Finally, the scrolling words began to slow, and a keen hush fell over the crowd, anticipation heavy in the air.

When the words finally stopped, my lids fell, and only one word came to mind. "*Fook.*"

Because we were, very much, fucked.

For the third time in history, I faced a battle to the death.

A battle I wanted neither of us to lose.

Chapter Fourteen

Josie
...To the Death

MY FILE ON Lachlan MacKeane had not adequately prepared me for the man facing me. Oh, I knew all his vital statistics, his likes and dislikes, the number of lovers he'd had, his addresses, a full list of aliases, the size and shape of the dozen tattoos etched up on his skin beneath his flowing white shirt. The two below his trousers.

The piercings.

I even knew what *size* clothes he wore.

Yet it all became meaningless in the face of his overwhelming...presence. That odd combination of rakish arrogance with an undercurrent of, dare I say it, honesty? Integrity?

I must be imagining things...the man was wanted for murder. Murderers weren't generally considered the compassionate, honest type. And he was Lycan, definitely clever enough to hide the scoundrel within.

Yet he gazed at me with an intensity that nearly held me in thrall.

And yet...none of these things mattered in that moment, because one of us was about to die.

And I wasn't about to let it be me.

The heavy weight on the air seemed to have silenced the crowd, or perhaps, they were just simply too shocked for words, unsure if any of this was real. Trust me; I had a thought or two in that direction myself. The day had started normal enough before rapidly falling to shite.

I stretched the muscles of my neck, tilting my head left, then right, then loosened my knees and took a fighting stance.

A disembodied voice shattered the silence. "This is a contest to the death. At the sound of the bell, both contestants will engage until one of ye is dead. If you choose no' to fight, ye will both die. Use of outside magic or weaponry will result in yer death. Attempts to escape will result in yer death. If ye have concerns regarding these rules or a dispute aboot a judgement against ye resulting in yer death, ye may take it up with management after the fight." *Assuming you win*, I muttered before the voice added, "Och, aye, enjoy yer battle."

I shook my head, and before the next thump of my heart, a bell sounded, followed by the deafening roar of a rapt crowd. Without pause, I leapt for to the nearest wall of the cage surrounding us and climbed, headed for a medium length sword I'd spotted when we'd first entered the arena. Still, I kept an eye on Lachlan's whereabouts; he had leapt to the opposite wall, intent, apparently, on retrieving a Scottish broadsword near the top of the dome. As my hand gripped the hilt of my acquired sword, I wondered if Lachlan had purposely left it for me. There were few intact weapons remaining in the arena, and had he taken this one, I would have been at a distinct disadvantage.

I swung down faster than I'd climbed, and the pair of us landed at precisely the same moment, our weapons held at the ready, knees bent, both of us prepared to lunge.

I swung first, pleased by how well-balanced and light the sword was in my grip; it was almost effortlessly maneuverable, even better than my own personal sword, which awaited me, presumably, like a checked coat somewhere within this massive network of tunnels.

Lachlan blocked me easily, and the match was on.

I swung, he parried, I stepped left, he matched me to the right. On and on and on we danced to a silent but deadly tune, and I couldn't help but be suitably impressed by his skill. I trained daily for battles such as this, while he wouldn't be used to working without his enhanced Lycan abilities.

But no amount of magic could diminish a person's inherent talent. And he had that in droves.

He aimed high, and I ducked while swinging out with my foot where I shockingly made contact, knocking him to his arse. The crowd gasped as I followed through, pinning him to the floor by throwing all my weight on one knee…the one I planted in the center of his chest.

Lachlan dropped his broadsword and blocked my sword arm with his, then reached behind my neck with his free hand and pulled me close. The heat from his hand seared the back of my neck, though not in pain…nothing even remotely resembling pain.

"I willnae kill ye." His eyes bored into mine.

I shrugged. "Well, that's your choice. But I will kill you." I pressed down a little harder, and bit out, "We don't have a choice, MacKeane."

His chest heaved beneath mine—for that matter, we were both breathless—and a surge of awareness jolted through me, surprising me with its intensity, not to mention its impractical timing.

He lifted his head, touched his forehead to mind. "There is always a choice, lass." His voice was deep, gravelly.

His lips hovered over mine, so close, yet not so much as a whisper of contact, still I could feel the heat of those plump pillows of skin, and something deep inside me urged me to close the gap, to take just a small taste.

In a blink, he flipped us, and for a moment, he lingered over me, but before I could even process the absolute hunger in his gaze, he slapped his hands to the ground, then leapt away leaving me ample time to roll to my feet, once I shook off a bit of a stunned delay.

A pause that in other circumstances, would have been lethal.

Dare I trust him?

I cannot deny I was (mostly) relieved.

Unfortunately, no one was fooled by what he'd done. In terms of brute strength, he had the advantage, no doubt about it. Instead, he'd let me go.

He let me go.

Disgruntled sounds rather resembling extreme disappointment echoed through the spectators, and the guards standing around the outside of our iron cage grumbled and adjusted their weapons to remind us they would kill us if we didn't comply.

Even Lachlan MacKeane, apparently…if it came down to it.

But would they? Would they really?

Lachlan swept up his broadsword and approached, whipping his sword left and right as if testing its weight and balance, yet loose-limbed and obviously prepared should I take the offense. But he stepped close enough so I could hear him when he murmured, "I have a plan."

When he drew back, he winked.

As if the arena *knew,* the cage surrounding us started to glow, and upon hearing Lachlan's uttered *Fook,* I understood the glow to be a warning we were about to die.

Chapter Fifteen

Lachlan
Let's Die Another Day

MY PLAN MIGHT not work. It was risky, insane, based on a hunch I didn't even *want* to be true, and it had never, ever been done before...but it was the only plan I had, and I was damned determined to see it through.

Sure, it was normal to feel attraction to a woman like Josie Bell...but this level of recklessness? For someone I don't even know, just what's written in my file on her? And sure, she was forbidden fruit, but... I had to wonder if she might be my mate, despite the lack of instinctive signs that should have told me definitively. For what other reason would I act so irrationally? She was a fucking witch for crying out loud.

Which mattered not, damn it. Neither one of us was going to die today if I could help it.

I prayed Josie Bell would agree. She was more than capable of killing me; even though I was stronger, broader, and likely faster. But she made up for it through impressive skill, training, and quick, intuitive thinking.

Unfortunately, what I needed most from her was trust and faith, which she'd already stated I unequivocally did not have. Who could blame her?

Still, I somehow needed to convey the details of the plan, without the guards or the magic surrounding us, catching on.

Easy.

I wasn't worried about the guards. The magic on the other hand…I was linked to it, and it to me, through my heritage as a MacKeane…linked as in connected *genetically* through my very origins.

Walk in the park.

But if we wanted to survive, I had to brazen this out. I tossed away my broadsword once again and charged her head on. It was risky but unexpected, and it was the surprise that allowed me to succeed.

We tumbled to the floor in a wild roll of arms and legs, and though ungentlemanly, I did not attempt to break her fall… I had to make this look real and keep an eye on that very lethal sword she still wielded with expert precision.

I blocked her sword arm, and though it brought me absolutely no joy to do so, I wrapped one large hand around her throat. I made all the appropriate faces—scrunched brow, gritted teeth, taut jaw—but we both knew I hadn't put any real pressure on her neck…it was all for show.

Fortunately, the spectators were buying it; the magic surrounding us, however, remained suspicious.

Still, Josie Bell had no choice but to relinquish her sword as I pretended to press down on her throat. Her sword fell to the ground with a loud clang, then she gripped my wrist with both hands as if to stop me from squeezing the very life out of her.

I pulled her up, close—more by the strength of her grip on my arm, than my own hold on her neck.

"Lass, we need to combine our magic." I whispered the words, doing my best to be clear whilst trying not to move my lips as much as possible.

With a burst of energy, she twisted, and we rolled across the ground once, twice, until I was back on top.

Gods, under any other circumstances, I'd be enjoying this

immensely.

She gave a pointed look at the cage surrounding us and its warning glow, which throbbed a bright orange, yellow color. What she didn't know, is that we were all right…until it turned red. For now, we were under a warning.

But I understood her question, and I leaned in close, until my head was beside hers. "Trust me. On the count of three, set yer intention and reach for yer magic."

She froze…stared at me as if to plumb the very depths of my soul, and I began to worry she wasn't going to agree, but then she managed a complicated maneuver with her legs—one in which I vowed to have her teach me after we survived this bloody ordeal—and flipped me once, before she released me and rolled to her feet.

I wasn't far behind, and as we circled each other, I noted the almost imperceptible dip of her head. *Och, aye.*

If this worked…well, *shite.* But at least we'd be alive to be concerned about the consequences, not to mention the implications.

I flexed my hands, then held one finger down. *Pause.* Two fingers. *Pause.* Three.

Together, we nodded, and I grabbed her the same moment I drew on my wolf, and she reached for her magic.

The result was *explosive.*

Individually, we never would have defeated the magic powering the arena. But together?

The discharge of our combined magic shook the very foundations of the system of tunnels and caverns. The cage itself exploded outward, tossing metal and weapons and guards, including two exhausted combatants, into the air.

The windows from the surrounding rooms shattered.

I landed amidst a pile of rubble, and for a moment, I lost consciousness. But I was Lycan, and with the magic dispersed, I began healing almost immediately. When I came to, chaos reigned as fires burned and survivors scattered like rats for the exits. I suspected I had only been unconscious five minutes at the most.

The arena's magic was gone, I could sense that through my connection to it, and I felt somewhat saddened coupled with feelings of guilt at the thought, but at that moment, I only really cared about one thing: finding Josie Bell.

"Josie!" I called out as I climbed over piles of debris. My left arm was wrenched, I was bleeding from my head, my shirt was torn, and I was covered in filth, but it didn't matter. We needed to get out of here before the whole cavern collapsed in on us. I doubted even I would survive that.

I received no answer, but I didn't need one. Now that my Lycan senses were back, I could smell her and unerringly made my way to her across a field of wreckage, tossing debris out of my way with inhuman strength as I went.

I was by her side in minutes, though it felt like hours, and when I found her, she was still unconscious.

With absolute care, I slid my arms beneath her and lifted her from the rubble, murmuring, "I've got ye, Josie Bell." I chuckled as I imagined she would not appreciate my rescuing *her* and added, "I suppose we'll just have to live to die another day."

Chapter Sixteen

von Rappoldstein
A Bane to Insanity

THERE WAS ONLY one spell The Lycans had repeatedly sought from me over the centuries, and I didn't doubt this was the same one my nameless MacKeane was after. Rarely had I agreed to a bargain to wield the spell, but then never before had someone offered me a nugget of the MacKeane Ore in exchange for services rendered.

If he could deliver…oh, the possibility had me increasing my pace down the stairs until I was practically jogging.

The spell was outlawed for good reason—it was dark magic, indeed—with a lengthy list of ingredients required to invoke it. Not to mention the toll it would take to wield it; I didn't doubt I'd require several Hellfire Brews—perhaps, more—to aid my recovery after.

I only hoped my broad-fisted MacKeane was prepared.

The spell itself was enchanted to ensure anyone who heard or spoke the blasted thing forgot the words and how to perform it. Fortunately, it was inscribed in detail in the Book of Forbidden Spells—*we magical folk weren't about to lose sight of a jolly good spell if we could help it*—a book I happened to possess.

A book only I had the means to access.

I performed the steps required to unseal the door to my underground workspace—it wouldn't do for the neighbors to see or hear what I was about—and tried, with extreme difficulty, to swallow my shock of surprise at the sight of one pest of a cat—clothed, thank the gods; it was beginning to feel weird to see Sophia unclothed for some reason—curled up atop the very book I sought.

"If I find any fur between the pages of that book, you're going to find yourself walking around hairless with a chronic case of boils."

In response, Lady Sophia slowly uncurled and yawned while arching her back into a stretch, her claws digging into the leather covering of the rarest book in the world as if it were naught but a pile of flesh-bound rubbish. When she was finished, she sat on her haunches, her back claws curling down into the leather as if to steady herself.

I had to grit my teeth to keep from trying to blast her to hell with a thought. Who knew what would happen if I tried now she'd claimed me as her familiar? Probably nothing, quite literally.

It was almost worth it to find out.

I flipped open my watch, glanced at the state of my soul, then snapped the lid closed with a decisive click. I was in the green. I had room to maneuver either way.

"Come on, shoo…" I nudged her to jump down, but instead, she leapt to my shoulder, her claws digging in through my robes, my coat, my waistcoat, and my shirt to unerringly find the flesh and muscle of my shoulder despite all the layers, and I had no doubt she did so with more savage intent than absolutely required.

But she didn't settle there…no…rather she curled herself around my neck and watched from over my shoulder as I flipped open the Book of Forbidden Spells.

"What are you looking for?" she mumbled after another deep yawn, her canines clicking together as her mouth closed.

When I didn't answer, she carried on, "Oh my. Is someone

annoyed I managed to find my way into his little playroom? Worried I might mess with your toys, von Rappoldstein?"

I snorted. "If you must know, I have a client in search of a spell."

"What sort of spell?"

"A Bane to Insanity."

Her ears perked forward at that. "Fascinating." She didn't truly look fascinated, what with her chin resting as it was on one outstretched paw, her eyes half-mast. "And you'll find it in there?"

I nodded as I carefully skimmed the pages.

"I can't imagine anyone willing to pay the price to make such a bargain."

"You might if your entire species was cursed to eventually go insane."

Her head perked up at that. "Your client is a Lycan?"

"He is." I saw no harm in telling her this. I suspected she'd find out eventually anyway. It seemed there were few, if any, secrets between a cat and her familiar.

Or at least, no secrets from Lady Sophia Tewkesbury-Smith.

"Are you this way with other people?"

She chuckled. "Not in the least. What can I say? You bring out the young woman in me."

"Provoking, mouthy, and irreverent?"

"Curious, yet lazy."

Eventually, she settled down and began to purr, her eyes closed as if sleep-watching over me, and I was startled to discover I'd been absentmindedly scratching her cheeks as I flipped through the book.

A few pages later, I found what I was looking for, and I skimmed over the list of ingredients.

Several different species of blood. Fur from the Lycan in question. Feather from a crow bathed in moonlight. Dragon's eye stone. Grasshopper oil. The list went on and on. Nothing out of the ordinary until I saw the last one.

A claw from a Class I Demon.

Now *that* was the truly difficult part. Not only were Class I Demons the strongest and most evil of the animalistic classes— meaning they couldn't be reasoned with, nor could they pass as human even with the right spell—but the moment one stepped foot on terra firma, the M.M.R. would be sending a Spellmaiden after it.

And I either had to pay a little visit to hell…something I was loathe to do…or I had to find one elsewhere.

"Sophia, have you heard of any Class I Demons being captured or trapped or even killed anywhere on Earth recently?"

With a yawn and a quick purr, Sophia answered, "Actually, I have…not recently, mind you…but there's one they call the Humpback Beast who is supposedly trapped beneath the little hamlet of Walrus, near Kent."

I nodded, recalling the event now with a measure of affection. Perfect.

But it was going to require reinforcements. I flipped to the Book of Forbidden Spells' index and scanned those listed under Temporary Mind Control, until I found one that looked promising.

The directions even made me wince, and I realized I might have to plan to comfort a few sick children in hospital in order to keep my scales in balance after this one.

Chapter Seventeen

Josie
Strange Questions

I AWOKE IN my own bed; George—the real one this time—sprawled across my legs; the aches and pains racking my body clamoring to make themselves known to me. My cat lay half on his side and half on his back, snoring, his forepaws up over his head, his pink tongue lolling out of his mouth more like a dog than anything, his dead weight making me desperate to move.

Thank goodness cats didn't drool, though I long suspected he had canine blood somewhere in his family tree.

I carefully extracted my legs from beneath him, wincing as every bone and muscle in my body screamed at me in protestation. I felt bruised and abused.

But I was alive and intact and in my room, thank the gods.

The real question was *how had I gotten here?* I had zero recollection after the blinding white light and subsequent explosion.

I rolled onto my side with a groan and buried my face into the pillows. They smelled different—mine, but overlayed with cinnamon, cloves, and…leather?

MacKeane.

I launched from my bed, my gaze automatically darting around the room to check the shadows. It was night, but a moon nearly full shone bright enough for me to see he wasn't here.

Had he lain in bed next to me?

I glanced to the bed, and there, on the pillow beside where I'd been sleeping, was a note.

I swiped up the letter, and for some reason, lifted it to my nose. It smelled like him, an exotic combination of leather and autumn spices embedded in thick, creamy parchment.

For a moment, I allowed my fingers to drift over the MacKeane seal on the back, fingering the edges and dips as I imagined him pressing the signet ring on his right hand into a deep, purple puddle of wax.

What was I doing?

With renewed fire, I broke the seal and opened the letter, lifting it into a ray of moonlight so I could read his words.

Josie Bell,

He wrote with a flourish, and I hated to admit I liked the way he added extra curlicues to the letters of my name.

Here's to living to fight another day. I look forward to our next encounter. I hope you can attend.

Yours,
—Lachlan MacKeane

In addition to his brief message, there was an invitation to the Duke of Abernathy's Ball scheduled for tomorrow evening.

A ball.

My instinct was to light the fire in my hearth and burn the note immediately; the contents were circumstantial but damning all the same. Should the M.M.R., or worse, the White Witch, get their hands on it, it would invite all sorts of trouble. Or *more* trouble. Certainly, a barrage of questions.

I kept the invitation to the ball, naturally. I wasn't foolish enough to pass on another opportunity to nab my Lycan.

My Lycan?

I could store the note away some place safe and decide whether to keep it later. My cloak and belts were hanging on the appropriate hooks by the door, as were my weapons from the looks of things—*oh, I have many questions for you, Lachlan MacKeane*—and I found my Purse of Possessions exactly where it should be. To anyone other than me, the purse would appear empty, but it was far from it. MacKeane's letter would be safe from prying eyes…

I stuffed the letter inside just as someone scratched at the door.

I opened it a crack and in slipped Sophia, who wound her way around and through my legs, which was oddly affectionate for her, before crossing my bedchamber. George remained steadfastly asleep on the bed.

Sophia sat at the foot of the bed, swishing her tail back and forth, back and forth, then jumped, walking right over George, who grunted before he rolled over and stretched fully on his side with a wide yawn, his head twisted upside down.

"Oh, do wake up, George," she admonished.

After yesterday's experience with Not Quite George, I felt an inexplicable urge to defend my cat from her scathing tongue, which could indeed flay a man with ease should she choose to do so.

But as I watched George crack open one lazy, watery eye, I recalled George never let a thing disturb him. Not even Lady Sophia.

I turned and checked my reflection in the mirror over my vanity. I had a cut, which had been bandaged with a small plaster, and as I probed at the bruising around the area, my thoughts returned to MacKeane. *Had he done this himself? Patched me up?*

"What happened?" asked Lady Sophia.

I jerked and spun around to face the bed, both cats were watching me now, though George remained fully reclined, of course.

"M.M.R. business. What day is it?"

"Tuesday."

I sighed with relief. I hadn't lost more than a day whilst recovering.

Sophia tilted her head, studying me. "Rumor has it Wolffe and Sons arena has been destroyed." *Destroyed?* "You wouldn't happen to know anything about that…would you?"

I frowned but held her gaze, wondering at the intensity behind her stare, then tossed her a nonchalant shrug. "I haven't the faintest notion."

I forced myself to maintain full eye contact while I lied between my teeth.

Sophia stood, paced in a circle, then sat once again, which was odd behavior for her. "But you did go after the Duke of Skye last night, correct?"

Was Sophia being a little more pointed with her questions this evening or was I being especially sensitive? I couldn't tell. But despite knowing I had been assigned to arrest the duke, Sophia well knew I couldn't discuss M.M.R. business…which reminded me of my probation and the strange fact that *no one* was discussing it.

Ignoring Sophia, I turned to George. "I have a ball to attend tomorrow night. I need…" I bit my lip, inexplicably feeling a touch of self-consciousness… "something appropriate to wear."

I could have sworn I heard Lady Sophia *growl*. I darted a startled glance her way, but she wore a look of supreme poise. I must have imagined it.

George, who had been swatting at a loose thread hanging from his waistcoat, glanced up, a delighted grin stretching over his face. He clapped his paws together. "Darling! I thought you'd never ask." He looked over my attire…loose shirt, rumpled trousers—I had just gotten out of bed after surviving an explosion, alright? "Er…yes. Leave everything to me. You will be the belle of the ball!"

I waved him off. "I don't want to be the belle of the ball."

George had already jumped off the bed and was making his

way to the door.

I followed, adding, "Make sure I have plenty of room to maneuver should the need arise."

"Naturally."

"And my sword, I'll need to bring it."

"Of course—"

"And my knives, my pouches… you know, the usual."

"Cherie, you will be… *perfection*."

But that's precisely what I was afraid of.

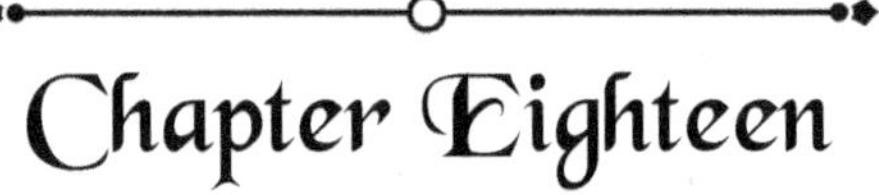

Chapter Eighteen

Lachlan
Must be the Season of the Witch

The Next Evening
The Abernathy Ball
Abernathy House, London

"HOLD STEADY, YOUR Grace."

I gritted my teeth and swallowed the urge to rip an arm off the man standing before me, a punishment any reasonable person might consider harsh given the circumstances.

For fuck's sake, the man was only doing his job—or trying to. I needed to appear at least somewhat tame this evening, precisely the sort of miracle a valet was *supposed* to accomplish.

Definitely not grounds for losing a limb.

Besides, the Duke of Abernathy would have my head if I maimed his personal valet. I didn't have a valet, there being no need of one in the Scottish Highlands.

Hugh laughed as he strode into my room without knocking. "Hold steady? That's a good one, aye? Lachlan has two speeds: breakneck and asleep, and I hear tell even in sleep, he's restless."

I rolled my shoulders. "All true," I bit out and darted a glance to the valet. "Apologies."

146

The valet stopped one step short of a full-on sigh. "Shall we try again, Your Grace?"

I nodded once and stared straight ahead, willing myself to hold steady as requested. But it was difficult to settle, when my mind kept wandering back to the impulsivity of sending Josie Bell an invitation.

Worse…I was, in truth, more concerned about whether she'd come than my reasons (or lack thereof) for inviting her.

Hugh was correct, though. I couldn't hold still at the best of times, much less when a man was tying what felt like a noose about my neck. Didn't the man know wolves were particularly sensitive to anyone messing around about their throat? He *should*, given he worked for the Duke of Abernathy, who was also a Lycan.

Objectively, it wasn't the valet's fault I was twitchy. I'd been out of sorts since the loss of my family's arena…and the unexpected questions I had about Josephine Bell…

An inner voice suggested, *mate*…but there was no proof she actually was. I should have known without question.

It seemed I was more out of sorts about *that* discovery than the arena, which was telling. Fortunately, I had some say in the matter. So long as I didn't kiss her…all would be *fine*.

I raised his arms and broke the valet's hold. "Give me a minute, will you?"

"Of course, Your Grace."

I paced a circle around my room, while I attempted to massage the tension from my neck. Hugh leaned against the wall by the fireplace, a glass of whisky in one hand. "Worried aboot the arena?" he asked.

"Nae." I meant it. There was plenty of ore on the island to recreate the arena if I felt so inclined.

An image of Josie Bell broken and sprawled across the debris, bloody and half buried under dirt and rocks, flashed across my mind, and I flexed the fingers on my right hand. "We can rebuild."

If I even want to.

The thought gave me pause. Since when had I tired of the thrill to be found in the fights?

Hugh raised a toast to that. "To rebuilding."

I shook off my doubts and changed the subject. "Heard from yer witch?"

At the mention of the wee plant witch we'd met at Willoughby's Curiosities, Lady Ivy, Hugh scowled. "Nae."

I suspected his ire was less about not having answers than about the lack of interaction with the witch, but honestly, I was in no real mood to tease the man about it.

I turned and could see the valet was all but grinding his back teeth. What was the man's name? John? George? Randall—yes, that was it. I nodded his way.

With an aggrieved sigh, he asked, "Shall we try this again, Your Grace?"

"Aye."

I tried to remain still, I really did, but I'd never been a man much capable of it.

Hugh made it worse when he decided to add his own irrelevant observations to our conversation. "Ye're an idiot for attending this ball."

I ignored him, which didn't deter him. "I've never seen ye quite like this."

"A person was murdered in my name. That's apt to change a man. Never fear, I'll be back to my charming self once I find the man responsible."

I could lie like the best of them when the occasion warranted it. Especially if I was lying to myself.

"Could be a woman."

For a moment, I thought Hugh had seen right through me to the source of what really bothered me, but no. "Could be, but I doubt it. And donnae worry aboot the ball. The Spellmaidens willnae be able to do anything inside. Abernathy has the best protection spells money can buy."

I'd later discover Abernathy's protection spells were less than worthless, but that was a realization for later.

Abernathy's valet interrupted. "All finished, Your Grace."

"Thank you, Randall. That will be all."

"Yes, Your Grace."

Hugh was like a wolf with a bone. "What if one entices you outside?"

I snorted. "Do you truly believe a witch could tempt me to do something so reckless? Even without a warrant for my arrest, I'd nev—"

Out of nowhere an enticing scent reached me, wafting in on the practically non-existent air. An earthy base, like cut grass, overlaid with a complex fusion of other scents: chamomile, lemon, and heather, teased my senses and my cock went fully hard beneath my kilt…*Gods.*

She was here.

I bit back a groan.

"*Fook me…*yer eyes," interrupted Hugh, "Ye've—"

I brought my head down and pinned my friend with a look, my gaze hyper-focused. "Gone wolf?"

I wanted to laugh, though I was far from amused. My tone held a definite edge.

Hugh dragged a hand down his face. "Aye, your eyes are full on wolf. All the gods, yer *mate* is here?"

"Nae."

It was true. I may have found her scent mouth-watering, but I still had no knowledge of her being my mate. I definitely would have known if she was. I certainly wasn't disappointed by that lack of connection either.

Still, I smiled, one thumb rubbed my lip as anticipation flooded me.

Hugh blocked my exit, his face a mask of fierce concern. "Who?"

"It's funny ye should ask."

"I'm no' laughing."

"I can see that." My grin widened. "Do ye really want to ken?"

Hugh folded his arms across his massive chest, which was answer enough.

I adopted a falsely serious mien and asked, "Fate certainly has a sense of humor. I wonder if Miss Bell will still arrest me if I tell her she's my mate?"

"I thought ye said she wasna—"

"She's no'. But she doesn't ken, aye?"

I made to step around Hugh, but he reached out and grabbed me by the arm. "Ye cannae mean to go oot there?"

I glanced down at his grip, which he dropped, then met his eyes. "I can and I will."

"Bloody hell, are ye mad?"

"Mayhap."

"But… fook. How did she get inside?"

"An invitation, I suspect."

"Funny."

I clapped my pack mate on the shoulder. "Hugh, my friend. Everything will be all right."

"Like hell it will."

"Trust me, friend."

Hugh dipped his head once, and I squeezed his shoulder before quitting the room.

I had trouble controlling my ferocious grin as I left to face my fate.

Alright witch, it's time to play.

Chapter Nineteen

Josie
Let's Try This Again...This Time Without the Oops

Abernathy House
London

I STOOD AT the top of the stairs and surveyed the thirty or so couples who waltzed below me in a colorful swirl of silks and sparkle as the majordomo, a black wolf whose deep voice seemed to rattle the very walls of Abernathy House, announced me with all the gravity of a bishop reciting his evening prayers. "Miss Josephine Bell."

I nearly cringed at the reminder I was the only untitled Spellmaiden.

Instead, I lifted my chin, signaling I had every right to attend this ball, even as abrupt silence blanketed the room and all movement ground to a halt. As if the world had just ended at the very mention of my name.

I had to remember I was here by invitation. But it didn't stop me from wishing my name was more forgettable and far less notorious.

I slapped on a deceptively bright smile and made a mental note to crucify George before dawn tomorrow, assuming I survived this encounter, for all his unwanted *assistance* in making me such a well-known celebrity amongst *the ton.*

A moment of doubt taunted me from deep within, but I relaxed my hands and shoved all uncertainty aside as I took my first step down into this den of formally attired wolves pretending to be as normal as the humans they mimicked.

Though a Lycan was, in fact, the host of tonight's rout, there weren't only wolves in attendance…it seemed the entire *ton* was present for the occasion, or at least, the lucky few who'd received an invitation and who had turned out *en masse*, resplendent in all their decadent glory.

I daren't allow them even a whiff of the anxiety I felt inside; they'd scent it like, well, like a wolf sensing the fox. I'd witnessed firsthand their tendency to strike… and with far less provocation…when they detected vulnerable prey nearby.

As every eye tracked my descent into the room, I'd have sacrificed my best bow to have the skill to read minds like other witches I knew, some who could read a man at fifty paces before he took his next breath.

Alas…

I had made it half-way down the long, curving stair when the hair at my nape lifted, not unlike the split-second before lightning struck, an apropos feeling, I noted, as the very man I sought exploded into the room with a force not unlike Thor's hammer as it split the sky.

But hotter.

Louder.

And far less tame.

As expected, he was here. Lachlan MacKeane. In the flesh.

He surveyed the room, his eyes sharp, and I catalogued every detail.

On the surface, he appeared civilized, but anyone who laid eyes on him in that moment would never believe it, despite the fitted black jacket, the mouth-watering kilt harkening to a bygone era, and the silver waistcoat which sparkled to life beneath the glow of hundreds of candles. He all but leapt off the pages of a Jane Austen novel, and I felt a surge of something I could hardly begin to describe.

I'd memorized every detail in his file. Obsessed over the photographs, which though only a snapshot in time, suggested the vitality this man exuded. Recalled our encounter in the arena *most* vividly.

Yet none of it had prepared me for the reality of his *presence* in such sophisticated surroundings.

His force throbbed with energy, pulsing brighter than every candle in this massive house, subduing the auras of every other creature in this room.

I was not alone in that respect for all at once, the entire room had turned from me as if enthralled to behold his captivating entrance.

As if he commanded everything, MacKeane dipped his head, and the earth began to spin once again. The dancers resumed their revelries, as if his very appearance was the signal that turned the world back on its axis. As if he alone held the power to either create or destroy…everything; it was an unsettling thought.

Relieved to no longer be under such intense scrutiny, I took a careful step, desperate to find somewhere less obvious to reconnoiter.

But then he winked at an elegantly clad woman as she passed.

I must point out, that under questioning, I would have a hard time explaining what happened next.

I sucked in a breath at the sight of that wink, and he froze. Just for a moment. A slight pause. A brief change in direction. *A knowing.*

I watched in helpless fascination as he closed his eyes, lifted his nose, and scented the air. I quivered at the sure knowledge he scented the air *for me.*

Then, he brought his head down and looked directly at me. Ready or not, it seemed I was about to discover whether the gold band encircling my upper arm was worth the price I'd paid for it, for I had acquired it for the sole purpose of having this man forget me until I had the opportunity to do what I came here to do.

Our gazes collided, and a line of pure power surged to life, connecting us, fusing us, pulling me forward—towards him.

The guests between us parted as one...as if he, too, had the power to cast a witch's spell, and I swallowed. His eyes drifted to my throat, and somehow, I knew he'd marked my reaction.

Gracious, what was wrong *with me?*

I gathered my composure and wrapped it around me like a protective shroud as I resumed my descent down the stairs. Despite his almost lethal vitality, he represented a duty, nothing more. He couldn't. I had to remember that.

I *had* to see this through.

He leaned in close the moment I stood before him, toe to toe, his hand landing at the small of my back precisely as if it had done the like a thousand times. Remembering Lady Sophia's warning about how Lycan's thrived off touch, I forced myself not to flinch away from his. Not because I found him objectionable, unfortunately. *Quite* the contrary, which was the problem.

I found his touch not to be the test of fortitude I'd anticipated, for it soothed as much as it excited me, an unusual dichotomy to be sure.

I knew I shouldn't but as I watched him watch me, I wondered what he thought when he so carefully blanketed me with his intense regard?

His warm breath tickled the shell of my ear, and I felt the ghost of his lips so very near as he whispered, "Yer name is upon everyone's lips, *mo bhreugaire beag.*"

I smiled and found the action far easier to employ than it should. "Do I need to acquire a fainting couch so I can be suitably melodramatic about that fact?"

What I really wanted to ask was, *'Does my name mean anything to you?'*

He shook his head, one side of his mouth hitched in a smile, and for a moment I was startled by the power of his grin and worried, briefly, he was answering the silent question.

Further, he clearly had no idea I spoke his native tongue. I feigned ignorance and laid my hand over his heart, my fingers walking a path to his shoulder before I slid them around his neck to play at the fine hair there. He'd pulled his dark locks into an unfashionable queue, and in that moment, I wanted to see them loose and mussed, which was patently ridiculous.

Focus, Josie Bell.

I widened my smile and leaned into him. "I shouldn't think the guests would spare me a second thought with *you* around."

His eyes flared, relating promises I daren't take the time to interpret. I usually failed miserably at flirting, but with him, it seemed I could play the coquette as easily as I donned my favorite cloak in the mornings.

He dipped his head, acknowledging my bold flirtation. Did he realize my words, deliberately chosen, could mean anything and nothing at all?

He tightened his grip, his fingers curled in my skirts, trapping me in his arms as surely as a nightingale in a wire cage. "I stand corrected, *Josie Bell*."

If his early words, '*mo bhreugaire beag*'—*my little liar*—hadn't already given it away, the inflection of his voice and the tightening of his fist at my back as he said my name, signaled he saw straight through my disguise, though his charming smile never faltered for a moment.

Later, I would have to work out why the circlet around my arm hadn't worked as it should. But for now…

I might be in a world of danger.

Then, I recalled, I was dangerous, too.

Still, if he knew who I was, why hadn't he done *something*— something more than stand there looking for all the world as if he enjoyed our overt flirtation.

Oh, the lies, how easily they tumble from our lips. Only the angels possessed the skill to ascertain the bigger fraud.

As his eyes slid over my body, I felt his gaze like a caress, and now that he held me close, I didn't think his flare of appreciation forged. To test that theory, I swiped a tongue across my lips, knowing he would note the subtle movement.

He did not disappoint.

His gaze snapped to my lips, lingered there, but only for a moment.

He fingered the band encircling my upper arm. "This is an interesting piece. Is it gold?"

I dipped my head. "I purchased the piece at a faire in Cornwall."

I lied. I'd paid a fellow Spellmaiden to create it for me.

"It's exquisite. Much like the lady who dons it."

I warmed at the compliment, even knowing how dangerous it was—the road to hell was a slippery slope, indeed—still, despite years of training, I all but preened beneath his appreciative gaze. "My, you are as charming as they say." *Truth.*

I needed to take control of this conversation; direct it to where I wanted it to go. So, I thrust my fingers into the queue at his nape and gripped him by the neck, to punctuate the meaning behind my statement, that was *all.*

It had the intended effect—on us *both.* He growled and pulled me close, my body fitting to his like a tailored glove. I felt the unmistakable evidence of his desire...his cockstand was large and hard and *insistent...* and I could not prevent myself from subtly surging forward with my hips.

To him, I was anything but subtle.

I realized the danger I taunted... knew full well I would not leave this place unscathed.

Because I *knew* I wouldn't leave without knowing the taste of his lips.

And yet...I did it anyway.

Knowing I'd still complete my task.

Did that make me a terrible person? Or merely human?

Regardless, sizzling awareness, an impressive cock, and a charming smile would *never* cause me to forget my oath to the

Spellmaidens of Coven Square.

As if he really could read my mind, he asked, "I understand Spellmaidens become Spellmaidens for life. Is that true?"

He knew it was true, but more importantly, any doubt he knew that I knew exactly who he was, was extinguished by his pointed question. I humored him and answered honestly. "More or less. And better still, the work prevents us from aging, so as you can imagine, the competition to become one is fierce."

"Indeed. So, ye remain a Spellmaiden until ye die."

I nodded.

"Well, I hope like hell ye get hazard pay."

I wasn't entirely sure how to take his remark. Was he being funny? Was he threatening me? Was he trying to compliment my skill?

His charming smile suggested he teased.

Lachlan's free hand, which had previously flirted with the loose strands of my hair, enveloped my own where it rested at his nape, halting my questions as well as my not-so-subtle exploration. But he did not pull away. In fact, his eyes flared as I simply slid my free hand up his chest.

Up and up and up, my questing, curious fingers skated across the exquisite fabric of his waistcoat and cote, then over his shoulder and further, until I wrapped my fingers around the front of his neck, imprisoning his vulnerability in the palm of my hand.

He might have flinched; I couldn't tell. If he did, he hid it well. His only reaction was a tightening of his hand at my back, where his fingers pressed into me, five points of blazing heat, though not enough to leave a mark.

Otherwise, he held steady in my arms as I searched his eyes for any hint of capitulation.

But he never submitted.

On the contrary, he leaned forward, *into* my grip, and his lips hovered just above the outer shell of my ear.

I *felt* it when he spoke, the heat of his warm breath a caress upon my skin.

"You. Me. Outside. Now," his voice sounded rough, broken.

Perfect.

I stood on my toes and whispered, knowing his keen ears would hear every word, "I thought you'd never ask, wolf."

Chapter Twenty

Lachlan
A Kiss to Mate—Or Die—For

*O*CH, AYE…*HUGH WAS going to kill me.*
Regardless, I winged my elbow and smiled as Josie Bell, Spellmaiden…*witch*…slid her hand into the crook of my arm and tossed me a welcoming smile. It took an extreme amount of effort to ignore the blast of awareness her touch produced as I guided her out onto the back terrace with no hesitation. I just might meet my death at the hands of fluttering lashes, brilliant, blue eyes, and vibrant, red hair.

Aye, I knew it was a terrible idea, an impulsive notion.

But something was *off*, and I needed to find out what.

She didn't smell like my mate…well not completely.

I suspected it had something to do with the cuff encircling her arm, but I couldn't be sure, and we were attracting far too much attention in the crowded ballroom for me to figure it out.

I refused to entertain the notion that that wasn't the *only* reason I wanted to see her alone.

Further…and inexplicably…I didn't want to consider she might be here to arrest me. I had no real desire to watch my pack tear her to pieces, literally or figuratively, to protect me.

It was strange—this warring feeling of both wanting to strip her disguise…figure out what she was about, what was *wrong*, and protect her.

I had a sinking suspicion that would *always* be the case.

Her hand slid down my arm, and I clasped it, entwining our fingers as I marched her to the far end of the terrace and down the half dozen steps leading into the formal gardens. The cool air was a welcome relief to my over-heated body, which ran hot at the best of times but had been *scorching* whilst I held her in my arms inside the Abernathy ballroom.

I'd both hated and welcomed the burn.

Eventually, I led her up the steps to an open-air gazebo situated at the back of the gardens, where we could be shielded from—yet remain surrounded by—the over-bright, nearly full moon. I needed enough light to see her without highlighting our presence to the rest of the world.

I turned to face her, though I did not relinquish her hand.

Without question, Josie Bell stood before me. I recognized the daring glint in her eye, the lethal air about her, and her unique scent, which wasn't the lemon and bergamot so many others of this time employed. But it was almost as if she stood beneath a shimmering veil of magic…her face, her body, her voice, her smell… all of it seemed muted to a fraction of her real self, but even then, her allure remained potent to me and my inner wolf, which currently prowled beneath my skin like an animal caged by desire and need.

Fook, I was in trouble.

Josie Bell flashed me a knowing smile. "You know why I'm here."

It was more a statement than a question.

"Yes…and no," I reached out with my free hand and fingered the gold band around her arm. "I suspect this is the culprit." I stared into her eyes. "Am I wrong?"

The dip of her lashes and the sultry curl of her lips should have had me racing back to the house. Hell, that wasn't the only reason. I wasn't a coward, no, but I was well aware I was bewitched. She could have me on my knees in the blink of an eye, and some twisted part of me *wanted* that.

She might very well be the architect of my demise, and still, it wasn't enough to send me running away.

Instead, my cock swelled ...I was harder than I'd ever been in my damned life...and like a fool, I remained rooted in place...very much willingly enthralled. Part of my brain screamed inside my head, reminding me—quite unsuccessfully—that I would regret this entire affair in the morning.

The rest of me held no such concern...wanted me to see where this thing between us led. Begged me to put my trust in fate. Reasoned what could possibly be the harm in accepting this gift of such a capable mate?

Mate? Since when had I felt more than a suspicion of what she might be to me? I didn't want a mate, so that wasn't it. Up until this moment, I wondered, but...well, she still didn't trigger my internal instinct that would tell me, without question, that yes, she was indeed my mate. It was very strange.

And she was very much capable. *Too capable.* Which was also part of the problem.

She shrugged. "A trinket I paid entirely too much for...apparently." The last was spoken so softly I wouldn't have heard her had I not been so attuned to her every move.

It was as much of an answer as I was going to get.

"Bold of you to come here tonight, knowing I'd be surrounded by my family, my pack."

She glanced around as if to ask, *where are they now?* She shrugged. "You all but dared me to come."

She wasn't wrong. I'd literally sent her an engraved invitation.

Perhaps, deep down, I wanted to be caught. By her. On instinct, I rejected that notion, but the lie was apparent for anyone to see. I was here. Alone. With her. Knowing exactly who and what she was.

I leaned close and whispered. "Take off the cuff."

She chuckled, pressed her body against mine and touched her cheek to mine. "I'm no fool, MacKeane."

Her hands slid up my arms, mapped my shoulders, and slipped around my neck, her fingers lighting a trail of fire beneath my skin.

I realized, in that moment, I was seeing a side to Josie Bell no one else had ever seen. But was it real or just an act?

I wanted desperately to find out. So long as we didn't kiss…and I didn't think she would take it that far…where was the harm?

I should have known better; fate would not be denied. It's why I hated that fickle bitch.

It was my last coherent thought before she closed the last bit of space between us and pressed her lips to mine.

Her taste exploded on my tongue…honey and spice and everything I craved…ambrosia igniting a hunger deep inside me the likes of which I'd never before known, making me forget the reasons why I ever hesitated to claim her—my mate.

I hadn't truly known before, but the moment our lips touched, there was no denying it.

In a moment, I would realize just why that was very, very bad.

Without pause, my hands cupped her face as I deepened our kiss, sealing our entwined fates.

Her tongue darted out, tangling with mine in a playful dance I hadn't expected, and I chuckled softly, my mirth quickly sliding into a moan filled with desperate *want* as our passions soared. She all but purred, and it nearly brought me to my knees.

This *woman*. I could not get enough of her.

I slid my palm down her side, tracing her luscious curves and slipping around the firm curve of her arse and alongside her muscled thigh, before guiding one leg up and over my hip, opening her to me, allowing me a hint of the scent blooming at her core.

My eyes rolled back in my head at the heady fragrance…

Gods, if this was a muted taste, I'd lose my damn mind when faced with the full, undiluted effect.

I nipped at her bottom lip, then soothed the sting with my tongue; pressed a kiss to the corner of her mouth, and another at the edge of her jaw. I needed to touch and taste and feast on her delectable skin. To discover my soul in the clutch of her arms. To take and give and give some more.

To mark her as *mine.*

Our bond locked into place a moment before an agonizing fire etched my wrists.

What the hell?

I stepped back and raised my arms before me, staring in shock as ink magically inscribed itself around both my wrists, forming an intricate Celtic pattern of symbols and swirls, rather like a pair of tattooed shackles. The wolf inside me howled in pain, and I pinned Josie Bell with a look of hatred as a second, less pleasurable bond snapped into place.

"What the fook have ye done?" I yelled.

"Just my job, Your Grace."

Chapter Twenty-One

von Rappoldstein
The Demon's Digs

On the Road to Little Walrus

THE ROAD TO Little Walrus was paved with ill intentions. Or so my watch accused as its needle vibrated between green and yellow…aimed towards evil, apparently.

I snapped the lid closed and glanced across the carriage at my newly hired first commander, Harry, who sat in a sulk on the seat across from me, grumbling a string of incoherent oaths and general complaints, or so I thought. I didn't really care.

"Well, that was a resounding success." I prompted, referring to the destruction a few days past of the Wolffe and Sons arena.

Harold shot me an incredulous look. "What do you mean successful? Nobody *died.*"

After only a few days in my employ, I had come to realize my new first commander was a trifle *bloodthirsty.*

"Yes, but the Scot proved himself, and that's what we needed to know." I crossed one leg over the other and relaxed into my seat. "Besides, several guards and a spectator died."

Harold brushed off my point with a wave of one tiny paw. "Yes, but nobody *important.*"

I ignored that. "Further," I gestured to the lapel of his coat. "You came out of there with your very own commemorative pin."

Harold glanced down at his Wolffe and Son's Queen Victoria's Diamond Jubilee commemorative pin, which was entirely too large for his diminutive size, but he didn't seem to care. He thrust out his chest and stared down at the pin with what could only be described as pride. "God bless the Queen."

"Indeed…anyway." I glanced out the window as the carriage began to slow. "We're here."

Here being the Cock and Bull Tavern, the social hub of the village of Little Walrus.

From outside, my manservant Baldor knocked on the door and with a muffled voice, said, "We've arrived, Your Munificence."

Harold looked at me, his brow furrowed. "Why does he call you—"

I held up a hand. "Don't ask."

The overly large hedgehog raised his brows and shifted his eyes away. "If you say so."

"You know what to do. Gather the men and cover every exit, while I go inside and *hire* the support for our…*dig*."

"Whatever you say, Your Highness."

"I'll send out the children before I start."

Harold scoffed. "Sure, sure."

SETTING ASIDE MY commander's odd behavior—for now, I picked my way across the murky courtyard, my robes lifted to avoid getting filth on my hems. For the first time, I actually wished Lady Sophia was here as witness to my conversation with Harry. Something was off and I could use her insight. Alas, she was a cat with her own damned mind and had wandered off again.

I was about to step onto the stoop before the tavern's front door, when a familiar Scot stepped in front of me.

"What are you doing here?" I asked to his chest. In my defense, it was a very large and distracting chest.

"I've come to protect my investment."

I *tsked*. How quaint. "You risk tarnishing that pristine soul of yours, Scot."

"My soul is already tarnished, what's a few more knicks and bruises."

I gestured inside, a cautionary tale. "You may not like what you see."

His nostrils flared. "Are ye sure about that?"

Wait. Was he *flirting* with me?

I narrowed my eyes. "How old are you?"

He crossed his arms. "Twenty-seven."

I nearly choked, a babe in the magical community, and an infant compared to me. But thankfully, he was an adult, at least. Still, on impulse, I patted his cheek. "Stay outside, little pup."

I couldn't resist that last bit, which was laughable seeing as how the man was nearly a head taller than my respectable six foot one, and much, much broader.

He gripped me by the wrist, which *burned* my skin on contact, deliciously so, and had the audacity to block me from entering the tavern with one massive arm across the door. "Ye're no' going to hurt anyone, aye?"

Oh, my naïve little wolf...that ship has long since sailed. Aloud, I asked, "Define hurt?"

"No blood or broken bones."

I nodded. "Unless someone injures themselves during the dig, which even I cannot prevent."

"No enslavement."

That was a tricky one. "What if I promise not to make anyone do anything they'd find reprehensible?" *Or normally find reprehensible, I thought to myself, giving myself a little room to push the boundaries while satisfying my Scot.*

MacKeane shook his head.

I narrowed my eyes. "I'll have you know, digging in the dirt is honest work."

The Scot recrossed his arms.

I wanted to belt out, *Vill-ain,* as I pointed to myself. I well knew the role I was created to play in this gods-forsaken world.

"Listen, lad. I can't promise anything, so you either need to reconcile yourself to the situation or walk away. Either way, at some point, you're going to have to realize there are times when we have to harden our heart for the greater good. What you're asking me to do? You know as well as I, you're already operating in the grey, murky areas of ethical certainty, so none of this should surprise you. The question is…how far are you willing to soften your moral certitude in order to procure this spell?"

A moment passed, then two, while the Scot stepped further into my personal space and glared deep into my eyes, and oh my, I felt myself harden deliciously in my trousers, which hadn't happened in…well, quite some time. With blown pupils, his gaze dropped ever so briefly to my lips, then, without warning, he punched the wall above my head and with a low growl, stalked away.

My throbbing cock twitched in response.

I suppose I had my answer.

AN HOUR LATER, after successfully enchanting the villagers using a compulsory spell (which used the power of suggestion to bend others to follow my bidding), I steadfastly refused to feel a lick of remorse.

I always had found the power of suggestion quite easy to use on others and this evening was no exception. Still, I found myself relieved the Scot hadn't witnessed the affair. I'd only thought of his possible reaction once or twice (or maybe ten times) and only hesitated to invoke the spell three, maybe four times on the few occasions I couldn't oust the bloody Scot's disappointed face from my mind. I had quite the imagination at times.

In the end, I'd followed through and, er, 'convinced' two dozen men and women (and no children, thank you very much) to dig beneath the old mill at the top of the hill, starting tomorrow. In truth, I didn't need the labor so much as I needed their cooperation. It wouldn't do to have them asking too many questions or attempting to stop the dig.

The mill itself had been derelict for years. My research indicated the demon we sought was trapped beneath it, deep underground. The place was surely bespelled with numerous wards, which was why my new recruits were not expected to report to work until the morning. Tonight, I had some wards to break.

But first, I found myself seated by the fire in a private room off the main tavern area, a skein of yarn wrapped around my outstretched arms, while an industrious old lady clacked away with a long pair of knitting needles.

"Where are you from, laddie."

"London," I mumbled.

"No, I mean before that. Originally?"

"Oh, um, Germany."

She nodded her head. "Explains the von Rappoldstein, but I must say, I don't see you as a Vincent…"

I refused to reveal my real name was Humphrey. Humphrey just didn't have the same villainous ring to it, so I'd changed it the moment I was old enough.

"…makes you sound like a villain in some horrid novel."

Exactly. I practically puffed out my chest and smiled with pride at her compliment.

She paused and took in my smile, then with a sharp scowl and a huff, resumed her knitting.

"What are you making?" I nodded at the pile of wool at her feet.

She immediately forgot her moment of pique and beamed at my query, and I swore I could feel my soul scales shift a hair towards good…*bleh.*

But also, quite necessary considering what I was about to do.

"Why I'm making a scarf; how kind of you to ask."

I tilted my head in confusion at the massive, knitted pile of yarn before her. The *scarf* must be twenty feet long at least, all told, with bands of random colors in arbitrary widths—as if she was simply using whatever yarn she could find, regardless if it was a pleasing color or even the same thickness. If that was a scarf, the recipient was either a really, really tall antifashion fiend, or just a blind creature with a really, really wide neck.

And, clearly, she wasn't finished.

She caught my gaze then, and I gave her a false smile.

She nodded. "I really appreciate the help, young man. It's the boils, you know…"

Ah. Here it comes—a long litany of aches and pains. The next half hour promised to be interminable, and I willed my watch hand to move faster.

Chapter Twenty-Two

Josie
The White Witch and a New Assignment—With a Twist

Three Days Later…

I'D FINALLY BEEN called before the White Witch, and as I waited outside her offices at the M.M.R., my mind wasn't on the upcoming conversation, though it, perhaps, should have been.

Rather, guilt pierced me between my ribs and straight into my heart with a keenness that *lingered*. As it had been for days. Particularly when the payment for Lachlan MacKeane's arrest landed in my bank account the very next day after I arrested him.

I couldn't seem to banish MacKeane's look of utter betrayal from my memory; it flashed across my mind with increasing frequency as I carried on with the basic motions of life. And when I wasn't thinking about that, I was reliving that kiss…

The dark circles beneath my eyes further reflected my remorse, as did the frequency with which I nodded off in front of others courtesy of a scarcity of sleep.

This morning, the M.M.R. ordered the entire Coven of Spellmaidens to its hallowed walls.

Outside of our rituals on the sabbats, general meetings were a rare occurrence, which only added to the feeling of dread which had been hanging over me like a black cloud since I'd arisen earlier that morning.

And what information did they impart at this all-so-important meeting? Nothing. Not. A. Thing. It was all very peculiar.

To take my mind off my troubles, I glanced around the room where I awaited my appointment. The place was almost completely devoid of ornamentation. I sat in one of five wooden chairs lined up along one wall, while off to my right, the White Witch's assistant—a quiet man named Jonathan—studiously ignored me, scratching away at his work with a long, white plumed quill. The relentless scratch of his quill coupled with the loud ticking of a clock on the wall did nothing to ease my nerves.

Besides the clock, the only other thing along that wall was a rough-cut piece of slate indicating how many days since our last P.E.E. (Potential Extinction Event if you recall). Someone with neat penmanship had chalked in an ornate number one, complete with dots and curlicues and other lacy adornments, and I briefly wondered who had written it. Definitely not the White Witch. I glanced over at her diligently focused assistant. *Yes.* My money was on Jonathan.

I turned away with a bored sigh. There were no windows, and the walls were painted black. Further, there were no lamps, merely a few braces of candelabras lit the room, which meant the lighting was decidedly dim…poor Jonathan was likely to go blind in a few years.

Good thing no one was in danger of tripping over a potted plant or other random pieces of furniture. I snorted. Even the wooden floors were bare of any rug to soften the surroundings.

Needless to say, my environment did nothing to calm the state of my nerves. Something was just so *off* about it all. Particularly, when I knew what I'd find behind her office door.

Suddenly, an orb of white light appeared over Jonathan's desk, and he looked up. "Ah…," he glanced my way, "the White Witch will see you now." He dipped his head towards the black door in front of me.

"Right." I jumped to my feet, swallowed my concerns, squared my shoulders, and opened the door.

The White Witch's office was also black, like the waiting area, but that was where all similarities ended. Magic gave the far wall the illusion it was made up entirely of windows through which the White Witch had an unimpeded view of a London that definitely didn't exist in any reality judging by the black buildings which appeared to drip with...I leaned forward. Was that blood running down the Buckingham Palace? That was...disturbing. But then I blinked, and a more normal looking view appeared in its place. *Bizarre.*

The rest of the room, overflowed with...stuff. Paintings, plants, books, capes, wands, hats, knickknacks, orbs, quills, papers, tables, chairs, a bar... my eye struggled to find a place to land; there was just so much to see. Yet, somehow, it was a controlled chaos, everything artfully arranged, but still...it was *a lot*, and I long ago suspected that was by design.

I focused my attention on the woman seated at the large desk in the center of the room.

The White Witch was a woman, middle-aged, with only a handful of very fine lines marring her otherwise smooth complexion. Her hair was white as snow, and she wore it, as usual, pulled into a severe chignon. Her robes were old-fashioned, apart from their color: a pristine white. Long fingered hands, each one adorned with multiple gold rings, were steepled before her, and both her elbows rested atop a black file folder, the only item in a small patch of cleared space directly before her.

I should probably note by now that over the years the White Witch had tried, in vain, to be a mother to me. And though most people seemed to think she was positively perfect; I didn't find that to be true at all. And I could definitely attest she hadn't a mothering bone in her body.

Today, her icy blue eyes and pinched lips did not bode well.

"Have a seat, Ms. Bell." She indicated the lone chair before her desk with a dip of her head.

I sat.

The White Witch opened the file folder before her and began to silently read the first page. Eventually, she turned a couple of pages, then cleared her throat.

"Cerberus has filed a complaint."

Which wasn't at all what I expected her to say.

She glanced up. "With regards to his fourth cousins—"

"Thrice removed," I murmured.

"—he claims you smote them too severely."

"They were attempting to eat the Earl of Pendleton in the middle of Mayfair. Naturally, I sent them back to hell." I didn't add that I wasn't the only person involved in that battle.

"Be that as it may, a petition has been filed, and an enquiry will commence immediately. During the enquiry period, you will be taken off rotation for assignments, as I stated in my message."

This was the moment I should mention the MacKeane case. Before she did. And yet, I couldn't force out the words.

Something was wrong. It was like the M.M.R. didn't know I'd been assigned the case despite the fact that everyone else in the world seemed to know. Worse, it was like they didn't know I'd *completed* it even though I'd been paid. I had a Receipt of Delivery in my Purse of Possessions at this very moment.

"Are we clear? Need I remind you that your house is already absent its third witch?"

"No ma'am." She really needn't. I had to bite back the words I truly wanted to say. Questions I wanted to ask, such as, *'Of course, I hadn't forgotten. Perhaps, you can tell us why she's gone. Or better still, how she died?'* I didn't want to believe she was dead, even though I knew the rules. Instead, I jumped to my feet. "Also, yes, ma'am. We are clear. As a crystal ball."

It wasn't fear that had me keeping my thoughts to myself. More like, following my intuition. Besides, I didn't feel like listening while she pointed out all my recent mistakes, which is what normally followed a conversation like this. That and, *'You would have been dead a hundred times over if it weren't for your special place in my heart, Josie Bell.'*

I only just refrained from snorting at the memory.

The White Witch narrowed her eyes.

I pasted on a bright smile and waited.

"Good," the White Witch finally said with her own suspiciously insincere smile, adding, "You're dismissed."

I all but raced out of her office, and promptly jumped in my boots when Miss Madeline Tenderbrush, a local animus witch and history expert who maintained our records along with all our important witch-related artifacts…art, books, curios, trinkets, talismans and the like, appeared beside me and whispered, "That was another meeting that could have been a missive."

I assumed she referred to the morning's coven wide meeting, and I chuckled, "Indeed," as I smoothed my skirts and worked hard to calm my still-racing heart.

I assiduously avoided glancing at the usual mess of papers she clung to, which looked on the verge of spilling to the floor and asked, "Madeline? Have there been any assignments recorded for me lately?"

For a moment, Madeline stared at me queerly—to be fair, my question *was* odd—but she was too much a kind and optimistic soul to remark upon the strangeness of my query. "Nothing since the Matilda assignment."

I bobbed my head. "Perfect, thank you." Matilda was months ago, and until this week, the last task I'd been assigned.

Together, we left the M.M.R.'s parliamentary building…naturally, the magical world had their own offices at the Houses of Parliament, directly next to the House of Lords, in fact…but as we stepped out on to Abingdon Street, a darkness blanketed us like a fog, and the door we'd just exited slammed shut behind us.

I glanced over to Maddie, who stood with her legs braced and, surprisingly, her wand aimed and at the ready, if a bit unsteadily. She ignored her mess of papers, which were currently dancing and twirling away with the wind.

"Be careful where you point that." I nodded pointedly (ha!) at her wand.

Madeline's wand was notoriously chaotic at the best of times, and she flashed me a look of chagrin. "Fair enough."

Rather than reach for my own wand, I slipped out my favorite daggers, comforting myself with their familiar weight and the smile it brought to my lips.

Fortunately, we didn't have long to wonder what manner of catastrophe was about to befall us. Between one thought and the next, a colossal green demon appeared at the end of the alley, limping and frothing at the mouth; its breath bringing the stench of sulfur and hellfire and an explosion of wind which swirled about us like a furious tempest.

The demon had massive appendages, six of them hooved and two with fingerlike digits between which flashed two sets of wicked, six-inch claws—ten in total.

Make that nine. A bloody hole gaped where the tenth claw should have been.

Madeline yelled over the wind. "A Class I Demon, and I believe one the M.M.R. had bound over forty years ago. I wonder how he got out?"

"I don't know," I called back as the beast roared and charged toward us.

"I suppose it's a bit irrelevant at the moment," she quipped, and we both chuckled.

I cringed when Maddie aimed a spell at the charging demon. Unsurprisingly, the spell missed, and a corner of the building opposite exploded into a burst of feathers.

Maddie winced. "Sorry, I'm not trained for the field."

"It's alright, just…stay out of this fellow's reach."

She nodded. "Good plan."

The beast had what appeared to be a metal collar around its neck and a scaled tunic which meant tossing my dagger at its heart or neck was out of the question.

I could go for the eyes, but…

When the moment was right, I leapt and slid beneath the charging demon, right between his legs. I swiped out at his left, but my daggers were utterly useless; his skin was thick and covered with oozing boils. My efforts were as effective as relying on a paper cut to stop a charging bull. It only enraged it further, if it even noticed the slice, which I doubted.

Behind it now, I rolled to my feet and charged its back, but it wasn't as slow as I'd expected for such a great big, lumbering beast, and it half turned as I launched myself. I had intended to latch onto its back. Instead, the beast snatched me out of the air by my waist and tossed me to the side as if I were a pesky fly, a minor annoyance.

Which, I was, in all fairness. To it.

The landing would have been excruciating, a few broken bones at the least, but just before I connected with a solid wall, Madeline, bless her, shot off a spell with her wand, turning the stone wall into a giant, fluffy pillow, so that I merely bounced softly before sliding to the ground.

"Thanks," I shouted when I could.

She sketched a quick curtsey and called back, "Don't mention it."

Which was a mistake as the creature turned and trained its beady eyes on her.

"No. No. No," I shouted whilst waving my arms wildly about. "Look at *me*."

I stepped to my left, slowly, trying to move away from Madeline whilst keeping the beast's eyes on me. A plan began to form...not a very good plan, mind you, but a plan nevertheless.

"Stay where you are, Maddie. I'm going to try to get it to charge me."

I could almost feel Maddie biting back words along the lines of, *Are you insane?* And I stifled a small smile. *Probably.*

I planted my feet directly before the M.M.R. door once again and held up one of my daggers. If I recalled my Demon Studies course, this type of demon was drawn to blood.

I was counting on that.

I drew the edge of the blade over the top of my forearm...not enough to require stitches, but enough to draw forth blood.

The result was almost immediate; the creature's eyes widened, his pupils blew, and saliva pooled, then dripped from its gaping maw. A second later, like a confused berserker, he charged.

I held my position, fighting against every instinct to run. I had to wait until the time was just...right...

I launched myself out of the beast's path at the last moment, and the creature crashed into the M.M.R. building with a loud *boom!*

And promptly disappeared along with the furious wind.

I pulled off my jabot and began wrapping the length of lace around my injured arm as Madeline raced to my side. "Are you alright?"

"I've been better."

"Where do you think it went?"

I shook my head. I truly had no idea.

"How did you know that would work?"

"I didn't."

"Do you think it was after us, specifically?"

I didn't think so. "I think we got lucky."

"Lucky? But the door..."

"Standard M.M.R. Procedures. The street locked down the moment the creature appeared... a safety measure introduced to prevent innocent humans from wandering into something they oughtn't." I didn't add that we'd been lucky to come across this demon during the day, when it was at its weakest. Had it been nighttime...things might have turned out very differently.

I brushed dirt and debris from my skirts as Madeline helped me stand.

A moment later, the skies cleared, and I glanced upward to see a purple paper bird flap about vigorously over my head. I held out my hand, palm up, and the bird twisted and turned in on itself until it landed in my open palm in the shape of a small purple file.

I flipped open the cover to reveal my latest assignment.

It read, Capture the Class I Demon.

Of course.

Maddie nodded at the file. "The Demon?"

I sighed, "Yes."

"You know, there is only one person who has ever successfully faced a Class I Demon on his own and lived to tell the tale."

Maddie really knew how to say just the wrong thing at the right moment. "Oh really?" Somehow, I knew I did not want her to finish that thought, but still, I said, "Do tell."

"Lachlan MacKeane."

Of course. How did I not know this? "MacKeane's safely incarcerated in Marshalsea."

Madeline shrugged. "Is he?"

"I suppose not." I ignored her confused look and raced off before she began asking questions I couldn't answer.

Chapter Twenty-Three

Lachlan
Lucifer's Lush Sure Gets Around

Marshalsea Gaol
Southwark, London

PRIOR TO 1849, Marshalsea Gaol was a human debtor's prison. Then, in 1849, the gaol went on auction, and the Seraph of Southwark purchased the buildings, refashioning them into a penitentiary for the most dangerous of magical criminals.

Now, almost fifty years later, the gaol had a fearsome reputation in the magical community. No one who entered ever got out. In large part because the angels in charge—the Seraph— didn't make mistakes, or so they claimed.

I laughed, feeling a point of pride that the government considered me so dangerous as to place me here of all places. Then again, it might have been the Seraphs' special blend of nitrous oxide, which left me feeling pleasantly amused.

They hadn't placed me in with the general population of magical criminals, either. Instead, I had my very own cell, thank you very much. And every time I laughed, the sound of my voice echoed strangely about the large room, which was made up mostly of damp, irregularly shaped stone. When I laughed, it sounded as if a dozen people laughed with me. I always had liked an audience.

Clearly, the Seraph weren't taking any chances with me. Not that it was going to matter in the end.

Deep in the bowels of their dungeons, where security was at its tightest, I relaxed in my cell and waited for someone to actually bring forth the charges against me before I completely descended into madness. I had been here for days now and so far I hadn't seen a soul since I'd been delivered here. Meals appeared magically twice a day.

Perhaps, I should have revealed I had a newly discovered mate when they'd tossed me in here, but to be honest, I didn't feel it necessary to give the Seraph an advantage by offering up a warning for free.

How did the old adage go? *Never come between a Lycan and his mate?*

Och, aye, I could no longer deny I'd found my mate.

And she was a *witch* of all things.

I should have been deeply concerned. I wasn't.

Hell, being locked away in Marshalsea Gaol wasn't even the biggest problem I faced. Not by a long mile.

No, my biggest concern was the fact that Josie and I hadn't fully completed the mating bond. We'd only triggered it with that knee-weakening, mind-bending, scorching hot kiss she'd wrecked me with at the Abernathy ball. A kiss that was *un-fucking-forgettable*, got me hard as stone every single time I recalled it (and I'd been recalling it an awful lot), and upended my entire life. Quite literally.

I chuckled. Again. Because if Josie and I didn't complete the mating ritual by the time the next full moon sets, I was going to become lethally deranged.

Forever.

As a species, Lycans go permanently insane if they trigger a mate bond but don't complete it by the next full moon. And when Lycans go insane, we lose all our humanity and become stuck in the form of a wolf for life.

But not a friendly domesticated sort of wolf. Oh, no. That would be far too easy and not much of a curse.

No, we become more like oversized and oversexed snarling, drooling, rabid wolves full of angst, rage, and unimaginable strength. It was part of the price all Lycans paid for the gifts of heightened senses, enhanced strength, and increased longevity.

And the next full moon was set to start rising in two days.

Two. Days.

I fell into a fit of laughter again, my ever present audience of echoes joining in quite merrily.

Was I concerned? Marginally.

Was I angry? No. Not even at Josie Bell for her role in all this.

I suspected this was due to the aforementioned nitrous oxide. Normally, it would keep a Lycan like me—a male in his prime— adequately subdued.

But a partially bonded Lycan male?

My current bemused state wasn't going to last. Especially while I was separated from my mate. For as the full moon closed in, the urge to get to her and complete the ritual would increase by the hour. Things were going to be especially dangerous the moment the full moon began to rise.

At that point, *nothing* would keep me behind these bars and away from Josie Bell. Then, I had until the moonset to complete the ritual or become permanently deranged.

I rubbed absently where Josie's tattooed bindings had appeared around my wrists. They weren't there anymore. The angels had removed them upon my arrival, and for some reason, I…missed them. They should have reminded me of her betrayal. I should be glad they were no longer there, not bemoaning the loss of another link to my mate.

I wanted to despise Josie Bell, but between the giggle juice and my general good humor at the best of times, even my fury towards her had withered over the days as I was left to cool my heels in total isolation. Knowing she was my mate, however it came about, helped even if my choice had been taken from me. Neither of us had known what havoc such a kiss might wreak, and to be honest, never could I imagine enjoying my own downfall more. I couldn't even be certain I wouldn't do everything exactly the same even if I somehow knew what was about to happen.

Hell, I could keep warm for days purely on the memory of that bloody kiss.

No, the fault for my possible impending brush with insanity lay with whoever cursed me to begin with, thereby, presumably the reason I could not truly sense my connection to Josie until it was far too late.

I laughed out loud at the absurdity of the entire affair, though no one was there to hear me.

Or was there?

A faint chirp in the corner had me staring into the shadows. "I ken ye're there, wee beastie. Come out, come out wherever ye are…"

Lady Sophia Tewkesbury-Smith strolled out of the shadows and arched her back as she rubbed up against the bars at the foot of my cell.

"Och, Lady Sophia, deigning to cross the threshold of Old Marshalsea. Careful, ye might get yer paws dirty."

Ignoring me, Sophia began to strut.

"To what do I owe the pleasure? Or should I say, to whom?" I didn't think she'd come out of her own curiosity.

I first met Lady Sophia after the accident that claimed my uncle's family, an accident that was my fault, and though she'd been a great source of comfort at that time, which was years ago, I no longer felt any sort of bond tying me to her for her grateful help.

But even without that connection, she was well known in the magical community, particularly for her powerful magic and notorious connections at every level of society.

She turned and rubbed against the bars with her other side.

"The silent treatment, Sophia?" I laughed, then pinned her with my gaze, allowing a touch of my inner wolf to show through as I did. "Why dinnae ye tell me Josie Bell was my mate?"

I didn't actually know Sophia had a connection to Josie Bell, but I strongly suspected and decided to go with my gut instinct. If I was wrong, Sophia would correct me soon enough.

Sophia continued to pace, but I didn't miss the flash of surprise in her eyes. She paused, shifting from foot to foot and shaking her tail as if about to mark the bars of my cell. "I didn't know."

"*Ye?*" I scoffed. My disbelief wasn't feigned. "How aboot this…did ye ken she was going ta arrest me?"

Yes. She didn't answer, but I could see the truth in her feline eyes all the same.

Eventually, Sophia sat and cocked her head. "You seem different…"

I laughed and raked a hand through my hair. The chains surrounding my wrists rattled with the motion. I tossed her my winningest smile while I gestured at the ridiculous tunic they'd made me don. "It's the prison stripes, ye see…they clash with my winning personality."

Lady Sophia turned her back and shook her tail at me as if she considered spraying *me*. Then, she glanced over her shoulder and asked, "Did you kiss her?"

I scratched at my chin as I cackled madly. "Oh, Sophia. I'm no' the kiss and tell kind of man, aye?" I knew Sophia wasn't actually asking for details. But she'd been acting odd, and I didn't trust her even before, so I withheld the truth. Lycanthropes and felines weren't the obvious choice of friends at the best of times, though I respected a good mouser, but Lady S was something altogether more, and my animosity towards her bordered on rude, which I knew was out of character for me, especially with females. I didn't care; I trusted my instincts.

My hands began to shake as I carded one hand through my

hair again, not a normal habit of mine, but then these weren't normal times. Worse, Lady S noticed.

"What is it?"

"Oh, ye didnae ken? She didnae tell ye?" I wasn't sure why that bothered me. Surely, Josie Bell updated her feline friend, an assumption I made, true. Cats of Lady S's type were well known to choose witches as their familiars, so I found it impossible to believe Sophia, with all her powers and infamy didn't already know herself. Was she testing me?

Sophia stared at me and gave a subtle shake of her head.

I chose to test her knowledge after all. "Yer wee protégé kissed me."

"She's not my protégé." The cat paused and pursed her lips. For a cat of her reputation and personality, this was akin to cursing loudly. "But it's only two days until the full moon."

She stated it so casually as if I didn't know exactly what sort of trouble I faced. But her response told me she had suspected we were mates even before now. I decided to play things close to my chest, for as long as I could. Impending insanity for a Lycan who never completes the mating ritual once started is a very real, very large concern, and Sophia would know that. "Tell me something I dinnae ken."

Sophia paced the length of the hall before my cell, clearly agitated and definitely not acting herself.

I smiled. "Never say ye care, Sophia?"

"You're angry."

"Och, well, let's give the professor a medal. I've known the moon cycles for more than 50 years, Sophia, but I also ken ye knew what was going to happen—do no' insult us both by pretending ought. The real question is, why?"

"How did you know?" Sophia lifted her chin as if to dare me to question her actions, her motives; the feline was far too proud for her own good. "Ah," she added as if inspired. "You like her."

I snorted my disbelief. As if that was any sort of new revelation. Or even unusual for me, and though my wolf suggested I was kidding myself and well-knew this Josie Bell was very different, I couldn't resist saying, "Ye ken me; I like all women."

"So how does this one end? What are you going to do?"

"What? Ye're asking me? No cryptic, sage advice? No forthright suggestions from the great Lady Sophia Tewkesbury-Smith?" Talk about acting out of character.

Still, she really surprised me when she didn't respond to my bait, and instead asked, "How come you're not insane right now?"

I could feel the tension tighten my jaw, and sought a handle on my notorious charm, though I'm sure my smile showed too many teeth, and my voice held an edge. "Who says I'm no'?"

She gave me a speaking look and ignored my question.

I chuckled but this time, I was not laughing. "We both better hope she gets me oot of gaol afore the full moon."

She lifted her chin, a too-proud feline once again. "I know the consequences."

"Do ye? Is this a game ta ye?"

She leaned against the far wall and made quick work of investigating her claws as she was wont to do, and I laughed. "Do no' tell me the infallible Lady Sophia made a mistake?"

She didn't even glance my way when she replied, "No, never."

Right. "Och, from where I'm sitting, it sure seems that way. What are ye going ta do ta fix this, Sophia?"

And that was when she smiled, her face a mask of pure mischief, possibly deceit. "Why, nothing, Your Grace. Nothing. At. All. See you around, wolf."

Bloody hell, I was fooked.

And with the full moon drawing near, everyone was soon going to know just how much. If Josie Bell knew what was good for her, she'd stay far, far, far away from Marshalsea Gaol.

Chapter Twenty-Four

Josie
A Good Day to Break *Into* Gaol

I WIPED CLAMMY hands down the sides of my skirts and sucked in a deep breath of air as I marched with purpose towards Marshalsea Gaol. Angels were notoriously overconfident, I reminded myself. A fact I intended to exploit.

I supposed the angels' excessive pride might seem reasonable given nobody had ever escaped one of their gaols—at least no one in recorded history. I could almost pity them their arrogance, but for the fact that the prospect of getting caught breaking a wanted criminal out of an Angelic stronghold had me quaking in my boots. Not that anyone could tell I felt even a modicum of concern—and in that moment, I suspected my greatest skill just might be my ability to look confident even when I was anything but.

Still, not taking any chances, I pulled on my extremely useful Raven Shroud before I'd even rounded the corner onto South-wark's High Street, where the latest iteration of the gaol stood. The Raven Shroud was a cloak fashioned from ravens' wings, which not only rendered the wearer invisible, but soundless, too, a feature I appreciated as I approached the infamous prison.

I risked a glance into the courtyard, but there was no one

about. The only interesting thing to remark upon at all was a washing line loaded with prisoner's garb that stretched between two buildings. Without slowing, I marched straight past the entrance tower and the gaol's forecourt and turned down the appropriately named Angel's Alley. It really was a shame the humans would never know the perfect irony of this street's name.

I could have entered through the nearby church yard, but despite being rendered invisible, it seemed too risky to enter so close to *Summer House*, the prison's public house. The last thing I needed was to run into a few drunken inmates.

No. I planned to enter through the prison chapel at the rear. Besides, I needed to take a detour via the booking department and review how they'd documented MacKeane's stay, and more importantly, where they were keeping him. Based on my research, entering through the chapel would require me to walk straight past the vital records department in order to get to where the Very Important Prisoners were incarcerated.

In the end, entering the prison proved uneventful. I literally walked right in. Had I mentioned my cloak also nullified all but the most elaborate protection spells and runes? As you might imagine, if this cloak fell into the wrong hands, the results would be quite detrimental, to say the least. Its loss would definitely register as a P.E.E.

Mindful of the time, I made quick work rifling through inmate files. After a bit of snooping and listening and the occasional whispered spell or two, I learned there was no trace of Lachlan MacKeane actually being in, or arriving at, the gaol...*Huh.* Well, that was interesting and inconvenient. Where was the flashing sign showing me precisely where to find him? Rude.

I didn't doubt he was here; I'd brought him here myself. I also didn't question, though perhaps, I should, why there weren't any angels around to not notice me walking amongst all the desks and file towers.

Wait. Why weren't *there any angels around, or other beings for that matter, magic or otherwise?*

I suppose the prisoners would be in their cells on other levels, but there wasn't even a prisoner being booked. Or released. For that matter.

Obviously, I hadn't the answer to those questions. Nor, I decided, did it really change anything. I actually had every right to be here. At least, up until the moment I did something illegal, which I hadn't decided to do yet. I only wore the cloak to hide myself in the event I did decide to—well, I didn't actually want to admit, even to myself, what I was considering doing.

Ultimately, I found him by reaching out with my senses and following the magical traces of spells and runes until I found the most powerful, most complicated reinforcements…and went that way.

It worked.

Somewhat unexpectedly.

For I merely followed the stairs to the lowest floor and had to swallow back a gasp of surprise as I turned a corner and spotted him pacing the back of his cell like a caged animal, oh the irony.

My first thought at the sight of him should have been disgust. Or indifference. Or any number of other, perfectly normal and acceptable thoughts than the ones that actually flew through my head. Dangerous thoughts. Ill-advised thoughts.

Thoughts like: When is that man going to kiss me again?

Argh!

I forced myself not to relive the meeting of our lips (for the thousandth time) and focused on feeling satisfaction because he looked…tired. Irritated. Disheveled. Magnificent—NO! Yes. No. Or, yes. It was *magnificent* to see him so out of sorts. Not, magnificent to just see…him.

Liar.

No. Kisses were not why I was here.

I needed his help. Probably. I hadn't decided.

Even though I knew he couldn't see me, couldn't sense me, I remained deep in the shadows, content to watch him while, once again, I argued with myself over the decision I didn't want to own. It wasn't too late to back out. To come up with an alternative plan, a better plan.

"I ken you're there, lass."

Impossible. Still, my heart skipped a beat, then began to race as his delicious brogue slid over my skin like a decadent caress. His voice was a raspy rumble that worked some sort of spell on me. Ironic, considering I was the witch.

I watched as he tilted his head back, his eyes closing as he inhaled deeply. "I can smell your mouthwatering scent."

My mind replied, *I can recall your taste.*

I shook my head in denial though there was no way he could see me.

He turned his head slightly to the side. "You smell of sunshine…bergamot…and rose?" He turned a little further towards me. "Interesting."

Beneath my cloak, I crossed my arms. Not because my nipples suddenly beaded beneath my shirtwaist or anything.

When he opened his eyes and looked down, his gaze unerringly pinned me in the dark. It shouldn't have been possible, but my body didn't care. I *throbbed.* My lips took the opportunity to tingle and remind me, again, of how it felt to kiss him. My tongue darted out without a thought as I wetted my lips at the intrusive memory. His own twitched as if he knew what I was thinking, and I had to admit he was—somehow, impossibly—telling the truth. He knew I was there. He could smell me. There was nothing for it; besides, I couldn't very well ask for his help from beneath the Raven Shroud.

Confident I remained in complete control, I pulled back the hood and stepped out of the shadows. Slowly, cautiously, I stopped before his cell door and clasped the bars with both hands.

His smile spread, and I nearly jumped when he winked at me.

And then he moved, and it was sudden and unimaginably fast, and before I could blink, he stood directly in front of me, his broad hands wrapped around the bars of his cell with white-knuckled strength. Though close, his hands didn't touch mine, and yet it *felt* like they did. I could feel the heat emanating off him…warming me, like a hard-working radiator.

The two-inch steel bars no longer felt like any sort of impediment separating us, but I refrained from leaping backwards in retreat.

Instead, I lifted my chin; I refused to be intimidated.

Once again, he inhaled deeply, and I could have sworn he groaned. His eyes flared with obvious desire, which I felt from the top of my head to the tips of my toes, a delightful but unwelcome sense, so I went on the offense. "You, sirrah, are entirely too bold."

My words might have held more power if I hadn't whispered them, or if my voice hadn't sounded somewhat breathless.

His lids lowered, slowly, then lifted once more, and he pinned me with another, lazy smile. "Mmhmm. Perhaps." I felt that rumbly response in places a witch didn't mention in mixed company. "And yet I'd wager ye *burn* ta know why…"

I scoffed. "To know why you're depraved? Not really."

"I think ye *do* want to know how I could scent ye through what is clearly a verra clever and convenient cloak."

I rationalized his remarks. "You're Lycan." But I made a mental note to research whether the Raven Shroud was supposed to block smells, too. That seemed an important thing to verify just then.

"I am. But that's no' why."

I remained mute.

"Don't ye wonder why?"

"Not particularly." I added a shrug of nonchalance I definitely didn't feel. I'd *never* tell him the truth—even on pain of death.

Which mattered not one wit. He seemed to know it. His lip hitched in a half smile as he whispered, "Liar."

"Mr. MacKeane—"

He chuckled. "Your Grace will do."

I knew that. *I did.* "I don't think you're in any sort of position to demand titular respect. You'll be lucky to leave this place with your life." I could boast at the best of times. Especially when it felt like a lie.

He shrugged as if his stay here was simply a minor inconvenience, then turned his back. I had to bite my lip to keep from calling him back and demanding he look at me. *What was wrong with me?*

He crossed the room as if he had all the time in the world, and I (quite shamelessly) embraced the opportunity to drink up the sight of his muscular backside.

And I gasped out loud—*Did he just laugh?*—when I noticed there was a hole in his prison-issued tunic. A. *Gaping*. Hole. The kind of hole that revealed (quite, quite clearly) he wore no small clothes. No under clothes other than the tunic. None. At. All.

I could feel my cheeks flame as the muscles in *his CHEEKS bunched* and clenched in very interesting ways with his every step. Was that a bruise blooming on his arse? Had he been spanked? I mean, beaten.

Gracious, what was *wrong* with me!? No...I lifted my chin. What was wrong with *him?* (I ignored the tiny voice that whispered back, *Not a damn thing.*)

Of course, something was wrong with him. The man was in gaol for goodness' sakes. Right?

I wanted to bang my head against the bars if only to knock some sense into my disobedient brain.

While I argued with myself, MacKeane settled onto the floor and leaned back on his elbows, his legs stretched out and crossed before him as if he hadn't a care in the world. A crooked, *knowing* grin curled his lips, then those lips of his moved. "Let's do away with this game, lass. Why are ye here?"

"Tell me about the time you escaped the Class I Demon," I demanded.

He smirked as if he knew that's not what I really wanted to ask. He was completely wrong. Really, really, super wrong. So, so wrong. I was only interested in the demon. I cleared my throat.

He shrugged. "I ripped its head off with my claws."

Gods, that must have been—no! I refused to be impressed. "Did it die?"

He gave me a *what do you think* look.

"There are demons who might have survived that." Not really.

And not helpful. My assignment made it clear I was to apprehend the demon, not kill it. Besides, killing it would involve a lot of unnecessary paperwork. And meant more time spent with MacKeane, a wolf I definitely wasn't marginally attracted to. Or attracted to at all, dammit. (Liar.)

"Why did you jump into the arena?"

MacKeane frowned. "I donnae ken… it seemed like a good idea at the time."

Typical impulsive, bored, I-don't-care-attitude. I hated it. Besides, his voice had ended with an inflection, which implied a question. "Are you asking *me*?"

"No." His response was short, clipped.

His sudden change in demeanor bothered me, and I didn't like *that* either. I began to pace, while more and more questions flooded my mind, and I began to fire them off in short, rapid bursts. "Why did the arena explode?"

"I donnae ken."

"Liar."

He shrugged.

"Were you the one who took me home?"

"Aye."

"That's impossible. How did you get past the dragons? And the griffin? And my roommates?"

His eyes lit up as if amused, but he didn't answer any of those questions. I refused to wonder what was going on in that impulsive, keen mind of his.

"Where were you when the murder occurred?" Dammit, I wasn't supposed to care or ask.

"Home."

"Did you know them?"

"Aye."

"Why did you invite me to the ball?"

"I wanted to."

He did? That stopped me in my tracks. Had he enjoyed our—

"Yes."

I paused my pacing; heat once again flooded my face, and I swallowed. "I didn't ask anything."

"I know."

I clenched my hands into fists to fight the urge to rub at the back of my neck or worse, enter the cell and rub MacKeane's backside instead.

"Lass, are ye here ta release me?"

"No."

He raised one brow.

"*No.*" I maintained, emphatically.

He stood and once more approached the cell door. And again, I held myself rigidly in place, refusing to back down or show any sign he might affect me. In <u>any</u> way. He didn't.

Once again, he settled his hands on the cell bars. This time, directly over mine; his grip firm and incredibly ~~hot firm~~ real. Real. Yes, that was it.

When had I reached for him—er, the bars. I meant the bars! When had I reached for the bars? I hadn't even noticed I'd moved.

"Josie?"

I answered him with a nod. I was too afraid my voice would crack if I dared to speak.

He touched his head to the bars and looked down at me.

For some reason, I nodded again. And wet my lips. He noticed. I didn't want him to notice. Or want to want him to notice. Or—shite.

"I can help ye, lass."

I nodded some more. My brain was officially lost.

He smiled. "*Let* me help you."

I returned his smile, and said, "No."

He shook his head. "But didn't ye come here to ask fer my help?"

"Perhaps. I know you can talk to your clan through your wolf, through a familial telepathy. If I release you, you'd have to promise not to contact them."

"Ye're asking an awful lot o' me. It goes against every instinct I have."

I nodded. "I understand, but this entire affair relies on very few of us knowing what's happening, so I will have to demand it of you."

"What if I lie and contact them anyway?"

I shrugged. "I'll know."

He narrowed his eyes. "My, aren't ye all powerful."

"It sort of comes with the job, duke. Now. Do we have an accord?"

Chapter Twenty-Five

Lachlan
A Bargain Made in Hell

M Y WOLF HAD all but demanded to be let loose the moment Josie Bell had appeared in the short hall outside my cell. Hell, before that. I'd known she was coming long before she'd even crossed the threshold of Marshalsea Gaol.

And yet I knew I couldn't manage the shift no matter how badly I wanted to make it happen, and my wolf knew it as he whimpered in my head in clear despair. Pick your choice of reasons; there were a whole host of them available to explain why that would be, none of them good, unsurprisingly.

I met her eyes and nodded to answer her question. "Aye. We have an accord."

She didn't even wait nor acknowledge my acceptance before saying, "Here. Put this on."

In her hand was a red leather strap, like a bracelet, with several knots in the strip of leather.

"What is it?" I asked as I put mine on. I didn't realize the significance of how much I trusted her that I didn't ask her many questions before donning it. Though she wore one herself, it didn't follow mine held the same magic.

"It's coated with a simple protection spell. It isn't foolproof, but it should be—" She stopped talking abruptly, narrowed her eyes, then added, "Something's coming."

I nodded my head. "Och, aye." Naturally, I could hear them.

"Run."

I looked around me and laughed. Where'd she expect me to run? *How* did she expect me to do it? I was going insane, magically sealed behind bars—all while fighting a strong instinct to fuck her right then and there. On the filthy ground.

But she did something with her wand and a murmur of words even I couldn't discern, what with the sound of rapidly approaching terror growing louder by the second. Whatever it was, I suddenly *knew* I could flee. As if to confirm this, the door to my cell clicked and slowly crept open as if of its own free will.

But I still couldn't shift.

"Shift if you have to."

I tried. I really, fucking tried. "Shite, shite, shite."

"Why can't you shift?"

"I donnae fookin' ken. Something's been off since Hugh procured that damned coin, and it's getting progressively worse." I don't know why I was being honest, though I suspected it had to do with our unanticipated link.

"Does wolfie have performance anxiety?" She thought she was amusing, did she?

"Verra funny, lass." But I shook my head, though my frustration was obvious.

"We don't have time for this. Run."

I opened my mouth to argue.

"I said, *Run!*" Josie repeated more forcefully while shoving me without much success...I was still a rather large man.

"Working on it." I launched back at her. Didn't she realize I wasn't quite myself just now?

If I didn't trust Josie Bell's skills so completely, I'd have worried the open cell door was a trap. But I truly did trust she knew what she was about, her success record provided incontrovertible proof, so I wasted no more time and sprang into action.

We reached for each other and linked hands as if we did this sort of thing all the time. I didn't know why, nor did I have time to reason it out. Well, for my part, I understood, it was the pending matehood in action, but her excuse? I had no fucking clue.

And did I really care? I didn't think so.

As we raced out of the cell, I decided that I didn't care, in fact. Probably.

And I still didn't care even after she tossed the magical befeathered shroud over our heads, which I immediately hated with a passion.

To my way of thinking, things would have been so much better if I could properly shift. I could carry her and run faster, and it wouldn't feel as if it was taking us forever to exit the gaol. Not to mention I wouldn't currently feel an icy draft caressing my buttocks through the hole in my prison tunic.

And Josie wasn't by any means slow. She was clearly in top physical condition, a thought which threatened to further disrupt my already distracted and impulsive mind which currently bounced about with random, racing thoughts as we dodged approaching angels and ran our hearts out, all the while knowing the prospect of insanity trying to snake its way into my mind and set hooks was very, very real.

After we'd finally flown from the gaol and crossed several streets and turned numerous corners. I pulled her a short way down a dark alley and stopped, then ripped off the shroud.

"Are you insane?" She mumbled a quick curse. Probably a curse that suggested passersby not glance down the alley.

"Funny you should ask." I was bent at the waist, attempting to catch my breath while Josie appeared perfectly composed, if agitated, which was absurd and alluring and *dammit.* "That appears ta be the question of the day."

She wrinkled her brow. "What?"

I waved off her query. "I'll explain later."

After a few more huffs as I tried to catch my breath, while

Josie Bell made it perfectly clear she was tired of waiting on me, I managed, "That was easy."

Her mouth dropped momentarily. "You call that easy? You have no idea all the spellcasting I had to perform while we ran, do you?"

I didn't. And I could only offer her a cocky grin in response. But really, how was I supposed to know and truthfully, it only made her more appealing, that much more competent, knowing she was doing all that while I simply ran for my life. Something told me she didn't prize my silent appreciation of her skill.

Josie shook her head. "Whatever you say, MacKeane. Just get back under the shroud."

Och, hell no. "I am no' going ta get back under that thing."

"Do you want to go back to gaol? I'll take you there myself."

I shook my head. "It's no' necessary."

She narrowed her eyes. "Why don't you humor me?"

I shook my head. "Look. No one will recognize me. I have a bit of a curse problem." I had so much more than a curse problem.

I could have sworn she said, "Don't we know it." And she definitely said, "Just do as I say or I'm taking you right back to gaol."

I shook my head. "No, I'd rather no', thank ye. I just left."

"I could force you…"

"You could, absolutely, but ye freed me fer a purpose, so I do no' believe ye would."

"Oh, trust me, I definitely would. I'd find another way to accomplish my task," she mused.

Josie Bell had a fair point, and it made me feel a trifle desperate. "Look." I raced, or limped rather, toward the mouth of the alley and reached for the next person attempting to pass. "Do you ken who I am?" I asked the man in my hands. For her part, Josie followed in my wake, or meandered more like, her gait casual. She was clearly humoring me.

The bloke in my hands looked me over. "Should I?"

I nodded my head while stealing glances at Josie Bell to make sure she was paying attention. "I'm Lachlan MacKeane, the Duke of Skye."

The man immediately started laughing. "Oh, aye. Tell me another one, *Your Grace*." More laughing. "You hear that, mates?" The man glanced over to the people who had stopped alongside him to watch our exchange.

I didn't care, even as they stormed off laughing and mumbling. "He should be locked up." They'd made my point, even if it was at my expense. To Josie, I asked, "See?"

She merely folded her arms.

I shook my head and marched to the nearest shop window. She trailed me with a sigh. I yanked one of my infamous wanted posters out of the window and held it up next to my face, then stopped the next bloke. "Och, do I look familiar?"

The guy stared at me oddly and shook his head. "No resemblance if that's what you're asking?" I let him go and grinned at Josie Bell, convinced I'd made my point, this time. The departing man added with a low mumble, "…crazy gin addict. Thinks he's the Duke of Skye. Ha!"

My grin widened. "See?"

She was *still* unimpressed. "Are you quite finished?"

I narrowed my eyes. "Aye." What the hell was it going to take to impress this woman?

She nodded and dropped her arms. "Good. Then, get back under the damned shroud."

Och, she was going to be the death of me, forget my impending date with psychosis.

"Ye ken, fer a witch, ye're magnificent," I complained. Bloody stubborn as hell, too, but bloody magnificent. "Still, I cannae believe you all aren't constantly magic this and magic that."

"All magic is unpredictable. That would be foolish."

"Ah…but it seems ye're doing a fair bit of magic around me."

She merely shrugged. "What can I say, MacKeane, you make me foolish."

For some reason I liked this sentiment. I refused to ponder why and echoed my earlier thought, murmuring. "Bloody magnificent."

Still, I got under the fucking shroud.

Chapter Twenty-Six

Von Rappoldstein
Extra! Extra! Read All About It—Or Perhaps, Not

"THE WOLF NEEDS to stay where he belongs…" Lady Sophia all but marched across the room and tossed the paper on my desk in proper disgust. "Nothing is in the paper. It's all very hush hush. Mum's the word." She all but mimicked some imaginary reporter, and I briefly wondered if my insanity was rubbing off on her.

Still, her uncharacteristic fit of pique had me whispering, "Honk like an enraged swan," beneath my breath, and I waited for some enraged honking. But alas, once again, nothing.

Sophia continued, "I have it on good authority even his family doesn't know where he is…before or after his arrest. As far as they are concerned, he disappeared from the Abernathy ball, but they're keeping it quiet." She threw herself in a chair and crossed her arms with a huff. "They're acting as if he's just gone home for mundane reasons."

As far as I could tell, and believe me, I'd asked around since Sophia had thrust herself into my life, this obvious bit of bother was uncharacteristic of my feline (my?) and I was amused to witness her ruffled feathers.

"Are you even listening to me?"

"Yes?"

She narrowed her eyes.

My lips spread in a grin of feigned innocence; I could feel their tight pull against my bared teeth.

We remained that way, in some sort of bizarre standoff, each one waiting for the other to budge, and I worked very hard not to move so much as a muscle as I thought, *'Start picking at fleas in your fur.'* Not that I thought she had fleas. That definitely wasn't the point.

Her eyes narrowed further. "You're not listening."

It was a relief to release the hold on my frozen facial muscles, and I very nearly burst out laughing, which made me scowl, and I had the sudden urge to go steal candy from children.

Steal candy from children?? How strange…

I dropped my head to my desk with a moan. *What was happening to me?* If I hadn't suspected I was well on my way to going insane from all the curses lodged at me, this entire conversation (even though most of it was occurring in my own damn head) definitely would have convinced me.

"Something wrong, von Rappoldstein?" Sophia wasn't laughing.

Neither was I. "Merely wondering who'd managed to turn my evil streak into rainbows that bit people."

"Biting rainbows?" Sophia now looked marginally concerned.

She wasn't the only one, and I bit out. "Well, it's definitely not much of an evil streak if it's just a plain rainbow, is it?" My petulant tone made me sound even more insane. Like a weakling playing at villainy. *Good Lord.* I banged my head once more on the desk for good measure. Maybe I'd knock some sense into my own damn head and find myself again. *Ha! How many years had it been since I knew myself? I couldn't even say.* No, really. Aaaaand…*Good gods,* I was one booted foot and well-placed curse away from Bedlam. Or the stage. It didn't matter which…one was just as bad as the other in my mind.

With near mythical strength, I forced myself to focus and

consider MacKeane's probable escape and found I couldn't decide if I was upset the damn wolf had gotten away or elated to think of how pissed off the angels were right about now.

Oh, Josie Bell, you really are a frightfully clever witch. Pride colored my thoughts, as if I had ought to do with her helping him escape. But worse than that, I didn't understand *why* I felt proud of her, a refrain that had entered my thoughts repeatedly over the years at odd times. And always about Josie Bell.

I didn't even know if she'd done the deed. Except, I knew. *I definitely knew.*

There was no announcement in the papers for any of it, there hadn't even been a notice regarding the initial arrest, and I realized in that moment I wasn't the only one stirring up trouble. *Interesting.*

My first commander stormed into the room unannounced—*where was my damn butler, anyway*—and honed in on the broadsheet straight away. Worse, all I felt was *amused.*

Even the hedgehog had ruffled feathers.

And why the hell was I thinking about birds?

"Don't bother." Lady Sophia piped up. "There's nothing in the paper—"

"How do you—"

"And he's…," she whirled her hand in my general direction, "*off.*"

Sophia ignored the lieutenant's question but not without giving him a withering glance and my amusement grew. It seemed Sophia *really* didn't like being questioned. That was good information to know.

Also, she was right. I was definitely *off,* and I began laughing. Out loud.

Chapter Twenty-Seven

Josie
Clothes fit for a—Nope, that's it. That's the Joke. You'll See.

The Sorcerer's Hound
The Rookery

THE SORCERER'S HOUND wasn't what one would call a respectable establishment, but it was outside the angel's territory, and for now, that meant we were safe. Here, there were rooms to let, which could be had with no questions asked for the right price…the proprietors being well-used to a regular clientele who were keen on remaining anonymous.

Based on the shiny gold buttons and fitted, custom suit the owner wore, he'd made a prosperous business off his willingness to look the other way.

Better still, the Sorcerer's Hound was situated near the docks in an area I knew well having grown up an orphan on these very streets.

I took my usual room whenever I stayed here, it had a lesser view but it offered a better chance to escape out the window should the need arise. I then ordered a bath and food for three to be sent up as soon as possible. After his time in Marshalsea, I assumed Lachlan MacKeane could eat enough for two.

The thought of a bath, though, made me realize I needed to find His Grace a change of clothes, and as I eyed the proprietor's questionable sense of fashion, a sort of plan began to take shape. A plan that was wholly out of character for me, but then that was my general problem of late…always trying…and failing…to act *in* character.

Normally, I would have been prepared for this eventuality and brought some clothes with me, but clearly, I really had managed to convince myself I'd not yet decided whether to break Lachlan out of gaol.

I suppose this all demonstrated how good I was at lying to myself.

Still, I glanced at the proprietor and put on a winning smile. "I'd like to make you an offer for a set of men's clothes."

OUR ROOM WASN'T particularly clean—but would suffice for our needs—and had a bed, a small, round table with two chairs, and a fireplace. Pulling out my wand, I lit the fire and the brace of candles on the table with a swift flick of my wrist.

"That's a neat trick," said Lachlan, but I ignored him and slid into one of the chairs. He seemed on edge, and I wasn't willing to inquire as to why. I was quite sure I knew, and I was equally sure his agitation was because of me.

The duke sat on the edge of the room's lone bed and bounced on his arse as if to test the bed's structural integrity, and for a moment, I could only stare and had to suppress a twitch of my lips at his antics.

Especially when he lifted his head and waggled his brows at me. Funny how even agitated, the man still seemed to find humor in the mundane. I hated how I desperately wanted to understand why…

"For a man wanted for murder and being hunted, you're

awfully jovial," I said.

He shrugged. "I'm no' worried, lass."

With a flick of my wand, the clothes I'd procured downstairs appeared on the bed before Lachlan, folded neatly and tied with a string.

Why the string? Don't ask. I don't know. Truly.

A pair of surprisingly well-polished boots appeared on the floor next to the bed. The entire ensemble was clearly several decades out of fashion, but I honestly felt that part wasn't going to be a problem for a man like Lachlan MacLean.

"For me?" he asked with false surprise. "Ye should no' have. I didn't get ye anything."

His remarks didn't deserve a response, and I reached for my Purse of Possessions, but not before I observed that while I had stayed at this very room plenty of times before—I had always thought the beds plenty large. But with Lachlan sitting there...no, now laying across it, the ridiculous man...the bed seemed preposterously small all of a sudden. Which was a patently absurd observation, but a real one, nonetheless.

And a problem for later.

"Are ye going to stay while I change?"

I could hear the humor in his voice, and though I paused, I didn't look his way, I had to force the onset of a very revealing blush down into a box buried deep. My voice was strong as I replied. "It won't be a problem."

"But what if *I'm* concerned about the state of my delicate sensibilities?"

That remark deserved the scoff I couldn't hold back. "Your sensibilities are no more delicate than a succubus's. As a matter of fact, a succubus and a nymph loitering in a well-attended bawdyhouse where they've played for hours while the worse for wear due to an overabundance of gin and a gluttony of sex, have more delicate sensibilities."

"Ooooh, are ye propositioning me?"

This time, I couldn't help but glance at him with a withering stare, while ignoring how much I seemed to be enjoying our not-so innocent banter, and noted he truly was teasing me based on his casual pose, amusing grin, and the light dancing in his eyes.

I immediately understood that this version of Lachlan MacKeane was far more dangerous to a woman's peace of mind—or at least, my peace of mind—than any other version I'd previously been treated to, and I swiftly repeated, "It won't be a problem," then cleared my throat nervously as I returned to my task.

What had I been doing before?

Oh, right. A letter to Daphne.

I swallowed, and ignored him as best I could, which wasn't easy. I pulled a quill, ink, and parchment out of my purse and proceeded to jot down a note to Daphne. Or at least, that was my intent as I fought to consider precisely what I needed to say to her. I was sure I'd known exactly what I wanted to say when I'd entered the room.

I was proud of myself for ignoring the sounds of Lachlan MacKeane changing out of his religious prison garb… You know, religious because it was 'hole-y'.

I snorted, then shook my head. *What was wrong with me?*

After a few hot moments, during which I wrote absolutely nothing at all, Lachlan's movements ceased—or so I heard.

"Well," he said, "I like the color, but we definitely have a problem."

The mere tone of his voice warned me I definitely didn't want to look, but that did nothing to stop me from lifting my head from my blank piece of parchment and face where I expected to see the duke.

And very nearly lost every bit of my hard-won composure at the sight of Lachlan MacKeane wearing a motley collection of last-century's clothes that were extremely and comically too small.

When I could speak, and to be clear, I never once let a single impertinent chuckle escape my flattened lips, I said, "Yes, I see the problem."

And the gods knew, I definitely could see. Everything. I could even make out the piercings in his nipples, and I very nearly reached for my damned blank paper to start fanning myself.

But I was far more in control of myself than that. Or at least, I was capable of controlling myself… I was supposed to be. Might have been. Until my gaze landed in the general vicinity of his groin.

Which, in all fairness, wasn't general at all because his, er, size and the, um, tightness of his breeches made it blatantly clear exactly what sort of situation was going on beneath his ill-fitted attire.

I blew out a long breath.

"We should have ordered larger attire," he supposed.

I nodded. To his *projection*. My eyes locked in place and had a mind all their own for it surely wasn't me who couldn't look away from his sizeable manhood…or the not-so-vague-nor-subtle-by-any-stretch-of-the-imagination outline of it.

"Especially in the groin area."

"Yeeeeeppppp," I agreed, still nodding.

"Josie…"

"Yeeeeepppp," I reconfirmed. *What was I confirming? Bollocks.*

I let out a long exhale, because *gracious me* the man was *massive,* and blurted out. "I can fix it."

And promptly groaned because that just made everything so much worse. And funnier.

"Oh, I'm verra sure you could," which didn't help. At all, "but ye're no' going to like me verra much if I don't try to—oh, lass, eyes up here, love."

"No really, I…" I finally tore my gaze out of its not so innocent stare and swept over the rest of his appearance as I sought out his face. I couldn't ignore that he was actually trying to help me, despite his apparently well-deserved *sizeable* reputation, and worse, I wasn't so lacking in self-awareness I couldn't tell I was more disappointed that he'd actually put a stop to this.

I cleared my throat just as more uncharacteristic mischief taunted me into how best to address his problem, and I glanced at my still-blank paper while with a wave of my wand, I cast another spell.

This time, his clothes were no longer way too tight.

"Josie Bell…," I heard him all but growl.

And I had to laugh.

For this time, his clothes were far, far too big.

Chapter Twenty-Eight

Josie
A Witch, A Fae, and an Incubus Walk Into a Public House...

I WROTE OUT detailed instructions for my roommate, while across the table, Lachlan MacKeane inhaled the food which had finally been delivered. When I finished, I folded my note, magically sealed it, and walked to the window to see what manner of creature I could find to coax into delivering it for me.

I opened the window, and a quick survey of the rear alley told me I had a choice of a squirrel, a cat, a hedgehog, and a raven. I had no idea what a hedgehog might be doing in this sort of area, which smelled like trouble, so I would definitely avoid that. The cat would have no sense of urgency and only deliver the note on its own time, and the raven might be too obvious were someone watching, so I chose the squirrel. There were times being an animus witch proved extremely useful.

MacKeane joined me at the window just as the squirrel settled herself on the sill. I studiously ignored how he'd managed to find (somehow) a makeshift tie to hold his trousers up and then rolled his now ankle length breeches up over boots which were better suited for a clown.

"Oh, my," said the squirrel as she fanned herself and eyed Lachlan, "What a strapping young man you've got there, love."

Did she seriously not notice the ridiculousness of his attire?

"What is it saying?" asked Lachlan.

"*She* says you're smelly, and she's seen better canines on a mangy bulldog."

Lachlan folded his arms across his chest. "Is that so?" He rubbed at his chin, a thoughtful look across his face. "She's a...she, you say?"

I folded my own arms, refusing to answer...to join in on this line of talk. I well-knew where this was headed.

As if he read my mind, his answering smile was everything mischievous. "She looks rather adoring if ye ask me."

The squirrel *did* appear to be making eyes at the duke, and I had to refrain from rolling my own. I had a strong suspicion I would have to grow used to this type of behavior where females where concerned...at least, while we were working together.

I turned my attention to the squirrel and away from the man who seemed to be standing entirely too close. I could actually *feel* the heat emanating off of him. I cleared my throat and addressed the squirrel. "I need you to—*ahem.*"

The squirrel jumped, having not been paying me the slightest attention. "Oh, um, yes dearie?"

"As I was saying, I need you to take this note to Miss Daphne Black at number One Coven Square. It's urgent."

"Are you sure?" I raised one brow, and she swiftly added, "I mean, yes, of course."

The squirrel looked adoringly at the duke again.

After a moment, I stressed, "We are rather in a hurry."

The squirrel clutched at her neck, and I was sure beneath her grey fur, she blushed. "Oh, oh, of course."

When she made no move to turn away, I dangled the note in front of her. And still, it took a moment for her to shake off her lust-induced trance and take the letter. I turned her gently, putting her back to the duke, which worked. Now that the duke was out of sight, the squirrel scampered away with all due haste.

I quickly closed the window lest she change her mind and

return.

"Can ye trust her?"

"I wouldn't have given her the note if I didn't. Besides, being an animus witch…let's just say an animal would never betray me." It was part of our special bond.

I turned to move away from the drafty window, but Lachlan remained in place, blocking my escape, searching my countenance for…something. I knew not what.

I no longer felt quite so chilled, and yet as I noted the man's long lashes and heated eyes, his pupils blown wide in the dim lighting, I forced myself to chant internally, *He's wanted for murder. He's wanted for murder. He's a rake and a rogue and entirely too impulsive. And murder, Josie Bell. Mur. Der.*

Yet I didn't move. Even when he dipped his head, closer. *Closer.*

But then someone knocked on the door, and the sound quickly flushed out the building heat arching between us.

I jumped back just as the door opened and forced myself to ignore the man's knowing smirk in the process.

In the end, it turned out to be someone at the wrong door, but the spell had been broken.

What was I thinking?

In a fit of uncharacteristic nerves, I magicked away the evidence of MacKeane's earlier dinner and proceeded to wait for the arrival of my roommate, which I imagined was going to feel interminably long.

FIVE HOURS LATER, a knock on the door signaled the arrival of my roommate. I don't know how I managed to wait five hours in a tiny room with Lachlan MacKeane and not kill him or start licking him, but somehow, I had.

"Josie, what is going on? A group of angels came to the house looking… for… yo—" Daphne's voice trailed off, and she froze in place the moment she noticed Lachlan reclining back on the bed, his long legs stretched out and crossed at the ankles as if he hadn't a care in the world. "Oh."

Like the love-sick squirrel, one hand moved to Daphne's neck, and a blush stole across her sharply defined cheeks.

Behind her the door opened further, and in walked Aiden Locke, the Duke of Anglesey. "Well, stop ogling the man and step aside." His voice a growl directed at my housemate. "And just what the hell are you *wearing*?" He gestured at MacKeane; his tone held a hint of laughter.

Lachlan smirked. "Clothes. From the House of Witch."

Daphne jumped and rapidly fluttered her eyes as if clearing her mind from a trance.

I hadn't anticipated the duke, and our little room grew quite a bit cozier, despite the frosty, dismissive attitude the incubus directed towards my roommate Daphne. The man was as massive as Lachlan MacKeane and normally appeared just as human. But since we were in private, I could just make out his demon's horns, and his skin was a dark, dusky red, which I supposed made sense for a demon who thrived off of sex.

I gave the pair a wide berth, and nearly closed the door on George who slipped in, quietly for once, behind Anglesey. But then he paused, his gaze locked on MacKeane, and he shook his head. "Helping others with their wardrobe again, Josie Bell? You should have waited for me, Your Grace."

For once, I ignored George's taunt and fought the urge to look back out into the hall to see if anyone else was coming.

I glanced to my roommate. "Daphne. I thought I made it clear we needed to be discreet." Anglesey was never discreet—it seemed the nature of demons. And George—ha!

Lachlan echoed my thoughts, in a fashion. "What did ye do, Red, take oot an advert in the Times?"

He called me Red?

Daphne spoke up in my defense. "I'm afraid I summoned Anglesey and George. You're going to need more than a couple of animus spells to do…well, whatever this is…"

Honestly, I'd tried hard not to contemplate just how difficult it was going to be to find and capture a Class I Demon while hiding from the authorities. Especially with a wanted man as striking and conspicuous as Lachlan MacKeane tagging along.

But making a deal with Anglesey? An Incubus? They're nearly as bad as the Fae when it came to striking bargains. Anyone with a modicum of common sense knew *never* to trust the Fae.

Ignoring Daphne and I, Anglesey nodded toward MacKeane. "Ye're wanted for murder, mate."

"I ken." The duke lifted one brow. "Are you here to take me in?"

The Duke of Anglesey barked out a sarcastic laugh. "Me, a demon, help the angels? Not a chance in hell."

"Good."

"Daphne—," I began.

Daphne stared at me with an intensity that made it clear she was trying to convey something she couldn't say out loud. Her eyes pled, *Trust me. We can trust him.*

The problem was, I trusted no one but myself.

Daphne turned to face MacKeane, and in an instant, her hard expression softened. For some reason, the sight of this ruffled my proverbial feathers, and if I didn't get a handle on myself, everyone in this inn was going to know just how ruffled they were. And I didn't even *like* the man. What was wrong with me? I'd always been the epitome of calm.

I slammed my mental doors closed on those thoughts and listened as Daphne said to MacKeane, "You're going to need more than a spell to hide you in plain sight. And you're going to need his help," she gestured over her shoulder at Anglesey, "to find and track this demon."

Behind her, Anglesey exploded away from the wall with a quick-tempered curse, his broad hands clenched into tight fists. "No… No. No. No. No. No. *Dammit.* I cannot betray my own kind. Not even for this. Daph, you can't ask me to do this." His voice softened the slightest bit. "Don't ask me to do this."

Daphne turned to face him. "Anglesey. It could attack people. *Kill* people."

He threw up his hands, "Then listen for the screaming and run that way."

Daphne, shaking her head the entire time, said, "Anglesey. No one will find out."

MacKeane snorted, and I could see the plea in Anglesey's eyes when he all but begged, "Someone always finds out."

Daphne crossed her arms, and the ever-present light in Anglesey's whisky-colored eyes dimmed just the tiniest bit, and I really wanted to turn him away if he offered to do this anyway.

Then, Daphne turned her back and looked at me with wide, worried eyes. "We don't have a choice." Behind her, the demon closed his eyes.

"Anglesey?" I asked. The demon looked as if he was asking a higher power for strength. When he finally tore his eyes from the ceiling and looked at me, I continued, "What does Daphne expect you to do?"

With a resigned sigh and an uncharacteristically, flat voice, he said, "*Dammit.* Everyone but Josie leave the room."

Apparently, Lachlan had opinions about that. "Incubus… I'm no' leaving this room while she's here." He jerked his head in my direction.

Anglesey pointed a finger at the Lycan. "Fine. You stay, but only you. And fair warning, if you stay, you have to be a part of it, too. Otherwise, the link is weak or worse, won't take at all."

MacKeane dipped his head.

"Fine," Daphne said and made to leave, but she stopped in front of Anglesey on her way out. "Duke—"

He turned his head the slightest bit, but it seemed he couldn't completely turn away from her. "Don't."

For some inexplicable reason, Daphne reached as if to cup the man's cheek, and he jerked his head back to prevent her. Daphne's hand fell, and so quietly, you could barely hear her, she whispered, "Thank you."

The demon didn't respond, and Daphne left the room after George, who I'd nearly forgotten was present, he was so uncharacteristically quiet. Perhaps, he was far better able to understand the tensions in a room than I'd ever given him credit for, which made me feel pretty rotten, but also, I didn't have the luxury of worrying about it.

The door closed with a deafening click. It sounded so final, and I suppressed a shiver.

After Daphne left, Lachlan broke the silence. "From where I'm standing, things would be a hell of a lot easier if you two would just fook and get it over with."

I spun to face him and jabbed a finger in his direction. Straight into his chest. Leading with the nail. "Not helpful!"

For his part, Lachlan merely grinned at me, then dropped a quick glance at my finger, which was still pressed into his chest, and which I promptly dropped as if scalded.

Meanwhile, Anglesey yelled, "Shut your gob before I make you, bastard."

Lachlan laughed, "I'd love ta see ye try. And I'm verra much no' a bastard."

Anglesey stepped toward the duke, his fingers curled into fists, and I stopped him with a gentle hand to his chest. "Wait." I glanced at Lachlan whose attention was pinned on my hand where I touched the demon. "Both of you."

Any moment now, they were going to start measuring their—well, manly bits—and I had no time for their nonsense. Nor any interest in seeing Lach Jr.

Well, any *more* of Lach Jr.

Worse, I realized I must be practically delirious with exhaustion when my mind found it rather appealing to consider how, precisely, Lachlan MacKeane referred to his…er, equipment.

I forced myself to glance back at Anglesey, who nodded, though his eyes held a wealth of emotion in their depths, and in that moment, I truly realized the sacrifice he was about to make.

Softening my voice, I asked, "What do we have to do?"

Anglesey nodded in acknowledgement, then released a long breath. "We have to make a bargain and seal it."

Behind me, Lachlan snorted. "With a kiss, I suppose?"

"Yes, actually."

"I was only joking, what the hell?"

Anglesey gestured to himself. "Incubus demon, yes? *Everything* is about sex."

Lachlan pointed a finger at Anglesey. "Ye're no' going to fook her." His voice was hard and stilted, practically a low growl.

"Lachlan!" I exclaimed, but internally, I had to admit his anger on my behalf was somewhat enticing—*no! Wanted murderer, remember? I did not find his sudden 'I'm the alpha' attitude attractive. At all. I am* not *one of thousands of other women.*

I was here, in this place and successful, through my own hard work. I didn't need him... I solicited his help because my assignment dictated so. That was all.

Right?

Lachlan turned to face me. "We do no' need this demon. All ye need is me; isn't that why ye broke me out of gaol?"

I shook my head and dissembled, "You defeated a Class I Demon by taking its bloody head off with your claws. My directive is to seize it, not shred it." I turned back to Anglesey. "Besides, we don't know where it is."

I swore I could hear MacKeane grind his teeth behind me, but he was all charm when he asked, "What do ye need me ta do?"

"Hold her."

MacKeane glanced at me and waggled his brows. I refused to be amused despite the small twitch I felt tugging at the corner of my mouth. I pointed a finger his way. "If you tell anyone about this..."

But then, Anglesey clarified, "If you tell anyone about this, anyone at all...she dies."

Well. That was rather unexpected.

"Ye won't lay a finger on her..." MacKeane's voice was low

and deceptively calm, and his vehemence on her behalf was…n't the tiniest bit appealing.

Whatever further thoughts I might have imagined contradicting this observation, died a swift death (thankfully) with Anglesey's sigh. "I won't have to."

Oh.

"Well," I rubbed my hands together, "what are we waiting for?"

Anglesey and MacKeane shared a commiserating look I didn't want to notice, and I continued not noticing it while also ignoring Anglesey's whispered, "Listen. You staying feels right, but I don't make the rules." Anglesey glanced at me. "Do you want him to stay?"

I appreciated that he asked my consent, if a touch belatedly, but I only had eyes for Lachlan MacKeane when I replied, "Yes."

It was because I didn't trust him not to run away while we were doing this.

That was the *only* reason.

I gave my best impression of acting thoroughly unconcerned about his reaction when I asked, "Is he going to have to kiss me, too?"

And yet, I still flinched when Anglesey responded. "Yes. Is that going to be a problem?"

I swallowed, but my voice cracked when I replied. "N-no. Of course, not."

And just like that, Lachlan's irreverent humor was restored. "Right. Now, what aren't ye telling us?"

To give Anglesey credit, he tried very hard not to wince. The attempt was ruined when he glanced away and carded one hand through his hair. "The demon could possess *you—*"

Well, that was…unfortunate.

"You might not be able to sever the connection completely when you're finished…"

Even better. Nothing to be concerned about. At all.

"The link works both ways."

Nice. I can sense it… it can sense me… To be honest, I seemed to be taking this alarmingly well, considering.

But, also, he wasn't finished…

"You might have some unusual…side effects. Tendencies. Some of Lachlan's—and the creature's—more persistent, er desires."

Great. Did I really want to know what turned on a Class I Demon? Or Lachlan for that matter?

Lachlan had a lascivious look on his face. Again. "Is she going ta want ta tup?"

I closed my eyes, which was rather silly, to be honest. Because I didn't want to know the answer to that. Mostly. And I knew my eyes didn't *actually* impact my hearing.

Also, perhaps, because I already knew the answer.

But I couldn't seem to find actual words as I absorbed the… risks.

And then, he added, "…And some of mine."

Great. I was probably going to start lusting after my roommate now, too.

I didn't have a problem with female relationships, but relations between witches in the same house were definitely frowned upon, and I didn't want Daphne the way I wanted La—

I opened my eyes when I felt Anglesey rest two hands on my shoulders, which was unexpected and kind. "It'll be fine. You're strong. Just…maybe…break the link as soon as you can."

He gave me a sheepish grin then, and I realized I actually *liked* our tortuous trainer. As a person, or demon, rather.

Anglesey cleared his throat. "Now, that we've established all that, and I've verified *his* motivations and other things," he jerked his head at MacKeane, "I can admit I had an ulterior motive in allowing the duke to participate."

I had a feeling I wasn't going to like this. The duke scoffed. "Allowed?"

Anglesey grinned as if he were suddenly enjoying this. "I don't really have any interest in kissing Josie, no offence, dear…"

I dipped my head. "None taken."

"But the attraction between the two of you is…"

Lachlan's subsequent grin was almost smug.

"Let's just say I can do this just by feeding off *that*. So, change of plan. I'll be doing the holding, with your permission—"

"Yes."

"Good, and you'll be…"

I'll be kissing Lachlan MacKeane. The Duke of Skye. Wanted murderer and infamous rake and on the run from the law. Well, the last part was mostly my doing.

"Lass…" I glanced at MacKeane, who stared at me with an intensity I honestly hadn't expected. He leaned in and his lips brushed my ear as he softly asked, "Are ye sure?"

Desire raced through my veins at the graze of his lips, and all I could do was nod for mere words escaped me. Yet I felt confident. Accepting.

And maybe just a tiny bit eager…

I fell into Lachlan's intense regard and barely noted Anglesey's presence, even as he gently settled one hand on my shoulder. Nor did I hear the words he murmured as he began the ritual.

No. In that moment, I only had eyes for Lachlan MacKeane.

Particularly as he began to lower his head.

I had kissed the man before and was used to closing my eyes upon receiving a kiss. But not this time. I couldn't. I didn't want to miss a moment and closing my eyes as his lips approached mine felt like missing far more than a moment.

Yet the instant his lips touched mine, I had no choice. My eyes shut of their own volition. It was as if I had no conscious control of my body, my mind, or my emotions.

And oh, did I feel. And sense. And want. Everything.

Yes, I wanted. This. Him. And it was this knowledge that transformed me into an active participant in our kiss.

With the change, I became almost greedy with desire, not that Lachlan seemed to mind, which was good. Because I didn't mind either. I *so* didn't mind, and in that moment, I wanted him to know it.

I slid my hands up his chest. Perhaps, slid was too tame a word. More like clawed. Raced. I suddenly couldn't get enough. "Take it off."

Not that I needed his help. His too-loose clothing was practically taking itself off.

But I didn't have the presence of mind to properly congratulate myself on my obvious *forward* thinking when I decided to make his clothing ridiculously easy to remove.

In the future, I would understand how fortuitous the thoughts about to bombard me truly were even though I didn't feel any such thing in this moment.

Thoughts of mine like:

"We're not alone."

"He's irresistible. And delicious."

"Anglesey, poor bastard, has to live with this type of sexual tension constantly?"

"How does he survive it?"

"Poor beastie."

And "Oh, Anglesey, what did you do…"

And theirs:

"What am *I* doing?"

"I want more."

"We don't have time for this."

"This is marvelous."

"I love her?"

"She's my mate."

That last one did the job. I abruptly broke our kiss, my mind swirling with the implications from all these revelations I'd somehow exposed, the last one standing out most prominently.

Witches didn't have mates.

But Lycans definitely did.

Why hadn't he said anything?

While I tried to make sense of that, I decided to keep the

knowledge to myself, for now, and instead asked, "How much time do I have… before I start to see signs." Then, I looked at MacKeane. *Really looked.* The onslaught of emotion that hit me like a charging dragon nearly knocked me off my feet, and I whispered, "Never mind."

MacKeane snapped out of whatever random thought was weighing on his mind, possibly about the complications of our impending *matehood*, and shook his head. "What? Look at me." MacKeane dipped to meet my eyes and studied my expression, obvious concern etched upon his face. "It's already started? What-what do you feel? Where's the demon?"

I laughed really, really, really hard. To myself. Because I sure as hell wasn't going to tell him I had the sudden urge to tackle him to the floor and rub myself all over him. No. Way. Nor was I ready to articulate my newfound discoveries. Even at the best of times, people struggled with the idea of someone peeking inside their head.

I closed my eyes and pictured the demon. The words *Tired, so tired* entered my thoughts, and I knew they weren't mine. I felt a pull, and though I couldn't explain how I knew, I tugged back, then mentally followed the return tug, which was far more powerful, more intentional. Had it been real instead of mental, the pull would have knocked me off my feet. I had no doubt it was the demon.

I opened my eyes. MacKeane still stood before me, his face scrunched with what looked like genuine concern. "He's found a cave to sleep in. He's fine."

MacKeane narrowed his eyes. "Are ye sure?"

I hated when men questioned me that way, and I could tell the moment that registered with MacKeane. My face must have betrayed my irritation, and he had the good sense to look somewhat apologetic, if a rogue could ever look apologetic. Still, I answered him. "He's been incarcerated beneath the ground for five hundred years. He's a touch…disoriented."

Behind me, Anglesey said, "Good. It worked."

I very nearly asked if there had been some doubt on his part, but since it didn't matter *now*, I merely said, "It did."

MacKeane's voice was soft when he asked, "Is that all?"

I wasn't about to answer him. Instead, I broke MacKeane's intense stare and turned about. "How long do I have before it all becomes permanent?"

MacKeane *might* have whispered, *"Coward…,"* as I turned my back on him.

But more important was Anglesey's rather unfortunate answer…

"Two days."

Two days?

"Maybe, three."

Bollocks.

Chapter Twenty-Nine

Lachlan
To Clean or Not to Clean

A FTER SUCH AN eventful day, everything following the ritual was remarkably mundane and anti-climactic. Anglesey mumbled, "I'll go get the others, while you two...," then he gestured vaguely at myself and Josie Bell. I appreciated his intuitive understanding and nodded my thanks as I began setting my clothes to rights—or at least, as much as I could with such ill-fitting, albeit comfortable togs. After he left to find the others, Josie Bell remained curiously quiet, and I, sensing her needs, let her be.

Ten minutes later, our friends, for lack of a better word, returned. Their stay was short, few words were spoken, and ultimately, they simply left. For such a motley collection of people, they all looked rather bored, if I had to guess, though the tension between Josie's roommate and the Duke of Anglesey was obvious.

I was not bored. And I suspected, Josie wasn't either, though on the surface, she appeared peculiarly calm, considering.

After I closed the door behind the last of our guests, I turned to find Josie Bell staring at the bed, a curious expression on her face, and then it dawned on me: there was only one bed.

I was about to say something, a jest regarding the bed, likely, but before I could, Josie snapped out of her daze and began turning down the blankets. Her practical behavior was admirable, and yet the site of her preparing *our* bed turned my mouth dry and the blood in my body raced south. *Fook me.* I didn't want this.

That was a lie; I did. And that was the problem. I could no longer deny I wanted Josie Bell with every fiber of my being. I could no longer tell how much was instinct due to the attempted matehood and how much was just me, my own wants and desires. I supposed it didn't matter; I wasn't cut out for matehood, and I refused to allow my choices to be taken from me. I'd rather go insane.

Maybe.

The entire situation was laughable; insanity was a very real possibility if I didn't find a way out of this mess by the full moon. As it was, my resistance was weakening, no question about it.

This was a disaster in the making.

"Could you answer that?" Josie asked.

"Answer what?"

As soon as the words were out of my mouth, someone knocked on the door, and Josie slid a sly smile my way. I felt that smile all over. *Dammit.*

I turned to answer the door. If my usual charm was absent when I barked out a "What?" could anyone blame me?

Turns out it was a maid and several young men. "W-we are here with yer bath?"

I groaned and shut my eyes.

From behind me, Josie Bell, who was clearly trying to torture me, exclaimed, "Brilliant. Thank you. If His Grace would only move out of the way, you can set the bath before the fire."

I moved out of the way and thought I might as well bend over and let Josie take off my head now, which merely served to send my mind spinning out of control with thoughts of Josie Bell bent over, my cock sliding in and out of her quim.

I turned to the wall and began banging my head against it.

I paused my act of self-punishment when a soft hand settled on my back, and an even softer voice asked, "MacKeane. Are you quite all right?"

"Never better." *Bang.*

"But—"

"Just clearing my head."

Not really.

"If you say so."

"I say so."

"Well, never say I interrupted your ritual or whatever it is you're doing."

"Thank ye." *Bang.*

"But there is a bath waiting for you should you wish to take advantage of it."

I paused. "For me?"

I had assumed she'd called the bath for herself, and I didn't know which was worse. Her in the bath, or me in the bath knowing she was near and thinking of my needs, which nearly had my brain racing away with other needs she could help me with.

Dammit.

I choked, then said, "I appreciate yer kindness."

I turned and focused on the bath; I could not risk seeing the concern on Josie Bell's face.

"You're welcome, but it's not kindness."

"If ye say so, I—"

"No, truly. You smell."

"I smell—" Before I could stop myself, I lifted one arm and performed a not-so-discreet sniff. Eh, it seemed she had a point.

And in that moment, I knew if I hadn't realized it before, I certainly knew now: Josie Bell was going to be hell on my self-esteem, which was probably a good thing.

"I suppose I'll be taking that bath then."

I heard her swallow. "Good. Yes."

I darted a look her way. Was she laughing? She'd turned her

back on me, so I couldn't be sure, but I suspected she was laughing at my expense. Fortunately, I wasn't so fragile I couldn't laugh right along with her.

"So, how is this going ta work? Are ye going to leave me here to tend ta myself?" I hadn't meant to say that, and I hadn't even realized how suggestive I sounded until the words were out of my mouth. I didn't mean it. Mostly.

She cocked her head as if to say, *well aren't you adorable?* But merely held up her wand and said, "Magic, remember? I thought I could put up a screen to give you privacy."

"Och, aye. That makes sense." I was making a muck of this, I knew it. My usual charm was completely nonexistent. I felt out of my depth, which was ridiculous. It was time to quit worrying about whether or not I would be able to get in the bath with Josie Bell in the room without wrapping my hand around my erection and stroking myself until I spent. It was time I took charge of the situation.

I began by unbuttoning my shirt.

Josie's look of alarm was almost comical. I might have been concerned if I hadn't also noticed her pupils were wide and not with fear.

Later, I would come to realize exactly why and how I knew what she was thinking, and it wasn't the fact that her irises had all but been swallowed by the black of her pupils. But in that moment, I was too emotionally crazed to see sense. I was a drowning man desperate to regain some sense of control over the things I was feeling. Things I hadn't wanted, but now wanted desperately.

"W-what are you doing?"

"What does it look like I'm doing, love?"

"Disrobing." Her answer was a whisper, and when she licked her lips after she spoke, I swear I nearly came on the spot.

But I was in charge now. Most likely.

"Would no' want to waste this lovely bath ye so thoughtfully provided, now would I?"

She shook her head, but otherwise appeared to be incapable of further speech.

I finally reached the last few buttons…not that I needed to undo them considering the oversized nature of my attire, but that wasn't the point. I reached for the makeshift rope holding up my breeches and began to work the knot loose. Josie Bell followed my every move; her eyes focused on my hands as if bespelled to do so.

She swallowed when I worked the first part of the knot free, and it became perfectly clear she had no intention of stopping me, which I suspected she would come to regret later.

"Ms. Bell, unless ye wish to see…everything, I suggest ye put yer mind to conjuring up that screen ye mentioned."

"Yes. I-I'll get to that straight away…"

Her voice trailed off at the end, and I nearly chuckled. She was fucking adorable, truly, and in different circumstances, we might have—

I didn't want to finish that thought.

And just like that, the knot released; the only thing holding up my breeches were my hands and one very erect cock.

"Last chance, Josie Bell."

She nodded; then bit her lip, which made me groan out loud as I released my trousers.

Chapter Thirty

Josie Bell

Mate Math: One Bath Plus One Bed Plus Two Mates Equals
Five O________s

I ONLY JUST raised my wand in time. And I wasn't sure what bothered me most about that.

I didn't actually see anything of note, not because the man wasn't spectacularly endowed, oh, he was; I could tell that much. In fact, he was so blessed, the only reason I hadn't gotten a glimpse of Lach Jr. before I'd conjured the screen was because his breeches had gotten caught on his fierce erection like an erotic coat rack.

Imagine that.

And yes, I was really, really imagining it. Lots of imagining going on here. Too much imagining. I needed to get a hold of myself.

Twenty minutes later, he was still in the bath, and I was nearly lost in a haze of desire. For once, the rules society tried to command made complete sense. With every splash of water and his every unexpected moan of pleasure, I wanted to magic away the screen just to see precisely what he was doing in there because I needed to know.

Instead, I flung myself on the bed, buried my face in the pillow, and screamed.

"Did ye say something?" he called out.

I lifted my head and shouted. "Nothing," then dropped my head into the pillow and screamed again.

"Are ye sure?"

I raised my head again. "I'm s—wait. Are you laughing at me?"

"Nooooo. Never. I would no' dream of it."

He was. That bastard was laughing at me.

I wanted to be irritated, I really did, but I couldn't because I could feel his deep throated chuckles everywhere. And I mean everywhere. I rolled onto my back with a sigh of frustration or tried to. How had I forgotten I wore a bustle? I magicked the inconvenient contraption away with a wave of my hand and finally settled into position, which only made everything worse. Every move I made launched a thousand promises of pleasure at my core, and it was glorious. Problematic, but glorious all the same. I lifted my head and glanced to where my conjured wall of smoke prevented me from seeing Lachlan MacKeane in the bath. The beauty of this spell was that he couldn't see me either. If only I'd thought to make it soundproof, too.

I refused to recall it wasn't too late to change that fact, either. No. It was definitely too late. For me.

Before I knew what I was doing, I was pulling up my skirts and fumbling with my drawers, desperate for relief. I wanted to blame the incubus and his sexually charged spell for my ill-advised behavior, but it would be a lie. Or not the whole truth anyway.

And even though I well-knew I would regret my actions later, in that moment, I could no more stop myself from touching my core than I could stop breathing.

When my fingers found my engorged, aching clit, I had to bite my lip to stop my moan of pleasure. I might have taken my time, but my need, not to mention the prospect of getting caught masturbating by Lachlan MacKeane, a man I was supposed to loathe, had my fingers flying as I raced to find relief.

I had never been so desperate for release in my life.

Behind the smokey screen hiding the duke from my hungry gaze, a rhythmic slapping sounded, and somehow, I knew Lachlan MacKeane had his fist wrapped around his cock. My imagination supplied the rest, and it only flung me that much closer to release. I should have been horrified. I might have been horrified, except I knew, somehow I knew, this was going to be the most powerful release I'd ever experienced, I wanted nothing more.

From the bath, Lachlan's own desire seemed to grow with mine, the rhythmic slapping increasing in speed alongside my own increasing desire, and at that thought, I could no longer hold back my moan of desire.

By now, neither one of us bothered to pretend we were doing anything but masturbating to thoughts of each other. It might have been the ritual with Anglesey. It might have been the partial matehood I'd initiated. I didn't care.

My hips began to thrust rhythmically as I raced to the finish, thoroughly unconcerned about remaining still or quiet, and when my climax tore through me, I shouted my joy to the heavens. "Oooooh!"

So did Lachlan MacKeane.

But I couldn't think about that, I was too saturated with pleasure, too content to float in the beauty of post-orgasmic bliss to worry about anything else. Too satiated to even be embarrassed though I was aware enough to know my tattooed wolf knew I'd just brought myself to climax.

Still, it was surreal to hear his delicious brogue call out, "Josie Bell, take the screen down."

I wasn't ready to face him, but still, I asked. "Are you decent?"

A pause, and then, "No."

No? His answer was rather unexpected, which only made me race to fulfill his request that much faster.

The smoky blind hiding him from my gaze disappeared in an

instant and so, too, went my innocence regarding just what Lachlan MacKeane was hiding beneath civilized clothing.

He stood before the tub, dripping wet, hands fisted at his side. His chest was covered in the tattoos I'd come to expect. His nipples were pointed and pierced. But what snagged my attention was his jutting cock.

"Oh."

He was rock hard, and Lach, Jr—which suddenly seemed a totally inadequate nickname for Lachlan MacKeane's massive cock—seemed to point directly at me. I nearly pointed at myself as if to ask, *who me?*

"Oh? Lass, that's no' exactly the sound a man appreciates when a woman is seeing his cock fer the first time."

I shook my head. He misunderstood. "It's just…" *Goodness.*

"It's just…," he prompted.

I swallowed. "I, uh, thought you'd, um, finished."

"I did."

"Oh… Oh!" and he was still erect? That was…well, it was impressive. I had never had sex before, but I understood the mechanics of it all, and to know he'd ejaculated and was still hard was *something.*

"Aye. I want ye more than I've ever wanted a good gods-damn thing."

"Oh." *What happened to my vocabulary?*

As I continued to rudely stare, MacKeane approached our bed, his rod bobbing to his gait. "And I ken…," his voice was a tight, growl. "Ye do, too."

I could only nod. Why would I lie about it? He knew the same way I knew he had.

Lachlan MacKeane placed one knee on the bed and paused. I had to bite back a command for him to not stop.

"I won't fuck you."

I shook my head in agreement. Was that disappointment I felt? "Of course not," I added to be clear, and for a moment, I could have sworn his smile slipped just a fraction.

"But…"

But?

"…with ye're permission, we could do other things."

"O-other things?"

He dipped his head. "Naughty things."

"N-naughty things?" *Was there an echo in here?*

"Verra, verra naughty things."

I nodded my agreement.

"Is that a yes? I need to hear yer words, Josie Bell. I want there to be no misunderstanding."

"Y-yes."

He let out a slow hiss before saying, "Verra good."

I nodded. Again.

"Shall we remove these—"

Before he could finish, I magicked away my clothes, and he chuckled. "Remind me later to teach ye the pleasure of undressing yer partner. Slowly."

"Slowly."

He pulled back from the bed, which was counter-intuitive to the proceedings at hand, and strolled to the window, the muscles of his arse flexing with every step, and I watched my fill as he flung open the curtains at the window, allowing moonlight to fill the room. "I want to see ye, properly. How about you light some more candles…" with a thought, lit candles appeared on every horizontal surface in the room—I always carried spares in my purse. For emergencies—and he chuckled before adding, "…and spread yer legs. I want a taste of that quim with the delectable fragrance I've been scenting for the last half hour."

His words ratcheted up my desire like he'd lit me from within, and I spread my legs so fast, I could have easily pulled a muscle. I couldn't believe this was happening, and yet I wanted it to happen more than I wanted anything else, which was frightening and something to consider…later.

His eyes flared with desire and a slow smile hitched one corner of his mouth as he stared at my dripping core. I could feel his gaze like a brand down there and I couldn't wait to see what he had in store for me next. At this point, any reservations I might have had were non-existent.

Once again, he set one knee to the bed. "Ye are beautiful, Josie Bell, and I am desperate to tongue yer pussy."

I inhaled sharply, and my eyelids swept closed. "I want that, too," I whispered, and if he didn't get on with it, I was going to scream my frustration. I loved every filthy word he uttered, but more, I wanted him to act on his vow.

He placed his other knee on the bed and crawled forward. "Och, Josie, I am going to devour yer quim until ye come, then I'm going to lap up yer release while I savor your sweetness."

Yes. I definitely wanted that, too. He crawled closer, and my legs moved restlessly while I ached for him to settle between them.

Lachlan's lids lowered, then raised, the look in his eyes almost feral when he added, "And then I'm going ta do it again."

I whimpered. It was the only way to describe the noise I made at his promise. I couldn't believe the sound had come from my own mouth, but it did… I wanted this to the point I might have begged if he thought to change his mind.

But despite his confident promises, a slight flush of excitement stained his prominent cheek bones, and I knew he would fulfill his vow.

And then he positioned himself between my legs, but before he dipped his head, he glanced up at me one more time. "Are ye ready, Josie love?"

I nodded.

"Words, Josie Bell."

"I'm ready."

I could have sworn a flash of relief flared behind his eyes, but he was already dipping his head before I could know for sure.

I had to widen my legs further to accommodate his broad shoulders, and I knew I would never forget this moment. No matter what happened.

I felt his breath, hot and wet, right where I needed him as he whispered. "Ye can stop me at any time."

There wasn't a chance in hell.

And then he shifted forward and dragged the flat of his tongue through my folds. The sensation was indescribable, and we both moaned our pleasure at the same time.

"Fook me," he stated. "yer taste...I could do this all fooking night."

"All night..." I echoed his words as he traced my folds with his tongue, then dipped inside before he swept up again and sucked my throbbing clit into his mouth. *"Goodness."*

"Och, aye. So good."

Before I knew what I was about, my hands were teasing my nipples, then slid down my body until they found their way into his hair. I gripped handfuls of his soft locks before I pressed my fingers into his skull and pulled his face into my core. "Harder."

He chuckled, and I felt his breath on my nub as he said, "As my lady wishes."

Before I knew it, my hips were rocking and my fingers flexing to his punishing rhythm. I knew about oral sex, but I had never imagined this...this wildness. My feet felt as if I danced on coals, the same with the blood racing through my veins, and I loved it. "More. I'm dying here."

"Ye're no' dying, Josie Bell."

"Stop talking."

He chuckled, then, and before I could berate him further, he touched his tongue to my nubbin again, and he launched me into my release. I couldn't stop from crying out, from thrusting my hips, from pressing his head into me while I rode my release against his face. I no longer knew myself; he'd turned me inside out and upside down, and I didn't care. I was flying with the stars. Soaring. Without a care or a worry, just pure heated pleasure.

The aftershocks seemed to last for days, as my muscles clenched and throbbed.

And then he said, "Again."

I shook my head. I didn't think I could, but Lachlan MacKeane, the Duke of Skye, was having none of it.

"Oh, yes, Josie Bell. One more time. I'm not finished with ye yet."

He wasn't finished with me, and I should have known right then that I was never going to be the same.

The second time, I came even faster, which I would have said was impossible, but it was as if after one time, Lachlan MacKeane had learned how to play my body like a violin tuned to him and only him.

After I orgasmed again, I was barely able to open my eyes and watch as he sat back on his heals and brought himself to quick release with his hand. Had I been capable, I would have offered to help, but I was too insensate to do more than watch from beneath the lashes of my half-closed lids.

He came with a feral growl that was definitely inhuman and his seed landed across my stomach with a heat that felt more like a mark of possession.

He collapsed next to me with a groan, one arm thrown over his head, and I smiled as I swore he mumbled, "Fook me." Again.

I might have dozed, I couldn't be sure, but one glance at the candles, half of which were spent, like me, half of which were barely hanging on, and another glance out the window to see the moon had definitely moved further along across the sky said I'd dozed for at least a couple of hours.

But I had awoken with one thought on my mind. "Lachlan?"

"Mmhmm?"

"Why didn't you tell me I was your mate?"

Chapter Thirty-One

Lachlan
Why Didn't You Tell Me We Were Mates

AND JUST LIKE that, I was awake, my post-orgasmic bliss gone almost as if it had never existed. My inner wolf howled against my denial. *Yeah, I ken. It did happen. I didnae mean it.*

I crawled out of bed, and Josie sat up, then pulled the sheets up to her waist. I liked that she didn't cover her breasts, but perhaps, she merely forgot because she was too concerned to think about it when she asked, "Where are you going?"

I laughed, but I felt no humor. "I need clothes if I'm going to have this conversation, Josie Bell."

"Oh," and there was that word again. I feared I was going to come to hate that word coming from her delectable lips. Then, she added, "Wait."

I waited, completely comfortable in my own nudity as she made some sort of complex gesture with her hands. In an instant, my clothes reappeared on my body, but in the right size this time. I was almost disappointed.

Almost.

"Thank ye," I mumbled, then, "I see ye didn't use yer wand."

She shrugged. "Technically, I don't need it. It really only helps me focus my intentions…my magic."

That was interesting and not something they'd taught when I'd taken witch studies at university.

I pulled out a chair and settled into it, angling it to face the bed…it was far too dangerous to join her on the bed after last night's mind-altering orgasms…and leaned forward, my elbows resting on my knees, my hands loose between my legs. "What do ye ken about the mating habits of Lycans?"

Had I not found myself in a suddenly disagreeable mood, I might have appreciated the slight blush staining her cheeks.

Still, she lifted her chin, and I truly was impressed by her confidence. "As a Spellmaiden, we are fully educated in all the major species of magical beings under our protection. For all shifter species, we are particularly educated regarding the differences between mated and unmated shifters."

She had an interesting way to put it…*our protection*. Particularly when she'd been engaged to arrest me, but that point was irrelevant for the purposes of our discussion. Instead, I nodded. I expected no less. "So ye think I kenned ye were my mate the first time we met?"

She dipped her head.

"I didnae."

"How is that possible?"

I carded a hand through my mess of hair and shrugged. "My best guess? My clansman, unbeknownst to me, had purchased a magical shilling that was supposed to protect me from those hunting me."

She cocked her head. "You mean me."

I nodded. "He was worried I would be arrested before I discovered who had framed me for murder." A small smile curled her lips, and once again, I couldn't help but admire her confidence. I felt, dare I say it, *pride*, at her capabilities. "Aye, turns out he was right to be concerned, clearly, but the coin didnae work." I couldn't help but narrow my eyes with a scowl, I was still somewhat irritated—and impressed—she'd done it; she'd taken me to gaol. "…but just before my arrest, we discovered there was more to the coin than Hugh had bargained for. Fortunately, I hadn't touched the coin myself. Still, it was powerful enough to curse me through proximity, and I think this curse affected my ability to detect my mate…you."

Josie Bell whistled. "That is some powerful curse. Where is the coin now?"

"One of yer sister Spellmaidens has it, a witch named Ivy."

Josie nodded her head. "She lives next door to me, actually."

I couldn't help but admire her in that moment. She looked deep in thought as she considered the implications of everything I had revealed.

"When did you realize I was your mate?"

It was a fair enough question. "I started to suspect at the battle arena, especially when we managed to escape what should have been inescapable. It should only have been possible if I had combined my powers with my mate, but I didnae ken for sure until—"

She groaned and squeezed the bridge of her nose. "—Until I kissed you."

"Aye."

She dropped her hand to the bed, "So why didn't you tell me when we were in the gaol."

I shrugged. "Ye might no' have agreed to get me oot. At the time, freedom was my biggest concern."

She seemed to think that was a reasonable explanation.

"Ye should ken, I would have escaped, eventually. But I rather preferred to do so before I turned insane with the moon rise."

She groaned. "You have to complete the mating ritual, with me, before that or you will go insane."

It wasn't a question, but I answered her anyway. "Aye."

"And there really isn't another option for you is there?"

"Och, love, there are always options, but sometimes, none of them are palatable, ye ken?"

I could see she understood me perfectly.

"I had thought something was wrong with you in the gaol."

"I was already showing signs of insanity."

"Why aren't you now?"

"Who says I'm no'? If anyone could make me insane, it's ye."

At this, Josie Bell smirked. "Goodness, MacKeane, do you flatter all the ladies this way?"

I shook my head. "Decidedly, no'"

"You seem perfectly normal to me now," she mused.

I stood then, stopping as my knees hit the side of the bed. "Oh, Josie, I am anything but perfectly normal, as ye will soon discover, but to answer yer question, being near my mate staves off some of the insanity, even makes me stronger."

She seemed to preen at this, just a bit, but then she frowned as she asked, "Is this curse why you couldn't shift."

"The curse, the spells on the gaol cell…there were a lot of things affecting my ability to shift. I'm not even sure I can now. Still," and it *chafed*. Inside, my wolf whined his agreement at this thought.

As if she could sense my inner wolf, Josie Bell flashed me a look of empathy.

Which made me wonder, "How did ye ken we were mates?"

"Oh, um, Anglesey's ritual."

Of course. "And do ye feel our bond?"

She shook her head in denial, but I wasn't sure she was telling the truth.

To test my theory, I crawled onto the bed, and leaned into her until my lips brushed the shell of her ear. "And now?" I whispered. "Anything?"

I heard her swallow, and I pulled back enough to see her bite her bottom lip. Still, she said, "No," though her tone of voice was unusually bright.

I leaned back in, and inhaled her scent into my lungs, right at the base of her nape where her neck met her shoulders. She smelled delightful, and my cock was definitely interested. So was my wolf for that matter. I placed a gentle kiss on her neck, then added a few more as I traced the edge of her jaw. "Nothing?"

I smiled when she stifled a groan, and my smile grew even as her husky voice said, "Um, yes. I mean; Yes, I don't feel anything. At all."

"Little liar…" I whispered, amused despite everything. She could deny it all she wanted, but I knew better.

And I knew better than to let this proceed any further.

Finally, I pulled back and rolled on to my side saying, "Go to sleep, Josie Bell."

I hid my smile when I heard her silent curse as she turned her back to me and settled into bed. She fluffed her pillow rather forcefully before she added, "Good night, MacKeane. Tomorrow, we have a demon to capture."

I let her believe that. I didn't tell her we had a different item to see to in the morning. I didn't want to ruin her rest, but there was no way we weren't going to do something about my curse first.

My life … and hers…depended on it.

Chapter Thirty-Two

Josie
We Have to See a Witch About a Curse

The next morning…
One day until the full moon…

THE NEXT MORNING arrived with Lachlan MacKeane wrapped around my body like a fitted glove. Or a tight coat. Or more like a customized curse based on the grumbling going on behind me as the duke pulled away leaving my backside feeling rather chilly.

He wasn't the only one. Normally, I wasn't at my best in the mornings, either, but this morning, despite the glorious orgasms we traded last night—and they were, indeed, glorious—I was feeling decidedly off. More so than usual. I would never admit this to him, but I was torn regarding which task we should accomplish today.

I had a job to do. As a Spellmaiden, I had taken an oath. An oath I took very seriously, and not just because Spellmaidens were Spellmaidens *for life*. I was already pushing the boundaries of that oath by breaking Lachlan out of gaol. That in itself was a gross dereliction of my duties.

I had convinced myself I could put this man back in gaol once he'd helped me complete my task, but now? I know he felt confident the gaol couldn't hold him completely, and I somewhat believed him, but that didn't matter, really. Sending him back to gaol with the full moon so near was akin to a death sentence and no amount of trying to convince myself it wasn't my fault, that I was just doing my job, sat well with me.

In fact, I was seriously contemplating just letting him go, and inexplicably my heart ached at the thought, and I nearly groaned. Sure, he'd tended to my quim wickedly well last night, but that was no reason to put my job, and therefore my life, on the line.

Though, goodness, the man did have a magic tongue.

I shoved that thought out of my head and rolled all the way onto my back. I glared at the ceiling while the duke, nakedly—the man had removed his clothes at some point in the night—crawled out of bed. In the cold light of day, I refused to admire his magnificent body. Refused.

He grumbled while he hunted for his clothes, and I convinced myself I was merely being petty when I chose not to use my magic to help him out again. It wasn't really because I kept peeking at him as he sauntered about the room in the nude and collected his things. Not at _all_.

I could tell he was pulling on his trousers when he grumbled, "Tell me again why we didn't hunt this demon over cover of darkness?" because I definitely wasn't watching. Mostly.

Huh. It seemed someone besides me woke up with clouds over his sunshine. "The darkness doesn't offer any advantage. The whole cover of darkness thing is a myth, magic being the great equalizer. So, we might as well go about in the day where at least we can see where we're placing our feet." An important consideration in some of the less favorable areas of London.

Lachlan growled. "Lycan, remember? Keen eyesight. I don't need the daylight either."

I snorted. "Sure, MacKeane. How about, then, so I can see where I am placing my feet?"

The wolf folded his arms across his massive chest. I knew this without looking his way. I steadfastly refused to look at him.

He all but barked out, "Somehow, I do no' think ye need to worry aboot that either."

The wolf was threatening to put me in a foul mood as well, and I threw back the bed clothes. I had switched back into my day wear while beneath the covers, and now, I dragged myself from bed fully dressed and in no mood for MacKeane's obvious cantankerousness.

I also ignored the rush of pleasure his compliment made me feel. "Whatever you say, duke. Then, how about we go get ourselves a Class I Demon. It is what I helped you out of gaol to accomplish." I really needed to just perform the task I was assigned. I wasn't responsible for his mating issues. The man could take care of himself.

Liar.

Lachlan didn't move. "Aboot that. We need ta take a wee detour. I need to go see that witch. Lady Ivy."

I shook my head. "I assure you, wolf, we do not."

Naturally, he had to argue this point. "If we don't do this, ye're going ta have more than just the demon on your hands. I'm going to become a very inconvenient hindrance to our success. Our close contact has staved off the insanity fer now, but as the full moon draws nearer—in just over a day, I might add—I'm going ta be fighting instinct and the onset of insanity. Do ye really want ta be fighting the demon as well as me?"

A burst of desire raced across my nerve endings as my mind immediately supplied very detailed images of me fending off the wolf's *need*. In that moment, I hated that I wasn't fully opposed to the idea of saving him with sex. The sex would be fantastic.

Out loud, I asked, "How can Lady Ivy help you?"

He rubbed at the back of his neck, and in that moment, I hated seeing such a competent man show any sign of discomfort.

"I do no' ken that she can, actually, but I'm hoping that since that cursed coin brought aboot our matehood—" he shrugged.

"You think by breaking the curse, it will take care of your

problem."

"Aye."

It might, but I wasn't actually convinced, but then what else could he do? There was no known way to stop the impending insanity other than death.

Well, besides, completing the matehood before the moonset.

Could I do it? For that matter, could he? He seemed pretty adamant that he wanted no part of a matehood. It wasn't personal. But to the point he'd die to avoid an unwanted matehood?

Everything in me rejected that idea.

"We need to see Lady Ivy."

"All right." He *was* right. It was his only palatable option at this point, and I was not so callous and cold so as to force him to see to the Demon first. The Demon was safely tucked away for now.

"Do you need to send Lady Ivy a note first, or something to that affect?"

Lachlan clearly didn't know about Spellmaidens and their special abilities to communicate with each other. I opened my mouth to explain when a knock sounded.

MacKeane turned to the door, and I had to suppress a small smile. He was quite agitated indeed if with his Lycan hearing, he hadn't noticed the knock hadn't come from the room's door, and while he futility went to answer it, I turned to the room's lone window.

He grumbled, "No one's there," as I lifted the sash.

"Good morning," I announced to our returned visitor.

In the alley below me, a curious vine of English ivy lifted a familiar squirrel to my window. This time, the squirrel was actually wearing clothes. Fancy clothes. And she had kohl around her eyes and a blush staining her cheeks. Or was that rouge? And was that a beauty patch on her left cheek? I only just refrained from shaking my head with a fond smile just as I spotted the tightly folded note within her small grasp. I crossed my arms, bemused, as the squirrel tried her best to see past my shoulder. Eventually, she asked, "Is that young man here?"

Behind me, the Lycan cursed, and I said, "He's busy."

The squirrel stood on the tip of her toes to no avail. "Are you sure?"

"Yes, I am, thank you," I nodded toward the note in her hands. "Is that for me?"

The poor thing definitely sounded bothered when she sighed and said, "Oh, well, yes, this is for you," and she reached out to hand me the letter.

I was just about to grab it when I saw the squirrel's eyes fill with complete adoration as a familiar hand reached over my shoulder and plucked the note out of her paws.

"I'll take that," came a familiar Scots brogue.

Before me, the squirrel actually giggled like a young school-girl.

I leaned over to block her view of MacKeane and handed her a coin, saying, "Thank you for your troubles."

She mumbled something about, "No trouble at all, dear," as I very carefully and gently closed the window, then turned to face the room.

Lachlan had already retreated to the far wall. He leaned against it; his arms crossed; his seemingly good humor restored.

I relaxed against the wall on my side of the room and returned his stance, fully unconcerned by his behavior. I knew better. He was about to find out.

Lachlan smirked as he asked, "Mind if I read this?" as he dangled the letter in front of him.

I tipped my head giving him permission but remained in place. "Be my guest."

His smile dimmed a little, likely at my confidence, but he didn't break eye contact as he opened the thing. He shook it out several times to flatten it, then eventually dropped his eyes.

He mouthed a few words as he pretended to read the thing to himself, but my own grin never faltered. I knew better.

Eventually, he refolded the paper and spent an inordinate amount of time recreasing the fold.

I raised a brow in the universal sign of 'Are you finished?' and he said, "That was utter gibberish."

"Imagine that." My voice dripped with sarcasm.

His eyes narrowed at my flippant tone, but he didn't say anything.

I shrugged. "Why don't you let me try?"

We met in the center of the room, but he didn't release the note right away. "Ye ken I would no' be able to read it."

I nodded. "Spellmaidens, and witches for that matter, are not inept. We well know the chances of our missives being intercepted is high considering the nature of our work."

With a grumble, he released the note, and then it was my turn to open it without breaking eye contact with him. "Don't worry, Lachlan MacKeane, better men than you have tried and failed to best us," which only made him grumble louder.

Eventually he asked, "Aren't ye going to read it?"

"With pleasure," and I glanced down.

The words, initially gibberish as Lachlan had discovered, began to swirl immediately until they reassembled into English, and I was pleased to see it was from Ivy, which I had suspected based on the vine outside our window. I read the note to myself first, just in case there were any private messages just for me.

For his part, MacKeane wasn't pleased with this, and he impatiently asked, "Well. What does it say?"

I didn't look up as I replied, "It says, 'Don't go kissing any wolves.'"

To his credit, despite the dire situation he was in, he chuckled. "Too bad the horse is already oot o' the stables on that one. What else? Or is that all?"

"Yes."

"Then, why are you still reading?"

"I'm not."

"Josie Bell, yer eyes are literally moving back and forth across the page as ye mouth the words with yer lips, and ye've clearly read more than five words at present count…"

"Are you counting?"

"Not really."

"Good."

"Wait. Now, ye're blushing? What the hell aren't you telling me?"

I shrugged. "Nothing that matters." How could I possibly tell him Lady Ivy's warning not to kiss him, which he knew as I'd already said as much, had led to a ridiculous and uncouth part of my imagination to follow up her warning by contemplating whether it counted if the kissing wasn't on the lips…or er, mouth?

And now, I was blushing all over again; I could feel the burn in my cheeks.

"Josie—," my name ended on a low growl, which I felt everywhere, though I refused to admit, even to myself, that I enjoyed teasing him, but since it all *did* affect him, very much, I decided to help a wolf out, and read:

"Dearest Josie,

Enclosed please find the coin which cursed our mutual friend.—"

"Wait," the duke interrupted. "I didnae see a coin."

I didn't even look up as I replied, "That's because she used a spell to hide it so nobody inadvertently touches the thing."

"Oh."

At his response, I couldn't help but glance up. "Shall I continue?"

He gestured at me. "By all means."

"I'm sure I don't have to tell you that the coin has an especially creative, ingenious, and dangerous spell attached, so don't let anyone, but especially His Grace, touch it. As you might have guessed, I discovered the witches echoed signature, but I can only determine that the witch who created the curse is one of

*our own and one of the witches from House Sermos. They will
explain everything. I'd make haste.*

Yours,
Lady Ivy"

MacKeane sighed. "Is that all?"

I shook my head and added, "*P.S. Don't go kissing any wolves.*"
I didn't add the part that read, '*not that I think you'd ever do that,*'
for obvious reasons. I wasn't naïve enough to invite the sort of
questions that remark would engender.

MacKeane laughed again. "So, she really did say that?"

"She did."

"Wonderful."

I wasn't sure what his tone implied. He seemed more
thoughtful than aggrieved in that moment, and I carefully
refolded the note, my own thoughts awhirl. Using magic, I sent
the note to my purse for safe keeping since the cursed shilling was
still hidden within. It didn't escape my notice I'd been using an
awful lot of magic…more than usual…since Lachlan MacKeane
had entered my life.

"So," I said, "I suppose we're off to The Dikter."

"The Dikter…," he groaned.

"It's the house for the Sermos witches."

"I ken."

I was reasonably sure he only thought he knew, and what he
knew was basically the same as what everybody knew: that the
place was the most unobtrusive…and deadliest…house on the
planet.

The Dikter was oh, so much more…so much *worse*…but it
wouldn't be very effective if everyone truly knew what to expect.
I thought I should probably tell him the truth of what we faced.
Later.

Lachlan's voice softened unexpectedly when he asked, "Josie,
are ye sure? You broke me out of gaol to capture a demon."

I swallowed. "Of course." *Why is he asking? Isn't this what he wants? Does he want me to risk his sanity by tackling the demon first?*

When I looked at him carefully, the confidence in his gaze provided the answer, '*Because he trusts you to make the right decisions.*'

I refused to be pleased by that thought. Refused.

"What about the demon, lass? Can ye sense him?"

I nodded.

"Have ye…I do no' ken…looked in on him? This morning, I mean?"

I shook my head and started putting away my things in preparation to leave. "I don't need to."

"Ye don't?"

"No. I can just…sense him. I don't know how to explain it. I think if he tries to do anything, I'll know immediately."

"Where is he right now?"

"Still in his cave, recovering."

MacKeane narrowed his eyes, clearly not liking my pronouncement. His response echoed that sentiment. "Then, we best hurry back and break this demonic link as soon as possible. Perhaps, we should—"

"No. You said it yourself, MacKeane. I can't fight you both. We go to The Dikter first."

"And then?"

"And *then*, we have a demon to capture."

"Agreed—"

"Followed by a couple of links to break."

"To the demon…"

"And…"

"And me. Before the moonset."

"Yes." Why did it feel like a lump was suddenly pressing down on my chest?

I shook my head and tried to steel myself. I determined right then and there I would make it right. Somehow.

Chapter Thirty-Three

von Rappoldstein
When an Insanity Spell Cast by The Insane Backfires
Otherwise Known As
Destined for Glorious Purpose

THE DAY BEGAN with an auspicious start. With me. Playing darts. I only ever partook in the past time when I needed to think. Deep thoughts. It was simply never a good day when I resorted to darts to figure things out.

As if on cue, I tossed three darts in quick succession. *Thunk. Thunk. Thunk.* And asked aloud, "Why did I go through all the trouble of releasing the most fearsome demon in a millennia, only for him to simply take refuge in a cave in the woods and contemplate—well, whatever demons like him thought about when they weren't doing other more destructive things? *All the gods*, you just can't find good demons these days." *Thunk.* "Bullseye!"

I threw both my arms in the air in a sign of victory. Unfortunately, there was no one about to notice or celebrate my skilled, er, dart-ing. Nor to answer my very important questions. Or at least, nod appreciatively at my clever musings. I was merely talking to myself. Out loud.

Sometimes, even I needed expert advice.

As I retrieved my darts from the board, I glanced over to my soul scales, which stood not-so-innocently on the small table by the window. The scales weren't at all in balance and were leaning heavily on the side of good, *dammit*.

"Your scales are out of balance," I remarked. Oh, I was still alone. That was just me. Talking to myself. Again. I returned to my starting position and lined up my next shot. *Thunk*. Twenty points.

"Tell me about it," I grumbled. *Thunk*. Forty-five.

I paused to glance over at my reflection in the full-length mirror on the far wall and raised a brow in silent query. My reflection did the same. Somehow, I felt less a candidate for Bedlam's Division X (where the magically insane were held) when I spoke to my reflection rather than just to the empty air surrounding me, though even I knew better than to think the very air we breathed was ever innocent of listening ears.

Nor that my reflection was blameless of any wrongdoing. *He* was guilty of a great many things.

That was especially clear, when I saw myself ask, "Why don't you try using Essence of Toad?"

Actually, it was an excellent idea, and I had to ask myself, "Why *haven't* you tried using Essence of Toad to complete the spell your favorite Lycan hired you to conjure?"

I'd been trying, with little success, to complete the spell for some time now, hours it seemed, but perhaps it was only a handful of minutes, and I was making little progress. I wasn't precisely sure where I'd errored. Or more importantly, where the book had gone horribly wrong with its recorded list of ingredients.

But as the possibility of success via the proper application of Essence of Toad began to suggest itself, I dropped my darts to the floor in wonder—fortunately, I missed all my toes seeing as how I was barefoot—and raced to my dungeon, murmuring, "If I only use part of the demon's claw again and try the Essence, I could make a very small sample, and—"

"Yes," I interrupted myself. "That could work. That could really, really work—"

"—And then our wolf will be ever so thankful, he'll—"

"—Oh, yes, I can envision it now. He'll gladly thank us in that way," I whispered suggestively.

I simply loved it whenever I could delight in my own clever ideas like that.

Unfortunately, my brilliant plan failed, which I only discovered when I woke up, somehow, on the chaise longue in my study, just as a beautiful red-headed angel came into my limited view above me, clear concern in his azure eyes.

As I reached out to touch his familiar face, he seemed to ask me, "What happened?"

Since when did angels start speaking with rough, Scottish brogues?

I shook off such a ludicrous question and asked one of my own. "Are you an angel, my pet?"

Why did my tongue feel fat? And why did my words sound slurred? For that matter, how did I end up here? Last thing I recalled, I was in my dungeon working on…something.

That familiar face offered what I somehow knew was a rare laugh, and said, "I'm far from an angel, my lord."

Indeed. I could see that. Angels never quite looked so wicked, though they definitely were, but I really didn't care in that moment, so long as my angel kept trailing his fingers through my hair that way. I failed to recall Angels never touched anyone. The thought seemed rather unimportant in that moment.

Especially as every bone in my body seemed to ache. I was quite sure something was broken. Perhaps, more than one thing. And I felt a trifle disguised. Very, very disguised…er, drunk.

My beautiful man opened his mouth to speak, when a disembodied voice (not mine this time) interrupted what I was convinced was about to become a very, very heated kiss. (In fact, I still had my lips wildly puckered in obvious welcome as I turned to face the voice, which said, "Vincent, what have you done with—"

My guardian angel was practically atop me as we both stared at Lady Sophia as she waltzed into the room speaking. When she finally glanced our way, she froze in place, her eyes wide.

It was my angel's delicious Scottish brogue which asked, "Lady Sophia? What are ye doing here?"

Startled, I glanced up at who I was coming to realize was my favorite Lycan and not an Angel, or at least, not an actual angel, and *dammit* I missed whatever name Lady Sophia called out in question. For I *still* didn't know my wolf's name, and I narrowed my eyes as I realized Lady Sophia *did* know, and had never said a word, curse her.

I needed to curse her. Unfortunately, courtesy of our odd bond, I had yet to succeed in that department, and on that thought, I realized, I was starting to come back to myself, if only a little at a time.

And really, it looked as if my little wolf had a few more secrets of his own I had previously been unaware of, judging by the look on his face as he stared at Lady Sophia.

I couldn't help but ask the obvious, "You two are acquainted?"

Satan's Best Friend replied, "We've met."

While my little wolf...fine, he wasn't so little, simply flexed his jaw before murmuring, "I've seen her around."

Now, they were *both* lying?

"You know," I pondered as I shoved the Lycan off me and sat up. *I was not pouting.* "I may be slightly insane, but I still know when someone is keeping secrets." I was the only one allowed to lie in these relationships, dammit.

Lady Sophia ignored me. "Where's your brother? And Josie Bell? Word has it—"

Was this her poor attempt to deflect unwanted questions? And truthfully, the real question was—is she working for someone else, too? Someone who is not me?

My wolf spoke up; his eyes narrowed. "What are *ye* doing here, Lady S?"

I liked the way my wolf seemed to be hovering over me, as if he wanted to protect *me*. The greatest villainous witch of all time.

"I don't really think that's any of your business, young man. What are you doing here?"

Neither of them seemed willing to answer the other, only deflect, and I scoffed at the entire absurdity of it all. As if on cue, they both turned to look at me, but it was Lady Sophia who asked, "What are you about, von Rappoldstein? You seem guilty."

I shook my head with a fond smile, and replied, "Oh, I'm guilty of a great many things…it's my purpose in life after all, but what specifically do you mean, this time?"

Lady Sophia

Five hours later

I WINCED UNCHARACTERISTICALLY as another chair flew through the air and crashed into a rather large mirror. It seemed overt insanity was the theme of the day today. Perhaps, the week.

The screeching voice pained my sensitive feline ears as this villainous witch proclaimed, "They can't be allowed to complete the matehood because then they would be unstoppable, Lady Sophia. You must interfere or all hope is lost."

I bit back an aggrieved sigh. We'd been over this before, more than once, but I reminded the witch anyway, "The coin is already doing its job, obviously."

Which wasn't the response anyone wanted to hear. Especially said villainous witch, who did not disappoint.

"I don't care. I don't want to take a chance. The coin isn't actually a sentient being—you are! I want no mistakes this time!"

Gracious, the absurdity was getting quite out of hand. As well, the mood swings, and I had to wonder if power without the caveat of being required to make anyone my familiar ever again was even worth all this.

It was a fleeting thought. One, that still had the same answer. Yes, it was worth it. I wanted to keep my powers without having to have a familiar. Ah, but this time? The villain was about to lose it, and I wasn't sure I wanted to be here when she did.

Chapter Thirty-Four

Josie
Your Secret is Always Safe With Us...Or You Die. Free of Charge!

Designed in the fashion of a storybook home, number Eleven Coven Square, also known as The Dikter, looked as if pulled straight out of a fairytale, complete with rolling roof lines, rounded windows and a charming, if antiquated, thatched roof. The blinding sun dazzled, shining brighter here than anywhere else in the whole of England, and I knew from experience, no cloud had ever dared hover over this particular house and its grounds. At least, as far as anyone could remember.

Perhaps, even the clouds feared The Dikter.

The front garden, a traditional-looking English cottage affair filled with an abundant mix of flowers such as roses, hollyhocks, and peonies, seemed to smell sharper and more fragrant than I thought possible. Even more so than Hage Hus (or Green House) which housed the Planta witches (witches who drew their power from plants, who, as you might expect, had notoriously green thumbs.) Even the birds here, which fluttered, darted, and danced about every corner of the lush grounds, appeared more numerous and more colorful and sounded *more* vocal and sweeter of song than any bird ever heard.

Sound too good to be true? Certainly.

And irrelevant because despite all of this incandescent innocence all but saturating the very air, The Dikter did not soothe. Rather, the *almost* innocuous façade elicited feelings of distress and discomfort, even fear.

Fear augmented by the antithetical contrast between what one *saw* and what one felt whilst standing before this particular house, and its singular, if deadly, power.

If that weren't enough (which it was plenty), there were the words, which literally floated about on currents of air—substantive and brightly colored entities that were such a peculiar and unexpected sight, you might question whether you were, in fact, hallucinating.

You were not.

The words were very real and every bit as conspicuous and compelling and *dangerous* as one might expect something so impossible to be. More so, even.

Sometimes, The Dikter house words proved brutally fatal.

Needless to say, it behooved everyone to tread carefully when approaching the home of the Sermo witches of Coven Square…witches who drew their power from the very words we speak, which is very much not the same as any other magical being using words to cast a spell, even a complex one.

Sermo witches could draw power from a poem. A thought. The very words themselves.

Oh, the women who lived here weren't, as a general rule, evil. The Dikter, as with all houses on Coven Square, simply had its own idiosyncrasies, its own dangers, its own unique defenses.

Visitors beware—even perpetually-happy-but-decidedly-deadly Lycans.

As if my thoughts bestirred him, Lachlan chuckled and lifted his arm, and quick as a cast spell, I slapped it away, then muffled him with a hand across his open mouth before he could speak. "Don't!"

Naturally, his eyes darted to mine, and he scrutinized me

with a thoroughness that left me breathless.

I shook off the odd sensation and gradually removed my hand, gingerly adding, "Don't touch. And try not to look too closely."

"Why—"

I mentally chastised myself for being so focused on getting to the next step, I hadn't taken the time to prepare Lachlan for what we would face here. Never mind that I was being considerate towards a man wanted for murder. Allegedly, if his claimed innocence was true.

When had I forgotten that important detail? And why do I keep forgetting it?

Despite that timely reminder and my uncharacteristic behavior, I carried on, convinced I simply didn't want to contend with the inconvenience his death on my hands would produce. "From now until we are actually in front of a Sermos witch we keep our voices down," I hissed. "There is magic here. Reading the words, *touching* the words, letting them touch you, even, might be construed as casting a spell. And such spells are often unpredictable. Sometimes, deadly."

"Fook m—"

I slapped my hand over his mouth once more. "Perhaps it's best if you just don't speak at all."

I nearly laughed at the very idea of a man like Lachlan MacKeane *not* speaking. Could he even manage it?

His eyes narrowed and my lips twitched at the unexpected laugh that tried to bubble up and out of me at the look on his face. I felt his smile, saw it reflected in his eyes, a moment before he nipped my hand, producing a bewildering shiver which bolted down my spine. Swallowing, I did my best to ignore the sensation and explained. "L-like all the houses on Coven Square, The Dikter has its quirks and randomly chooses to assume a person speaking out loud is, in fact, casting a spell. The results are always—er, unexpected."

Gracious, had I just stuttered?

Lachlan winked but had the good sense to *not* point out what might be *misconstrued* as discomfort—or worse, *awareness*—on my part. In that moment, I was quite sure my face warned what I daren't put into words: speak aloud what's on your mind and I will make you regret being born.

His sense of self-preservation appeared to be in good working order because what he asked was, "So what's the trick ta gaining entrance to The Dikter? I assume there's a wee key to unlock the door *and* survive the experience."

Boy, was there ever—I hated *the key to unlocking the Dikter over every other house on Coven Square, and if you knew what some of those keys involved, that was saying something.*

Only a fool would think something as 'simple' as the perfect secret *wasn't* dangerous.

Aloud, I said, "You're smarter than you look."

At his are-you-mocking-me look, I had to fight back an unexpected grin, which wouldn't do *at all*. Locking such thoughts away, deep down in my dark, little metaphorical box of emotions, I continued, "Naturally, the house has a unique key. They all do, and as you might expect, the key is tied to the type of magic the witches who live in it have."

"Och, aye. Let me guess…words are involved."

I nodded just as a brief burst of laughter escaped my lips. Worse, I felt a corresponding flash of heat dust my cheeks. I wanted to pretend neither had happened. And yet I dared him to remark upon my aberrant behavior with a brief but pointed look and said, "You have to tell it a secret."

"Surely, no' just a secret."

I scoffed. "Of course, not. If you lie, you die. If it's not actually a secret, you die. If your secret isn't deemed worthy enough, you die."

"What if ye do no' have a secret?"

"Don't be silly," I answered. "Everyone has at least one secret."

He flattened his lips.

Ha! The fool. Fine. The answer was simple, after all. "If you have *no* secrets, you die, and," I nodded toward the almost-but-not-quite-innocuous looking slate with ears mounted by the front door, "If you walk over there and state your secret out loud—"

"Och, let me guess." He pretended to think for a moment. "Ye die."

I patted his arm. "Gracious, I dare say you're getting the hang of this."

Judging by his low growl, I don't believe he appreciated my obvious sarcasm. "Anything else I should be aware of—any more trivial details ye've yet ta impart?"

"In a nutshell? Every person has only one secret The Dikter will accept, and it already knows what that secret is. Get it wrong…?"

"Ye die." He said it as if he still didn't quite believe me, the fool, and he appeared every bit unconcerned for his own safety, despite my dire warnings.

I gestured at the house. "Magic." Which, to be honest, really said it all.

"Och, aye. Magic," he agreed.

And like the optimistically-leaning—dare I say, fearless—man I was beginning to know (if reluctantly, right? *Right?*), he clapped his hands together and with a voice laden with amusement, said, "Well, then, what are we just standing aboot here for? Let's share secrets."

"…with the door," I clarified.

"Aye, lass. Whatever else could I mean, love?"

I wisely refrained from answering that. He wasn't the only one with a honed sense of self-preservation.

An unexpected shadow fell over us, and I winced when I realized I'd forgotten one small little detail—the Poet.

"Er, duke?"

"Aye?" Thankfully, the duke stood immobile, as if aware that nothing here was as it seemed.

"Do you see that shadow?"

Lips barely moving, Lachlan replied, "Ye mean that shadowy wee outline aboot ten feet away of a man in historical garb wearing a tricorne with an ostentatiously sumptuous feather, which is currently floating a few feet above the ground and whose posture suggests, if one didnae ken better, he is simply a harmless, jovial sort? *That* shadow?"

Ah, he understood. "Precisely. He is not."

"What? No' harmless? No' jovial?"

"Yes. To both."

"Enlighten me. Does he spit fire from his non-existent eye sockets? Or, since this verra house is full of word witches, from his mouth?"

"Er, not exactly."

Though I daren't remove my eyes from the shadow before us, I could sense Lachlan's growing exasperation. Perhaps, it was his second, low—barely discernable growl. I smiled, despite the seriousness of our predicament. "He's called The Poet."

Lachlan sighed. "The Poet. As opposed to the house, which is also the poet," he said, and I found myself pleasantly surprised he understood The Dikter reference.

I nodded confirmation, though Lachlan didn't so much as glance my way.

"I ken I'm going ta regret this, but please, tell me more."

"Well…he might whisper soothing words in your ear and entrance you through suggestive reasoning."

"Och, is that all," his tone was decidedly sarcastic.

"He can fill your head with ideas not your own, including ideas that are not remotely in tune with your personal desires, wishes, morals…"

"I've heard worse." I knew he was being sarcastic.

Speaking of, "He's been known to interpret your own words as indicative of wants, desires, and spells and can take your words quite literally. Sarcastic idioms are particularly dangerous. With careless words, one could inadvertently create a new spell and execute it without even realizing it, and with unexpected, sometimes lethal results."

"Fook m—"

He cut himself off. *Fuck me—or us—indeed.*

"Oh, and try not to face him when you do need to speak because he can read lips, which is just as effective as if he heard you say them."

"Of course." His voice dripped with heavy sarcasm.

At this point, I honestly felt I didn't need any further words from Lachlan to know precisely what he thought, so after a pause, I carried on. "The house can perform the same, er, trick." I imagined Lachlan figuratively dragging a hand down his face. "As can the house's resident soul."

"I'm almost afraid ta ask, but who—"

I nodded. "Shakespeare."

"Of course. So why have they no' tried anything."

"Technically, we haven't crossed the official line of the house's property. For now, they're just warning us."

"Anything *else* I should ken?"

Once again, I winced internally. "The witches here are responsible for, er, keeping a couple of important books here."

"Oh? Which ones?"

"Well, there's the *Book of Bargains*, the *Book of Arcane Thought*, and the *Book of Enchantment*."

"Children's books, perchance?"

I snorted. "Hardly." Why did he bring out this side of me...a better side of me?

"Right. Deadly books."

I nodded. "And the *Distinguished Book of Runes, Sigils,*—"

"For godssake—"

"—*and Symbols of Greater England, Scotland, Wales, and Ireland*—"

"All the gods—"

"—*not Counting the South Downs*."

"Why not the South Downs?"

I shrugged, and he gave me a look.

"Yes, it's a ridiculous title."

"But deadly."

"Precisely."

"And we're just going ta walk inside."

"In theory."

"In theory."

"Do you often repeat things people say?"

"Only when I'm overcome with disbelief at the utterly outrageous things coming oot of her mouth."

"Oh."

"Right. So, tell me this, then. Why are we just standing here talking aboot it all as if there's no' a deadly, dangerous shadow standing ten feet away, staring at us…or whatever the equivalent is when it's a thing missing actual eyes or anything physically corporeal?"

"Listen, it actually helps. Keeps him from dropping suggestions in your mind if you keep your mind occupied this way, or at least, away from him. And do stop staring at him."

Lachlan shook his head.

"Turn your back if you have to."

"Lass, a wolf never turns his back on a threat…"

Gods, that was sexy.

So far we'd managed to mostly turn our faces when we spoke or spoke out of tight lips, but I could sense Lachlan grew tired of all this talking without any forward action, but The Dikter was no laughing matter.

I chose to ignore his last comment, and suggested, "Thinking about utter nonsense helps," I added, "Gibberish is especially effective."

"Wallysuperfrasticmaston."

"Quite."

"Will he try ta stop us if we attempt ta go inside?"

"Who knows."

"Right," he said with a sigh. Then without warning, Lachlan reached for my hand. "Come. Let's go."

I didn't want to release his hand, which was concerning. I certainly didn't want to entertain precisely why I didn't want to release his hand. I let go anyway. "The secret, remember? I can't hear your secret."

"Right," he all but growled.

I let him go first. I needed to watch in case he tried to tell The Dikter he didn't have any secrets, which would consequently lead me to having to save him from certain death.

My eyes followed his form as he climbed the steps of The Dikter. I was impressed when he didn't even hesitate. He simply leaned in and, presumably, whispered what could only be a small, handful of words before he straightened, confidence apparent in the way he held himself. Without pause, the magic dispersed, and I well knew I was in trouble.

For in that moment, I *desperately* wanted to know his secret.

Chapter Thirty-Five

Lachlan
A Curse Upon You

Inside The Dikter...

I REALLY DIDN'T appreciate the secret I had to reveal to enter this house, and it turned my general good humor foul, but the moment I crossed the threshold of The Dikter, I knew I had better focus on the here and now over anything and everything else. Besides, there'd be time to contemplate what I'd revealed later. Unless things didn't go my way. Like if I went insane and died. Unfortunately, the chances of that eventuality were remarkably high.

The House Sermos witch who greeted us looked more like the type of witch humans imagined when they thought about witches (if they thought about them at all) than any actual witch I'd ever met in my life. She wore a black, pointed hat with a band of leaves of all sorts, which might have made you think she was a witch from House Planta if not for the odd words that appeared and disappeared in various places in the very weave of the hat's fabric, none of which made any sense at all to the casual observer. Based on what I'd already experienced, that was probably a good thing. Who knew what sort of demon I might summon or what spell I could cast should I actually be able to read any of the words, particularly while standing in the receiving room of The Dikter?

And just in case I was fooled into thinking that she was a mostly harmless young woman, the wide brim of Lady Samantha's unusual hat shaded the top half of her face such that the only thing one might make out about that general area, was her piercing grey eyes, which seemed to understand who you were down to your very soul with just a look and could curse you just as quickly, if not faster.

And just to remind me that the witches of House Sermos were as contradictory as the innocent-but-far-from-it house they lived in, her personality was such that she was everyone's best friend.

Until she wasn't.

And let us not forget all the dire warnings one hears about the house itself. Things like, 'it puts ideas in your head not your own,' and 'say one word wrong, and the house thinks you're casting a spell or conjuring something you shouldn't.' By all accounts, we should be quaking in our boots. How did the witches who lived here survive with their own sanity intact?

Perhaps, they didn't?

Five minutes after our arrival, Lady Samantha (the aforementioned Sermos witch) asked, "Who wants you dead, wolf?" Obvious humor colored her tone even though my situation was far from humorous. Without awaiting my answer, she continued, "This has to be one of the most interesting curses in all my thirty years of being a Spellmaiden." (She didn't look a day over twenty).

Lady Samantha looked up and glanced at me over the top of her spectacles, spectacles which hadn't been there before I'd blinked, but could somehow make out through the shade of her hat like a frame for her piercing grey eyes, "Someone went through a lot of trouble to curse you and drive you insane. Who would do such a thing?"

Josie Bell snorted. "I'm sure the list is long and distinguished."

I tossed a low growl in Josie's general direction. As for Lady Samantha, she called this interesting? Rather than convey that thought, I waited for the witch to elucidate. She hadn't actually told us what she'd uncovered in the space of a glimpse. For a coven of witches who drew power from words, this witch, I would come to learn, had a very roundabout way of getting to the fucking point.

Josie nudged my arm, rather uncharacteristically, I thought. "Must be someone who knows you. Right, MacKeane?"

"No." I shook my head in denial, and I knew I was being abnormally serious and curt. Josie Bell knew it and tossed me a speaking look. I couldn't help but explain, "Lass, I'm impulsive at the best of times, but in a day or two, my normal is going ta seem perfectly staid by comparison, and then I'll be more dangerous than that Demon who's running loose. No one I ken would risk unleashing such havoc on society."

Josie tossed me a wry smile. "Relax wolf. I wasn't serious." When had Josie and I changed personalities?

I shook off that thought. She might not have been serious, but the possibility of it being someone close to me could not be ignored, despite my clear denial and the very real reasons behind it. My heart *ached* at the very idea, even as my mind rejected such blasphemy. Which one of my friends, or worse, my family, wanted me dead? Or at least, insane and out of the way? I knew the obvious answer but I daren't give voice to my fears, my mind so thoroughly rejected the idea.

I shut the door on such thoughts and turned my attention to Lady Samantha. I dipped my head toward the coin on the table between us. "Tell us about the curse."

Lady Samantha nodded her head in agreement. "It really is rather clever. From what I can tell, the coin was designed to make you insane."

Josie nodded, adding, "But everything backfired when Lachlan never actually touched the coin."

Lady Samantha pointed a finger at Josie Bell. "Precisely. And as we are all aware, employing magic can have unintended consequences."

Josie Bell seemed to grow more excited by the minute, which made me frown. They appeared to momentarily forget my presence, their mounting enthusiasm at solving the riddle making it seem as if they forgot the consequences to me were very fucking real.

"Yes!" Josie all but exclaimed, "so the coin, rather than just outright making him go insane, found another way."

Together, they turned to face me, twin smiles of delight spread across their respective faces as, together, they said, "An unrealized matehood."

"Wonderful." My tone was decidedly sarcastic, though I felt my lips twitch as Josie and Lady Samantha all but celebrated over their own cleverness. I shook my head, somewhat bemused, somewhat exasperated. "But if the coin brought Josie and I together wouldn't that go against making me insane? Wouldn't the verra real possibility of us actually becoming mates, therefore becoming stronger together, be considered a major flaw with this plan?"

Lady Samantha agreed. "Yes, but I think it's safe to assume the coin intended for you to trigger the matehood but planned to throw obstacles in your way to prevent you from finishing the deed, but then the coin moved out of close proximity, and though the curse was very real, it actually comes down to pure luck that you cannot yet complete the ritual. Not until the full moon, at least."

They called this lucky?

Josie asked, "I don't understand why it would mask the fact we were mates. If it wanted us to k-kiss? Wouldn't Lachlan knowing I was his mate actually ensure that eventuality?"

"Nae," I answered, "I never had any intention of taking a mate. Ever. I suppose this coin or spell or whatever the fuck we're calling it would have known I had no intention of claiming a mate. My entire family knew I hated the prospect of having no choice in the matter."

Josie frowned at that, and I rubbed at the sudden ache in my chest.

Lady Samantha confirmed. "Yes. That makes sense. The coin would have anticipated that."

I was still confused over Josie's sudden change in demeanor, the frown still turning down the corners of her mouth. Out loud, I asked, "Ye speak as if the coin is sentient in its own right."

Josie shook her head. "I-if that were the case, the coin would have all but leapt in your hand the moment it came near you, for there are far easier ways to achieve the same result."

A moment of real terror flashed across my mind at the thought of that happening as I ignored Josie Bell's uncharacteristic stutter. Worse, I knew I wasn't terrified of actually being rendered instantly insane, but rather, of the very idea of never having had the opportunity to experience…everything—hell, anything…with Josie Bell. The shocking ache that followed had all but exploded behind my chest and had me rubbing at the area almost absently. My wolf agreed and echoed his displeasure.

I was sure I was missing something important; I just couldn't put my finger on precisely what. Or maybe, I just hated the feeling of everything being wildly out of my control. I valued my freedom to choose above all other things, which was ironic for a Lycan. "We still don't know who created the curse?"

"Actually," Lady Samantha interjected, "we do know it was a Sermos witch, all curses like this leave an echo, a signature of sorts that points to the type of witch…"

"Aren't there only three of ye living here?"

"Yes—"

"So, it should be easy to figure oot who did it."

Josie nodded her agreement, after wiping the sweat from her brow, but said, "Sure, but who created it is rather irrelevant."

"It doesnae feel irrelevant to me." Also, it wasn't actually hot in here.

Josie Bell flashed a sympathetic look my way, but disagreed as she fanned herself, "Of course it doesn't feel that way, but the real problem isn't who created the curse…various people hire witches to do this sort of thing all the time…the real question is who actually paid to have it done."

"Exactly," Lady Samantha agreed, and she reached for a thick, ornate book on the table at her elbow, which wasn't there two seconds ago. "This is our spell log, a record of every curse, spell, potion or magical object ever created by a Sermos witch."

The tome was monstrously large; someone the size of Lady Samantha shouldn't even be capable of lifting the thing, which she absolutely did, without magic backing her up. Or at least as far as I could tell.

Josie nodded. "All witch houses have one; it's actually required by law."

"So, we look to see who requested and paid for my curse?" Somehow, I didn't think it was going to be that easy, and my impatience to find answers grew as Lady Samantha thumbed through the book, her frown deepening as she continued. Based on the size of the book alone, we could be here awhile.

Eventually, she stopped, her face grim all of a sudden. Then, she looked up and caught my eye. I simply returned her stare, and I sensed Josie shift uncomfortably beside me.

It was Josie who asked the question on both our minds. "What did you find?"

Lady Samantha tore her gaze from mine and looked at Josie Bell. "I see where the curse should be registered, but the information is missing, which is impossible, or rather, should be.

Of course. Aloud, I said, "Clearly no'." I shoved away from the table and began to pace the room. It seemed we were wasting time. Still, I pressed for more information. "Why don't we interrogate all the Sermos witches, starting with ye?" Lady Samantha scoffed, and I added, "I may be just a man, but I can be verra, verra persuasive."

I could have sworn Josie Bell mumbled, "You are far more

than just a man," which we would definitely be discussing at a later time. Still, she stopped me from making a mistake I'd regret with a gentle press of her hand on my arm. "Lachlan…"

I'd never heard her tone of voice sound so soft, so concerned, and I couldn't look at her. I *couldn't*. Despite everything in me demanding I glance her way. Instead, my furious gaze pinned Lady Samantha in place, who merely smirked. The witch clearly wasn't as concerned as she should be. Or I wasn't as concerned as I should be.

Josie continued as if I weren't minutes away from removing Lady Samantha's head from her shoulders, "We needn't bother. Whoever did this was powerful enough to remove the log entry; she wouldn't have overlooked a little thing like erasing the memory of the witch who created it. It's a cold trail."

"So, we're no' going ta try?" I thought I might find immense satisfaction if only I could knock a few heads about, never mind I'd never actually harm a woman, call me old-fashioned. Or at least, I wouldn't harm one without just cause. Though right now, I felt like I had more than enough reason to justify such a course of action.

I locked eyes with Lady Samantha. "It could have been you."

Unsurprisingly, she agreed. "It definitely could have. It's highly likely, in fact, but I'd never even know it."

Exasperated, I glanced at Josie. "You said she? Why do you think it's a she?"

"Oh, that's easy. Because only a woman would be so clever."

I laughed, I couldn't help it, and after everything I'd heard this day, I would have been foolish to doubt her, or any woman for that matter. Still, I wanted to pull out my hair. Or run away with Josie Bell, I couldn't even tell which; it was like I had already gone insane, forget about waiting for the full moon. "Bloody hell, doesn't all this bother ye? The verra idea of someone fookin' with yer mind…" The very thought was anathema to me.

"Of course, it does," Josie confirmed.

Yet they seemed far too calm about it to be quite believable, but then I knew I wasn't in the best state of mind to judge. Talk about insanity. Being a Spellmaiden clearly wasn't a decision one made lightly.

It only made me admire Josie Bell all the more, though in that moment, I wasn't even close to realizing it.

"So, the question remains...," Lady Samantha was the one asking it, "Who the hell wants you dead, wolf?"

"Och, that appears to be the question of the day, aye?"

I felt the urge to release my inner wolf and run off my frustration; I was all but climbing the walls at this point. Thankfully, Josie Bell was keeping a far more level head than I. She asked the questions I was too agitated to consider. "I assume if we destroy the coin, we break the curse?"

Lady Samantha nodded. "In theory. But it won't be easy."

"Will breaking the curse break the triggered mating bond?" I asked.

Lady Samantha shook her head. "Sorry, wolf. The curse merely brought you two together. The rest you did on your own."

"Fook me."

Lady Samantha shrugged. "The obvious and easiest solution is for you to complete the matehood...that would invalidate the coin." My inner wolf desperately agreed with that plan and all but howled his enthusiasm inside my head.

I laughed like a maniac. "No."

While Josie Bell sputtered, "Definitely not." She wiped the sweat from her brow, which by now was starting to grow alarming and obvious.

Lady Samantha had the good grace to wince (though the mean look in her eye said she didn't regret a single word) and added, "If there is a way to destroy this coin, I don't know of one."

The witch was serious and for a brief moment, I thought these women were simply too dangerous to be unleashed upon society. Their power was immense, and I suspected Josie Bell was the most powerful of the lot.

"Fook me."

"We'll find a way, duke." I was glad Josie Bell was confident in our ability to do so, but the pinched look on Lady Samantha's face suggested she didn't quite believe it.

"Maybe, we *should* keep the coin with us."

My head spun toward Josie Bell with almost comical swiftness. "And they say I'm the one losing my mind."

"No. Think about it. Neither of us want this matehood, correct?"

I dipped my head in agreement, though the ache in my chest flared once again and my inner wolf very loudly and very clearly rejected the idea. But *I* didn't. I'd only ever wanted complete autonomy over my own life. And besides, I didn't deserve a mate, did I? But I said none of those things, and I ignored everything in my body which rejected the very suggestion of not completing this matehood. I convinced myself we'd finish what we set out to do, and somehow, I'd either find a way out of this situation, which was so remote as to be laughable, or end it all through the regular means of every Lycan throughout history who didn't die in battle.

Finally, I realized what I was missing about the entire affair. "So how, then, did Hugh manage to find the curiosity shop but seemingly end up somewhere else?"

Lady Samantha answered, "Oh, that's simple, actually. Someone put a curse on the door and redirected him."

I laughed but I found none of this even remotely amusing. We were touching on what I didn't want to consider, after all. "Och, is that all? Ye witches really are frightening. People don't realize the danger, do they?"

The two witches shared small smiles, then, together, said, "We know."

"But how did this person hunting me know Hugh would be the one to go to the curiosity shop?"

Josie said, "I suspect she didn't know. All a witch need do is anticipate it would be you or someone connected to you, particularly someone from your pack, and you must admit, the chances of it being one of those people would be very high... So, again—who wants you dead and are you sure it's not someone you know? I suggest you find out who decided to go pick up this coin and work from there."

"You think it's a witch..."

Josie shrugged. "It seems the most obvious answer."

I wanted to deny the obvious.

Oblivious to my inner turmoil, Lady Samantha said, "Surprisingly there's no time constraint on the coin, someone made a lot of assumptions."

Josie Bell quipped, "I take it back, a man must have done this."

I growled, but neither woman cared.

Lady Samantha continued, "Destroying the coin itself will be next to impossible."

"But not impossible," Josie interjected.

"Nothing's impossible," I added.

"You both maybe right. Since you two are so keen on not completing the matehood, why *don't* you keep it as you suggested?"

"And literally go insane?" Were we really going to seriously contemplate keeping the coin with us? "I thought we were just tossing oot ideas no matter how ludicrous."

Lady Samantha shrugged.

And Josie added, "Well, it will ensure we don't accidentally have sex."

Perhaps, I was already in Bedlam's Division X? "How often do ye accidentally have sex, Josie Bell?"

She all but rolled her eyes. Or was she about to faint? "You know what I mean."

I did, but it also wasn't in my nature to ignore any references to sex, especially, if it involved myself and Josie Bell. "Since I'm the one who will end up dead or insane if we don't fix this, excuse me for having a lot o' opinions on the subject."

"What you two need is something more powerful than witchcraft." This from Lady Samantha.

Josie scoffed, clearly unable to imagine anything more powerful than witchcraft. And five minutes ago, I would have agreed.

Instead, I just realized I held the answer in the very ground of my homeland on Skye. We'd both have to go back to Scotland to do anything about it, and we really didn't have the luxury.

I glanced at Josie Bell, and in those moments, I saw everything I liked about her in a glimpse. And fuck me, but it seemed it came down to a matter of choice after all. Ironic, in a way, since that's all I'd ever truly wanted in my life: choices.

I could save myself.

Or, and don't ask me how I knew this, but somehow, I did, I could save Josie Bell. My instincts were never wrong. As strong as she was, as capable as I knew her to be, she needed me there. Fate had decreed it.

Fuck me.

I looked at her. Really looked. My eyes narrowed at the sheen of sweat on her face. The paleness of her skin. Wait. She truly was about to collapse on her feet.

In a flash of understanding, I grabbed her hand and pulled her back the way we entered with an angry, "Let's go."

"What? Wait. MacKeane? Wait. We have to fix this."

"Let's go catch ourselves a demon," I commanded, while I ignored thinking about the only obvious person to question about my current situation…the person who tried to hand me the coin in the first place.

Even my inner wolf all but shook his head in denial from within me, rejecting the very idea as inconceivable.

"But—" Josie sputtered.

I spun to face her and leaned in, fury making my voice low and dark, "Listen. Ye need me for this. I made a promise. I don't go back on my promises. Besides, I have a solution for my problem," *mostly*, "It will work," *probably*, "I'll be fine," *I hope,*

"For now, let's go catch ourselves a demon…*after* I reprimand you for spending the last hour using magic from within the most powerful house in the world in order to protect me in some sort of misguided—" I was so angry, I couldn't even complete the thought. I had to refrain from pulling at the ends of my hair in wild frustration.

"How did you know?"

I ignored her question and marched on, which conveyed in no uncertain terms just how pissed off she'd made me for she simply followed without complaint even though I hadn't answered her question. No wonder she'd looked overheated back there. She'd even had the nerve to suppress my instinct to wonder why the big bad scary house hadn't even tried to fuck with me in there. She'd been using some serious magic back there. It had taken a toll.

To say I was angry would be an understatement.

Lady Samantha called out to us from the room we'd just left, clearly happy to let us find our own way out, "So long as you stay together but don't accidentally have sex, you should be fine, right?" and her laughter, which sounded like more of a cackle than a laugh, followed us all the way to the front door and outside…

…While I ignored the raging cockstand her suggestion all but ensured, which made it all almost surreal.

Almost.

Chapter Thirty-Six

Josie

I Don't Think This Song is About Us, Do You?

LACHLAN MACKEANE WAS in a fury, that much was obvious. He all but marched down the front steps of The Dikter, all the way to the pavements of Coven Square, and even the words floating about the Sermos Witches' house moved out of his way, which was brow raising to say the least. As for the Poet, he was nowhere to be found.

I couldn't blame him. Lachlan MacKeane in a fury was a fearsome sight to behold.

Surely, I was having my own brush with insanity for liking it so damn much.

Neither of us spoke as we marched our way past number Twelve Coven Square, or the Mareritt (The Nightmare), where the Somnium witches lived, witches who could harness power from dreams.

And we'd almost made it past the pile of rubble in the center of Coven Square, when Lachlan MacKeane drew to a halt, then began pacing silent circles. After a few moments of repeated cursing, he let out a long, slow breath and turned to face me.

He leaned in. Close.

Suddenly, anger was no longer at the forefront of either of

our minds.

I licked my lips and watched his eyes darken with desire. "Are you trying to kiss me, duke?"

He chuckled lowly, and I felt his rumble of laughter in every place on my body that housed a nerve. "The thought might have crossed my mind. Afraid, love?"

"I-I'd have to care to be afraid," I teased. But gracious. His presence was *potent*. How did this man have the power to distract me so easily?

"Oh, you care. I can see it just…here." One finger caressed the place in my neck where he likely *did* see evidence of my heart thundering behind my breast, and a shudder lovingly slid down my spine. He noticed that, too, naturally.

Still, I shook my head. "Perhaps, it's fear that drives my pulse to race like a stampeding herd of rhinoceroses?" *Rhinoceroses? Where had that come from…my wits must be positively scrambled.*

His lips twitched in response. "Fear? From ye? I donnae think so. You're the bravest, most capable lass I've ever met."

The bravest, most capable lass he'd ever met? I practically purred in delight as I savored the compliment, *Dammit*. He knew just the right things to say to me. As if he *knew* me.

"No," he proclaimed, "Fear is never what drives you away."

"Of course not," I acknowledged for I definitely understood that denying myself the pleasure of his kiss required bravery…but I could never admit that out loud.

"Lass, what is our next step?"

He was asking me? My heart melted in that moment, just a little bit. He said he knew what to do about his problem, though he hadn't told me. Still, it mattered that he allowed me the choice when I knew what he was up against. It *mattered*.

He leaned even closer, his eyes on my mouth. We shouldn't kiss. It was a terrible idea; not to mention terrible timing.

Still, I found myself closing my eyes.

When I did not feel his lips caressing mine, I opened my eyes, observed Lachlan looking over my shoulder, and cursed the damned bespelled coin in my possession, which was clearly busy employing its powerful magic to keep us apart now that it had successfully brought us together.

For a moment, Lachlan looked thoughtful as he stared over my shoulder, and as I waited for him to speak, I imagined there were a million things he wanted to ask me. Turned out, none of those imaginings where what he actually asked me instead.

"What is all this?" Lachlan nodded his head toward the pile of stones in the field behind me.

"What is all what?" I asked as I searched his eyes for clues. I was so caught off guard by the unexpected query, I had to clarify he meant the pile of rubble that had lain there, in exactly the way it currently sat, my entire life.

He jerked his head toward the obvious again. "The huge pile of wood and stones and weeds in the middle of Coven Square. Ye can't miss it. So, surely, ye have no'."

"What about it?" I know I sounded obtuse as I turned to face the neglected center park of Coven Square, but there were too many other things he probably should be asking me about instead, that I couldn't quite believe he was asking about *this*. It had nothing to do with us.

He released an exasperated sigh, "What is it?"

I finally realized he was serious. "Oh, um, no one knows."

"What do ye ken no one knows?"

"Precisely, that, actually. No one knows. I've even asked our witch historian about it; she's a national treasure by the way."

I couldn't blame him for the look of disbelief he tossed my way.

"Yes, quite so," I reinforced. "All anyone seems to know is it's always been there. Even better, they've tried for at least a hundred years to remove the debris, and the next day it's all simply there again, exactly like you see here, as if no one has ever bothered to try."

"*Exactly* like this?" I could tell his question was rhetorical, and that he no longer doubted me.

"Yes."

"What do ye think it is? I'm willing to bet ye have a theory."

He was correct. "*I think?*" as if I needed to clarify whose opinion he sought, "I believe this is the rubble of number Thirteen Coven Square."

"I suspect ye're going to tell me there is no record of a thirteenth house."

"You really are a rapid learner...for a Lycan." I couldn't help but add the quip at the end.

He laughed, then mumbled, "These women must have nerves of fooking steel."

I couldn't prevent the small smile which curled my lips as I overheard his admiring remark. I cleared my throat. "If I may? Why do you ask?"

"Does something aboot it look different to ye?"

I wanted to scoff and question whether he'd been listening to me at all. But we had walked past this very spot on our way to The Dikter, and Lycan's were notoriously observant with all their heightened senses, so I followed his gaze, but it all looked the same to me...like the remnants of another Spellmaiden house which had fallen into severe disrepair. If by severe, one meant there were no longer any walls, roof, or floor to speak of, just a reasonably large pile of wreckage and debris.

Unfortunately, that day, I didn't even think to use magic to further investigate. There were simply too many other, more important things threatening our continued safety, or mainly, his continued safety, for me to give any of it more than a second thought. Besides, it seemed all that rubbish had been sitting about in the middle of this field for as long as anyone could recollect.

For his sake, I did look. And I shook my head when I saw nothing, just as I had expected. "I don't see anything."

I started walking again, hoping he'd follow, feeling a slight surge in my desire to go find my demon even though I knew said demon was still sleeping happily in his cave. It was probably a feature of the power I'd appropriated.

I didn't even realize I'd grabbed his hand as I began to walk away, until he pulled me to a halt, saying, "Stop. I think I saw something."

Once more, I followed his gaze. And once more, I didn't see anything amiss. But then again, he did have a Lycan's sense of sight. I supposed I could always draw on the magic from, of all things, a common horsefly, an insect with notoriously keen eyesight, but without having a before view with that level of detail (worsened by the fact that it was something I saw every single day and I didn't truly believe something was actually happening), I was just wasting energy and time. "I still don't see anything."

With a frustrated sigh, Lach moved to continue our way, only this time, we'd only taken a step, when once more he drew to a halt. "Stop—"

"I don't see—"

He held up a hand. "I think I *heard* something."

I darted a glance his way and discovered his lips were shaped into a smile, and I knew he teased me but was also very serious. I briefly considered calling on a friendly bat in order to borrow a small measure of their keen sense of hearing, just so I could one up his Lycan senses, but that would be petty of me, wouldn't it?

Instead, as a witch, even a powerful one, I didn't bother trying to listen for whatever sound Lachlan had heard, and I realized somewhere over the course of this adventure, I had begun to trust my wolf. I mean, the duke.

"What's this about, duke?" I only just refrained from calling him, Your Grace, even though I'd hardly done so the entire time I'd known him, despite it being the correct form of his address. I was not a Lady. I was breaking all sorts of societal rules.

I didn't care.

I suspected he didn't either.

And I considered him as he shook his head while he studied the mysterious pile of rubble. "I donnae ken…"

"Are you worried?"

"No."

"Are you sure?"

"Yes."

"Then, why are we whispering?"

He laughed good naturedly, for we were, indeed, whispering, and he said, "Fook me," but his words held no heat.

We were just turning to leave, when this time, I was the one barring our departure with a hand across Lachlan MacKeane's broad chest. "Did you see that?"

He thought I was teasing; I could tell.

"What?" he asked, his mouth shaped into a grin of pure mischief.

"Something's off. Don't you feel it?"

"Naturally, I feel it. Ye ken it's why I've been stopping ye every two feet to ask?" He laughed.

We both did. Then, we both drew silent, and I knew we both saw it this time, something had moved. One of the stones, which had been half buried in the grass, was now situated perfectly atop another stone, which had previously been sitting next to it.

"Is that normal?" he asked.

I shook my head. "Absolutely not. I think I'd have heard about it happening before."

"I didna think so."

"I don't like coincidences," I added, rather unhelpfully.

"Aye, me neither. But I donnae think this one has anything ta do with us."

"What a novel concept of late," I observed.

"Josie Bell?"

"Yes?"

"I do no' mean to sound as if I'm afraid."

I laughed at the very idea. Like me, this man was not afraid of anything. "Me either," I echoed.

"Och, aye. But also? I ken we should go now."

As another stone shifted out of the corner of my eye, I nodded my agreement with his suggestion and added, "Yes, let's go catch ourselves a demon instead."

I turned to leave, which was fine. (Despite the sudden change at the site being somewhat alarming.) Besides, I well knew I'd find myself ineffectually contemplating what might be happening here, sometime around three in the morning if I had to guess.

"Och, I never kenned I'd look forward to hearing such words from anyone," Lachlan agreed.

And as we left Coven Square and Lachlan MacKeane shook his head in mild disbelief, I could have sworn he added, "nerves of fooking steel."

Chapter Thirty-Seven

Josie Bell
The Witch's Circle

SINCE I HAD gone through the risky, though decidedly erotic ritual of borrowing a little bit of Incubus demon power, it was about time I truly employed my newfound skills. Besides, I had grown weary of sensing the demon's wants and desires, even if his thoughts manifested themselves as merely a low-level hum emanating from somewhere at the back of my mind, not to mention we didn't have the luxury of time. Fortunately, avoiding an investigation into a Class I Demon's innermost desires was a simple matter, for gaining such knowledge was something I really, really wanted to avoid if I could.

Therefore, five minutes later, Lachlan and I were well out of the magically protected Coven Square, and somewhat vulnerable, when we crossed into Mayfair proper, the human side. Fortunately, we had gotten an early start and it was still morning on a Friday, so there would be few people out and about where we were headed.

I hailed a hackney, then once we reached Hyde Park, we walked toward a remote area where I knew I could safely employ a protection spell before starting the demon's ritual. The red bracelets we wore were simply not enough protection while my attentions were so narrowly focused to risk doing it anywhere near Coven Square, particularly with the angels and bounty hunters about who we both knew were searching for us.

My favorite protection spell was quite a simple spell, really, which only required me to cast a circle, then make proper use of a bit of rosemary and some candles. Most people didn't even realize that a large part of witchcraft, including some of the most powerful spells, required very little tools to be effective. Our red bracelets were a perfect example.

Still, staying truly safe while I accessed my new abilities, required something a little *extra*.

So, while Lachlan earned my eternal gratitude (or at least slightly more than lukewarm affection for the next handful of minutes) by keeping watch for any interested parties, I began by clearing our chosen location of any debris, such as stray branches, rocks, or loose leaves while keeping them near at hand. Then, I turned to more spiritual matters and cleared the area of any negative energy by making use of my wand and some basic meditation along with a dash of crystal, clear intention.

To cast my circle, I gathered the cleared debris and created a definite ring of stones, twigs, and leaves about ten feet across, making sure the entire circle was complete from beginning to end. Naturally, I wasn't tall enough to require a ten-foot diameter, but I wanted to bring Lachlan inside with me since I couldn't offer him any assistance should trouble arrive despite my precautions once I'd started the ritual. Knowing I had everything I could need on my person or in my purse, it was time to invite the duke inside.

Fortunately, few people had come near our spot in the park while I prepared the area, and those that had, found their attentions redirected by design, and weren't in any way curious about whatever mischief we might be up to. Thus, Lachlan was once more set to his usual factory settings...playful and just a little bit charming...when I invited him inside.

He winked, and teased, "Och, apart from being brilliant,

capable, fierce, and stunning, what else do ye do for a living, Josie Bell?"

Brilliant, capable, fierce, and *stunning? Had I said a little bit charming?* He might have been teasing, or worse, handing me an obvious line; he might even be a little bit inane, but as I walked, clockwise, and placed a candle in each cardinal direction, green for the earth and north, yellow for air and east, red for fire and south, and blue for water and west, I was so unexpectedly flattered, I nearly stumbled over my own two feet. I caught myself, just, and ignored Lach's light chuckle. Naturally, he hadn't overlooked my misstep.

"Och, is something bothering ye, love?"

"N-no," I cleared my throat, "Nothing at all, Your Grace."

Honestly, all teasing aside, this time, it felt necessary to put a measure of distance between us by reminding us both of his lofty station in society. I was just a simple Miss, the only Spellmaiden who wasn't a lady, and he was a duke, practically the highest title in the land and certainly the most sought after by the unmarried female population of the *ton* (or at least, their matchmaking mamas). Still, I didn't miss the brief frown that turned down his lips as he no doubt made a note of what I'd done, and possibly why, and I felt a corresponding flash of despair. *Where had that come from?* I also, foolishly I might add, ignored the little voice in my ear who whispered, "He doesn't *have* magic; he is magic."

She sounded remarkably like my little imposter fairy, who was always prepared to remind me when I was about to chalk something up, even when I wasn't.

I shook off such maudlin and definitely-not-rational thoughts; it was time to Bless the Circle, and I turned my attention, fully, to the task though my every ritualistic action at this point was deeply ingrained and familiar. We couldn't afford for me to get caught up worrying about Lachlan MacKeane, and my unconscious partiality for him that I should really quit trying to deny. We would have quite a disaster, perhaps a deadly one, on our hands if I couldn't remain attentive to my task.

I briefly wondered if the coin in my possession was at work, using its own magic to interfere with our plans, but the exercise was pointless; we didn't have a choice, and in that moment, I knew I had to believe in my own skills if we were truly going to succeed. In my defense, I hadn't had the presence of mind to realize my errant thoughts were far from pushing me away from Lachlan MacKeane, which would be the coin's aim were it trying to expend its magic against us, and so I walked the perimeter of my circle, leaving a trail of salt while lighting each candle along my way without the proper care I needed to be aware of my surroundings.

Instead, despite my extraordinary efforts to focus, I was constantly aware of Lachlan MacKeane's *presence*, though he remained quiet as though he understood how important it was for me to concentrate, and simply watched my every move with an intensity I genuinely believed he couldn't help.

Oh, Josie, love, he is clearly anything but simple.

For a quick second, I actually envied him his ability to focus so intently, for though I normally didn't have any cause for concern, I also knew I was in danger of inviting real trouble with my distraction. Plus, negative energy, even in the form of thoughts and words such as envy, worry, and despair, could destroy my intention or create cracks in even the most reliable incantation as effectively as any purposely cast hex by any well-read witch, or villain, directed our way.

I did my level best to find the right words to establish my purpose for the circle as I circumnavigated the stones three times, while once more sending any negative or malevolent energies packing, clearly a few were quite determined to stay. And as my attention was caught once again on Lachlan doing literally nothing wrong, I knew I needed to reevaluate my normal circle casting routine. It was a matter of weighing the options against the risks. I was finally listening and hearing my intuition, which told me the longer I took to close the circle, the more distracted by Lachlan MacKeane I would be come. I had to decide which was worse, skipping a step that I traditionally included or risk the additional time and further inattention.

I chose to move forward with actually entering the circle myself, and as I did, I knew intuitively, I would be calling on Medusa, the Greek Goddess and one of three 'monstrous' *gorgons*, for help.

As if listening to my intuition opened an erroneously closed door in my mind, I immediately recalled how George had curiously been gifted a different type of gorgon and knew it hadn't been a coincidence, thanks to Lady Sophia's warning.

I knew it was important. For now, though, I had to ask the goddess, Medusa, for help.

On the heels of that thought, I realized someone was trying to push me into making a mistake, and I only grew frustrated at myself for being so distracted by Lachlan MacKeane, I hadn't even noticed the malevolent intent aimed in my direction. Only another witch would understand a witch was at her most vulnerable while she was concentrating on casting a spell, and the best way to find her at her most vulnerable, was ironically, (or perhaps not so ironically) while she's inside her cast circle. And the only way to penetrate *that*?

Forcing her to make a mistake while casting it.

Who would want to force me into making a mistake? I circumnavigated the inside of my circle knowing full well the other witch might have already succeeded in tricking me into casting an imperfect one; I was far too distracted. I needed to search for the mistake I undoubtedly made; I certainly wasn't about to begin my ritual when I knew I was ripe for an attack.

I don't know what prompted me to look. It might have been that Medusa had already decided to help, I thought I sensed her attempts to guide me, but as I looked at Lachlan MacKeane, I suddenly had to wonder, was it me they were really after?

"Josie?"

It took me a while to realize Lachlan had called me by name despite the fact I was looking right at him. So much for my inattentiveness.

"Yes?"

"Why Medusa? Isn't she one of the villains?"

Only if you're a man…

I swallowed back a smile at my own sense of humor, though I couldn't resist saying, "It's a common misconception, even amongst well-educated men."

Lachlan MacKeane chose to laugh and admire the quality of my wit. "Humor this rather unfortunate, inferior man."

I snorted at the very idea this man was unfortunate or inferior. He really, really wasn't. Further, I truly admired his ability to remain generally positive and optimistic, while I had to work hard to ignore my opposite attitude towards his entire species before I'd ever given him a chance. I managed to stifle a wince at the reminder of my own flaws.

Or so I thought.

An idea I completely discounted immediately as I turned to explain. "Witches have long known Medusa has been a victim of vicious vilification over the years; not that the goddess considers herself a victim by any measure of consideration. But tell me this…why would a woman, any woman, vilify another of her kind who was literally punished for being the victim of rape at the hands of a man?"

It seemed Lachlan MacKeane was smarter than he sometimes looked, for he said, "They would no'."

I had begun pacing as I lectured my man (my man?) and stopped to emphasize, "Exactly. They wouldn't unless they'd been fooled into believing a lie."

He nodded his head in thoughtful contemplation. "So, who would most benefit from having women believe such a thing?"

After a short pause, together, we faced each other and replied, "Men."

Lach's face took on a look of supreme satisfaction, while I suspected I suddenly looked genuinely confused. Because in that moment, I *felt* confused. No, I knew I was confused. I hadn't wanted to like this man at all, I could at least, admit that, and I knew, it really was rather obvious, that I was truly beginning to like this Lycan who was helping me. Who'd have thought it?

I forced myself to cease progress down that train of thought. I wasn't afraid, I just knew I was focusing on the wrong questions, knowing someone was clearly planning an attack.

Still, I couldn't help but add, "Many witches think Medusa's curse was actually a gift, for it was a woman who 'cursed' her, after all, and few women I know would understand how a woman could be so jealous as to curse another woman for the actions of a man. Even one she thought was her own. So, what if…"

It was Lachlan who showed me he truly understood me when he finished, "What if instead the woman really wanted to give Medusa the power ta never be a victim that way again?"

I smiled, then, a genuine smile since I *was* pleased by his accurate deduction. "Why, indeed. A gift, you see? Not a curse. For it gave her agency, something women so often lack. And since you're asking, I did summon Medusa to ask for her assistance, because I definitely believe the lesser-known version of her tale. Why didn't they teach you that while you were busy getting a degree in witch studies?" I knew I smirked then; I couldn't seem to help myself.

But Lachlan, who I was really beginning to understand, smiled with a pointed, sexy look and said, "I see someone has been thoroughly studying my file…did ye see something ye liked?"

Did I ever…

He chuckled and I briefly wondered if he'd read my mind.

His ever-present mischievous grin widened. "But honestly," he continued, "need ye ask?

I shook my head. "The course was established by a man…"

"Exactly," he replied. As if he were lecturing me. I had to laugh at the very idea.

His implication, though, had been obvious, and I responded with yet more out-of-character behavior, when I suggested, "Well, I am a *thorough* kind of woman."

I felt his breath dance across my cheek, *When had I drawn so close?* as he asked, "Oh, ye definitely are. I'm beginning to realize just how thorough, Josie Bell."

Was it getting really hot out here?

He closed the last of the space between us, his body now lined up tight with mine, and added, "It's one of the things I've admired about ye most from the moment ye entered my life. Right next ta your skill with taking down the villains in our world...," his voice had grown softer, if a little less smooth, and his eyes held an intensity I was beginning to crave.

I tried hard to resist; I had to lick my dry lips in order to reply, "Flattery won't get you anywhere with me."

He shook his head. "Och, Josephine Caroline Bell? I'm no' quite sure I believe that one, love."

The sound of my full name on his lips, with his delicious brogue had me feeling decidedly weak in the knees, assuming we weren't currently under attack. I couldn't precisely tell in that moment. *Mmmmm.*

... What the hell is wrong with me? I knew I was on the verge of climbing this man like one of the Duke of Anglesey's more challenging training hurdles.

But I chose to stop my ill-advised behavior with the perfect response. "I guess you'll just have to trust me." And with a small pat to his stubble covered cheek, and a quick glance down at not-so-little Lach, Jr, who was clearly harder than one of the stones making up my witch's circle, I turned and stepped away from this hard to resist man.

My own traitorous brain supplied, *And by hard, you literally mean it. Sigh.*

"Ouch," I heard him say from behind.

Which drew forth another small smile from somewhere deep inside me. This was beginning to become a habit.

For some reason, I wasn't bothered by what definitely would have bothered me before.

I refused to look at him when I asked, "So shall we continue with the proceedings?"

"Lead on, Josie Bell."

He really was a fast learner.

"All right, but first, I have to say I think someone's trying to interfere with our success."

From behind me, Lachlan growled and I could feel instant fury rolling off him in waves. I glanced his way and was relieved to see he was alert and scanning the world beyond our circle, looking for threats. It was exactly what I needed him to do.

"Keep an eye out for anything odd while I look for the mistake."

Lachlan's eyes remained alert, even while he snorted and said, "Ye? Make a mistake? No' possible."

I warmed at his compliment even as I replied, "Everybody makes mistakes…," for a moment he frowned, and I added, "but yes, I make fewer than most."

His eyes never ceased his vigilant search, though he smiled now, and added, "There's my witch."

My witch?

I ignored his remark and focused on locating the error.

In the end, I almost missed it; Lachlan's presence remained difficult to ignore. It turned out to be a small break in my circle of stones, barely discernable, but enough to have allowed *anyone* to slip inside while I was vulnerable to attack.

Relieved, I said, "Found it."

Lachlan moved to stand over me, his gaze never ceasing his endless search for threats. "The mistake that could have ruined everything."

"How long before ye've repaired it?"

I love that he didn't ask me *if* I could repair it. "It's already done." And I dusted my skirts as I stood, then turned to face him. "Lachlan, you can relax your guard." His eyes dropped to mine. "We're safe."

I hadn't even processed the meaning of his words before his lips crashed into mine.

Or had mine crashed into his?

I hardly knew who started what, and honestly, I didn't care. In that moment, I simply wanted his lips against mine...his tongue sliding against my own.

He only pulled away long enough to say, "Raise that clever little privacy screen of yers, love," before we were kissing again, and yet the entire time he spoke the words, my lips chased after his, desperate for more.

I moaned my relief the moment his lips settled upon mine once again. *And* I managed to raise the screen, which was a miracle, to be sure for I was already all but mindless with desire.

I reached for the old-fashioned cravat wound round his neck and began tugging at it, attempting to pull it free, my lips still locked with his, when something crashed against the circle's magical barrier, and we jerked apart.

What am I doing? This is the worst timing? What is wrong with me?

Or at least, any of those thoughts would have made perfect sense.

Unfortunately, none of those things were what really tugged at my mind, instead I thought, *Why did I ever decide to keep the coin with me?*

Because I knew the coin was actively trying to drive us apart.

Lachlan rested his forehead against mine, and I closed my eyes as we both worked to get our breathing under control.

And it was Lachlan who spoke first, "Are ye all right?"

"Yes." I loved that he asked that first.

"Are they gone?"

I reached out with my witch's sense even though I knew the answer without looking. "Yes."

"I presume the loud crash was someone trying to get through the circle? Or was it the coin?"

"Both."

"Bloody Hell."

I chuckled. And I knew he felt the same as me regarding the stupid idea of keeping the coin, though we both understood it was for the best.

It was for the best. It was.

And with a sigh, I pulled back from Lachlan MacKeane even though every inch of my body and my mind rejected my actions.

"We should finish this."

Lachlan dragged a hand through his hair as I admired his kiss swollen lips. "Aye."

Chapter Thirty-Eight

Lachlan
Catch a Demon By Its Toe

T HE RITUAL ITSELF was uneventful and felt disappointingly anticlimactic after everything else, but now, it was done, Josie's circle was closed, and I tried to feel some measure of relief. Now, Josie could use her borrowed power to take us directly to the demon.

"We best hurry," she urged from beside me.

I nodded but didn't speak.

"The demon now knows I'm coming."

I combed a hand through my hair. Of course. It was why we waited to activate this last bit, but it didn't make me any happier to know she stirred the creature's notice.

For some reason, I grew less and less thrilled at the very idea of Josie Bell in danger, which was ridiculous since it was the very nature of her job, and her skill was something I'd found so attractive and admirable about her to begin with. My alpha tendencies wanted nothing more than to put her somewhere safe, even though I knew she would have my bollocks strung up if I so much as hinted at trying to keep her safe, or worse, prevented her from being *her*. From doing her job. Hell, for even *suggesting* she wasn't more than capable.

I was so fucked.

In my defense, which really was more of an observation, half my brain seemed to be permanently lodged in my genitals, particularly whenever Josie Bell was around, which was all the time. Not that I wanted her anywhere else.

Fuck me.

I knew my voice was uncharacteristically gruff when I grabbed her hand, and said, "Let's go."

We had only taken a handful of steps, when Josie pulled back. "Lach?"

I spun around, the tone of her voice putting me instantly on alert. "Yes?" I scanned her face, looking for a hint of what drew her concern.

She closed her eyes briefly and said, "It's too late. He's already here."

Fuck.

I glanced wildly around. "I thought he was in a cave."

"He was."

She seemed entirely too calm. And his arrival was way too fast. "How do ye ken—"

She tilted her head with a pointed look, but I already knew it was an idiotic question.

Still, she answered me anyway, "As soon as he sensed me, he came to us."

As if summoned by her words the sky darkened ominously and a massive demon appeared about six hundred yards ahead of us…and bloody hell, I'd never seen one so large.

Nor one so dammed fast.

Josie Bell shoved me to the side just in time for me to avoid being trampled by the creature, and I nearly laughed at the irony of it all.

Wasn't I here to help?

I rolled to my feet, spun around, and could hardly believe my eyes when I caught sight of Josie Bell atop the creature's back. I was equal parts amused and terrified and knew right away, I was going to be hard pressed to help Josie Bell catch him rather than kill him.

My claws exploded from my hands as I raced towards them, my wolf and I equally determined to save Josie Bell at all costs.

"Stay back!"

It was Josie who said it.

Her words did nothing to stop my advance; I was too mindless with rage; my only thoughts being: *Danger. Danger. Save her. Save her.*

My mate.

I was so narrowly focused, I was stunned when Josie Bell whipped out her wand, all while riding the creature's back, and tossed *me* so hard I landed at least five hundred yards away from the creature and Josie Bell.

I was on my feet in an instant, racing back, single-minded in my purpose.

Even though I was somehow aware of what I was doing and what she wanted, but unable to change my actions.

Inside my head, Josie screamed, "I said, 'Stay *the hell* back.'" And followed that up with another blast aimed my way, which sent me another six hundred feet further.

This time, I could feel the weight of her magic upon my chest, holding me down. I roared my outrage, desperate to get to her.

My frantic desire proved successful. Even Josie's unimaginable power wasn't enough to stop a Lycan from trying to reach his mate, and I was on my feet, pushing towards her, though she fought me with her magic, every step of the way.

Worse, I knew I needed to stop. I was making everything *worse*. Josie Bell didn't need to be fighting us both, but I was only a man. And a wolf. My logical half was at war with my inner beast, and I briefly entertained the idea that Josie Bell would argue my inner wolf was my more rational, better side.

Was this the moment I ended up insane?

Because I surely felt insane in that moment. The very idea

Josie Bell was in danger was enough to do it.

Once again, I roared my frustration as now together, Josie and I fought against my own instinct to rescue my mate.

I had to do something. I could very well kill her with my desire to save her, talk about lunacy.

For a brief moment, everything seemed to slow as I caught Josie's eye, and we stared until I nodded her way. When she returned the gesture, I knew she understood, and with a third roar, which was echoed by Josie Bell, I was struck with such power, I flew through the air once again and landed hard with a painful, bone rattling thud.

My last coherent thought before everything went dark, was "Be safe, Josie Bell. I lo—"

Josie Bell
These Arms of Mine are Chewy

THAT MAN. IF witches had nine lives, I'd just lost at least one as Lachlan MacKeane went down. Before that, I had been all but stupefied by his immense power. I didn't believe I would have been able to defeat him had he not tried to fight himself.

I wanted to race to his side. To ensure he was all right. But I was first and foremost a Spellmaiden, and I had an assignment to complete. Humans to keep safe.

I hung on for dear life as the demon tried to force me off his back. I don't know how I managed it, but while I held on, I reached out to every animal in the vicinity and requested they do whatever it took to see no humans came around. As it was, I cringed every time this demon roared his fury. Someone was bound to come looking. I managed to hold on long enough to also send a raven to my roommate. She would make sure no one else got too close.

The moment the raven took to the skies, I relaxed just a bit in relief. It was enough of a distraction to see me flying through the air as the demon finally threw me from his back.

Thankfully, I landed in the opposite direction from MacKeane who still hadn't moved. But I couldn't worry about that. At least, I'd be able to keep the demon from turning his attention to the wolf.

"Good morning. Nice to see you again," I called up to the massive beast.

I could sense his confusion, and he suddenly stopped growling his ire and tilted his head at me, desperately trying to work out the reason for the change in my demeanor and tone.

I almost felt sorry for the beast. I had no idea why. He'd kill me if he had the chance. I knew that through our bond. He might have been curious about me, but he definitely thought I'd make a tasty snack.

"I wouldn't make a great meal, actually." I held up an arm and waved it about, showing him how thin it was. "You see this? Very little meat and what's there is tough and stringy. Even if you cooked me on a low, slow heat." I had no idea if that was true. I just wanted to distract him long enough to work out a plan. So far, it seemed to be working. He still just stood there and stared.

At least, he was quiet.

In fact, with all the animals off running interference; it was very, very quiet. So when Lachlan groaned, the sounded echoed through the clearing as if a cannon had exploded.

The beast turned toward the sound and I shouted, "No! No! No!"

I jumped up and down and waved my arms, but the creature seemed to have decided that MacKeane would make a tastier meal, the lazy beastie. He simply ignored me. For the first time in my life, I was tempted to disobey the parameters of my assignment. If I killed the beast, Lachlan MacKeane would be fine.

But that wasn't my directive. Even then, it still wouldn't be easy. Class I Demons were classified as such for a reason. With all my power, most magic I tossed his way would be about as effective as a finger poke in his side. And for a moment, a small moment, I doubted my ability to defeat this creature.

Unless.

My eyes narrowed.

For some reason, the beast had settled his hands on his massive hips as he looked MacKeane over. I could sense him contemplating how to handle the wolf, even though the wolf wasn't moving. His thoughts were slow and simple, but still, I couldn't blame him for his hesitation after MacKeane's brilliant display of strength.

But that was neither here nor there. The demon's stance had me scrutinizing his missing finger. It was still oozing green blood. What if I sent a spell directly into the open wound. It still wouldn't be easy. It's not like the beast would hold still for a moment while I got close enough for a direct hit. Most spells don't require a high level of accuracy to be effective, but with this beast...I didn't want to take any chances.

More importantly, though. I had a plan. Of sorts.

My plan settled; I didn't allow myself to question it; I simply charged him, thinking the element of surprise would work best.

I wasn't stupid enough to announce my charge; I just ran as fast as my legs could move me. I managed to latch onto the finger next to the beast's missing one before he even knew I'd started running. Thankfully. Or things would not have turned out so well for me.

On instinct, the demon raised his hand in the air. I knew he would only be stunned for a moment before he would finish me off. I was in a vulnerable spot, holding on to a digit so large I could barely wrap my hand around it. My fingers definitely didn't meet on the other side.

I only had seconds to act.

I only had one shot.

I drew out my wand, jammed the pointy end in his wound, and screamed the words of a spell to make him sleep. "Sove Somnum!"

He flung me, and as expected, I could not hold on. But I was alive, and had the skill to land on my feet, "Thank you, Anglesey."

The moment I landed, I locked eyes with the beast, who hesitated only a moment before he crashed to the ground with a loud snore.

I crumpled to the floor, laying supine and let out a long sigh of relief.

Gracious, that was close.

Chapter Thirty-Nine

Lachlan
Goodbye, Josephine Bell?

I CAME TO, sprawled on the ground, Josie Bell's beautiful face hanging over me. Her breathing was a bit heavy and erratic, proving I hadn't been out long, and her eyes were narrowed in anger. I laughed at the perfection of the moment.

Had I really thought Josie Bell would be standing over me with her brow furrowed with concern?

Not *my* mate.

Not Josie Bell.

"Welcome back to the living, wolf."

I nodded my head, or tried to, for I had a splitting headache. I froze and allowed myself to briefly imagine waking up differently, my head on her lap as she soothed me with worry and concern and love coloring her words.

But then had that been our reality, she wouldn't *be* Josie Bell.

"So much for my helping ye catch yer demon, aye?"

My eyes were closed as Josie remained close-mouthed for a bit and merely brushed her fingers through my hair.

"Josie?"

"Yes?"

"Ye ken ye never really needed my help, aye lass?"

She let out a long drawn-out sigh, and her voice was unusually subdued when she replied, "Actually, in a way, you did."

"Oh?"

She shrugged and bit at her lip, finally saying. "You managed to distract him."

"While unconscious?"

She nodded. "Yes."

I feigned a long-suffering sigh. "Och, aye, it was difficult, but someone had ta do it."

She shook her head, seemingly exasperated.

"But ye really did no' need me, ye ken?"

She absent-mindedly threaded her fingers through my tangled hair. "I know it."

I grinned, happy she had the confidence to admit it…to know it…and fucking proud she *could* handle such a feat on her own. I was man enough not to feel less than in the face of her immense strength and power. I *loved* that my woman was so damn formidable. I had to wonder at who her parents were. I supposed we would never know.

I climbed to my feet with more than a few groans of discomfort. I had acquired several new aches and pains I would likely feel for a week. I dusted off my breeches before standing tall.

Naturally, Josie hadn't helped me to my feet, which I definitely didn't need, but I craved her touch too badly to not crave that very thing.

For a moment, I caught sight of Josie's clenched fist and wondered if she fought against herself to reach for me.

I knew without asking, she'd successfully captured the demon—she'd not be standing there so calmly—despite my attempts to make everything worse, and a glance beyond her to an unconscious and bound nine-foot demon confirmed that fact.

I dipped my chin at the creature. "How—"

She raised a brow, her arms crossed, and I chuckled, "Never mind… So."

"So…," she echoed, but her voice was less questioning and

more just tossing my words back with a hint of anger to back them up.

I swallowed and rested both hands on my hips. "I-I cannae go with ye. To the gaol."

Finally, her fierce gaze softened. "I know."

I nodded my head, my throat felt *thick* for some reason. Still, I couldn't help but ask, "Are ye no' supposed to be taking me to gaol, too?

She inhaled, slowly, then added, "I suppose I should."

I froze. What was she saying?

She stared at me hard as she explained. "You need to take care of the coin first. You seemed to know what to do, right?"

"I have an idea, aye." I hoped she didn't press me with too many questions. I didn't want to lie to her. I wasn't sure if I could.

For a moment, we both paused, saying nothing. Then, she brushed some loose hair away from her face and asked. "Look— Will you tell me how?"

I knew she was asking how I planned to destroy the coin. "I can no'. I really can no'."

She nodded her understanding, but I could tell she was disappointed.

Fuck, I hated this. So damn much. But I couldn't tell her my family's secret and about the power of the ore. Even though I trusted her; it wouldn't be safe to even say the words out loud; here in the wide-open space. Where someone might overhear.

I wanted to ask her a million questions. Though I knew the answers to most. An important one being how had no human in London noticed what was going on, but I knew that the Spellmaidens had ways to handle such an eventuality, and I trusted she knew what she was about.

Then, she said, "Well, fix that first, and then I'll take you to gaol." And she handed me Ivy's letter, which still had the coin tucked magically away.

I took it, my fingers playing with the creases, but I only had eyes for Josie Bell. Somehow, we'd drawn close while we'd stood there awkwardly, a thousand unspoken words between us.

I chuckled as I tucked the letter in an inner pocket, then rested my forehead against hers.

She teased, "Oh, you think I couldn't find you, wolf?"

I was at a loss for words for once, yet every fiber of my being kept chanting, "Don't go! Don't go! Don't go!" in loud silence, but I knew I couldn't say it. She had a job to complete, and I wouldn't be the one to stand in her way if I could help it.

Then, she added, "I'm pretty sure I could find you anywhere, Lachlan MacKeane."

Wait. I pulled back and searched her eyes. "Josie? What does that mean?

Her smile was small as she pulled back, shook her head, and said, "See you around, duke."

Then, she turned on her heel and left.

Chapter Forty

Lachlan

Why Does Purgatory Resemble My London Bed Chamber?

IT HAD ONLY been a few hours since Josie and I parted ways and already I felt wildly unsteady…as if my impending insanity had simply been building up and then unleashed all at once the moment Josie Bell stepped out of view. As if I hadn't slept a wink in weeks. I felt drunk on lunacy. High on betrayal. Delirious with unfulfilled desire. This was the end; I just knew it.

Hell, the cracks had started showing before she'd even turned to leave, and it had taken all my remaining strength to simply disguise them from her notice, so she wouldn't even consider…not even for a moment…giving up on her mission. And, oh, I had wanted more than anything in the world to call Josie Bell back. Fuck, to never let her go to begin with. But I simply couldn't. For nothing had truly changed; we were never truly destined to be together.

To make matters worse, I hadn't told her I was off to confront my best friend in the world about the role he played in my impending demise, rather than see to the coin. It was better that way. She might have fought me on that and the thought had me smiling despite everything.

After preparing for the very real possibility of my death, I spent some time in a park just outside of London watching the sun set. Despite the urgency. I figured this might be my last chance. I would have loved to have spent my time on Skye, but I never would have made it in time. I just hadn't had the heart to tell Josie that before she left. She might have tried to do something inadvisable. Like release the demon and help me instead. I couldn't put her in that position. I couldn't ask her to make that choice.

And now, with the onset of insanity upon me, it seemed especially fitting to bring my best friend down with me through the very thing he sought to bring about, for tomorrow the moon would rise, and then, there would be no turning back.

I forced myself to follow through with what I had to do, not what I wanted to do. I focused on my very best friend and his clear betrayal.

That was enough to reignite my fury, though I still didn't want to believe he could do this.

Insanity needn't take my mind to end me, for my broken, shredded heart was going to do the job first.

Almost comically, I found my *friend* at my own damn house in London.

"Hugh Fooking MacKeane, ye arsewipe," I bellowed from the pavement outside my home. It was very late in the evening now, and still Friday, the day before the full moon, but why the fuck did I care what the neighbors thought of my belligerent cursing from the street? My very world was ending before my eyes.

I didn't wait for my so called friend to respond, I simply raced up the stairs, fury and desperate pain fueling my flight, and literally shoved the front door straight through and off its hinges as I exploded across the threshold.

The wood which used to make up a quaint exterior door landed twenty feet down the front hall, taking a few priceless vases and a bit of plaster out in the process.

My traitorous friend peered down over the railing of the third floor, a bizarre look on his faithless face. "Lach?"

The sight of my packmate's familiar visage left a crack in my very soul, and I let out a roar of incandescent rage which I couldn't even hope to hold back.

I was too infuriated. Too incensed. Too *maddened.* By everything.

Too maddened to notice how quickly I tore up the stairs.

Too maddened to consider why my friend just stood there and waited for me to reach him.

Too maddened to understand what his thoughts told me. Thoughts which might have said *if I were guilty of this, I surely did deserve to die* and *I already forgive ye.*

Too maddened to hold back my strength as I wrapped my hands around my best friend's neck.

Too *lost* to make sense of the look of understanding and forgiveness in Hugh MacKeane's familiar eyes.

Almost too maddened to hear the unexpected yet well-known voice enter my mind.

Almost too maddened to comprehend the words my very own *brother* spoke with uncharacteristic softness. "Lachlan…Lach. He didn't do it. It was me."

It was me.

It was me.

It was me.

Like a warning bell clanging in my mind, those words counted out the last of my sanity in seconds.

Had I thought my best friend's betrayal might end me?

Ha…how did I not realize that would have been far too easy. Not even close to being equal to the punishment I deserved.

But this? *This* betrayal. It was fitting. Merited. Necessary.

It was almost poetic, when I thought about it. I was the reason my brother and I were alone…the reason the rest of our family had died. Naturally, then, it fit that the only possible end to me would be at the hands of the very person I had failed the most.

And it worked. It broke me. Or really, I broke me, for wasn't this exactly what I just said I deserved.

I only had myself to blame. Never him. Never.

At my end, my fractured mind only managed to supply one final word, one final thought, and it was, "Jack?"

Five Months or Five Minutes?

Twice in one day?

Insanity, I am in your grip. Take me away.

I came to expecting to see something wildly different from what I actually saw about me, but I supposed it only fitting that the criminally insane went to Hades in a place which looked remarkably like my own London bed chamber. But really, I expected Hades, or some level of purgatory even, to be a lot darker, a lot hotter, and a lot more *eau de burnt dog hair* smelling than something so remarkably close to the average smoggy London air in the early spring of 1897.

I turned at the sound of voices, and at the sight of my brother Jack and my best friend Hugh standing in a shaft of bright moonlight and speaking lowly, I feared I'd somehow brought them to hell with me.

I must have cried out in distress because the pair suddenly turned my way, then raced to my bedside, calling my name and welcoming me back to the land of the living. My mind began to process and discard thoughts at an alarming pace, and yet a feeling of peace seemed to blanket me out of nowhere. That was when I registered a few other familiar, friendly faces.

Crowded along the far wall, I could see Lady Daphne and Anglesey and Lady Ivy (who I somehow understood was the one who calmed me) and George even, but the most important one of them all, I did not see.

It almost sent me into another fit state.

I looked to George, who had leapt onto my bed and began

kneading the mattress, for answers; she was his familiar after all. "Josie?" I croaked out.

He turned around once, then laid down along my side and started purring, and though he hiccoughed as if he'd had more than a few drams of whisky or two, his voice was steady, if a touch sleepy, as he said, "Relax, Your Grace. Josie's fine."

Of course, she was. I should have known. I *did* know, and yet I didn't quite believe it. Not yet.

My strength returned rather quickly after that, along with my focus, and I sat up in bed, though Lady Ivy warned me the rebound would only be temporary, possibly very temporary, which only increased my urgency in figuring out what I needed to do next. Rationally, I thought my next step should be: Find Josie Bell; the hell with everything else. I just wanted one last glimpse…one last taste of her sweet lips…before this evening's moonset made the insanity permanent.

I reached out with my Lycan senses, and determined the moon would be up in five hours and based on the strength of the pull; it had to be the full moon.

Which didn't make sense to me, I was disoriented and could have sworn that I had months of memories of hell.

Yet my Lycan senses were never wrong. To be sure, I asked, "What day is it?"

George laughed. "Still, Friday, lad."

Hugh laughed. "ye've been oot for five whole minutes."

I scoffed, and out of habit, said, "Five *entire* minutes. Not five half minutes?"

George shrugged, adding, "My watch says four and a half."

This was met with a few groans.

"That doesn't make any sense," I stated. "I've got weeks' worth of memories of hell in here. Months even." I pointed to my head, while everyone else eyed my brain box with more than a little suspicion. Fair enough. *Dammit.*

Anglesey offered a perfectly logical explanation. "It could be that fate had a hand in this." Everyone else seemed to think it a reasonable explanation, for they all nodded their heads in thoughtful contemplation with a few 'quite right's' thrown in for good measure.

I rejected the very idea out of hand, though a part of me...the often overly optimistic positive part of me...wondered, could it be? Could fate, after all my bellowing against her involvement in my life and all my belly-aching about how much I hated the way she threatened my own agency, could *that* fate have made all this possible?

I was afraid to hope.

But I could only hope.

Based on the look in everyone else's eyes, they were entertaining the same sort of hope I was.

I was too stunned to ask any more questions, and it was Jack who filled the silence with, "How did ye become separated from Josie Bell?"

I answered out of hand, "I let her go," because it was the truth. "Or rather, she left me. The result is the same."

Anglesey frowned with confusion, and asked the pertinent question, "What do you mean you let her go?" while several others scoffed with soft, but very real outrage.

Hugh added the expected, *"Fook me,"* to which everyone glanced his way with open questions on their faces and he added, "He loves her, of course."

Of course. I echoed in my mind, followed by *Wait. What?*

Like some sort of lunatic version of a Punch and Judy show, our audience turned to me, and I stupidly asked, "I do?" followed by, "Shut up. I can't even keep her safe." I laughed. "She had to fight me *and* the demon. And I don't...," love her. I couldn't even say it out loud, even in denial.

Which really didn't matter because everyone else replied in perfect synchrony, "Yes, you do."

"And ye *can* keep her safe," added Hugh.

"But she really doesn't need it," chimed in George.

A small smile began to form and I noticed everyone about me

was nodding their heads in agreement, every one of them wearing silly, ridiculous smiles on their faces.

Hugh slapped me on the shoulder and said, "Well, then you better go find the girl ye are definitely not in love with and tell her someone else is out there doing all this because she could be in verra real danger."

Fuck me. She *could* be in danger. I *should* go. But then hadn't she demonstrated time and again she could handle herself? Besides, if she were in imminent danger, I'd *know*. Right?

Besides, of the two of us, I was the one in bigger danger. I'd had a brief reprieve. Somehow. I knew better than to question such a gift.

I also knew not to squander it.

These reminders allowed me to keep my tone light despite the urge to go find Josie Bell right this minute. "You're right, mate. And I'm not in love with her."

I said it with a smile I knew Hugh didn't believe for a minute.

"Of course, ye aren't," Hugh confirmed.

But then a familiar throat cleared and I hesitated. "Wait... Jack?"

Jack wore a look of pure misery.

Och, my brother.

Despite everything, I no longer felt compelled to attack him the way I'd been after my best friend earlier when I thought he'd betrayed me. Hugh squeezed my shoulder in a show of support, and the small bubble of joy we'd momentarily enjoyed dissipated. The air grew palpable, the mood almost somber. I nodded at my brother. If Hugh and Jack stood there together without killing one another, there was a perfectly good explanation I needed to hear, and though I did want to go find Josie Bell, and I did need to save myself, I was also the head of this family, and I had a duty to them. I loved them. All of them. I could take the time to hear what my brother needed to say.

I reached over and slid my hand behind Jack's neck, bringing my forehead to his. "Och, lad. Tell me, brother. I'm listening."

I sensed Jack's wolf's whimper of misery, could sense Jack squeeze his eyes tight. His voice was gruff when he spoke. "I-I needed time. I just needed time."

"Time for what, *dearthái̇r?*"

Jack released a slow sigh. "To save Uncle."

Our Uncle, whose family had perished through my own impulsive actions had gone insane at the loss of his mate. It was my fault, and I had to live with that. But our uncle had gone through the ritual years ago. One last act of heroism to save human and magic-kind from the insanity of a Lycan without his mate...every mated Lycan was doomed to the same fate eventually, where reason would be lost to wild insanity. There was honor in death before that eventuality. So, I didn't understand. I thought back to those dark days. Normally, I would have performed the ritual for Uncle. Not just because I was responsible for his family's demise through my own reckless behavior, but I was the clan Chief. The duty fell to me. But I was also young. Grieving the loss of my own parents. Angry at our cursed fates. Angry at our lack of choice. My thoughts raced back to memories I had long sense buried. I recalled Jack comforting me. Owain, too. Hugh even. I remembered them being patient with me every time I had drunk myself into oblivion, which had been often in those days. Then, a memory surfaced. One so innocently sweet. Jack pledging a vow. Jack telling me I could count on him. Promising me he'd take care of it. Take care of everything.

I pulled back and met my brother's eyes and saw shame and grief and guilt in their tormented depths. I shook my head, rejecting what I knew he was going to say. My wolf howled his grief and whimpered his support, and I, aye, I knew. Oh, how I knew. "Ye did no' complete the ritual," my voice was barely a whisper.

Jack nodded; his eyes bleak; his voice choked with emotion. "I-I thought I could save him. I thought I could find a way..."

He didn't finish that thought, but he didn't need to. Yes, he wanted to save our Uncle. But really, he wanted to save *me*.

I shoved back the tears that threatened. I wasn't angry. I knew his actions came from a place of love. If anyone was to blame, it was me. I hadn't handled it well. I hadn't…

Jack put his hand on my shoulder and squeezed. "No. Och, no more blaming yerself, either brother. We're only perfectly flawed beasts. But ye, my brother, ye are the most honorable of us all. I failed ye. I tried ta make it right. I failed. I should have come ta ye. We both made mistakes."

"Aye, brother. I ken. We did. Both of us. And ye're so, so right." I pulled him close again, to let him feel my acceptance. My continued love. To know it. "Who killed the man I've been blamed for? Was it ye?" I hadn't wanted to ask. I was prepared for the worst, already knew I had forgiven him.

Jack looked so forlorn, but this was important. And yet, his answer surprised me. "Uncle did. Somehow, he escaped…"

Och, of course. It made so much sense now. And would have made my brother's feelings of guilt so much worse.

This time, I pulled him in for a full embrace, my arms squeezing him, patting his back, stroking his hair. "I forgive ye, brother." He needed to hear the words as much as I needed to say them. Family was everything for a Lycan. I needed mine as much as they needed me. Perhaps, at times I had forgotten that.

Someone cleared their throat, and Jack and I pulled apart; the pair of us swiping away the tears in our eyes.

"So, ye are responsible for my little cursed coin?" I tried to keep my tone light. To make him truly understand I already forgave him. That they weren't just empty words I'd said, but it was important to have this conversation. To know for sure…

Something's no' right, my inner wolf warned.

Aye, I ken, I replied.

I learned long ago to listen to my wolf whenever he sent such a warning.

Jack sighed and answered, "Aye, but I just needed time ta fix everything. I did no' plan for it all ta go wrong…"

I nodded. Even the best laid plans went astray. "Who even

gave ye the idea to get such a coin in the first place, brother?"

Jack scowled. *Ah.* He hadn't quite told me everything.

"Who?" I reiterated.

My hackles raised their warning a moment before Jack answered, "Lady Sophia."

Fook me.

I knew there was more to discuss, that I should seek out Lady Sophia, though she would be almost impossible to find. Instead, I felt compelled to find Josie Bell. My wolf echoed his agreement with an urgency I had never heard from him before.

I was desperate to know she was safe. Though, I felt more than a little bit of concern regarding how Lady Sophia was involved in all this, I still felt joy, pure joy, at the idea of going to find my woman.

My broad grin gave the truth away, and in that moment, I knew I really did love her. I would do *anything* for her. Even seek her out before handling my own cursed coin, I loved her that much.

But I wasn't about to tell all these arses that *before* I told the witch herself.

And if I had doubted for even a second longer whether I was in love with her, the fact that I could once more shift into my wolf laid the question to rest. I wouldn't have been able to manage it so close to my pending insanity if I hadn't. Not even to save my own skin, for we'd long understood as a species that Lycans could be mates, even perform the ritual, without first falling in love.

But that was definitely not the case for me and Josie Bell.

Through our bond, I heard my pack mates encourage me to go after her. Hugh vowed to go with me. To watch my back. While Jack said he would explain the situation to the others, who'd been largely left out of our conversation being that it was mostly a family affair.

I let out a wolfish howl as I raced on all fours across London just to catch up to my mate. My Josie Bell.

It was time to find all the answers.

And if fate was willing, it was time to end all this. One way or the other.

Chapter Forty-One

Josie Bell
What Do We Do With the Time We Have Left?

I LEFT MARSHALSEA Gaol after a very unsatisfying delivery of a certain problematic demon and after hours of bureaucratic nonsense, my normally calm thoughts were more chaotic than usual. I had so many questions on my mind. The biggest being, "Why did I involve Lachlan MacKeane when I had the power to catch this demon all along?"

I supposed I just didn't believe in myself. I thought I needed his help. Perhaps, I harbored some guilt at my role in arresting him, which meant at some point, I'd quit thinking about him as a job and started believing in his innocence.

As far as the angels who ran the gaol where concerned, I desperately wanted to ask *them*, "What happened to the Lycan I brought in a few days ago?" but then I might as well have walked in with a waistcoat bearing the words, "It was me. I released him," in big, bold, flashing letters.

That could prove somewhat problematic.

I had just crossed Angel Alley and turned a corner, when I drew to a halt, my heart pounding loudly in my chest at the sight before me.

His best friend, Hugh, stood a few paces behind him, but I

only had eyes for one man, Lachlan MacKeane. I just didn't know why he was here.

My face must have registered my bewilderment because he chuckled and asked, "Do you think I would really let you go to an *Incubus* to break yer connection to a demon?"

I laughed at that, but then his smile dropped, and he stood taller when I stated. "It's already taken care of."

He began to growl, and I shook my head saying, "Relax, wolf. I didn't have to pay a visit to the Incubus."

His shoulders visibly lowered, but only a small amount. "How?"

"I don't know, truthfully, though I intend to find out. The power just sort of snapped, and I could tell it was gone. It's likely a simple result of the spells warding Marshalsea Gaol coming into effect when I turned him over."

I could see my reply didn't help and added, "It *is* a concern, but I have enough power of my own to understand the bigger concern isn't about me. I'm more concerned about Anglesey, actually. Have you seen him?"

Lach nodded. "Not long ago; he seemed fine."

That was interesting, and not what I'd expected, but in light of this new information, a new plan began to form, but first. "Did you take care of the coin?"

Why did I feel a surge of hope as I anticipated his affirmative reply?

"No."

Wait. "What do you mean, 'No,'?"

"It's all right, Josie Bell. I've got it handled. Where are ye off to?"

My instinct was to argue this, but I had the thought I needed to trust him. To show him I trusted him, so I said, "Home, actually. Then, tomorrow I planned to go pay a certain friendly neighborhood villain a visit."

I felt something wasn't quite finished. For years, von Rappoldstein had been behind all manner of trouble the Spellmaidens had to clean up. This entire affair reeked of his involvement, and yet, surprisingly, I'd heard very little from his quarter, and that didn't sit well with me.

And then there was the matter of my probation, the lack of record of MacKeane's arrest, the lack of record of my getting the assignment in the first place. So much didn't make sense, and it all pointed toward a very powerful being, indeed. Very few had that kind of power, and I well-knew von Rappoldstein was one of them.

There was a long pause where we both stood there a bit awkwardly before Lachlan broke the silence. "I see," he laughed, "It seems we're both dragging our feet before completing our tasks, but I do agree. We need more answers."

"We do. And speak for yourself, wolf. I've just been busy."

The man standing behind MacKeane shoved Lach in the back and said, "She's got ye on that one, friend."

Lachlan had a look of bemusement, and when I raised a brow, he said, "Forgive me my manners. This big, idiot behind me is my pack mate and friend, Hugh MacKeane. He's been dying ta meet ye. He's a big admirer of yers."

Hugh narrowed his eyes and growled at his friend.

"A pleasure to meet you," I said.

"The pleasure is all mine," came his gruff reply.

I nodded. "I thought about going to von Rappoldstein's tonight, but…"

"Ye're exhausted."

I nodded. I was. I pulled at my jabot. "And my clothes are being held together by the magical equivalent of adhesive tape." I laughed. "Not to mention, I smell."

Lachlan waggled his brows, and I shook my head at his ridiculous sense of humor.

Behind him, Hugh cleared his throat. "I'll just meet the two of ye in the morning. We'll confront the villain together, aye?"

I nodded my thanks. They didn't have to help me, but it said much about their character that they were willing.

Lachlan clapped his hands together and rubbed them expectantly. "Well, then, however shall we pass the time?"

I could think of a few things… I wanted to argue that he should take care of his curse problem, but I didn't think he'd appreciate the lack of trust if I told him so, and after everything, I didn't want to disappoint him in that way. I was mature enough to admit I'd been very wrong about the man. And after feeling a bit lost as I wrapped up things without him, I had to admit that perhaps, I might be a little partial to him as well.

If he said he had everything in hand I had to believe him.

So instead of asking what, perhaps, I should, I asked instead, "How about we go somewhere less crowded?"

Lachlan's grin was wide when he replied, "Aye, lass. I thought ye'd never ask."

Chapter Forty-Two

Lachlan
A Whole Lot Of Loving Going On

The Langham Hotel...
London...

THE LANGHAM WAS a grand hotel and quite a bit more fashionable than the place we stayed last night, but that was neither here nor there. We entered its infamous courtyard, Josie and I were suitably impressed. The hotel had just this year installed electric lighting around the perimeter of its courtyard— the first hotel in London to do so. The Langham had always been a leader when it came to innovation; it's why I loved to stay here.

Even better, it pleased me to experience the look of awe on Josie Bell's face as she twirled in place and appreciated the artificial light. I imagined it was difficult to impress someone of her caliber, so to witness it firsthand felt like a gift.

Speaking of gifts, I still couldn't believe she had agreed to come here with me, but I was not about to turn down such good fortune. I felt a little bad I had to evade the truth about my handling of the partial matehood....Josie Bell thought I had everything under control...but there truly was nothing I could do at this point, and as a last meal, so to speak, I intended to make

322

every moment count without taking away Josie's agency.

I was going to love her so thoroughly; with her consent.

We took the modernized hydraulic lifts to the top floor; the two of us like a couple of eager children as we ascended to the top, and before she knew what I was about, I'd lifted her into my arms, thrown open the door, and carried her across the threshold.

She giggled, a delightful, carefree sound, if uncharacteristic of her as I spun her around once, then let her slide to her feet, but her laughter was cut short when we heard, "You two need to find a bed chamber."

Josie spun around, and I frowned at the familiar cat laying sprawled out across the massive bed.

"George!" exclaimed Josie.

"Och, this *is* a bed chamber," I pointed out.

The cat dipped his head in acknowledgement. Man to man, I returned a look that said unquestionably, *your timing leaves a lot to be desired.*

The cat merely shrugged, thoroughly unbothered by my point.

"What are you doing here?" asked Josie.

"Can't a cat just go about his business in peace?"

Josie scoffed. "Since when have you ever desired peace?"

George seemed to think it over as he looked off at nothing and scratched at his chin. I adamantly refused to follow his gaze; I was convinced all cats did this sort of thing on purpose to make one look foolish.

Eventually, he said, "Your point is fair, Josie Bell. I don't. So you wouldn't mind if I have a wee dram of whisk—"

"I mind, ye ken," I bit out. There wasn't room for the three of us with what I had planned.

George looked to Josie for confirmation, and I actually appreciated that he checked with her rather than just leave on my account.

"George," she said, her voice softer than normal. "I know I don't say it often…"

The cat snorted at that.

"All right. I've never said it, and that's my fault. But I'm saying it now. I appreciate you."

The cat lifted his chin as if to indicate he deserved any and all accolades attributed to him and to please continue offering such praises, thank you very much.

Josie looked back at me, winked, and when we faced forward again, George was already busy bathing. It was a weird sight to see, with him all adorned in a top hat, a cravat, and a waistcoat while licking his backside with one hind leg in the air.

I cleared my throat. "Ahem."

George ignored me.

Josie added, "Do you mind, George?"

And with a put upon sigh, George dropped his leg, snapped his fingers, and vanished.

Then, we were all alone. *Finally.*

I didn't waste a second more and with her eyes wide and her pupils swallowing her bright irises, I knew Josie Bell was right there with me.

I twirled her around and pushed her gently but purposely against the wall. Then, I stepped into her space, pressed one knee between her legs, and *leaned* in, my lips skimming her shoulder, her neck, the edge of her jaw...

I felt on the verge of losing control. My wolf knew this was our last time to be together and even though I knew I would not be sliding into her warm, tight sheath, I was still so ridiculously out of my mind with love and lust, I worried I would not be able to *last.*

"Lachlan..." Her name on my lips, drawn out with her low, throaty voice made my cock pulse and harden further. "I ache," she added on a slow moan.

"Aye, love. I ken. And I am going ta take care of ye. Make ye feel so damn good."

Inside my head, my wolf growled, '*Mine.*' But no, I could not claim her as such. Not when I knew we were never going to be more than what we were right now, so I bit my lip and swallowed such words, and instead warned her what was about to happen. "Josie Bell, I want nothing more than ta be inside ye… Nothing would give me greater pleasure, ye ken? But not tonight, aye? I will no' take ye unless we're both free to *choose* with open consent."

I rested my hand over her heart, feeling it beat frantically, then slid my hand up and around her neck, gently holding her there, so I felt it when she spoke, when she nodded, when she confirmed, "Yes, Lach."

"Yes, what, love. Tell me what ye expect. What ye're willing ta take."

She dipped her head, then wet her lips, and I swore I almost ejaculated right then and there. "I want you to make me come. I want your mouth on me. On my breasts. On my quim. *Everywhere.* And when you've forced me to my release, I want to take you in my mouth."

"Josie…," my voice broke on her name. I was wrecked by her words. A woman who knew what she wanted was my *fantasy*. I should have known that when I asked, Josie would more than deliver. "*Fook me—*"

It seemed my own coherent thoughts had abandoned me, so I decided to replace words with deeds. I was better at action anyway.

Her skirts were unusual, split down the center and only there, really, to hide the fact that beneath the lengthy fabric, she wore trousers. I suspected trousers made it easier to fight. I'd seen other Spellmaidens wear the same type of garment and I knew she could pin the sides back and out of her way. I was just glad she wore them because it meant I could do this: I lifted one of her legs and wrapped it around my hip, then thrust my hard, aching length against her, mimicking what I truly wanted but couldn't have.

And Josie Bell loved it. Her moans increased in intensity as we set a slow, steady rhythm. Och, my woman wasn't a silent one, and I relished every sound she made.

But if I wasn't careful I would come before I wanted to, and that wouldn't do, so I lifted Josie Bell, wrapped her other leg around me until she could lock her ankles behind my back, then I carried her across the room, my hands boldly gripping her arse, and lowered her in the middle of the bed. I followed her down, her legs still locked behind me, and I knew in that moment the next few hours were going to be the best sex I'd ever had in my gods-dammed life.

But first. I was going to unwrap her, like an erotic present. My manhood leapt with excitement, but my inner wolf whined his impatience.

All in good time, I admonished him. Tonight, I had to give Josie Bell enough pleasure to last a lifetime.

I started by removing her voluminous skirts. My hands unexpectedly shook with pent up desire as I loosened the buttons. Being a Lycan and nearly out of my mind with desire, I feared I would ruin her clothes.

Josie must have noticed my struggles, for as I unhooked a third button, she touched a hand to my cheek and lifted my chin to face her. She wiggled the fingers of her other hand and said, "Magic, remember? If you rip something, I can fix it. You don't need to take care."

Gods. This lass.

After fumbling with a forth button using fingers that were way too broad for such delicate fastenings, I took her words to heart and ripped her skirts in two, then tossed them over my shoulder to the floor.

Josie bell laughed, and I genuinely smiled in return.

Now, she was down to her custom trousers, a shirtwaist, and all the other lacy trappings of the modern woman, plus the unique straps and pockets and *weapons* I might have expected on a Spellmaiden who was at the top of her field.

Discovering what lay beneath all those trappings was going to be a fucking delight, and I was going to take all night to discover her secrets.

"Lachlan…"

"Aye, love?"

"Must go faster."

And oh, how I found a new thing to adore. I loved how she struggled to string together words…because of me and what I was doing to her. Out loud, I said, "Och, lass, donnae rush me. I'm enjoying this far too much."

I unpinned the brooch holding together her jabot and set it on the table beside the bed.

Josie Bell followed my actions with a growl of frustration.

I paused, "Problem?"

She shook her head frantically, her legs twisting and moving beneath me and her arms sliding up and down my shoulders and chest the entire time.

I grabbed one end of her jabot and pulled it from around her neck, nice and slow.

Josie Bell was all but panting now, and I was loving every minute of it. All this pleasure beforehand had never been quite so riveting. And I hadn't even touched her intimately yet.

I decided to give her a little more and pressed my knee between her legs just there, and Josie wasted no time; she began undulating her hips all but riding my thigh and seeking her release.

I moved on to the buttons of her shirtwaist.

I had a similar problem with the fastenings there, but I loved this shirt on her. Equal parts functional and feminine, it fitted her in such a way I felt desire every single time I saw it. It told me she was a woman, feminine *and* capable, and I loved it. I couldn't destroy this one, so I tried my best to take care.

Josie wasn't having it. Before I knew what she was about, she sat up, grabbed ahold of my shirt, pointed her wand at her chest, and before my wide-open eyes, her shirtwaist and corset disappeared and her breasts bounced free, her nipples puckered to hard points and straining at me.

"Fook," I groaned. I'd never seen anything so erotic in my long life.

As if of their own accord, my hands cupped her, and I was leaning down and drawing one large nipple into my mouth before I even knew what I was about.

I focused on her right breast, sucking and nipping, and her taste was ambrosia exploding on my fucking tongue. She whimpered when I rolled and pinched the other nipple while I suckled her.

"Lach. Don't stop. Don't. Ever. Stop."

"Aye, lass. I've got ye."

"More. *Harder.*"

Who was I to ignore her command. I wrapped my lips around her other nipple, and bit down lightly, then soothed the sting with my tongue.

"I'm close."

Those two words almost sent me over the edge. I could not believe I had her there after only attending to her breasts. I hadn't even touched her quim. "Not yet, Josie Bell, or I'll just have ta make ye do it again."

"Not. A. Punishment."

I laughed. "I suppose no'."

And then, fuck me, she did come with a long drawn-out moan. I pressed the heal of my palm over my erection to stop myself from following her over the edge.

"Och, ye naughty woman."

Josie nodded her head. "You're definitely going to have to make me do that again."

"Aye, I suppose, I'll just have to remove these trousers now," I said with an aggrieved sigh, "But, och, there appears ta be an awful lot of straps ta unbuckle."

I bit back a chuckle as Josie Bell decided she wasn't going to stand for that and magicked away the rest of her clothes, just as I'd hoped. At this point, I was growing too impatient to unwrap her like I'd imagined, and my inner wolf echoed his agreement with a howl.

For her part, Josie sat up, having recovered her wits, tossed her wand in the air and magicked it away with a flick of her wrist, then began tearing at my clothes with her bare hands.

I wished in that moment I had a lifetime with her, seeing her so capable and unafraid to take grasp of what she wanted, I knew, would never grow old.

And I liked that Josie Bell wanted to use her hands to unclothe me. Then again, I had far less to remove. Basically, a kilt and a shirt at this point, and even those were optional, to be honest.

Josie Bell had me in nothing but my skin in a matter of minutes, and I was so damned thrilled by that, I wasted no further time. I dropped down, tossed her legs over my sweaty shoulders, and dragged my tongue up her delicious quim.

Her taste exploded on me like ambrosia. She was so very wet for me, having already orgasmed once. I couldn't wait to feel her coming on my tongue again, to taste her release as it happened.

I kept my hips elevated less I find myself rubbing my cock against the bed like a young pup; as it was, my hips jerked of their own accord, and I thrust against air, mimicking the act I so desperately wanted to perform. I couldn't help myself; I was so far lost for her. For her taste. For her smell. Everything about her seemed designed to destroy me for anyone else.

I supposed fate knew what she was about after all.

Her honey coated my chin, my tongue, and now I was sucking on her clitoris as Josie Bell began chanting my name like a benediction. "Lachlan… Lachlan… Lachlan…"

My name in her lust crazed voice was almost too much, and I used my hand to pinch her clitoris as I jammed my tongue in her core as far as it could go.

She orgasmed that way with a scream of pleasure, and once more, I had to squeeze the base of my cock to keep from falling with her into the abyss of mindless delectation. I was going to explode when it was my turn to release, so damn hard.

But Josie gave me only moments to pull back from the edge, before she rolled me over, wrapped her hands around the base of my aching cock, then followed it all by enveloping the bulbous head with her delectable lips…then, she began go suck.

My eyes rolled back in my head, and it was my turn to scream. *"Fook me!"*

I was embarrassed to say I lasted mere minutes.

Like a gentleman, I warned her ahead of time…as best I could. At least, I think she understood my odd grunts.

And just like I'd come to expect of my woman, Josie Bell held on for dear life as I shot to the stars and unloaded every bit of my essence into her willing mouth.

If I hadn't suspected before, I knew it then. I was absolutely ruined for anyone else.

◦

Chapter Forty-Three

Josie
von Rappoldstein's Lair

S ATURDAY MORNING ARRIVED bearing clear skies and a bright, brilliant morning sun. It was so at odds with the troubles we were sure to face today. I wanted nothing more than to lie in bed and drape my body over my duke, and wallow in the beams of light shining through the large windows of our room, but time was working against us, and we had no time to dally.

We'd brought each other to orgasm so many times throughout the night, at some point, I'd lost count, and I had to work extra hard to focus on what was important. My eyes were bleary, but I was so unbelievably relaxed from pleasure. I didn't regret a moment of our loving.

I was marginally embarrassed by just how many times in the night I begged him to complete the matehood, but he remained stalwart, adamant that we would discuss this again after the threat to his sanity had been addressed and we could discuss things without coercion.

I respected that. I did.

And he was right to take that firm stance. I approved, heartily, of his ability to be level-headed about this and not be ruled by his lust.

I was so wrong about him in so many ways, and I looked forward to apologizing to him after we settled this unfortunate business.

The von Rappoldstein House in London covered an entire city block and would have garnered far too much human attention without the use of magic to create the type of façade a human might expect. For one thing, the real house had over twenty chimneys, which were crooked and angled in every imaginable direction. Worse, half of them expelled smoke in various colors, all of them shades far different than the various shades of grey a non-magical person would expect. Also, the front door appeared to randomly change size. No one in the magical community understood why, just that sometimes, the door was as tall as a field mouse and virtually undetectable apart from the odd blank wall of stone where an exterior door might be expected, to a door that stood higher than the house's own roofline. Further, the house changed color every single day.

Today, it was entirely black, which might have seemed ominous if it weren't for the rainbow of brightly colored smoke spewing from seven of the home's twenty chimneys.

The *style* of home also changed, from an expected Victorian to something even the most creative individual couldn't begin to describe.

I suspected it all hindered upon von Rappoldstein's present mood, which to be honest, really didn't help. What was a black Romanesque villa spewing colorful smoke meant to convey? Lunacy?

Lachlan, Hugh, and I (Hugh had met us in front of von Rappoldstein's home) climbed the ivy-covered steps leading up to the front door, which, fortunately, stood about twelve and a half feet tall today. Before I could knock, the door opened revealing an overly-tall, perhaps nine foot, butler with long, grey hair. Most of his height appeared to be from the waist down, which was a bit odd. Regardless, he answered the door as properly as any of the highest-trained butlers found in any society home across London might, "May I help you?"

I stifled the urge to ask how the butler managed when the door was only two feet tall. "Josie Bell and company to see Mr. von Rappoldstein," and with a flick of my wrist, my calling card appeared in the butler's hand.

"Ah," the man bowed and stepped aside, allowing us to enter, adding, "the master's been expecting you."

I nodded my head as if it made perfect sense to be expected.

Once inside, the butler turned on his heel, clearly expecting us to follow, and I shared a look with MacKeane as we did.

The butler walked remarkably slow for a man with such long legs, which gave us the opportunity to study our surroundings as we headed deep into the bowels of the house. Once again, what we saw offered no clues apart from lunacy, for every door, wall, stick of furniture, room we could see into, and painting shifted from style to style with alarming frequency and covered everything imaginable from overly frilly to starkly barren.

Lachlan leaned in, "Do ye think it's a trap?"

I supposed it could be, but said, "No."

"Do ye think he's behind…everything?"

"It would make sense." Which really didn't answer his question, but my instincts told me von Rappoldstein was guilty of quite a lot, just not this. It made no real sense to be honest. What would be his motivation?

I supposed, historically speaking, von Rappoldstein didn't appear to need much in the way of motivation to perform nefarious deeds. It was precisely this reason…or at least one reason…why it was always so bloody difficult to charge the man with any real crimes. Even though we all *knew*.

He was the villain to our hero. For as long as we could recall.

I wasn't even sure quite what we'd do without him, to be honest. Historically speaking, more than half of the P.E.E.s could be attributed to him alone. More, when we counted the collaborations he'd had with other would be villains. Cerberus was a consistent favorite of his.

Eventually, we stopped before an ordinary door (all the others along the way had been anything but ordinary, of course) and the butler opened said door, saying, "Yer Munificence, Josie Bell to see you."

A voice from deep within the room exclaimed, "Dammit, Baldor, I've told you thousands upon thousands of times, it's Your Highness." This pronouncement was followed by Baldor stating, "Yes, Your Wonderfulshipness," and then, silence, followed by an aggrieved sigh, followed by, "Show them in."

After the insanity of the various rooms and design styles along the way, it was shocking to walk into what appeared to be a very normal-looking Victorian library.

As for the room's owner, von Rappoldstein appeared, on the surface, to be perfectly ordinary as well, if a bit young, for all he'd been credited for over the years. I'd seen him before, naturally, he was practically a legend, for a villain, but every time I came face to face with him, it struck me how I always expected someone far older and definitely not this, perhaps, forty-year old man with dark hair and a definite twinkle of delight in his eyes. Complete with a gracious smile curling his lips from where he sat behind a large mahogany desk.

It was all very…strange. Every single time.

But not as bizarre as the raccoon sized hedgehog like creature to his left. That one had a manic look about the eyes I did not trust.

Then, there was the man wearing a kilt like the one Lachlan MacKeane normally wore, who was in the process of standing upright after having been leaning over von Rappoldstein as the three of us drew to a stop before the desk. The Scot now stood at von Rappoldstein's right elbow.

I sensed both Lach and Hugh stiffen behind me, while von Rappoldstein said, "Josie Bell, at last," then he glanced at MacKeane, looked pointedly at his garments from last century, and winked. "Now that I've seen you in the flesh, I'm so glad I had all your bounties removed…" Well, that explained why we hadn't had any trouble from that corner. von Rappoldstein clapped his hands together with obvious delight and added, "Might I say, your clothing, Your Grace, I heartily approve."

Never breaking eye contact with von Rappoldstein, I stepped in front of Lachlan and hastily swapped out his borrowed clothes for his normal ones using my wand, which I held behind my back, then I slid back into my previous position front and center.

von Rappoldstein followed my actions with obvious delight, and merely said, "I see."

Usually, Lachlan might have growled his ire, and I very nearly turned to see what was the matter, but when I looked at the Scot I didn't know facing us, I could tell by his strange stare that MacKeane only had eyes for this man, who was clearly part of his clan.

Lach's voice was filled with tension and emotion when he said, "Jack? Brother?"

The Scot nodded and released a long, slow exhale. "Aye, Lach. I hadn't told ye all of it, I ken."

I couldn't help but turn to look at MacKeane, something I never would have done and something that went against every bit of my training as a Spellmaiden, for I was effectively giving the enemy my back. But the sound of bleak pain that came out of Lachlan's mouth was a sound I could not ignore. I only just refrained from reaching over and grabbing his hand; but more importantly I was about two seconds away from harming Jack for causing this man beside me so much pain, which I well knew would have been a disaster.

It didn't matter. I wasn't prone to impulsiveness, but in that moment, I felt on the verge of being very spontaneous, indeed.

That was when I knew my feelings had been engaged. I could no longer deny it.

But now was not the time for that sort of revelation.

Lachlan stiffened, and I once more looked at our adversaries, my arms crossed, as Lachlan said, "Explain yourself."

I narrowed my eyes, echoing the duke's command.

The man, Jack, nodded. "I approached von Rappoldstein and offered to pay him an extraordinary amount to create a spell."

Lachlan muttered, "…not another godsdamn spell," while from my right, Hugh cursed rather violently.

"My cursed coin?" Lachlan asked.

At this, Jack shook his head. "I genuinely thought it was for your protection, as we discussed, but no. That happened exactly as I said. I went to von Rappoldstein for a different sort of spell."

Even I could tell Jack was serious about that part. He crossed his arms as if he wouldn't budge despite the obvious pain contorting his face.

"Go on," urged MacKeane, "what was this *other* spell supposed to do?"

"Stop a Lycan from going insane."

My anger softened the tiniest degree as I considered whether Jack might have done something terrible in order to do something good.

Lachlan's voice gentled as well when he said, "For our Uncle…"

For a moment, Jack glanced at the floor, then lifted eyes bright with tears, and whispered, "Aye, Uncle."

I actually felt sorry for the big man in that moment, while beside me, Lachlan MacKeane exploded into movement. Hugh and I stood to the side and watched, giving the brothers space to come to terms with these revelations, while Lachlan paced.

He froze and glanced over his shoulder. "Where is Uncle now?"

Jack shook his head. "I do no' ken."

von Rappoldstein decided, to add, "Isn't this exciting" at which we all turned to glare at him, after which, he adopted a very serious look, adding, "I mean, yes, this is terrible. Terrible." He wasn't very convincing.

From beside me, Lach released a heavy breath, which sounded almost defeated and before I knew it, Jack had rounded the desk and the brothers had their foreheads together, Jack offering apologies and Lach, who I'd never admired more, offering forgiveness and understanding, again apparently.

For his part, von Rappoldstein appeared more normal than ever for he looked at the two men with an intense amount of compassion before turning his attention to me.

For some reason, his glance startled me, and I had the strangest sense that I knew this man, and as a witch, I learned long ago to always heed my instincts, which were practically screaming at me the same message: *you know this man.*

I just couldn't see how. I mean, despite the obvious interactions in the course of my job as a Spellmaiden.

von Rappoldstein seemed to be equally confused by similar thoughts, I don't know how I knew that, I just did.

Finally, his thoughtful look cleared, but before he could speak, I asked him, "Why did you do it?" Why did he interfere in these men's lives? Because to me, it was clear someone else was involved. I knew Lachlan's past from his file. I knew his Uncle would have been put to death after the loss of his family. I hadn't known that actually hadn't happened, though it seems it hadn't. I don't know exactly what happened, but I didn't believe for a moment, that their uncle had just escaped on his own. These men were far too capable to bollocks up something so…simple.

My instincts screamed someone else had a hand in this.

von Rappoldstein folded his hands on the desk before him and answered, "I'm guilty of a great many things, but, maybe, not this."

"Maybe?"

He shrugged and gestured at his own head. "Memory problems. They're a real bitch."

I actually believed him, but I had to ask.

von Rappoldstein didn't help his denial though, when he thoughtfully added, "Well, naturally, I do my part to keep the Spellmaidens employed as you know. Just not this time. Probably."

Probably. His doubt almost made me laugh.

And that was when I wondered, "Jack? Who told you where to go to purchase a spell for protection?"

His voice was grim when he said, "Lady Sophia Tewkesbury-Smith."

"WELL, WELL, WELL. I never knew you had it in you."

We all spun to face the newcomer, whose familiar voice had just joined the discussion.

Lady Sophia stood with her back against a nearby bookshelf and studied her claws.

Everyone but Jack asked or stated, "Lady Sophia…" in varying degrees of wonder, but for my part, I couldn't believe I hadn't seen it all before. All at once, it made perfect sense. Even as far back as Lady Sophia appearing almost immediately after I'd taken care of George's escaped gorgon, the answer had been there all along. It made a sick sort of sense. Mostly. A few things didn't add up.

Rather than ask her why, I thought about everything I knew. I considered my training. Human, or in this case cat, motivational behavior. For her part, Lady Sophia observed me, clearly eager to watch me figure it all out with a sort of misplaced sense of pride in her lifted chin. As if she had any claim to why I had the skills to work it all out. She didn't. Hell, she'd never even considered making me her familiar. Something which I was no longer bitter about, it seemed.

Villainy tended to do that for me.

And then I knew. One of the oldest motivations in history. "Power."

Lady Sophia nodded. "Go on."

"Your kind are required to have familiars in order to retain your powers…"

von Rappoldstein interjected, "She chose me as her familiar."

An interesting fact, I tucked away to consider later. For now, I ignored him.

Lady Sophia simply nodded, though I didn't really need her confirmation.

"…and you hate that," I continued. "You thought that by doing all this, you'd be able to somehow free yourself from that constraint."

"Very good," she answered.

It was but I was missing something important here. "How did you expect to do that?"

It was Jack who knew the answer. "MacKeane Ore."

I turned to face him, a mistake I would later pay for dearly, while Lach, Hugh, and even von Rappoldstein had an even more violent reaction than mine, which was more along the lines of disgust.

Ignoring their outbursts, I asked, "What ore?"

Lachlan's soft voice spoke up, "Ye cannae answer that, brother."

While von Rappoldstein exclaimed, "The ore you were planning to pay me in for your spell!"

Jack simply nodded, and I felt sorry for the man, just a bit, for I knew for sure he was only ever doing it all for love, to help ease his guilt, I said, "Your uncle didn't escape on his own. Did he, Lady Sophia?" From behind me, she confirmed this herself, but I already knew I was right and added. "It wasn't your fault, Jack." I glanced to Lachlan. "Yours either."

He looked at me, a question in his eyes. "What do ye mean?"

"You're not responsible for the death of your uncle's family." Of course, I knew about his past. "It was all part of the same plan. Every last bit of it. Someone wanted you out of the way. Someone killed for power."

I only had a moment to witness the love and dawning realization on Lachlan MacKeane's face as he finally forgave himself, when Lady Sophia said, "Your uncle really was a right pain. I don't know what she wants with him?"

No one missed the slip. Lachlan spoke first. "She? Where's my uncle?"

As I might have guessed, Sophia refused to reply and changed the subject to me. "You really are the cleverest, most skilled Spellmaiden we've ever had. Unfortunately, you aren't quite as clever as me."

And with that, my friends, von Rappoldstein, the entire room, and worse, the man I loved, vanished before my eyes.

Chapter Forty-Four

Josie Bell
The Cat is Out of the Bag?

W E REAPPEARED SOMEWHERE in London. The space was intimately familiar, and I knew without question this rundown back alley filled with trash and debris and such foul smells I wanted to vomit, was within a block of the very streets I'd grown up on before I was discovered by the White Witch. Ah, the Rookeries. Sometimes, I still recalled this odiferous stench in my dreams, and I nearly gagged as unwanted memories threatened to resurface.

I forced myself to look around, an effective distraction technique, thinking, *surely, this location wasn't a coincidence.* I hoped beyond hope Lachlan MacKeane was taking care of his matehood problem and not spending time worrying about me.

He was too clever to do something idiotic and come for me, right? I had to believe that.

But I knew better.

On the tail of that thought, Sophia sauntered into my line of sight, her gate smug; her chin lifted. I admit, I was somewhat disappointed in myself for not seeing what now felt painfully obvious. Sophia's odd behavior. Her general air of disappointment and discontent. The knowledge she shouldn't have had.

Even her own damn warnings. She'd probably laughed as I fell for every line she fed me with superior conceit.

I narrowed my eyes as she tilted her head my way, saying, "I can see you working everything out." She shrugged. "Well, almost everything."

I fought to remain collected. Poised. Despite internally berating myself for why I'd ever wanted her to claim me as her familiar…she was so arrogant now. Not in the slightly aggravating, slightly endearing way of George—*Blast,* I was going to owe him an apology or ten—but in a far less attractive manner. Haughty. Smug. Overly confident.

It seemed I had been too caught up in admiring Sophia's apparent competence and had ignored all signs warning: danger.

But here? Now? I was proud of myself for not allowing my frustration to show. In fact, it was Sophia's infamous composure I could see beginning to fray around the edges. Her eyes were almost manic; her pupils rounded. "You were right. I want to be free of the less desirable aspects of my powers. But I'm not the villain here. Not really."

I had to chuckle at that. If anything, she was delusional. But I couldn't resist a petty taunt, something guaranteed to pick at the worn outline of her crumbling self-possession. "I see." I smirked. "Someone more powerful than you is really in charge. You're just a pawn. *They're* the one who promised they could fix your little 'familiar' problem."

My taunt worked. I could practically see the steam pouring out of Sophia's pointed ears. I couldn't believe she was at the mercy of such obvious manipulation. Or was she?

"Ah. You've been trying to make your own plans. You should know by now, those types of betrayals never end well for the betrayer."

Sophia began to uncharacteristically pace. I could feel her growing anger. "The gorgon was supposed to kill you."

"You gave George the gorgon?" I admit that surprised me.

Sophia shook her head. "No. That *witch* did. I tried to stop it, actually. Knew the plan was unhinged. I did warn you."

Her warning hadn't saved me. That was all me, though I suppose she did suggest George's acquisition couldn't have been a coincidence. I'd give her that much.

Everything still pointed to von Rappoldstein. He often bragged about being a witch. Being powerful. Being a villain. And someone was powerful, indeed, to manipulate so much.

But he'd never hidden behind someone else's actions before. I hated to give the man credit, but he certainly liked to get recognition for the havoc he wreaked, and that hadn't been happening.

Further, I still didn't know *why*. For all I knew, I was collateral damage. Lachlan? Perhaps, not. And while I easily understood Sophia's motivations, it wasn't enough. I needed to know what this villainous witch wanted. Then, I hoped I would have my answers.

"What about Lachlan, then?" I had to keep her talking while I worked out a plan. "Why try to drive him insane?"

"He's too strong. We need the power he keeps. It's the key to everything, but the man can't be corrupted or manipulated. He's too *good*."

My chest wanted to puff with pride even though her praise had nothing to do with me. But he was my mate. Or I was his. And I liked his abilities a little too much. I liked *him* a little too much. "Yes. The man is imposing and imminently capable. More so than anyone I know."

My mind raced through the implications of this new information. If Lachlan had such power, they might have been trying to get at it for *years*. They might have—Oh… On a hunch, I said, "It wasn't Lachlan's fault his uncle's family died. They weren't even the target."

Sophia shifted her balance, clearly agitated. Impatient. And I knew I was right. He'd also told me his family's deaths occurred around the time he'd first met Sophia. I narrowed my eyes as I looked at her in such a new light, and I realized she was almost desperate to tell me everything. Mayhap, all I really needed to do was ask. It had worked thus far.

So, I did. "Who really is behind all this?"

I could see she wanted to tell me. She even smiled before she spoke, and I held my breath as anticipation raced over me. I would have answers. Finally.

She opened her mouth to say his name. I was sure of it.

And that's when everything went to shite.

In a flash, every villain I'd ever apprehended surrounded me in this dark, cramped alley. But none of these creatures were behind all the nefarious events of the last weeks...none were powerful enough. Nor clever enough. No. They weren't any more in charge than Sophia, who I could no longer see through the creatures now surrounding me.

And at the moment, I couldn't care.

Not when they suddenly attacked *en masse*.

Chapter Forty-Five

Lachlan
Who Exactly Needs Saving Here Because I'm Confused

THE MOMENT JOSIE Bell disappeared, Hugh and Jack exploded into chaos. Even von Rappoldstein seemed more than a little bothered by how events had unfolded.

As for myself, I was strangely calm, when normally I would be anything but. Perhaps, it was because I couldn't accept I'd ever lose Josie Bell. I had already concluded we were a fixed point in this universe. Fate wouldn't have created the perfect mate for me only for me to lose her before I ever really had her.

Despite everything, I didn't believe fate would be so cruel, which was ridiculous considering the moon was set to begin rising in a matter of hours.

Hugh stopped before me and looked into my eyes. "Lach?"

I could tell he was worried. I wasn't behaving as I normally did. And then I started laughing, which only deepened my friend's concern. I could feel their worry, Hugh's and Jack's, in my mind, but they needn't be. I was calmer than I'd ever been before.

It didn't help when I laughed and said, "All this time I worried I didn't deserve her because I couldn't keep her safe."

Hugh whispered to someone else, probably Jack. "I think he's finally gone insane. This must have pushed him over the edge."

I shook my head and smiled. I knew I was as level-headed as ever, though I still wasn't out of the woods yet, what with the aborted matehood, the full moon, and all.

Jack stepped into my line of sight, too, with his own thoughts and concerns. "You ken Josie Bell isna the type ta need saving, aye?"

I nodded. We'd gone over this before. I did know. It's one of the things I loved best about her.

Hugh asked, "So, are ye finally going to admit ye love her?

I smiled but shook my head. "No."

I still believed strongly I needed to tell Josie Bell first.

"All riiiiight…." Hugh drew out. "Well, thank the gods ye did no' break the bond, then, and that Josie Bell's yer mate."

It was true. "Aye, I can track Josie Bell through the incomplete bond."

When I didn't move, Hugh slowly suggested, "And ye're going to use that bond, now, aye?"

I smiled. "Of course, I will, but you don't know those witches. They're verra clever and skilled and tricky."

Hugh agreed. "I ken."

Which caught my attention and I looked at him more directly. "How?"

He slapped me on the back. "I'm not telling ye shite, friend."

Somehow, I suspected Lady Ivy had something to do with his thinking in that direction, but I really wasn't in any frame of mind to pressure him about it.

My tone was serious when I met his eyes again. "Ye ken what ye have ta do, aye?"

Hugh nodded once. He would respect my wishes on this. Not only was I his alpha, but he knew there was no other choice in the matter.

Relived Josie Bell would ultimately be safe from me; it was time to run.

It was time to go save Josie Bell even though she didn't need saving.

Besides, at this point, I needed my last moments on this earth to be with her, watching her be the amazing Spellmaiden she was.

WE ARRIVED IN a dilapidated back alley in the middle of Southwark to utter chaos.

Various magical creatures were running wildly about, and I could barely tell who was fighting who. That was the problem with such mercenary villains with little higher reasoning; they often lost sight of who they were meant to be fighting.

That thought had barely formed when a voice I had come to adore called out, "It's about time you showed up." As she raced past us, chasing after some sort of three-armed demon.

With a chuckle, Hugh leaned into me and called over the sounds of battle, "What were ye saying about not being able to keep her safe?"

I laughed and shook my head, then crossed my arms, adding, "I ken. If there's anybody in this world who does no' need help, it's my woman."

Hugh shook his head. "Somehow, I do no' ken she'd appreciate ye referring ta her in that way."

I chuckled again, "Och, aye, I ken."

I followed her actions a moment, completely absorbed in admiration, then finally, I called out to Josie Bell, the love of my life. "Ye ken we could use some clothes right aboot now."

Aye, we were naked. It's what happens when you're a Lycan and you shift to get somewhere, but don't have a spare set of clothes close at hand.

Josie Bell threw a knife into the jugular of another demon and yelled. "I'm quite busy right now."

Being Lycan, we were used to nudity, and were in no rush to cover ourselves. And, we were definitely distracting a few interested parties.

I grew marginally concerned when she raced by again with a wicked smile etched on her face. She waved her hand but didn't stop to look too carefully.

I knew why when a few moments later some bloodstained clothes from a couple of fallen adversaries appeared on my body.

Enemies who were clearly female.

I glanced at Hugh who returned my look with a shrug. At least we were no longer vulnerably naked. We could join the fight now.

I nodded and proclaimed, "Ye ken, that dress suits ye, aye?"

He nodded, adding, "I ken yer bustle makes yer hips look quite slim."

This was why Hugh and I were friends, or one of many reasons, and I said, unnecessarily, "My witch has a sense of humor aboot her."

I glanced down the alley and caught sight of Josie Bell. I couldn't help but admire her skill, and in that moment, I wondered if she had enough space inside her for two hearts, because mine was surely stolen. It certainly wasn't still inside my own imperfect chest.

Hugh nodded his agreement about her sense of humor, and asked, "Shall we?"

"After ye?"

We turned to join the melee only to discover everyone, apart from Josie Bell, was either dead or gone. Josie herself stood amidst the carnage with her arms akimbo and tapping her foot. "Are you finished admiring each other's frocks?"

Hugh and I glanced at each other one more time, and I couldn't help but point out, "That jabot really brings oot the color of yer eyes."

Then, I grinned and stepped forward, while Josie Bell shifted her stance, her arms now crossed and one brow lifted as if to say, 'You could have helped.'

As I approached, an overly intrepid cockroach dared to cross in front of me, and I used my heeled boot, which was open at the front, exposing my toes where they hung a few inches off the front end of the sole, to squash it, then gestured at the remains as if to show Josie Bell I had, indeed, helped.

She shook her head, but smiled as she said, "Lachlan MacKeane? You're an idiot."

I reached her then and pulled her into my arms. I touched my forehead to hers, saying, "Perhaps, but I'm ye're idiot."

Josie shoved at me, laughing until she snorted. "You're ridiculous."

It was true. I was.

I kissed her quick, then asked, "What happened ta Lady Sophia?"

Josie rested her hands upon my chest and said, "She disappeared in the melee."

I promised. "Ye'll find her. Ye have nothing ta concern yerself with on that score."

"I know but that's not what's bothering me."

"No?"

"I still don't know who is behind all this." Before I could say anything, she added, "It's not Lady Sophia. Not really. She's guilty, definitely, and has her own agenda, but she's not the real villain here, and I don't think it's von Rappoldstein, either."

"I believe ye. Ye're the brilliant one. I'm just the hired muscle."

She scoffed, which was fair. I hadn't really done much, simply watched her back and let her be herself. Trusted her.

I suppose, then, I knew there was nothing simple about it after all.

Unfortunately, I hadn't noted how dark the sky had turned. Somehow, I had forgotten the passage of time… or what state the moon was in, I suppose I was too caught up in my love for Josie Bell. I was too happy.

Suddenly, my body forcefully bent at the waist, then I collapsed to the ground, already starting to shift uncontrollably. I couldn't help but want to curse at the moon as it rose in all its glorious fullness. "Hugh—"

Josie screamed and called out my name and yelled. "You lied to me?"

Aye, Josie Bell, I thought. *I had no choice. There wasn't anything to be done to save me.*

I had cursed fate and my lack of choices too thoroughly and too long to ever get my happily ever after, right?

Josie practically pulled me up by my elegant, if bloody jabot. "Listen to me, Lachlan MacKeane. I command you to survive, so that I can *murder* you."

I laughed at that. Aye, love. I couldn't speak now, my entire body wracked with pain as everything tried shifting forcefully and if I tried to speak; I was likely to bite off my tongue more than anything. This change was nothing like when I *chose* to shift. I could feel my bones snapping, reshaping. This wasn't a magical change; this was a biological change.

Still, hearing her tell me in her words that she cared…it helped. Somehow, it helped. And I hoped she knew that. I was sure Hugh would tell her if she didn't.

That was my last thought as my back bowed from the sheer force of changes occurring in my spine. At this point, I was no longer able to suppress the unimaginable torture and I screamed out in acute pain.

Josie Bell
What is Fate?

LACHLAN MACKEANE, THE man I loved, was turning into a mindless wolf. The very thing he'd been trying to avoid. And the sound he made…*dammit.* The sound of such excruciating pain broke something inside me. I never wanted to hear it again.

The only solution now was to ritualistically end his existence the way all Lycan did before turning insane.

At some point, I had fallen to my knees and cradled my shivering wolf in my arms, and now, I looked to Hugh, pleading, "*Do something.*" For once in my life, I reached out for help.

Hugh sobbed and shook his head. In his hand, he held an ornately bejeweled *sgian dubh* close to his chest. I hated it on sight. I knew he planned to use it to take MacKeane's life, but I refused to accept there was nothing we could do. Not after all this. I couldn't lose this man before I'd ever really had him.

And yet I knew Lachlan was beyond help. He was mostly unconscious now, thankfully, the only sound was a heartbreaking whimper that occasionally broke free. I just didn't want to accept that this was it.

Suddenly, the wind picked up and a voice whispered in my ear...a voice remarkably like von Rappoldstein's...and it said, "Use your pendant."

My pendant? I didn't know how he knew, and I didn't question him now. There wasn't time.

For the first time ever in the presence of others, I spoke a quick spell and retrieved the small disk hanging around my neck. The pendant itself wasn't any sort of precious metal at all, but more like a mineral or rock, and I yanked it free, ignoring Hugh's gasp of astonishment.

Only then did I hesitate. Why was I trusting a man I'd always known as a villain? It was so at odds with my current instinct to follow his advice.

As if to address my concerns, von Rappoldstein spoke on the wind once again. "Trust me. It's what I've been working on with Jack."

How had the thing he had not finished for Lach's brother found its way in a pendant I've had in my possession my entire life? It made no sense.

"All in good time, my child."

His answer was strange, but then it was clear the man was going insane for reasons I couldn't begin to imagine.

Still, I hesitated. Or perhaps, it was the coin we had yet to destroy working against me. I didn't know, but I glanced down, and I could see Lachlan's beloved countenance behind strange, wolfish eyes. And then he growled out, "R-run."

I shook my head, and his eyes flared with a whole range of emotions, the strongest of which was anger. But I knew we could solve this problem if we just completed the matehood. There was time.

As if he understood my way of thinking, Lachlan ground out. "Won't take ye. Like this. I'll…insane…before I take away…"

"What? Lachlan, take away what?" I shook his shoulder carelessly. He could take it.

He smiled then, slow and steady, and said, "Yer choice, my love."

This man. I both hated and appreciated his desperate desire to ensure I had a choice. And I wanted to argue, but I knew my stubborn wolf would not budge, nor was he in any frame of mind to be reasoned with. It all came down to this, and in that moment, for better or for worse, I made my decision.

Operating on instinct, I palmed my pendant, slapped it down on his chest directly over his heart, and with all the power inside me, said, "No. I love you. I will not run, and you will not die. Not today."

Chapter Forty-Six

Josie
Magic and Mating Under the Rising Moon

I HADN'T EVEN realized I'd closed my eyes. But when I opened them, Lachlan and I were alone and in a strange, new place. A place I'd never been. I suspected we were somewhere on the Isle of Skye, his home. I could see a green hill, dotted with sheep in the distance, and there was a dense forest behind me. From my left, came sounds of the sea along with a hint of briny sea air on the steady wind. We were in a grassy glen, surrounded by beauty, everything so lush and green, and we were alone. Blessedly alone.

I glanced down, expecting to see Lachlan unconscious for he had yet to move, but he was wide awake and staring at me with absolute devotion shining from the depth of his eyes.

I swallowed, my throat suddenly tight, almost afraid to hope.

"A-are we on Skye?"

Inane, maybe, but important.

"Aye, love," Lachlan lifted one hand, and tucked some loose hair behind my ear, then demonstrating immense strength, he stood, pulling me up with him and keeping me in his arms. His brawn was something I knew I'd never grow tired of. He carried me in silence for a few minutes and I was content to simply hold onto him. He stopped at an especially beautiful patch of grass surrounded by wildflowers.

He lowered me to the ground once again, saying, "Do ye mind, Josie Bell? I like this spot in particular."

I shook my head, astonished. He'd just come back from the brink of death and he was asking me if I minded? This man.

I magicked a large blanket on the ground beneath us to make things more comfortable.

Once we were on the blanket and laying side by side, I watched him as he closed his eyes and reached out with his senses. When he looked at me once again, he was all smiles. "It's Saturday morning. The full moon is just cresting."

I nodded. He would be able to sense the moon phase unerringly, but more importantly he was sane, and he was alive. This was a chance to make a different choice, and I wanted it so much, I didn't want to question *how*. Besides, I well-knew just how powerful magic mixed with faith made anything possible. This wasn't even the strangest, most impossible thing I'd ever seen in my years as a Spellmaiden. Not by a wide margin.

I reached out with my own senses and knew our partial matehood had been removed. He was no longer in danger of becoming unhinged. And yet... a part of me was disappointed, and for a brief moment, I felt bad for having such a dark thought. I was also remarkably calm, and I did wonder at this, but decided I was more confident in us, than actually calm. Fate was on our side, right? And, by now I was an expert at moving from lethal danger to a boring day filled with nothing in the blink of an eye...it was practically written in the job description under Spellmaiden.

On the heels of those thoughts, I swallowed, fearful of his answer, but I had to ask, "Am I still your mate?"

He slid one arm beneath me and pulled me close. With a gentle squeeze, he answered, "Aye, lass. Ye are. So if ye kiss me now..."

As his teasing voice trailed off, I searched his face for the lie, but he was telling the truth, and my heart leapt in unexpected relief. Fate might have suggested we should be mates, but the choice to move forward as *bonded* mates was now completely ours.

His eyes dropped to my chest, and he fingered the pendant I wore around my neck, now visible for his perusal. He nodded at it, saying, "This is made from a special mineral ore, which can only be found here, buried on my lands. It is only able to be harvested by the Lairds of Clan MacKeane."

"It seems your ore is very powerful stuff."

"It is. It fueled my family's battle arena for so many years. Very few people, however, ken its existence and the full extent of its magic. *Usually* only a laird can choose to reveal details about the ore, even its existence, to another, and only someone in my family can even remove it from the island."

"That's incredible." And he was telling *me*. "So does your telling me about this mean you're planning to keep me then?" I was only half teasing.

Lachlan laughed and nuzzled my nose, whispering, "Just try ta stop me, lass."

I walked my fingers up his chest. "Then, tell me more about this ore of yours, wolf."

He nodded. "There have been rumors, naturally, but even when people suspect, they can no' get their hands on it unless it's through someone in my family."

I nodded. "So, your brother was being used…"

"Aye, though even he can no' find new ore, but if he has some already, he could take some from the island."

"I wonder how someone in *my* family got it."

"I wonder, too, and I suspect we're going to find oot sometime soon, though perhaps, no' today."

I laughed. "Perhaps, not." I couldn't stop the blush from dusting my cheeks.

"Is that a symbol of yer family, etched there in the center?" he asked.

I glanced down at my pendant, noting the entwined letters

which looked like, perhaps, a V or a J, maybe an R? It was very stylized if so, but without a frame of reference, I couldn't be sure. "I can only assume so. Orphan, remember? I usually keep it magicked out of sight. I've never shown it to anybody."

He nodded; his eyes studying the ore. "It sounds right, at least, to my ears."

"So, what do you think happened?"

He let go of my necklace and answered. "I think ye're pendant, coupled with my ore, and ye're love for me—"

I shoved at his shoulder playfully. "My love for you?"

He looked up at me and grinned, nodding, "Och, aye. Yer love broke the coin and the curse *and* reset the matehood."

"But I thought von Rappoldstein…," at his questioning look, I clarified, "I heard his voice telling me what to do. He told me this would only buy us a little time. My instincts told me to trust him, but now, it seems he might have been mistaken? Or did he lead me purposely astray?"

Lachlan settled me more firmly in his arms now and began to stroke me absent-mindedly. "I suspect he did no' ken how yer love for me would enter into the equation."

I playfully bit at his chest. "You know, you're supposed to let *me* say it rather than just assume, you cocky bastard." My voice was teasing and held no heat.

He laughed, then groaned. "Now, where would be the fun in that?" He was a little worse for wear and I suspected his sides pained him somewhat, though he made a great effort to hide any lingering effects of what he'd been through. He *looked* like he'd been beaten half to death.

He'd never looked better to my eyes because in that moment, I knew he was all mine for as long as I wanted to keep him.

Good thing I wanted to keep him forever.

His face took on a serious mien then, and he rolled onto his side, then cupped my cheeks in his large, warm hands. "Ye ken, I love ye, Josie Bell?"

"I do, but I certainly like to hear it."

"Aye, I do love ye, Josie Bell."

"And I'm pleased to know it, but first, I'd like to discuss…what in the *hell* you thought you were about before I saved *you*?"

He had the good sense to wince. "If the ore on its own could have saved me; we would have discovered that a long time ago, aye? Lycans have been searching for a cure forever."

I shook my head. "At the hotel, we could have completed the bond. We were right there. You knew then what was going to happen. You knew you were going to die." My voice cracked on the last word.

"Aye, lass, but I would no' be me if I had given ye no choice in the matter."

I punched him in the chest, hard. "But that was my decision to make. Not yours. Do you understand me, you fool-headed man?"

Lachlan laughed. "Och, I will listen ta ye're wise counsel from now on, aye?"

I punched him in the chest again for good measure. "Good. Now, how about you tell me all the ways in which you love me?"

He allowed a quick smile, then turned serious once again. "I never wanted a mate."

I narrowed my eyes. "Too bad and too late."

He dropped a quick kiss on my lips. "Aye, love. In the end, I love ye too much ta let fate's desire thwart my happiness."

"Don't you realize, Lachlan MacKeane? Fate may have thrust me into your path, but you always had a choice. You didn't have to choose me, and I certainly don't have to choose you, but you do choose me. And I choose you, too. So, while we may be fated to fall in love, we also chose it. I love the very idea of a fated soulmate, myself, but a chosen soulmate feels even more powerful than fate. And for a witch, that is everything. We never underestimate the power of mindset and choice. After all, at the very heart of a witch is our belief in manifestation."

"So, then you do choose me?"

"I think it's rather obvious, but you do realize, you just kissed me, even if it was only a peck, we've restarted the matehood."

Lachlan fell back with a groan and shook his head. "*Fook* me, but I'm an idiot," then he smiled, "but not so much of a fool as to let this stand in the way of our future."

I nudged him and added, "*This* time."

"Aye," he laughed, then touched his forehead to mine, "this time."

"So, what are you waiting for, Lachlan MacKeane. Kiss me again and make me yours. And *this time*, know I could have stopped that kiss just now had I truly not wanted this. But I didn't. I choose you. The full moon is upon us. Let's make this binding. Together."

"Aye, lass. Forever."

And with that he kissed me with purpose.

We wrestled about on the blanket, which was so soft over the lush grass. And since I wanted nothing to get in our way, I used my magic to will away all of our clothes. When I landed atop him, we were both skin to skin. Nothing had ever felt better.

Lachlan laughed. "I could get used to magic, but one day, ye're going ta let me undress ye and take my time."

I shrugged. "Sure. One day." Maybe. But today was definitely not that day. I wanted him too much. Out loud, I confirmed, "But today, you don't really have a choice, my love." I rolled us over, so he was on top, adding, "And this time, I want *everything*. Do you hear? I'm making my desires known: No holding back."

His eyes flared with hunger, and his voice rumbled when he flexed his hips and said, "Aye, love, no holding back."

He did have a point though. I still remembered how his cock sprang free when I undressed him last time. A woman could get used to a sight like that. His cock was beautiful. A work of art. I wanted to study it. Enshrine it. Worship it. I already suspected it was going to give me pleasure like I'd never imagined. I could hardly wait.

Speaking of his cock, I wrapped one hand about his manhood,

which stood stiff as a pole, and stroked his length from root to tip.

And it *wept* for me.

Copious amounts of his liquid dribbled from the tip, which was plum-colored and soft as silk.

Gracious, the sight of his physical desire *for me* was one of the best things I'd ever seen. It made me feel *powerful*. Adored.

Loved.

"Josie, what ye do ta me, love…"

"I know, Lach. I know."

"Ye're mine, love. Do ye hear me?"

His voice was fierce when he said it, growly. I didn't normally react well to that sort of sentiment, ownership, but coming from the mouth of Lachlan MacKeane, I *coveted* hearing it. Goodness, I nearly *released* over it.

"I'm no' sure I can take my time. Wanted ye for so damn long it seems…feels like a lifetime."

It hadn't been. I knew that well enough, but I understood the sentiment. When your life thus far was unnaturally long and the intimacy you'd experienced to date had been mediocre at best, finding the right partner made you feel as if you'd longed for each other forever. A lifetime.

We'd pleasured each other enough by now to know it was going to be life-changing when we finally came together, and I was unbelievably impatient to reach that next step. Now, when it mattered most, under the rising of the full moon.

My eyes dropped to his magnificent body, taking in every bit of flesh in sight. I stopped to flick one of his nipple rings. I knew many people had them; I never realized how exciting I'd find them, but oh, how I did.

My questing fingers slid further down, mapping out his sides, his stomach, tracing his tattoos, feeling the trail of hair that led to his cock, which was distended and as solid as a rock, and I couldn't wait to have it in my hands again.

While I was distracted by his beautiful penis, one of his broad fingers reached between my thighs and stroked my quim. I had to fight to keep from closing my eyes, the pleasure was so intense. Heat burned the bottoms of my feet. I was already so very close, and we were only just getting started. I swear the anticipation was going to be the death of me.

I didn't want to miss any moment of our joining, so I forced my eyes to stay open. To take in everything. Every sight. Every smell. Every sense. Every touch. Every word that fell from his kissable lips.

Lachlan's eyes blazed with intensity and fierce love. "Ye ken I love ye, Josie Bell."

I laughed between moans. "I believe you've said that quite recently, my love."

He responded with a flick of my clitoris, then quickly sucked on my left nipple, both of which were tightly furled and pointing skyward.

"Saucy lass," he growled out.

I was too lost to sensation to respond; I could only whimper my need. I loved it when he played with my nipples.

Between my legs, his fingers started up a persistent rhythm, strumming my distended bundle of nerves, and I knew I was already so very close. I groaned, "More."

He chuckled but complied as his fingers played me like an instrument, dipping into my dripping core, then returning to tease my engorged clitoris.

He did it once. Twice. A third time.

The third time did it, and before another thought could register, I was racing to the stars, riding the strength of my orgasm, which was *fierce*.

Lachlan wasn't satisfied with that and kept stroking me, commanding, "Again."

But I'd grown sensitive to his touch and tried to shove him away. "Who are you to command me?"

He didn't answer; nor did he allow me to push him away, tenacious bastard.

"Push through it, Josie Bell," he commanded.

I shook my head. "I can't."

"Ye *can*," he countered.

Turned out he was right. He pushed me through my discomfort, this time with his mouth in tandem with his fingers, and almost immediately, I was releasing built up sexual tension again. I knew in that moment, I would always feel this way. And this time, I could feel the difference in our loving now that it was happening under the rising moon. I knew magic was at play here, my witch's eye open to sensing its presence. There was comfort there, knowing the magic was not my own but there for me anyway, providing protection. Never to harm me. Quite the opposite, in fact, for I knew that together we would be greater than we ever were alone.

Lachlan licked me again, one last time, and then, just as the aftershocks began to subside, he was there, his cock poised at my entrance.

"May I, Josie Bell?"

I laughed. "I'm likely to kill you if you don't."

He touched his forehead to mine and whispered, "I need yer words, love. I need ye to say it."

I knew what he needed and didn't even think about denying him. "Yes. Make love to me, Lachlan MacKeane."

He didn't hesitate then, and I was so beyond ready, so *wet*, he slid in with very little resistance. I was still feeling the aftereffects of the last orgasm, and when he filled me with his thick length, I suddenly spiraled straight into another one.

Add that to the sudden surge of magic as the matehood began to fall into place, and I knew this was a once in a lifetime event.

Lachlan groaned as I squeezed around his manhood. "Good gods, Josie Bell, you are so incredibly perfect. Like you were shaped just for me. I'm going ta come so *fooking* hard."

I could only nod and say "yes," and nod some more and hold on to his broad shoulders as he began to move, establishing a steady rhythm I would dream about for years.

"Can ye come for me again, love?"

I shook my head and whimpered. He kept hitting a spot inside me that had me seeing stars, but I didn't think I could release my building tension again, could I? Not yet.

"Try, love. I refuse to stop until ye do. *Gods.*"

I laughed, an almost mindless chuckle. I was so lost to pleasure. "Not. An. Incentive." I managed to warn.

He added a snap to his hips and adjusted the angle of his thrusts, and my goodness, I swear my eyes rolled back into my head and I lost consciousness for a brief moment. I wasn't a woman to write poetry, but right then and there, I wanted to write a bloody sonnet to his thighs, his hips, and his magic-fucking-rod.

I didn't curse often, but apparently Lachlan MacKeane's magical cock could draw forth the filthiest words out of me.

But, oh, we'd been building towards this for far too long to take it slow, I knew. This was raw. This was necessary.

I wouldn't have had it any other way.

The pace he set was brutal, now. The sounds we made together, erotic, filthy, *insane,* but I loved hearing every bit of it. This was the music and magic we made together when we were intimate and nothing about it could ever be less than beautiful, less than perfect.

"Och, fook, aye. Too… So… Damn…Ngh…"

Gracious, hearing Lachlan MacKeane unable to form complete thoughts was powerful, and I relished seeing him so delirious when perfect pleasure was the source of his distraction.

Then, he picked up the pace, again; he was almost savage in his thrusting, and I, too, found myself unable to even think coherently.

The slap of our skin as he pounded into me punctuated each fractured thought and I loved it—*Gods,* I craved it. Then, he froze for a moment, swelled to an unimaginable length, and with a loud growl, he latched onto my neck, marking me magically at the same moment he exploded inside me. Together we fell over the cliff and into pure, flawless bliss.

He growled his continued release, his hips still thrusting as he held on with his mouth, his arms, his very sex. Until right at the end, he unlatched, leaned up, and roared, "Josie Bell, yer mine!"

The magic surrounding us was something I knew you could only experience to understand. Possibly, the experience differed for everyone. But for me? I truly didn't know how to describe the completeness I felt in that moment. And the heat of him….*goodness*, I swore he scorched me as he flooded me with his fiery essence, which had seemed to surge over and over and over again. My magic and his magic…coupled with the intimacy of sex…I could only describe it as thus, every feeling I had in that great moment of intimacy compounded with his feelings and getting to experience them as if they were my own; so not only was I feeling my own enjoyment, but his as well. Add that to the love I felt for him and it made it all the better…

That's when I knew that intimacy moving forward as bonded mates was going to be nothing either of us had ever known before.

Feeling equally possessive of my new mate, I clung to his slick shoulders, my nails digging in and staking my claim. This wolf was mine.

It might have been moments or perhaps even hours, I didn't know and couldn't care less. All I knew was eventually, we rolled, switching places, and he pulled me into his side and my arm slid over his chest as if we'd practiced this move a thousand times before.

I gasped, startled, when I saw the new brand on his chest. I'd always wondered at the small circle of unmarked skin about where his heart should be. It was no longer empty, though, for there, in its place, was the same symbol from my pendant, and the right size, too, as if the pendant had burned a new tattoo right over his heart.

Lachlan clasped my hand and offered me a smile. "There's another one you can't see, branded on my soul as well." The sentiment brought tears to my eyes, and they fell as he added, "but I don't need either of them to ken ye're forever in my heart and forever mine."

My heart full of love, I kissed this man…my very own wolf…and knew everything between us was going to be all right.

Chapter Forty-Seven

Lachlan
The Future Begins Here

Two Months Later
London, England

J OSIE AND I were in our bed chamber in our house in London, a place we could be frequently found…when we weren't staying at The Kameleon that was. We planned to have a public ceremony in the future, but as far as anyone we cared about was concerned, our matehood was official, unbreakable, and *definitely* raising some eyebrows, even sparking more than a few intense debates amongst politicians at the M.M.R.

And among various local squirrel factions for that matter.

But as a general rule, people were beginning to accept that not all Spellmaidens would be unmated. Or a maiden. As Josie so often proclaimed of late, it was time for the Spellmaidens to face forward into the upcoming 20th Century with a more modern view. The National Union of Women's Suffrage Societies had formed seven years prior and already most within the magical community supported their manifesto, even predicted women would eventually earn the right to vote early in the next century at the latest.

The White Witch, despite being in a position of authority and a woman, did not approve for some reason. This perplexed Josie to no end, and we discussed the witch's behavior at length more times than either one of us cared to.

But for now, I held her in my arms, a place I would never tire of having her. We spent a lot of time here discussing our future and our past. Tying up all the loose ends in the aftermath of such a whirlwind courtship, if you could call it that, and subsequent mating.

"Tell me, MacKeane," Josie asked as she absentmindedly traced the tattoos covering my chest. "What was the secret you told to enter House Sermo?"

I chuckled. "Are ye sure it's safe to say?"

"Of course."

I squeezed her tight. "The truth, naturally. That I was in love with ye."

She sat up at that. "Really?"

"Really. Oh, I denied it to myself and others a dozen times after, but I really did ken, even then, as the house obviously knew. And ye?"

Without missing a beat, Josie said. "I told it my greatest wish was to know who my father was."

I pulled back to better see her. "Truly?"

She nodded but avoided my eye, laying her head back across my chest. "Someday, I still hope to find out."

I squeezed her affectionately. "I'm sure one day, ye will. I still can no' believe the White Witch just dropped yer probation enquiry. It seemed rather pointless to begin with, all told."

"I don't know what that was all about. I think it is related to whoever is doing all this."

"We will find oot, ye ken? Eventually, the truth will come oot."

"I know it."

Our conversation was interrupted when someone knocked on the door.

"Go away," I called out. Then, turned to Josie. "How could anyone get past yer magic to even knock on our door?"

I dragged myself out of bed thinking to intercept whoever it was, for if they could get past Josie Bell's magic, I couldn't imagine they were going to allow a measly door stop them from entering our bed chamber.

I stomped across the room, naked…I wasn't about to cover up to protect someone else's delicate sensibilities if they didn't have the presence of mind to leave a wolf and his mate alone when they wanted some peace. But eventually, Josie's giggle from the bed pierced my high dudgeon. I turned back and raised a questioning brow.

Josie laughed again, then jerked her head toward the window.

I pointed to the window as if to ask, *that window? Are you sure?*

She nodded but continued to laugh. I still didn't understand why, and I blame all the orgasms for not recalling who normally visited us via the window. I said normally, but in truth, she hadn't visited us since that fateful morning when she'd delivered a note from another witch, Lady Ivy.

I didn't recall all of that, however, not at the time. So, I wasn't sure what to expect when I threw open the sash.

I should have known. I really should have.

For there, standing before me, was a very impudent squirrel, whose wide eyes and red cheeks were all too familiar.

In the next moment, I recalled I was naked, and with unimaginable speed, I dropped to my knees so only my head cleared the windowsill. From the bed, Josie now laughed uncontrollably.

"May I help ye?" I choked out.

The squirrel was at a loss for words for once, and I called out over my shoulder. "I think she's having some sort of fit."

This made Josie only laugh that much harder.

Honestly, the squirrel was still standing under her own power, but she seemed unable to form any words. Her mouth was just frozen in the shape of an 'O.'

I noted the folded missive in her grasp and asked, "Is that fer me, love?"

She didn't respond. In fact, there was no change in her demeanor at all.

I called out to Josie once again. "I'm serious, Josie Bell. I ken something's wrong."

This time, Josie managed. "I'm sure you're doing just fine, MacKeane. You can do this." Another laugh and a snort sounded, then, "I believe in you, w-wolf." She was laughing so hard, she almost couldn't get the words out properly.

Grumbling, I looked at the squirrel again. She hadn't moved. "I'll take this, if I may."

I pinched the corner of the missive and tugged, gently.

Nothing.

I tugged harder.

Nothing.

I tugged once again.

Finally, the note came free. I almost ended up on my arse for my efforts. Startled, I glanced up and the squirrel had completely frozen, then tumbled backwards as if she fell from the window in a dead faint.

I launched myself up and leaned out the window, hand outstretched and calling, "Nooooo…"

But the squirrel merely waved as if to say *Goodbye* as she slowly descended, and I knew Josie Bell had intervened with her magic. Our friend would be all right. Probably.

I closed the window and spun around. "That was a cruel punishment, Josie Bell, and ye ken it."

She shook her head. "I know no such thing." Then, she extended her arm, and said, "well, let's see what it says."

I paused, just out of reach. "Perhaps, *I* should read it."

She raised one brow, and aye, I remembered what happened the last time I tried to read a message from a witch. I wanted to try anyway, just to prove…something, but even I wasn't that foolish. So, with a sigh, I handed over the note.

She opened it, saying thank ye, then dropped her eyes to the paper in her hand.

Her gasp made me realize something was very, very wrong. "Josie?"

She glanced up, her concern clear by her furrowed brow. "It's from Daphne. It's about Anglesey. He's missing."

THE END
FOR NOW

This adventure will continue with Daphne and Anglesey's budding romance in book 2, A Duke to Scry For...

Appendix A

Fun Items of Note for 1897

1. Queen Victoria's Diamond Jubilee:

    June 20 – private celebration in St. George's Chapel, Windsor

    June 21 – Dinner at Buckingham Palace for royal visitors across Europe

    June 22 – Festival of the British Empire – carriage procession from St. Paul's Cathedral (after a short outdoor service held) through the City of London, across London Bridge, and through south London before returning over Westminster Bridge to Buckingham Palace

    June 23 – 10000 school children gathered outside Buckingham Palace

Events for the rest of the week, included a state banquet and a (June 28) garden party.

2. Noted Books Released:

    Dracula by Bram Stoker published May 26, 1897

    Lady Godiva by John Collier

3. Type Writing Machine Patent Feb 2, 1897

The Houses of Coven Square

#1   Animus Witches

Magical Affinity: Animals

Common Personality Trait: Fierce

House Sentient Soul: Mac (A Shifter)

House Name: The Kameleon (Norwegian means The Chameleon)

Known Books in Possession: Book of Anti-Venom, Book of the Wild

#2   Planta Witches

Magical Affinity: Plants

Common Personality Trait: Versatile or tenacious

House Sentient Soul: Elf (A Brownie)

House Name: Hage Haus (Norwegian means Green House)

Known Books in Possession: Book of Apothecaries & Alchemy, Book of the Poisoned Heart, Book of Poisons

#3   Terra Witches

Magical Affinity: The Earth, The Land

Common Personality Trait: Cunning, Stubborn

House Sentient Soul: Dimitri (A Vampire)

House Name: The Steinblokk (Norwegian means The Boulder)

Known Books in Possession: Book of Snares

#4   Coleus Witches

Magical Affinity: Space, Stars, Planets

Common Personality Trait: Bright (all versions of the meaning)

House Sentient Soul: Celeste (A Fairy)

House Name: Himmelsk Hus (Norwegian means Heavenly House)

Known Books in Possession: Book of the Sun, Book of the Moon, Book of Celestial Wisdom

#5   Sensus Witches

Magical Affinity: Emotions

Common Personality Trait: Wistful

House Sentient Soul: Delphine (A Demon)

House Name: The Klarsynt (Norwegian means The Clairvoyant)

Known Books in Possession: Book of Divine Wisdom

#6   Tempestas Witches

Magical Affinity: Weather

Common Personality Trait: Fervent

House Sentient Soul: Blackbeard (A Human Pirate)

House Name: The Uvær (Norwegian means The Tempest)

Known Books in Possession: Book of Fury, Book of Storms

#7   Incendium Witches

Magical Affinity: Fire

Common Personality Trait: Fiery, Volatile

House Sentient Soul: Saint (A Demon)

House Name: The Helvete (Norwegian means The Inferno)

Known Books in Possession: Book of Fire and Ice

#8   Glacies Witches

Magical Affinity: Ice

Common Personality Trait: Stoic, Cold, Aloof

House Sentient Soul: Senna (An Angel)

House Name: The Glacies Hus (Norwegian means The Ice House)

Known Books in Possession: Book of Seduction, Book of Hoarfrost, Book of Fire and Ice* a constant battle with the Incendium Witches

#9   Artem Witches

Magical Affinity: Art

Common Personality Trait: Perceptive

House Sentient Soul: Theodorus van Gogh (Human)

House Name: The Kunstgalleri (Norwegian means The Art Gallery)

Known Books in Possession: Book of Arcane Secrets, Book of Illusions

#10   Musicorum Witches

Magical Affinity: Music

Common Personality Trait: Enchanting

House Sentient Soul: Theodorus van Gogh (Human)

House Name: The Sirene (Norwegian means The Siren)

Known Books in Possession: Book of Enchantment

#11   Sermo Witches

Magical Affinity: Words

Common Personality Trait: Witty, Clever, Charming, Weird, Dangerous

House Sentient Soul: Shakespeare (Human)

House Name: The Dikter (Norwegian means The Poet)

Known Books in Possession: Book of Accords, Book of Obscure Knowledge, Book of Runes

#12 Somnium Witches

    Magical Affinity: Dreams

    Common Personality Trait: Intuitive

    House Sentient Soul: Sandman (Centaur)

    House Name: The Mareritt (Norwegian means The Nightmare)

    Known Books in Possession: Book of Absorption, Book of Shadows

#13 Met...

About the Author

USA Today Bestselling Author Amy Quinton writes humorous fantasy and historical romance, often from her back porch in Summerville, South Carolina, but only when her dog and two cats allow. (She's guilty of spoiling them horribly.) She's susceptible to shiny things, soft things, leather, trips to the thrift store, Whisky, tattoos, witchy things, and men in kilts (particularly her husband)-but not necessarily in that order.

She adores her children (most of the time), finds a lot of humor being married to a Brit (usually), cusses (probably more than she should), and loves to read and write romance (always).

When she finds the time, she loves to crochet, knit, embroider, go thrift shopping, and make jewelry. And she longs to travel to the UK every chance she gets.